THE LOYAL DAUGHTER

THE LOYAL DAUGHTER
a novel

Nancy Lam

WINNIPEG

The Loyal Daughter

This book is a work of fiction. Names, characters, businesses, organizations, places, events, and incidents are the product of the author's imagination or are used fictitiously.

Copyright © 2022 Nancy Lam

Design and layout by Matthew Stevens and M. C. Joudrey.
Cover illustration by M. C. Joudrey

Published by At Bay Press September 2022.

All rights reserved. The use of any part of this publication, reproduced, stored in a retrieval system, transmitted in any form or by any means electronic, mechanical, recording or otherwise, without prior written consent of the publisher, is an infringement of the copyright law except if photocopying or reprographic copying in Canada with a license from The Canadian Copyright Licensing Agency.

No portion of this work may be reproduced without express written permission from At Bay Press.

Library and Archives Canada cataloguing in publication is available upon request.

ISBN 978-1-988168-65-4

Printed and bound in Canada.

This book is printed on acid free paper that is 100% recycled ancient forest friendly (100% post-consumer recycled).

First Edition

10 9 8 7 6 5 4 3 2 1

atbaypress.com

To Mom and Dad
Two very important Canadians

Cast of Characters

Mai Gum (Beautiful Gold or American Money) Lee (née Chung)
Bak Lai (North Reliability) Chung
Ping Hao (Steady Bright) Chung
Lei On (Thunder Peace) Chung
Su Ling (Gentle Compassion) Chung (née Yu)
Jung Sum (Loyalty Heart) Chung
Mai Jie (Pretty Pearl) Chung
Dai Sang (Big Mountain/Life) Chung
Fy Sing (Flying Star) Chung
Dai Hong (Big Healthy) Chung
Yaing Gong (Sunlight/Winning Light) Chung

Dat Wah (Done/Capable, Abundance) Wong
Fuk Sau (Happiness Longevity) Yu

Hao Ming (Good Light) Lee
Bo Chang (Waves Prosperity) Lee
Bao Jun (Gem Truth) Mak (née Lee)
Chung Lung (Intelligent Dragon) Mak
Fai Nguk (Great/Beautiful Jade/Flesh) Yee (née Lee)
Wang Dei (King Earth) Yee
Fai Lok (Great Happiness) Yee (née Lee)
Ho Choi (Good Luck/Good Fortune) Yee

Vikki Wei Qi (Valuable, Energy) Lee
Mark Wei Mak (Powerful, Mark) Lee
Amy Wei Ping (Valuable, Peace/Steady) Lee
Billy Wei Sum (Powerful, Heart) Lee

Andrew Benjamin Nesbitt
Zoe Lai Wah (Able Abundance) Nesbitt

Joseph Anthony Gallino

Her paternal grandfather (Yeh Yeh)
Her paternal grandmother (Mah Mah)
Her father (Abah)
Her mother (Amah)
Her first younger sister
Her second younger sister
Her eldest younger brother
Her youngest sister
Her second younger brother
Her youngest brother

Her ex-fiancé
Her male maternal cousin

Mai's husband
His father (Abah)
His younger sister
His brother-in-law
His elder paternal aunt (Dai Gou)
His uncle (Fai Nguk's husband)
His younger paternal aunt (Sai Gou)
His uncle (Fai Lok's husband)

Mai and Ming's eldest daughter
Their eldest son
Their youngest daughter
Their youngest son

Their son-in-law, Amy's husband
Their granddaughter, Amy's daughter

Amy's ex-fiancé

PROLOGUE

At St. John's Anglican Church, the female guests shed their wraps to show off their finest spring dresses while the men saunter comfortably about in their dashing wool suits. The onlookers watching Mai Gum Chung climb the steep concrete steps to the entrance, in her white gown and flowing veil, would never guess they were witnessing anything other than a true love story. Mai has known since she was a little girl that she was meant to accomplish more than her parents, her six younger siblings and everyone else from their small village in southern China. And here she is in 1966, about to marry a man she met seventeen days ago when she first arrived in this remote northern city in Ontario, named North Bay.

1

One day, after completing her morning chores on their farm, Mai is placing a bowl of water on the kitchen floor for their pet pig when Ping Hao Chung, her paternal grandmother, rushes in.

"Mai! Mai! You're here. Perfect!"

Mai grins at her. Where else is she going to be? It's barely past 7 A.M. and for over a year she's had the same schedule, which means she's in the kitchen feeding the pig at this time.

"Before anyone else woke, I shook the can of a hundred fortunes in front of the Gwan Yum, the Buddhist Goddess of Mercy. Listen to what I learned," she gushes to Mai, ignoring her son, Mai's father, Lei On Chung, who is sitting at the kitchen table reading.

Mai automatically looks at the Gwan Yum, who sits in her shrine next to the front door of their home. The can of fortunes is an old food can, wrapped in red paper. She had helped her grandmother write the numbers one to one hundred on individual bamboo sticks cut to the length of an adult hand. Each number relates to a fortune found in the tattered book her grandmother keeps at the bottom of her cubby under her pile of clothes. Mah Mah Ping received this book from one of the monks at a Buddhist temple she visited in Hong Kong, long before Mai was born, long before the Japanese took over the island.

"This morning as I shook the can I asked the Goddess to bring you great success and wealth in the future. To ensure you achieve all you can. And then I asked, what does your future hold?" She pauses. "Guess what fortune came out?"

"Which one, Mah Mah?" Mai is now caught up in her grandmother's excitement.

"Number ninety! It says: 'Both achievement and fame. Keep on as you are, and go forward without hesitation. All good wishes will be realized. Good fortune and luck will be yours always.'"

Mai feels a tingle travel across her shoulders, and blood wells up inside her chest until she cannot help but allow the corners of her mouth to turn upwards. She rushes to the sink to wash her hands before fetching a cup to pour her grandmother some tea.

"Good, isn't it? But vague," Mah Mah continues, "so, I went to the blind soothsayer to ask him the same thing."

"What?" Mai sets the pot down so quickly at this news she nearly topples the cup she filled. She knows they only ever go to the soothsayer if they need very important advice. It is far too expensive to go more frequently. She also knows from Mah Mah that in exchange for lacking the ability to physically see, the blind possess a greater gift, the power to see the future.

"When I asked my question, his head tilted toward the sky and it looked as if he was watching the hawk glide by. I thought for a minute he was only faking his blindness and I was ready to take back the sweet potato offering, when his head jolted haltingly back and forth, and I saw his clouded, vacant eyeballs failing to focus on anything."

Her grandmother now pauses to sip from the teacup, thirsty from her chatter and re-enactment of the exchange. Mai glances nervously at her father to gauge his reaction. He is scowling but Mah Mah doesn't notice, and Mai can't tell if it's worse than his usual expression.

"His words shock me. Do you know what he said?" She pauses for effect before deepening her voice to imitate the soothsayer, 'I see her forging a path. To North America. She is your family's route to a better life.'"

Mai opens her mouth to speak but finds she has no words.

"I start asking questions. *How? Will my husband somehow send for her? Will the family finally be together in Gold Mountain?*"

Mai finds her voice. "What did he say, Mah Mah?"

"He told me he only knows what he already said. He bowed so deeply I thought he might fall over but then he scooped up the sweet potato, and I knew it was the end of the reading."

Her father slaps his hand on the table so hard, a bit of Mah Mah's tea jumps out and Mai's certain her siblings will wake from the noise.

"The sweet potato was a meal for our entire household of nine. Why did you give that con man our dinner? It's not like anyone around here has extra food! You crazy *lo gwai*, old ghost. What a load of nonsense. Mai? Mai, a fat girl from a dead village in China who at best is an average student, leading us across the seas to Gold Mountain? We are almost related to that con man, he knows we have family over there, and he knows what you want to hear. Aaahh! You're delirious with fever. Crazy old woman!"

Mai thinks her grandmother must be going deaf because she simply shrugs at his words not seeming to notice he is shouting and answers as if they are having a conversation about the weather.

"A small price to pay to learn what lies ahead for my first grandchild."

Her father throws down the book he's read multiple times and storms outside, slamming the door behind him. Her grandmother flicks her hand behind him dismissively as she walks over calmly to reopen the door. She turns back to Mai and the two are giddy talking about what might happen as Mah Mah gets paper and ink to write down the words of the soothsayer.

Mai does not care or blame her father for his skepticism. After all, Mah Mah's husband left when Abah was still a baby. The idea was that Mai's grandfather, Bak Lai Chung, uncle and great grandfather were to work hard in the seafood business they established with partners in San Francisco, sending money home when possible. Mai isn't sure if they intended to funnel money back forever so they might eventually retire in China like royalty or if the whole family was expected to leave China for the Gold Mountain someday. Either way, the plans changed.

Bad things happen in three. After Abah's grandfather died, Abah's father, never sent money home. No one really knows why. Around the same time, Abah was gambling a lot, eventually losing the family savings. It got so bad, they had to sell most of her mother's family heirlooms to pay his debts. Then their baby sister died after trying to care for their other pig who got sick. Amah cried for days and Abah grew angrier. They were never the same. At least as far as Mai saw it. The only person who didn't change was Mah Mah.

Maybe it was a blessing they were suddenly poor because if they had a lot of money before the Communists took over, they might have been tortured, killed, or sent for re-education like other wealthy neighbours. Mai just witnessed the family who occasionally gave her candy being forced to kneel back for hours in the hot sun with a stick across their calves. All for having ambitious relatives who made them wealthy. So unfair.

Abah never said a bad word about his father, but he was unable to hide his frustration or anger when Mai and her siblings complained about being hungry after dinner. Now they're almost like everyone else. They grow some vegetables on the land, they own a few animals, and they gather what they need from the forest areas surrounding the village farms. Their house is made of stone though, and it's a bit bigger than those of the neighbours but not big enough to draw too much attention. Sometimes Mai wonders if Abah and Amah had her and her siblings just to fill up the house and look poorer. As if that was possible.

But how, after all these years was her grandfather ever going to help Mai get all the way across the ocean to Gold Mountain?

2

Surprising her teachers and most of all her father, at the age of twelve Mai excels at the provincial exams, out-scoring thousands, earning a spot in high school. It is one of the few times and certainly the only time since her siblings were born that Abah compliments her. This is of course after he confirms with her teacher there wasn't a mix up of Mai's grades with one of the actual top students.

Mai ignores her father's doubts and does not hesitate to pack up her few essentials, leave her family behind and move to the larger city to room with several other girls to continue her studies. Accustomed to keeping her own company within her crowded household, and truthfully embarrassed by her family's poverty, she quickly earns a reputation for being a polite recluse. Over the next few years, she only returns home for breaks, which include the random government announcements requiring everyone to stop their schooling or work, and farm the communal lands for the "greater good." When she was young, Mai always asked, "If it's for the greater good why isn't Brother Mao, leader of the Communist Party, farming too? His idea after all."

A few times Mai feigns sickness after arriving at school and hearing it is a farming day. But instead of going home to bed as expected, she wanders the open market reading all the notice boards.

One time she didn't wait long enough for her classmates to march off to the fields before going off on her own and they spotted her.

"There's Mai. She's not sick," she heard them shouting behind her as she tried to run away. Being fatter than all of them, though, she was slower and couldn't find anywhere to hide. That day, she ended up farming and hating it.

At sixteen, she finishes her schooling and is back at home when she receives an acceptance order from the Chinese government to study chemistry in Kunming. Her father's excitement quickly turns to anger when, rather than accepting immediately, Mai writes to the government thanking them but declining the offer advising that she wants to study nursing or chemistry in Jiangmen. Months later, much to Abah's surprise, the government writes back, issuing her an acceptance order to study nursing in Nanning.

"What do you mean you're not going? Again." Her father is ready to turn Mai in himself for her insolence.

"I don't want to be in Kunming or Nanning. It's nowhere close to Hong Kong. I want to study chemistry or nursing in Jiangmen."

"What you want is not important. And why are you worried about being close to Hong Kong? Not like you're going there. They can arrest you and send you to one of those re-education camps if you don't comply. You *ngow nai*, crazy daughter."

As her father rants, she sidles toward the door. "Going to collect some kindling for fire," Mai says as she dashes out while he continues his lecture.

Months later, everyone is relieved and a bit shocked when Mai is not arrested but issued an acceptance order to study nursing in Jiangmen, the city she wants to be in.

In nursing school, Mai somehow sidesteps the government culling of the student body, not once, but twice. The first morning Mai sits in class running through her mental to-do list, expecting to half listen to the usual administrative orders for the day before lessons begin. The teacher enters, looking a bit dishevelled and skittish. Her usual mannerisms and appearance are dull and she runs on like a tap, so when she stutters to get words out, Mai freezes and pays full attention.

"Those who are not within the top five per cent of the class," the teacher begins, followed by a long pause, "are to pack their belongings and return to their homes."

Her classmates start to murmur amongst themselves as the meaning of the words sink in. Mai's stomach curls and she feels like throwing up the little they received for breakfast. She did well on the last exam but top five per cent? She forces herself to calculate her grades if for no other reason than to distract herself from the thought of returning home, to village life, and farming. After all these years of study? She can't.

Mercifully, she is safe.

Mai knows she must prepare better for the next time. The top student is truly brilliant; inquisitive, learning for the sake of learning, an academic who epitomizes the image of a quiet, docile professor-like person. Mai knows this is not her. Mai's dedication to her studies is fuelled almost entirely by her determination to survive the next culling. When her remaining classmates take the weekend off to see the latest big picture release, Mai stays at the dormitory to study and clean her area of the room she shares with three other classmates. She hates the idea of wasting hours simply watching a film, accomplishing and gaining nothing practical. Never mind the cost.

More importantly, Mai felt she had more to lose than most of her classmates if she was forced to return home because she was poorer. This was clear when everyone unpacked their plastic wash basins while she took out her wooden one. But her classmates knew better than to bully her, not only because of her size but after an obnoxious roommate used Mai's basin to store her shoes, Mai promptly whipped the shoes out the window. When the roommate confronted her, Mai looked straight at her and calmly said, "If you ever touch any of my possessions again, I'll whip you out the window next."

When the second culling occurred, Mai was confident she was safe. In the back of her mind though, she knew even if she started a career in nursing, there was nothing to stop another random government culling, a call to farm, or something worse. Look at that teacher from last semester: accused of spreading anti-government views, she escaped a public beating, but disappeared. To where, no one knows. Witnessing this, Mai kept to herself so when the time came to leave, it was going to be easy. And it was. Except for him.

3

The first time they meet is in the hospital. Mai spots him limping into the crowded waiting area by the entrance as he winces. Being quicker and bolder than any of her colleagues she is the first to approach him. It helps that for months Mai has made a habit of approaching everyone in a uniform, especially the Russians. Her inability to speak their language never gave her reason to hesitate. As Mai sees it, how does it hurt to help those who might hold a bit of power?

"Officer, you need not wait here. I can escort you to an examining area with some privacy. Can you walk?" Mai grabs a clipboard to collect his personal details for the hospital records.

"Thank you," answers the young officer. "I may need help. Feels like a jagged chopstick is inside my ankle."

"Do you need a wheelchair?" Mai is already moving away to find one.

"No, but a crutch or a cane will help me keep the weight off the ankle."

Mai turns back to him. "How about you lean on me? We need to get over there." She points to a curtained area at the end of the hall. "It'll be faster than finding a cane from upstairs."

"Will work perfectly."

Mai positions herself beside him before noticing he's grinning broadly. She blushes as he tosses his arm around her shoulder and continues to stare at her. She places her left hand on top of his, surprised at how velvety his hand feels despite its large masculine size. The sign of a person who does not have to endure physical labour. She slips her right arm around his back and under his armpit to support him. They limp their way along, and with a simple nod and eye motion to the nurse managing the patients, Mai signals she is leading the officer to the open examining cubicle.

Inhaling exaggeratedly as they shuffle, the officer asks, "What lovely scent are you wearing?"

Mai answers seriously, "Rubbing alcohol."

He laughs out loud, and in the process accidentally steps down on his injured ankle.

"Ahhhhh!" he cries out.

"Oh no." Mai stops. "Are you ok?"

"I'm fine. But you must stop being funny," he says, catching her eye as he rights himself and motions her to continue.

Mai tilts her head slightly and unintentionally meets his gaze. She takes in his perfect set of teeth before proceeding to assess the rest of his face. Square. According to Mah Mah, men with square shaped faces are destined for prosperity. It means he is methodical, practical, reliable, down to earth. He will never rush into decisions or be influenced by the opinion of others, unlike women with the same shaped face who are pegged as unhappy. She can't help but notice his large warm eyes with their double lids, study her. His prominent Roman nose with narrow nostrils, do not resemble the common flat bridge and wide nostrils of the Chinese. His lips are not too thin—which would represent a silver tongue—and not too thick—symbolizing low intelligence. His complexion is fair. Objectively, Mai labels him handsome, and hopes the nervousness she feels is not outwardly apparent.

When they reach the curtained area, she helps him to the bed where he sits perched.

"I will take down your information while we wait for the doctor to come in. Your name, officer?" She could not match Abah's artful characters, but the head nurse and doctors regularly express their appreciation for her notes and information on the intake records.

"Wong Dat Wah."

"Position in the military?"

"It's actually the air force. I am a pilot."

Mai raises one eyebrow, impressed. Before she can gather any more information, the doctor comes in, to her disappointment. Dat Wah explains that he hurt himself trying to sidestep some horse manure at the home of an official. He neatly hopped over it but did not see the rock where his foot landed, resulting in his ankle twisting awkwardly and him collapsing. Mai laughs out loud. The doctor frowns at her much like Abah might when he disapproved of her decisions, but Dat Wah chuckles, clearly delighted by the reception to his story.

The doctor instructs Mai to fetch a cane while he completes the paperwork. She nods curtly and hurries out. Despite being larger than most of the petite women that surround her, Mai is quick. Many of her co-workers and classmates, who do not notice her worn shoes or see her wooden wash basin, assume she comes from considerable wealth that affords her the luxury of extra food and girth.

When Mai returns, the doctor directs her to help bandage Dat Wah's ankle. For the first time Mai suddenly feels self-conscious about her size, movements, and actions as she feels Dat Wah's eyes following her intently.

Dat Wah ensures he bumps into Mai at his follow-up appointment. Three dinners later, Mai excitedly anticipates their weekly meetings. As they walk through the market their chatter is non-stop.

"I feel there are no boundaries. Everything is within our grasp. We can do anything," says Dat Wah as he clenches his fists and raises his arms like he's won a race.

"Yes, if you are a friend of the government," responds Mai with her chin raised.

Dat Wah looks at her, uncertain if she is kidding. "And are you?" he asks.

"I am but a lowly student nurse. The government does not care for my friendship like it cares for the friendship of men like yourself. I humbly follow orders and I am always at the service of the government and its friends." She curtsies and lowers her head in front of him.

Dat Wah laughs heartily as he offers her a hand to stand up straight again. "You are far from a servant or a follower, Chung Mai Gum."

Mai points to herself mockingly. The reservations that initially inhibited her from speaking her mind due to her learned suspicious instincts and his professional rank, quickly give way to her natural outspoken personality. She comfortably shares her views. Perhaps, as Abah often scolded, it was because her young brain had yet to fully form and understand how sometimes speaking her mind, especially about or to the government, might lead to trouble. At the moment, Mai believed herself invincible, like most teenagers.

"Perhaps when you graduate and start running the hospital officially, the government will seek out your friendship as I do," Dat Wah responds. "The government takes care of everyone, but I fear stepping out of line too."

"What can you possibly fear from the government?"

"One of my first flights was disrupted because I bumped a lever during a sneezing fit. If it had not been for my flying record from the past, I am sure I would have been relegated to the fields as a farm hand, permanently."

"Let me know if you're ever scheduled to fly over this area so I can take the day off and hide." Mai laughs and cowers slightly.

"Funny now," says Dat Wah, "but not when we had to explain to the higher-ups why the plane was veering wildly off course." He stares at her like the first day they met. "Nice to hear you so relaxed."

"Perfect day, isn't it?" Mai says as they reach the edge of the market, looking off at the fluffy, pink-tinged clouds framed by trees in full bloom.

"Except you have to get back to the hospital and I, to my meetings."

"Now who needs to relax?" Mai says.

"Yes, yes. We need more time like this."

"You would grow weary of me."

"Never. For many reasons, never." Dat Wah stares at her until she looks away blushing.

He grabs her around the waist with one arm and pulls her tightly against him. With his other hand he firmly but tenderly cups her right cheek, so she has no choice but to look into his eyes. Mai feels flush.

"Never will I be weary of you," he whispers quietly into her ear.

"Stop. People are staring," Mai says, half-heartedly trying to pull away.

Dat Wah rubs the tip of Mai's nose with his own before releasing her from his embrace so they can continue to walk but his hand keeps a firm hold of hers.

"You're fine drawing attention arguing with me but not when I hold you?"

"I never aim to draw attention," she says. "But someone must keep you in line. You get away with too much because of your position."

Dat Wah roars with laughter as they continue to walk along the water's edge, hand in hand. The damp fresh smell of the recent rainfall fills their lungs. Mai wishes she could suspend time.

***

The morning of her wedding day, Mai stands at the edge of the large dining room looking around the empty restaurant that belongs to her soon-to-be in-laws and takes a deep breath. Her sister-in-law carries in the tray of longans and red date tea. Mai wears casual trousers and a polyester lilac blouse, typical Hong Kong attire. No need to be formally or uncomfortably dressed for this ceremony involving only family, her fiancé's aunt, Fai Lok, told her.

Her fiancé is setting two chairs in the middle of the room where a table has been moved to the side to make space for everyone to gather round.

"Good morning," her fiancé's uncle, Ho Choi, says aloud to everyone.

Mai and the others respond in kind as Fai Lok and Ho Choi, each take one of the seats. Everyone else stands a respectful distance around them, encircling them. Mai takes a deep breath and pours a cup of tea. She carries the first cup to Uncle Ho Choi, kneels, raising the cup in front and over her head, and presents it to him. After he sips and sets down the cup, Mai repeats the ceremony for her fiancé's aunt. Done. Mai rises. Her fiancé joins her by her side. With the tea ceremony finished, she is now officially part of his family. Mai looks around as chatter fills the room.

Her mind wanders to another time she stood in the middle of a room filled with people chattering around her.

***

It is more than half a year since she and Dat Wah met. Mai is in the hospital waiting room and she is aware of the hushed conversations surrounding her, but her focus is on her hand, tucked into her pocket, feeling the ring inside the velvet pouch.

When Dat Wah arrives, they embrace.

"Do you not like the ring?" He asks, as he examines her hands.

"How can you ask me that? You know I adore it," she responds as she furrows her brow.

"Then, why are you not wearing it?" He whispers into her ear, his lips grazing her cheek ever so lightly sending a tingle up her spine.

"I just don't want others to know my business," she replies taking the pouch out of her pocket to put it on. "Do you never take yours off?" Mai admires her finger as she stares at the dark yellow gold band protecting the striking leaf-shaped jade centerpiece. Dat Wah's ring is made of the same gold but the band is twice as wide as hers, and the jade center is cut in the shape of a rectangle.

"I haven't taken mine off since the day I gave you yours," he says.

"Well, I'm constantly washing my hands at work. I do not want to damage or lose this beautiful stone." She looks up at him.

"I always have it with me though."

He takes Mai's hand which now wears the ring. "I went to the best jeweller my family knows. This stone is not coming off. Do you see how many prongs of gold hold the jade in place?" He moves his hands and places one on each side of her face gently. "But even if the ring is lost, it will not matter as long as you are with me." He stares into her eyes before kissing her forehead.

The next time they meet, he presents her with a gold chain that matches their engagement bands.

"This is for work, so you can wear the ring always, and keep it hidden," he says as he takes the ring off her finger and threads it onto the chain.

Mai protests the cost, but Dat Wah shushes her.

"Don't worry. I know you did not ask or intend for me to buy you anything. You never do. But this ring is my way to remind you I am always with you, even when I'm physically not," he whispers as he fastens the chain around Mai's neck and hugs her from behind.

With her back to him Mai inhales and stifles the urge to cry. When she turns around, in an uncustomary public show of affection, she throws her arms around his neck and holds onto him not saying a word, not wanting to let go. After several minutes she brushes her lips across his. After he leaves, warmth spreads inside her as she imagines their future together.

***

The stuffy room at the back of the church is not helping Mai's mood. The hem of the borrowed tea-length taffeta wedding dress itches her calves. The pointy kitten-heeled shoes her fiancé's aunt insisted she buy matches the colour of the dress but squishes the balls of her feet even when she is just sitting.

Fortunately, there is a window. She stands to open it, over

the protests of the woman asked by Aunt Fai Lok to help her style her hair, apply makeup, and dress. Her hip short bob hardly needs products to stay in place, but her hair feels as hard as a helmet from all the Vaseline and sprays the woman insisted on applying. She knows the woman is trying to prove her services worthwhile—in hopes of a generous payback in cash or favour—and that is apparently measured by the quantity of product used.

Mai returns to the seat, twitches her face, and wriggles her nose to try to loosen the mask of makeup. No luck. The attention and fuss over her appearance makes Mai even more apprehensive than the day she arrived, just over two weeks ago. As hard as she tries, she cannot rid her mind of Dat Wah even if it has been years since she last saw him. She inhales deeply and reminds herself that this is a practical choice, much stronger than the immature feelings she had for him.

4

"I've been promoted. We're going to Nam King," Dat Wah announces, jumping up from his restaurant seat as Mai walks toward him. His eyes are larger than usual, and he is beaming from ear to ear.

"For how long?" asks Mai.

"Permanently with any luck," Dat Wah says grinning.

"I see."

"I can make the arrangements for us to travel together. There are other officers I know who have purchased homes in the area. I am the youngest though. I cannot believe our luck. I never thought this would happen so early." Dat Wah rattles on like a child in a candy store.

"It sounds wonderful for you," says Mai.

"Well, this is a first. *You* don't know what to say?" Dat Wah teases until he studies her face. "What is it?"

"I can't go," says Mai, "You know I want to but—"

"What? Why not?"

"—Gold Mountain," Mai gets out.

When he next speaks, Dat Wah's voice has dropped a few octaves. "When are you going to give up your fantasy about Gold Mountain? This is real. A great opportunity."

"It is not a fantasy. I am here studying nursing instead of farming in a forsaken village in southern China. That, too, would have been considered a fantasy," Mai says, her voice rising.

"But you are here now. And so am I. Maybe someday we will visit or live in Gold Mountain," says Dat Wah, softening, "but right now, this is where we need to go. It's a step in the right direction."

"For you," Mai says quietly and as her mind churns, she says more loudly, "Can't you request a posting elsewhere? To Macau or maybe even Hong Kong?"

"What? No. I cannot." He shakes his head and wrinkles his brow. "There are no postings of this kind there. You don't seem to understand how rare this promotion is."

Mai can't tell if he's annoyed or disappointed. The dark skies seem to creep out of nowhere as their conversation continues. Rain is suddenly coming down in sheets against the roof of the restaurant, and Mai feels it weighing her down.

They eat their meal in uncharacteristic silence. Mai's outspoken and staunch attitude, which normally draws adoration from Dat Wah, now seems to frustrate him as she remains adamant about not going to Nam King. He avoids looking at her and pushes his tofu and rice back and forth in his bowl.

When they finish and he walks her back to her quarters, he only squeezes her hand tightly instead of snuggling like they normally do. A part of Mai wants to hug him and not let go but a part of her, the stronger part, is upset that he expects her to just follow him because the government is dangling this carrot. Before he leaves, she searches his face for answers. Finding none, she releases his hand and marches decisively to her dormitory door, her head held high, forcing herself not to look back. A tear escapes as she enters the building.

More than angry, she's confused. What does it all mean? She thought he understood that there will never be any true freedom with this government. Does he not know this? Does he not care? Does he truly believe her desire to escape to Gold Mountain is nothing more than a fantasy? It's her destiny. She told him about the soothsayer and the fortune. What does he really think of her ideas and opinions? He was so attentive and complimentary, but maybe he was only humouring her. She spends the rest of the evening flip-flopping between wanting to see him and being incensed by his words. Has she misjudged him? Mai gets ready for bed and prays to Buddha for a sign of some sort before Dat Wah returns from assignment in two weeks.

***

Mai is grateful the woman helping her, leaves, so she has a few moments to herself before the ceremony begins.

When the hair piece is arranged and the veil set in place, Mai feels as if she is balancing textbooks on her head. She examines herself in front of the full-length mirror and bursts out laughing at the reflection. From the waist down, the poufy full skirt is so wide, she resembles a bell. The makeup is so heavy, trying to move her mouth seems to crack a spot on her cheeks.

She takes a sip of tea, losing a significant amount of lipstick on the rim of the cup. She quickly grabs a few tissues and blots at her lips, the way the woman showed her. Then she takes a deep breath, and stands like a warrior ready to battle. She is presentable. She is ready and anxious to finish what she travelled so far to do.

***

The sign Mai wished for, came in the form of a letter that arrived two days after she and Dat Wah argued.

May 17, 1962

Mai Gum,

Amah has taken Yaing Gong and Jung Sum to Hong Kong. Your sister needs a real doctor to look at her leg, not just the village healer. It is terribly swollen. Luckily, they received the medical visas for three years. I told Amah to leave Yaing Gong, but she says he is too young to stay here without her. Amah will have to get a job and see if any of her relatives can help them while they are there.

Write to her when you can, the address is below. We are getting by, and everyone is healthy. I trust your studies are going well.

Abah

Hong Kong? How bad must Jung's leg be that they finally issued the special visas? It's nearly impossible to secure entry to Hong Kong from China these days. Mah Mah Ping said Abah used to travel back and forth freely until the Japanese invasion forced him to hide out in the village during those last few years of the Second World War, around the time Mai was born. Then the Communists took over in 1949 and Hong Kong had no choice but to shut its doors to the overwhelming number of mainlanders seeking refuge from a government they didn't support. Perhaps, this is another reason Abah frowns more than smiles. China may take back Hong Kong one day but until then, it's the closest haven from Communist rule available.

How is Amah going to care for the kids and work at the same time? Yaing Gong is a baby. Jung helps on the farm, but what will she do in the city? If Amah loses her, like their other sister Jie, she will surely lose her sanity. Who is going to help them in Hong Kong? At home, even if Abah does not do much, at least he and Mah Mah are there. Amah has half siblings in Hong Kong who are all very polite but there are no immediate family members, no one they can impose on for longer than a week or so. Besides, they have their dignity, they can't live on charity. Now that they're out, chances are they won't have money to return home often, if at all.

What is Mai going to do? Does she really have a choice? Her family needs her. And this is an opportunity to get to Hong Kong finally. But what about Dat Wah?

How could he ever think I'd follow him to some distant city without at least a plan, a timeline, to get to Gold Mountain? But how will I return his ring and chain to him? Other than the military base, I have no idea who his family or friends might be. With whom do I leave these valuables? What if someone takes them? Or they get lost?

After two sleepless nights, Mai finally decides she can't wait any longer, especially if it's just to say goodbye. For the first time since they argued, Mai forgets her anger and the sense of betrayal. There is no time for any of that now.

The next day seems to last forever. Mai finishes her shift mechanically. With her school identification and residency documents in hand, she rushes over to the local city hall shortly before it closes.

"I need an application for a visitor visa to Macau. I am a

student here," says Mai to the officer breathlessly.

"Your proof of study and identification, *fai moi*, fat little sister?" the officer replies. He takes the documents Mai hands him, reviews them, checks the shelves behind his seat and pulls a form out. He makes a few notations on the paper and hands it to Mai along with her documents.

"Fill in the rest and return it to me quickly, *fai moi*. We are closing soon so hurry if you want this done today."

Mai quickly fills in the rest of the form, inserting Amah's cousin's address as the place she plans to stay, returns the form to the clerk, and pays the nominal fee.

"Takes a week to process. Pick it up here," the officer says as he walks away from the window.

A week later, she picks up her visitor visa to Macau.

Over the weekend, when everyone is out enjoying the sunny weather, Mai packs everything she wants to keep. She no longer has any use for the books and notes. Her few clothes fit into one small bag. Her hand travels to her neck feeling for the chain and the ring she has kept around her neck since Dat Wah left. She hopes he receives the note she left at the base with the security attendant. If he truly knows her, he will decipher her message and find her.

She scans the room one last time to ensure there is nothing else she needs or wants. Her eyes land on her cot and she decides to make a trip home to return the blanket Mah Mah gave her for the dormitory. It is one of the warmest the family owns. It is a three-hour trip, but it will only delay her departure to Macau by a day.

***

"Mai, what are you doing here?" Mah Mah Ping seems both happy and concerned to see her granddaughter.

"I came home to give you back the warm blanket," replies Mai casually. "Not staying. Leaving for Macau tomorrow."

"What? Why on earth are you going there? And you'll need the blanket when you get back."

"It's just a short trip. Blanket's too warm for me. You can use it more here. Where is Abah?"

"Your sister and brothers will be home from school soon. Abah is tending to the vegetables."

"I'll go help him," says Mai.

"Come into the house and have a drink of tea while I make rice for dinner. Your Abah will be fine," says Mah Mah as she pulls Mai toward the house smiling and patting her arm.

Mai sits and sips her tea as grandmother measures, washes, and starts the rice. Mai tells Mah Mah about nursing school and the hospital and listens to her stories about what's been happening at home. When the tea is done and Mah Mah is concentrating on the vegetables and eggs, Mai takes the opportunity to rush out, intending to find Abah and make her way to the edge of the property to gather some kindling. As she walks out the door, her siblings, Dai Sang, her eldest little brother, Dai Hong, her second little brother, and Fy Sing, her youngest sister return from school and start running towards her when they realize who she is.

She feels guilty for all the extra weight she carries on her body when she sees their back bones and ribs when they inhale deeply. She attributes her glowing fair complexion to sitting in classrooms and working indoors compared to their dark tanned skins and bruised limbs from working on the farm and daily chores. They appear to take no notice of their differences as they dump their school sacks by the front door and pelt her with questions.

"How long are you staying?" shouts her happy-go-lucky sister.

"I leave in the morning for Macau."

"You just got here," Fy Sing pouts. Before Mai can console her, Abah comes back from the garden and walks past them.

"Why are you going to Macau now? Did you not get my letter? How do you have time for a vacation when Amah is away with your siblings? Not very responsible. Your brain has not fully formed."

Mai says nothing. Accustomed to Abah's criticism, she lets him rant until he tires out.

"I won't be gone long," says Mai heading to the edge of the property where the large trees lie. She purposely leaves out the rest of her plans despite how satisfying it would be to prove him wrong. It is better her family know nothing in case they are ever questioned. Besides, Abah might think she's gone insane, and Mah Mah Ping will just worry if she reveals her plan to sneak into Hong Kong. Maybe Jung's bad leg was a blessing in disguise, giving them, and her, a reason to get where she needs to be.

Mah Mah comes out hearing all the voices.

"All of you, come in for dinner. You can gather kindling later." Mai's shoulders sag, but she does as her grandmother instructs.

As they sit down, Mah Mah beams. "Mai, eat some fried egg. You've a long journey tomorrow. Need the energy." She pushes the dish toward Mai.

"You don't think she eats enough? She has an extra layer of fat on reserve," says Abah, gesturing at Mai with his chopsticks.

"Are you blind? Look at her. She's lost weight working so hard at that hospital," says her grandmother as Mai soaks in their banter with a laugh.

"I will, Mah Mah, don't worry." Mai devours the simple meal of eggs from their chickens and the garden-grown greens with rice while her siblings pester her to describe Jiangmen and her job.

She cheerfully answers them and imitates some of the patients she treated, thinking of but never mentioning Dat Wah. A part of her wants to stay longer but the duty to help Amah seems to have grown in importance since she arrived home. Besides, this may be her only chance to leave farm life behind. Maybe even get to Gold Mountain to join her grandfather. As predicted.

After helping with the dishes everyone but Mah Mah walks to the edge of the farm to gather kindling. Abah and Mai create the largest bundles, before they start back toward the house with her brothers and sister chasing each other, occasionally running ahead and then falling behind, chattering amongst themselves. Mai pauses, looking back and waiting for them to catch up, trying to forget that she has no idea when or if she will ever see them or this place again.

5

Mai travels faster than she anticipates, thanks to her excellent sense of direction and a shortcut, arriving close to two hours early for the ferry. She sits on the rough bench someone has nailed together and waits.

With nothing else to keep her mind occupied, thoughts of Dat Wah take over. Did he receive her note? Did he understand her plan? Did he care? Any other girl would have followed him to Nam King without question. Would anyone in their right mind be sitting alone waiting for a ferry to Macau?

By the time the ferry arrives, thoughts of her walks with Dat Wah, their conversations, and his arms holding her, run through her mind non-stop, bringing her equal parts joy and anguish. It's as if she picks at a wound, and it lies raw and exposed now. She keeps her eyes on the water, ignoring the other passengers trickling towards her, in wait of the ferry. Tears well and she wipes them away harshly with the back of her hand. Maybe she should return to the dormitory and wait. Maybe she should agree to go with him to Nam King. But what of her family? Even if he supported her, she would never want or expect him to rescue her family from poverty.

Mai automatically follows the moving crowd.

"Hey, why are you crying on such a perfect day, young lady?" asks the woman standing next to her.

"It's nothing." Mai acknowledges her but looks at the ground.

"Be appreciative. You still smell of your mother's milk. Plenty of time for you to change what makes you so sad."

Mai sniffles, "Thank you, *Dai Je*, elder sister."

"Ha! I am a grandmother not an elder sister. One day you will be too. Enjoy yourself now when you can run without aches, eat spicy food without getting diarrhea, and show our great leaders how wrong they are."

Mai nods and stops crying. She says nothing more as they board. For the rest of the trip, she listens to the woman talk about her life and her youngest daughter who died because of some unknown illness reminding her of her deceased sister. Looking at the horizon, she takes in the pastel blue sky, the strong ocean breeze, and the warm noontime sun that makes her glad she has a hat. The old woman is right, she is lucky to be healthy and alive.

***

When the ferry finally docks in Macau, Mai nods to the old woman, who remains seated waiting for the crowd to clear, and wishes her a safe trip. She joins the long line to walk across the plank to land but moves deliberately slowly. Her pace annoys but does not stop other passengers from pushing past her.

Mai is soaking up the spring weather and the excitement at the dock like any other tourist. But her ulterior goal is to talk to the crew without being overheard. Most of the passengers have made the trip to sightsee or gamble and Mai blends in, gawking at various buildings. As more people walk past her, she feels sufficiently isolated to ask the closest crew member, a young man, if he knows of a boat that will take her to Hong Kong.

He narrows his eyes, looks her up and down and scans around. After a moment he appears satisfied her inquiry is legitimate and no one else is listening. He motions for Mai to step aside to let those passengers still lingering get by as he quickly whispers to her about a man with a moustache, wearing a green T-shirt, with a tattoo of a dragon on his left arm and a tiger on his right. The man loiters at the end of the marina from around five o'clock to midnight. Mai thanks the crew member, rejoins the passengers exiting the ferry, and walks down the plank.

As her feet touch land, Mai turns in the direction indicated, in search of the "Snake Head" smuggler. At first, she overlooks the small statured man whose sharp eyes dart about probing the area and assessing her long before she is close enough to speak with him. Feeling his eyes on her Mai looks at him and can't help but to notice his sun-weathered skin before she confirms a long dragon tattoo sprawling the length of his left arm while a tattoo of a tiger sits ready to pounce off his right arm. As she nears, the smell of cigarettes oozes from him. Mai is unsure if he hears her as his eyes continually searches the marina while she speaks.

"Arrive Friday night at the dock furthest from here," he points ever so quickly and says in a gruff low voice. "End of the line by the white and red boat. You see it?" Mai looks in the direction he pointed in and picks out the boat. "Wear dark clothes, no more than one bag. We deliver you to your address."

"How much?" Mai asks.

"Hundred Hong Kong dollars, half before we leave, half when we arrive."

"If I give you a gold chain now, I get it back when I pay the amount in cash?" Mai asks.

"Depends on the chain." Mai hands it to him to examine. After a few seconds, he releases it. "Bring it Friday."

She walks purposefully toward the buses and taxis feeling both excited and nervous about her plan.

"I need to get to *Dai Gai*, Big Street," she says to the first cab driver in the queue as she reaches the area where they linger. It is the address of one of Amah's cousins. She hopes the relatives are as kind as Amah.

"Get in, get in," says the cab driver as if he is herding cattle.

"What's the cost to get there?" Mai asks before stepping in. The driver smiles showing off his gold tooth, taking in her mainland clothes and accent.

"Don't worry. I'll get you there. Very cheap."

Mai ignores him and starts to walk toward the next cab in line.

"Come back, come back," he shouts after her.

By this time, Mai's reached the next cab and asked him the same question. She gets in only because he gives her the price and says nothing else.

Amah's cousins agree to let her stay with them for a few days despite her unexpected arrival. With everything settled, Mai has nothing to do but wait for the boat. She decides to spend the time touring Macau, as she knows it is unlikely, she will ever return.

When Friday afternoon arrives, Mai thanks her relatives for their hospitality and leaves behind a few sweet desserts she picked up at the market. It is all she can afford as thanks. They assume she is headed back to her nursing quarters in China.

Instead, she wanders the main street and at dusk makes her way to the marina and the designated dock. She spots the Snake

Head and reluctantly hands him the gold chain Dat Wah gave her. Her heart flutters as she climbs aboard the rickety boat overcome with fear, not for what may happen on the voyage, but because she may not see the chain again. She begins to descend the staircase when a commotion at the front of the boat draws everyone's attention.

"You cannot come tonight. Come back tomorrow," the Snake Head is saying to a woman.

"Why not? I paid," says the woman, who Mai guesses to be in her mid-thirties.

"We told you no bright colours. Your yellow shirt is like a beacon. It'll be spotted in the trees. Go. Come back next week." He waves the bills she gave him back at her.

The woman wisely shuts up and leaves. The boat starts to move shortly after the incident. Mai shuts her eyes.

The two-hour trip seems much longer given the turbulence and darkness at the bottom of the boat. She considers sleeping but the stench of body sweat and bad breath from herself and the other passengers keeps her awake. The little boat is so unstable Mai is convinced she will join her ancestors in the next life at least three different times as she swallows to force back the rice she ate before she boarded. Only then does she think to pray for her life.

Thankfully, the boat docks. Everyone is ushered out quickly and silently. Another man leads them as they climb through a pitch-black area, ascend a mountainous terrain, trek through trees, and cross a sandy patch. Even if she wanted to, Mai would not be able to retrace her steps or identify her whereabouts.

Eventually they see city lights. The passengers are divided into smaller groups headed to different areas of Hong Kong. Mai's group has five people. They cram into a car with the Snake Head as their driver. Mai watches as the first person reaches his destination. The Snake Head exits the car with him, and they disappear into the darkness for what Mai guesses is fifteen minutes. The Snake Head returns alone.

Mai is next. As before, the Snake Head exits the car with her, and Mai takes in the laundry hung out on balconies around them, a couple of broken windows and the buildings crammed tightly next to each other. She follows the Snake Head into a building, recognizing the number on the front as Amah's address. The Snake Head motions for Mai to knock at Amah's door. A woman answers. Mai asks for Amah. The woman walks down the hall yelling Amah's name, and Mai glimpses a room at the end of the hall where Amah is feeding little Yaing Gong something from a bowl, before the woman's back blocks her view.

Mai hears the flap, flap, flap of slippered footsteps.

"Mai? Mai? What are you doing here?" cries Amah as she opens the door wide. "Are you okay? Why are you not in school? What has happened? How—"

"Amah, not now," Mai says, "I'll explain later. We need to pay off the Snake Head." Amah finally sees the man standing behind Mai and understands the urgency. Amah quickly canvasses the other boarders to borrow the money Mai needs.

Mai counts it and hands it to the Snake Head. He nods and turns to leave when Mai calls out, "The gold chain. I get it back."

"Mai, don't," protests Amah, looking nervous.

"You should be more appreciative," the Snake Head says. Mai's only concern is he might not return the chain. After a moment, he reaches into his pocket, fishes out the chain, and studies it for a second before he mutters, "Not worth it," and tosses it behind him before walking away.

Mai picks up the chain that lands by her feet and stands up. She sighs aloud, leans against the wall, and closes her eyes.

"You foolish girl. Why would you risk angering a Snake Head for some cheap chain?" Amah pulls her inside.

Mai takes in the shabby conditions she now calls home.

Jung jumps up from her seat the second she sees Mai, bumping the table and toppling the bit of congee left in her bowl.

"Big sister?!"

"Hi, Jung. Your leg okay?"

"Much better," chirps Jung as she pulls up her trouser leg to show Mai.

To Mai's disappointment, the leg is clearly smaller than the other and the skin looks pulled and tight where they operated. Her sister might feel better because it no longer hurts but she is unable to bend the leg at the knee and she limps when she walks. Her face has matured, but she is much smaller than she should be at a mere few years younger than Mai.

"*Bebe sai lo*, baby brother, you are all grown up now!" Mai says smiling at Yaing Gong in his highchair. His now empty bowl is overturned, and he is hitting it with his spoon like a drum. He looks at Mai curiously, but he has no idea who she is. The boarder who answered the door leaves the kitchen to give them some privacy.

"Sit. Eat a bowl of congee. Tell me what happened. How are you here?" Amah asks Mai.

Mai washes her hands at the sink. She can't help but to notice the spots of rust around the drain that desperately need to be scrubbed away. She sits at the kitchen table and hungrily eats the congee Amah sets out for her. She wants several more bowls, but she does not want to pillage what she knows is their paltry supply of food. Besides, she's excited to explain everything to Amah.

"I received Abah's letter. I thought you might need help, so I came."

"Abah sent you?"

"No. Don't be crazy. Abah! Abah's more afraid of violating government edicts than he is of dying. Only the Snake Head knew I was coming. I knew you'd need help." Mai concentrates on scraping her empty bowl with her spoon avoiding eye contact with Amah.

"Mai, you're lucky to be alive. A Snake Head. So dangerous. Why? We'd be okay."

"I went home to see everyone. Brought them the warm blanket from school. Didn't want to see it go to waste. Helped them gather kindling for fire. Fy Sing and the boys were trying to make their bundles as big as mine." Mai laughs at the thought. "They are good. I left for Macau early the next day."

"Ohhhh," Amah says nodding as if it was all clear now, "You came from Macau."

"The ferry was full but not as crowded as the market in the city during the main shopping hours."

"Where did you stay in Macau? Those Snake Heads stay in dangerous places. You went and sought them out?"

"I stayed with your cousin."

"Did you tell them what you were doing? You're so lucky nothing happened to you." Amah clucks her tongue worriedly.

"Cousins were fine. And no. Why would I tell them what I was doing? If I did not tell Abah and Mah Mah, why would I tell your cousins who I hardly know? I don't know if I should tell you the rest if you're so upset already."

Amah says nothing else and starts to clean up the dishes as Mai continues with her account.

"Ai yah, Mai. You want me to die? They can kick you back to China tomorrow if they choose." She pauses before saying, "Or kill you."

"Amah. Do not worry. I will figure something out. Need to clean and sleep."

"Oh, Mai, you are so concerned about being clean. I'll boil some water, so you can wash." Amah's hands shake as she fills the kettle.

"You should've seen the people on the boat and then what I climbed through. You'd clean up too," Mai says.

Even though she knows Amah is right and she could be deported to China, arrested, or worse, she is inexplicably confident everything is going to work out as Amah and her siblings crowd into one of the two beds they rent at the rooming house, leaving the other one to her because of her size.

6

Mai inhales deeply as she sits by the bay window overlooking the enclosed garden of the church. The blanket of fully bloomed red and yellow tulips is stunning. The sight calms her momentarily.

A knock at the door and the grating voice of the woman who helped with her dress and makeup brings Mai back to her appearance.

"Mai, did you want me to fix the veil again? They're almost ready to begin."

"No, thank you," Mai responds, but the woman has already rushed in and starts to fuss with her hair and veil before she finishes answering.

"Isn't this exciting?"

"Mmm … yes," says Mai.

"Ai yah! What did you do to your lipstick?"

Mai ignores the woman and stands by the open door, waiting to be told to come out. A few minutes later, a voice in the hall announces, "They're ready."

Mai takes the bouquet from the woman's hands. She takes another deep breath, and they walk to the room outside the main hall. Her fiancé's uncle stands proudly in his suit. Mai looks at him and returns his smile before they link arms. He is her escort down the aisle.

Despite her fiancé encouraging Mai to invite her grandfather from San Francisco to the wedding, Mai had declined. He is no more than a stranger to her. Besides, Mai is unsure what she feels toward him. Uncle Ho Choi on the other hand, has been making efforts to make her feel at home since she arrived. Even if they just met, she senses he is genuinely happy to play a prominent part of the ceremony.

The music begins and they start down the long red carpet between the church pews. The walk is uncomfortably long, at least the width of six homes. The cathedral ceiling and stained-glass windows darken the room, and an ominous feeling passes through her. Knowing the eyes of all these strangers are on her is unnerving. She forces herself to look straight ahead as her thoughts return to another walk, one she took alone.

***

The morning after Mai's surreptitious arrival in Hong Kong, once Amah leaves for her job, sweeping up in a factory, and her siblings for school, she too exits the rooming house and walks in the direction Amah had outlined. She feels calm being lost in the crowds.

Before long, she reaches the immigration office. A large flag of China flaps over the front door of the cleanest building in the area.

She walks in and waits as the only other person in the room speaks to the clerk. When she walks up and explains her situation, the clerk pulls out a form and starts to fill in sections. She then marks a few spots and hands the form to Mai to complete.

Mai reads and pauses to consider the best way to explain how she came to be in Hong Kong and why she is applying for permanent residence status. Mai watches the clerk read her explanation and a contemptuous, lopsided smile takes over her face. Mai readies herself for a fight.

"Wait in front of the door."

"Which door?" asks Mai staring at the five doors in the direction the clerk pointed.

"Are you dull, farm girl? I told you the one over there."

"I know you may have trouble seeing at your age, Grandmother, but there are five doors there," says Mai.

The clerk meets Mai's eyes and pleasant smile. "Hmmm. Second from the end."

"Many thanks." Mai tips her chin, ignoring the clerk's snarl.

Mai sits down and nearly falls asleep waiting over an hour before a uniformed officer throws open the door and shouts, "Chung Mai Gum."

Given that no one else is in the room, Mai does not see the point in him shouting except to scare her. She walks over quickly. It turns out the door leads to a hallway with several other closed doors. The officer opens the third one on the right and orders her in.

The small room is brightly lit with a rectangular desk and two chairs. Another man dressed in the same type of uniform is sitting in one of the chairs studying what Mai sees is her form.

"Sit down," orders the officer who led her there. Mai does as she's told and sneaks a look at the officer's face. He has a scar across his right cheek, beady slits for eyes, and a wide mouth with crooked yellow teeth. His nose is pushed upwards like that of a pig. Mai turns to the plain-looking officer who sits directly across from her behind the desk, as the ugly one paces behind her.

"Tell us how you arrived in Hong Kong," asks the ugly officer.

"I came by ferry," Mai says.

"Everyone comes by ferry," he shouts. "Where is your passport? You know you cannot gain permanent residence status here without three years residence in Macau. So where is the proof you have lived there that long?"

"Unfortunately, I lost my passport and all my identity papers on the ferry ride over," Mai answers calmly.

"Who did you pay? What route did you take?"

Mai watches the other officer writing each time either she or his partner speak. He says nothing. He doesn't even look at her.

"I paid the man at the ferry. I've no idea what his name was and I don't know which route we took. We passed mountains, trees and a sandy area."

"There are mountains, trees and sand all around here. We're on an island!" shouts the ugly officer. "If you don't start telling me what I want to know you will regret it. What did the man look like? Was he a Snake Head? What was his name?"

"I've no idea what his name was. I don't ask such things usually. Do you, when you book a ferry?"

"Where is your family?"

"I have family everywhere, in America, here in Hong Kong, and even in Macau," Mai responds without blinking.

"We will deport you within days so you may as well cooperate," he threatens. The "interview" goes on like this for two hours before they excuse her with instructions to return the next day at the same time.

***

"How did it go today, Mai?" Amah asks with a furrowed brow

as she did the day before. Mai considers not telling her as she watches the greens for dinner quiver in Amah's hands like the money she held out to give the Snake Head the night Mai arrived.

"Same as yesterday. Need to go back in a few days. Do you have Fuk Sau's phone number?"

"My half-brother's son? Yes. Why?"

Amah came from a wealthy family. So wealthy, her Abah had three wives at the same time. Mai's maternal grandmother, was only his second wife. Amah and her mother left Hong Kong and hid out in the village like Abah did when Hong Kong was seized by the Japanese. Amah's mother died in Amah's arms before the war ended. Amah was younger than Mai is now when it happened. Who knows how life might be different if they had stayed in Hong Kong like Amah's half siblings who survived and are now flourishing.

Amah's half family has always been kind to her but Mai has only had occasion to speak with this cousin she is inquiring about a few times in the past. "I just want to say hello," Mai answers.

"He's very busy running the hotels. I don't know if he'll have time to speak with you. His sister was already kind enough to help your siblings and me when we arrived. I can't even repay her for that." Amah looks down at the floor.

"That's fine. I'll call to thank him. I don't want to be rude, coming to Hong Kong and not even paying my respects."

Amah looks at Mai quizzically but she doesn't ask anything more as she sets the greens on the table to free her hands to write the number down.

The next day as soon as everyone has left for work and school, Mai dials her cousin's number.

"How nice of you to call, Mai," answers Fuk Sau. "Your Amah didn't mention you were going to be joining her here. How are she and the family doing?"

"We are generally well. I came unexpectedly. It's complicated. But Amah needs the help. How is your family? Your mother and sister?"

"Everyone is well. Good of you to ask. What is complicated?"

"I'm having a little trouble getting my immigration papers sorted. I've been for two interviews already and I'm due back in a few days for a third. It'd be nice to see all of you soon."

"What is this problem with immigration? You know my sister is dating the head of the new immigration department. He's a decent man."

"They are questionning whether I've spent the required three years in Macau before applying for my status. I can't imagine what Amah will do without some help."

"You are brazen, Mai. I can't imagine how you survive otherwise though." Her cousin chuckles and declines to ask Mai outright whether she has in fact spent three years in Macau. "Take this number down, 826438576. Give it to the officers questioning you next."

"Amah and Abah always say my brain isn't fully developed. Probably true. Thank you for your help, cousin. "

He laughs. "I was your age not too long ago. Once this business is sorted out, you, your Amah, and your siblings must come out to visit."

"I will let Amah know. It will be nice to see all of you. And thank you again."

***

At the next interview, Mai sits waiting in the main area for the officer to call her in. She purposely sits upright and looks about casually, careful to exude more confidence than she feels.

"Chung Mai Gum," shouted an unseen voice Mai now knew

belonged to the ugly officer.

"No need to get too comfortable as long as you tell us the truth today," the officer says as she steps into the same room with the stiff wooden chairs. His partner is seated poised to take more notes.

"I've answered all your questions so far and I'm happy to repeat the information to you again."

"Start with the truth today," says the officer. "Now what—"

"Excuse me officer, before we begin, I was asked to give you this number." Mai half stands and hands over the piece of paper.

"What is this nonsense? Another delay tactic? Stop interrupt—"

"Wait. Let me see that," says his partner, speaking for the first time. He takes the paper and studies it before leaving the room without a word.

The ugly officer, clearly uncertain as to what is happening, barks at Mai to not move before he follows his partner out the room and shuts the door.

Mai never even thought to ask Fuk Sau whether he had given her a badge number, a telephone number or something else. Mai starts pacing. After what seems like forever, the officers re-enter the room. The ugly officer smiles, which unnerves Mai as he appears even uglier and she is unsure what is happening.

"Miss Chung, so sorry for the inconvenience. Would you like us to escort you home?" says the plain officer.

"Umm … no. It's fine … ummm … what does this mean?"

"I'm sorry for not explaining. You are free to go," says the plain officer.

"When am I to be interviewed again?"

"No, no. We are done. Your registration for permanent residence to Hong Kong is being processed right now. You will have a temporary card before you leave and we will send a courier with the final documents. No need for you to return here."

"Would you like some tea while you wait for the card? You can wait in here or in the main room." The ugly officer follows his offer with another smile making Mai shudder.

"No. It's fine. I'll wait outside." Mai quickly takes her bag and hurries out of the interrogation room.

Mai collects the temporary card within five minutes from the clerk she called a grandmother. As she heads out the front door, the ugly officer calls after her, "Have a lovely day and welcome to Hong Kong, Miss Chung."

Mai looks back at him and nods haltingly but she's not ready to smile at the man who had yelled at her for two days.

As she walks down the street, an overwhelming sense of relief washes over her. And the further she gets from the immigration building, the larger the feeling becomes. She breathes deeply trying to calm herself but tears of relief flood out. People walking past, eye her suspiciously or study her, confused at the public display of emotion, but no one approches or says anything.

For a brief moment, Mai doesn't care if she is breaking accepted customs. She doesn't care what anyone else thinks right then.

7

In the church, Uncle Ho Choi and Mai reach the minister. Ho Choi is waving his nephew over to stand beside her.

The minister speaks, and Mai focuses on his lips, not understanding anything he says. She blocks out the audience standing around her, the chill she feels in the church, and the part of her that wants to cry. She concentrates more fiercely on the movement of the minister's lips.

To the delight of the crowd she finishes with an attempt at the English words she practiced with Ho Choi over the last few days.

"Yeees." She pauses. "I do?"

Those within earshot laugh and clap at her efforts.

The minister directs her to sit down at the little wooden table while Ming stands behind her pointing to a line and gesturing for her to sign her name. Luckily, she'd been practicing the curves and shapes of the English letters that make up her phonetically translated name since before she left Hong Kong for all the immigration documents and forms that needed her signature. Except for "1966" and the "18th", Mai has no idea what the rest of the writing on the paper means.

Flashes mostly from the camera of the official photographer, Ho Choi's son, go off like a fireworks show on Canada Day. It was his wedding gift to them. Mai smiles as guests follow them out of the church throwing rice and flowers.

Mai and her husband stand outside the church doors, shaking hands with the guests, smiling and posing for the odd guest photo. It is an exhausting hour. All the smiling hurts Mai's cheeks. It is so unnatural. The watch on her husband's wrist shows they aren't quite due to return to the restaurant. She wishes they were. In contrast, her husband seems giddy with the attention and the company. Of course he is. He's surrounded by family and friends while she's alone.

***

To celebrate her acquisition of Hong Kong residency, Amah prepares Mai's favourite dishes that evening, salted preserved fish, pickled cabbage, and extra rice. They chat about their days but mostly Mai re-enacts the ugly officer during the interviews, making everyone laugh. However, Mai shushes the family when one of the boarders walks in. The shared accomodations and lack of privacy reminds her that only one of many challenges they face in Hong Kong has been settled, putting a damper on her mood.

Her frustration grows at the end of the night when Amah and her two siblings crawl into one bed while Mai crawls into the other alone. They desperately need money.

Within two days, a factory hires Mai to sweep up while the regular worker is away. Unfortunately, the pay is low and the hours are unsteady. Mai then finds work at a textile mill where she cuts the loose threads off the material being produced. The problem is, one day she has a full day of work, followed by a half day, followed by nothing for several days. After weeks of Mai offering to stay to help with everything and anything, the manager advises her to take a course to learn to use the loom because there is a demand with all the textile and garment factories popping up.

Mai follows the advice and saves enough after a few months to learn to weave the strands of thread through a loom. Some who take the course have trouble learning the art and never get the hang of it; others take several months to learn; still others, like Mai, learn most of what they need by the end of the first week. It pays off.

"Show me what you can do, *fai nai*, fat daughter," says the factory manager at one of the largest mills near the shantytown where they live.

Mai takes her time to assess the giant loom where the tall Shanghai woman she is to copy is working. At barely five feet, Mai knows she will be unable to reach the heddles to thread them like threading a needle. She spots folding chairs near one of the walls and sets one up at each end of the loom. Once in place, the factory manager looks at her, confused, but signals the worker to let Mai step in. Mai climbs onto the chair, threads one end, climbs down, trots to the other end, climbs up, and repeats the process. The manager and the Shanghai woman laugh as she runs back and forth like this for the next ten minutes until she is told to stop.

"Clever, fat daughter," says the manager.

Mai begins her steady full-time job that afternoon.

She works at a furious pace, sweating profusely and requiring several breaks in an hour as she runs back and forth climbing the stools at each end. As the weeks pass, she requires fewer breaks and does not breathe as hard. When bored she starts to time herself to see how long it takes her to complete one lap around the heddles. The ten-hour days are physcially exhausting but she eagerly accepts extra shifts on her days off, mostly for the money but also because it means she can collapse into bed each evening too tired to recall dreams and too tired to wonder why Dat Wah hasn't contacted her. Perhaps he didn't know her as well as she thought.

Before long, Mai finds her clothes have now thinned so much from use and her excessive washing, she can no longer take them in without tearing the fabric. When she visits a shop to buy a new *yi chang*, traditional two-piece Chinese outfit, she notices the posters of movies featuring the famous Betty Loh Ti and Jenny Hu hanging behind the cash register as she walks to the fitting room. The owner insists she try on at least one of the pre-made outfits from the rack even though Mai tells her she always needs her clothes tailor-made to fit. It is easier to comply than argue with the pushy owner.

Mai is surprised to find the off-the-rack *yi chang* fits, if a little uncomfortable. When she comes out to look in one of the large full-length mirrors, rarely available and usually of no interest to her when they are present, the image of a woman catches her eye. The woman has the figure of one of the famous actresses but not the same facial features, not the same large eyes they and the westerners have. It takes her a second to realize she is seeing herself. Mai knew she'd lost weight but for the first time in her life she can buy off the rack. She insists on buying a size up from what she tried on just in case she gets bigger. Perhaps it's a good thing Dat Wah hasn't come looking for her. He might not like what he sees now.

A year after Mai's arrival in Hong Kong her earnings

combined with Amah's, affords them a whole private room in the house, ten by eight feet, making them the envy of the boarders who rent only individual bed spaces.

Amah, Mai and the siblings enjoy a period of stability in their new routines, sending money home to Abah and the rest of the family regularly. Amah and Yaing Gong can even afford a trip home to visit. Mai loses herself in the frenetic pace of the mill factory, which gives her a sense of purpose and the perfect excuse to push aside her nostalgic thoughts about her less encumbered life as a student and everything she left behind.

***

"Mai, do you feel well?"

"What? Of course. Why do you ask me, Amah?"

"You're working a lot. There's no need to take every extra shift they offer. You won't be young forever."

"I'm fine."

"I worry. I don't want you to be alone. Most of the girls your age are married by now. It's maybe time for you to—"

"What? You're worried I'll be an old maid? You sound like Mah Mah Ping."

"No! I don't think that. Just want you to be happy."

Mah Mah's relatives had been forwarding photos of prospective mates to Mai since she turned twenty. Mai's comments about the potential mates were *too old*, *too short*, *too bald*. The truth was, none of them compared to Dat Wah. A part of her wanted to show him she was right to follow her destiny. Prove him wrong. A part of her hoped he might still send word or come to Hong Kong to find her. But he can't find her if she's not there—and what could he do if she was betrothed to another?

"Your grandmother probably wanted you to marry that postal worker in the U.S. because she wants you where your grandfather lives, San Francisco in America. The great Gold Mountain. Oh, Mai. I just don't want you to work so much. If you marry well, you won't have to. You're only young once."

"Didn't like the one in San Francisco. Who cares if he works for the postal service. Did you see his teeth? Yellow like morning pee. Imagine kissing that!"

Amah laughs. "What about that other one in Canada you were writing to for a bit?"

It was true. Mai took an interest in Lee Hao Ming's photo during one of the times she had worked herself up, decided she was angry with Dat Wah for not even writing, when she'd made up her mind for the hundreth time to leave the past in the past. Ming looked healthy but he didn't live where Grandfather lives. He lives in Canada where his relatives own a restaurant.

"Mah Mah said Ming has bad ancestral lines. His father married three times. First wife left after a few months. Second wife was Ming's mother who along with his two youngest siblings perished during the Japanese occupation here. And now he's married for the third time. Ming has a bunch of younger stepbrothers. The odds are whoever becomes Ming's wife will have a less than healthy future. Besides, he doesn't live in San Francisco like the soothsayer predicted.

"Mai, Mah Mah has brainwashed you since you were a child. You can't believe in those predictions one hundred per cent and you certainly can't make such important decisions in your life based on it. Besides, the soothsayer never said you were going to San Francisco, he said you were going to *North America*. Your grandmother assumed it was San Francisco because of your grandfather. Gold Mountain can mean British Columbia or all of Canada too. Just want you to have an easier life. To be happy."

"Easy and happy life like yours?" says Mai, knowing Amah's

regrets and nervous that Amah might be right. Amah looks hurt and pauses before responding.

"Had I a choice, I would never have chosen your Abah. He has a terrible temper and he thought he was so good at mah-jong. He is the reason we have no money and barely any valuables to hide from the Communists. Almost all of my mother's rings and necklaces, gone. Lost it all. Stupid man. My family thought because his father is in Gold Mountain, they had money. Who knew!" Amah leaves the room flushed, and with watery eyes.

Mai is too stubborn to apologize. She doesn't want to share the true reason she doesn't want to marry yet. Dat Wah was a part of her life no one from home knows about. But what if Amah's right? What if Mai's been foolish to make all her decisions based on some soothsayer's prediction? A prediction she may have misunderstood. Should she have followed Dat Wah to Nam King?

She quickly goes to her bedside where she hides the velvet pouch with Dat Wah's ring and chain and digs to the bottom. She takes out the triangular folded slip of rice paper.

July 12, 1950

I see her forging a path. To North America. She is your family's route to a better life.

Amah was right. The soothsayer predicted she was going to North America. All this time, she assumed it was Gold Mountain because it made the most sense.

Mai sighs as she gathers rice, bean curd, greens, and a thermos of water. She feels too guilty to say anything to Amah before she leaves for work. Soon after this conversation, the realization that she may have been making incorrect assumptions all this time inspires Mai to take an uncharacteristic step.

***

Mai awakes early one Saturday morning and does not want to stay inside to help with breakfast dishes, or the laundry. She offers instead to get the groceries for the next few days. While she wanders around the market streets picking up some fresh vegetables, a can of oil-preserved fish cooked with black beans and salt, and some Chinese sausages, she reads a crudely put together sign propped up beside a clothing shop.

WESTERN EYELIDS. UNDER AN HOUR. BEST PRICE HERE.

She walks up the narrow staircase and an hour later Mai exits with bandages over the tops of her eyes covered by a complimentary pair of cheap plastic sunglasses. She walks home feeling satisfied.

Amah screams when Mai removes her glasses.

"Mai, what happened? What are the bandages? Why are you bloody?"

"I just got the double eyelid procedure done. I'm fine. Here are the groceries."

"You what? Are you crazy? You're lucky you're not blind!"

Mai ignores her and lies down. By the end of the weekend, there is slightly less swelling but there is bruising and patches of blood forming scabs over each eye. Once they fully heal, Mai marvels at her double lids in the little mirror they have in the rooming house.

A distant relative of Mah Mah Ping sees Amah in the streets several months later. They catch up and eventually the relative asks if Mai has married yet. Amah relays the conversation to Mai when she gets home from work that evening.

"I ran into Mah Mah Ping's cousin, today. You know, the one

who knows Ming's aunts. She asked about you and she said Ming is still not married."

"Really?" It had been a little over a year since they stopped corresponding.

"Do you want to write to him again? She gave me Ming's aunt's number again. Do you want me to call? Or ask your Mah Mah to write to his other relatives?"

Mai sighs as she sips her tea. She knows she can't wait for Dat Wah any longer.

"You can ask for Ming's address again. I'll mention it to Mah Mah too when I next write to her."

Dear Ming,

Much time has passed since we last wrote to each other. I'm sorry for not responding to your last letter but I was working a lot at the factory. The manager keeps offering me more shifts because he tells me I'm quicker than all my co-workers. Helps to pay for the larger quarters we now have. We're thinking of getting a bigger place soon.

I decided to get a little cosmetic surgery. Western eyelids. It's the latest thing here.

Grandfather tells us the family seafood store and the half dozen cabs they operate are all very busy in San Francisco. You remember our family has been there for decades now. Perhaps we can visit him at some point.

I'm enclosing a recent photo of myself. Hopefully you and your family are doing well. Please send my best to your aunt and uncle at the restaurant.

I hope to hear from you soon.

Chung Mai Gum

Between Mai's letter and Amah's call, Mai is soon invited to the home of Ming's eldest aunt, Fai Nguk Yee, and uncle, Wang Dei Yee, in Hong Kong. Mai saved the bus fare and walked the eleven blocks to their home. The family was wealthy because of the husband's architectural business.

Knowing she had to impress them, Mai wore her newish *yi chang* and put on a fake jade bracelet she bought in the market. Thank goodness she did. The home they rented was something to admire. An entire ground floor of a building, consisting of three bedrooms, a living room, kitchen, bathroom, servant quarters and a yard all for themselves. The servant was apparently a woman that Ming's eldest aunt was friends with from their village in China. It was strange for Mai to have someone serving tea and clearing dishes. She almost wanted to help but knew better.

"Ming's father and half brothers are staying with us for a while," says Fai Nguk. "His Abah wanted to be here but he's at work and the boys are at school."

"I'm sure there will be other occasions to meet them. He travels here often?" Mai asks.

"Too often. He's taken over our son's room." Mai can't help but notice Wang Dei's eyebrow rise in annoyance.

"Your son is away, Uncle?" Mai asks even though she already knows the answer.

"Yes. He is at the University of Toronto! Very hard to get in. Studying architecture."

"He must have been born with geometry skills like you. I practically failed that subject. Any home I tried to design would be lopsided or fall over."

Wang Dei laughs and starts talking happily about the projects he's working on and bragging about his son.

"Do you like the city, Mai?" asks Fai Nguk at the next break in the conversation.

"I like the city better than the country. More to do and see. Even more than I thought possible as a nursing student."

"Yes, your grandmother told us you did very well in the provincial exams. Turned down two orders to report for studies. Brave. Why did you leave?"

Wang Dei leans in for the answer.

"School taught me two important things. First, to seize opportunity when it presents itself, and second, that under Communist rule no one will ever be truly free."

Wang Dei laughs. "Mai, you sound like a true Hong Kong person. You sure you weren't born here?"

"Well, you know my Amah's family has been here all their lives. It must be their influence. Perhaps you might know them, the Yus, they own hotels here and all over the world."

According to Mah Mah and Amah's sources, Mai heard this uncle of Ming's, was a bit of a snob and he usually ignored guests, especially relatives from his wife's side. So, Amah was surprised to hear he not only greeted Mai warmly but stayed for the entire visit, chatting away. Shortly after that, Mai received a letter from Ming.

Mai,

It is nice to hear from you.

I hope the weather is not too hot in Hong Kong. It's been a few years since I left. I miss parts of it but I'm glad it doesn't get quite as hot here in Canada. We're not too far from a lake so it helps a bit for the few months of summer we enjoy. We also eat a lot of fish. No crabs and lobsters though. Sounds like your grandfather might be able to get us some if we visit him in San Francisco.

I work a lot too here in my uncle's restaurant. It's pretty busy but I like a good day's work. Sounds like you do as well.

I took a trip out to a French-speaking area of the country with some of the other workers. They had a lot of stone houses there. And Uncle Ho Choi and I went to his cottage. Like living in the village.

My eldest aunt and uncle were very happy to meet you. They hope you will visit them again soon.

I liked your photo and here is one of me and a friend, in front of the restaurant. I'm on the right. The other is a passport photo.

Lee Hao Ming

Enclosed with the letter and photos is a bit of money to show his interest in her. Unlike Abah's calligraphy-like characters, Ming's were large and appeared to be written by a child. But she'd heard he didn't have much education. Just very hard working. His rectangular face showed he was stable and balanced, like Dat Wah. His lips are full, clearly indicating he is not silver tongued but honest. Plus he has a perfect set of white teeth. A prominent nose like Ming's is a well-known indicator of great wealth, now or in the future. His eyes are a bit small but that's the only negative Mai can see. He is fit and appears quite tall in his photo. He's not Dat Wah, but handsome in his own way.

Mai assumed her not-so-subtle allusions of family riches made a good impression because she was invited to visit as often as she liked by Ming's eldest aunt and uncle.

Mah Mah's letters no longer voiced her concerns about Ming's ancestral shortcomings and instead praised the fact that he and his relatives are settled in Canada. Even if it isn't the exact Gold Mountain where her grandfather Bak Lai lives.

8

After one of her shifts at the factory, Mai comes home to find Amah sitting at the kitchen table with a man she's never seen. When he gets up to introduce himself, she finds he is very tall, almost six feet, she guesses. He looks familiar but she can't figure out from where. He also has noticeably attractive dark eyebrows shaped like the peak of a triangle. It turns out he is Ming's father, Lee Bo Chang, and he has dropped by unannounced after his shift at the silk framing factory to meet Mai and her family.

Mai is surprised at how casual and informal he is compared to Ming's eldest aunt and uncle. He's more interested in talking about farming techniques than school and sharing his staunch support for Communism, which explains in part why Ming's uncle cares little for his company. She knows there is no need to keep up any charade of family wealth with him and, in fact, it might be dangerous to do so.

He readily accepts Amah's invitation to stay for dinner and

Amah sends her out with a bottle to be filled with a drink of alcohol for him. When the unexpected visits become almost regular, Amah and Mai calculate it is cheaper to buy a full bottle and keep it on hand for when he drops in. To further ingratiate herself with him and his family, Mai purchases fabric from Amah's factory at a discount and borrows a neighbours's sewing machine to sew Ming's young half brothers pyjamas as gifts.

Before long, the relatives are finalizing plans for Mai's trip to Canada and the wedding, even though there is never a formal proposal from Ming. Once they consent, Mai and Ming simply follow directions and attend appointments as directed by the elder relatives, writing occasionally to each other.

***

With the photos finally finished, Mai and Ming pile into Uncle Ho Choi's car with his wife and their son. They arrive at the restaurant, just down the street from the church, within minutes.

Mai tries to help unload items from the car, but everyone tells her not to get her dress dirty. She steps back alongside Aunt Fai Lok and watches for a few minutes before finally walking into the restaurant. It is now bustling with friends and staff setting up for the evening banquet, unlike the quiet she had enjoyed during the tea ceremony.

Mai makes her way to the back room she will soon share with Ming. There are still a few hours before guests arrive for the dinner, so she changes into comfortable slacks and slips into the kitchen.

"Mai, what are you doing?" asks one of the cooks she met on her second day there.

"I was going to help chop." Mai continues to tie up the apron she picked up.

"You can't help! It's your wedding day. The guests will arrive soon. Go change into your *cheong sam*, traditional Chinese wedding dress."

"Hours before guests arrive. There is lots of time. I can help," says Mai desperate for activity, desperate to keep her mind from missing her family, from thinking about Dat Wah, from what will be expected of her later in the evening.

"And big boss will yell at us if he sees we let his new niece prepare her own wedding meal! Get out," says the cook good-naturedly as he pushes her out.

Mai reluctantly hands over the apron and retreats. She straightens the already tidy room, her new home. Bored, she grabs her favourite navy-blue cardigan and walks out the back door quietly. The sunshine blinds her momentarily as she begins to walk.

***

Mai scans her side of the bedroom in the boarding house as she packs up the few belongings she owns. In two days, she will climb aboard an airplane for the first time, leave her family behind again, and start a new life. Amah enters their room and closes the door behind her.

"It's hot in here. Open the door, will you?" Mai says not looking at her mother while she sorts and folds the piles she's gathered.

"Mai, you had visitors the other day."

"What are you talking about? Who?"

Mai does not notice Amah's lower than normal tone.

"Jung says two young men came to the door looking for you a few weeks ago."

"Really? Were they from the Hong Kong Immigration Department? Offering me more gifts if I leave faster?" she says, laughing at her own joke as she hurries about.

"They were friends with someone named Wong Dat Wah."

Mai freezes and looks up at Amah for a second.

"Did they leave a number? An address? She feels faint and perches on the bed. "Did you say weeks ago?"

"Jung just told me today before I left for work. They came the day you were getting fitted for this—your wedding *cheong sam.*" Amah points to the gown hanging behind the door.

"What? Why didn't she tell me right away? Did they leave a phone number?"

"No. They did not. Mai. Mai, look at me. You don't have to go to Canada. We'll be fine either way."

"What did they say?"

"They said they were friends of this Dat Wah. They said he is your boyfriend. Your fiancé?"

"What else?"

"Jung told them you are getting married. Going to Canada."

Mai's left hand drops to her side, dangling the shirt she was about to pack, as she closes her eyes.

"Did they ask for the ring back?"

"What ring?"

"Go. Leave me alone."

"Mai. Mai. What are you going to do?"

Mai says nothing but sits down on the lower bunk bed. Amah eventually leaves but Mai doesn't even notice.

The next day Mai visits with Ming's eldest aunt and uncle as planned. She also visits cousin Fuk Sau, his sister and their mother, leaving everyone with fresh pastries as a parting gift. Amah had tried a few times to ask her about Dat Wah, but Mai changed the subject each time. However, idle time was all Mai had on the plane ride to Canada.

"Are you feeling all right Miss? Do you need some water? A

paper bag in case you get sick?" asks the pretty stewardess.

"Thank you. Maybe a pillow and a blanket so I can rest a bit," says Mai.

"First time flying?"

"Yes."

"It's a long trip we have ahead of us."

"Have you been there before?" Mai asks.

"Only for a few days, but it's beautiful. A little cold."

"Heard the mountains are gorgeous, like in parts of China."

"Yes, those are in Vancouver where we'll land first. Are you staying there or going on to Toronto?"

"Oh, Toronto."

"How long are you staying?"

"I'm getting married."

"Oh! Congratulations! Very exciting."

"I don't know what to expect. Don't know anyone there."

"Except your fiancé, you mean."

"I'm excited to meet him," says Mai. "We've written quite a bit."

"Ohhh, traditional," answers the stewardess stiffening a bit before recovering with, "I'm sure you'll be very happy. But you are looking a little worse. Shall I bring you anti-nausea pills?"

"I think rest will be best."

The stewardess returns quickly with a pillow and a blanket. "Call me if you need anything else, Miss."

"Thank you."

Mai leans her head back. She stares out the window past the man sitting to her left, but the cloudy clear skies grow boring after a few minutes. She is glad Ming's family did not pay extra for a window seat.

Unable to concentrate on much except trying to get rid of the pressure in her head and the nausea in her stomach, she dozes in and out of a fitful sleep. She awakes sweating, her head pounding, tired and disoriented. The restrictive dress she chose, to impress Ming's family with her ladylike appearance, is rumpled, and Mai is sure the seams are about to split.

She dozes off again and dreams of Dat Wah. They stand in the kitchen of an unfamiliar home. She apologizes for leaving, for being selfish, for choosing her goal instead of their life together. She wakes crying.

The stewardess rushes over. "Miss, miss. Are you in pain? Are you okay?"

"It feels terrible," Mai says through tears.

"I'll bring you some water and those pills," the stewardess answers.

All Mai can do is nod as the tears continue to fall. Eventually she is led to the small bathroom at the back of the plane, thankful for the privacy. She continues to cry for what seems like hours. She finally starts to calm her breathing and the tears dry up. In her head she yells at Dat Wah.

How could you dismiss my dream, my fate so easily? The Gold Mountain is not a fantasy. I didn't turn you down. I imagined our children. I imagined our home. I imagined us, but not in China. Maybe your promotion, your career might protect me but what about my family? I have a duty to them. You don't. I wanted to spare you, protect you. And if you really wanted to be with me, why didn't you send word earlier? Where were you all this time? Did you think I would just wait around for you? Forever?

A part of Mai hopes he finds someone but someone *less*; less attractive, less clever, less ambitious. She does not want him to suffer or be unhappy. She struggles with a vision of this lesser mate for him, reasoning that everything he professed to her came out of the ignorance of their youth and fleeting desires. Yet a part of her, the part now crying uncontrollably at the thought of him with someone else, even someone less, hopes he never finds happiness without her.

She leaves these thoughts in limbo. She longs for a glimpse into his life now, his life without her. She desperately wants to know the impossible: whether they were right for each other, whether they could have been happy together, somehow. She always thought hearing from him would bring her closure one way or another, but instead it has led to greater uncertainty.

Taking a deep breath, she pulls herself up to her full four feet, eleven inches, looks in the mirror, and scolds herself for crying, and crying in public no less—not the most fortuitous way to start a new life. Luckily, no one in her new, or old life, is there to witness her breakdown. She steps on the foot pedal to allow the water from the tap to flow, splashes some on her face, and grabs some of the plush paper towels to wipe up. She straightens her dress as best she can, leaves the stall and walks back to her seat avoiding the eyes of the passengers.

***

The Toronto airport feels as chaotic as the one she left in Hong Kong. Mai loves the frenetic energy. People wander around in every direction in both places but here, there seem to be conversations in many different languages. Despite many of the passengers on her plane being Chinese, they make up a small minority in the airport.

The steady jumble of unintelligible conversations follows Mai as she looks around for Ming, secretly enjoying the tapping sound of her new leather flats against the shiny ceramic floors but hating how they pinch her toes. Occasionally a voice cuts through the others, like that of a child crying for food or those of boisterous young men excitedly hugging each other, but for the most part everyone seems reserved and gentle like the British citizens she was familiar with in Hong Kong or the Russian soldiers she treated in the hospital.

Then she spots him.

She knows immediately that Ming is as honest as they come. Although he is quite broad shouldered, he stands, if not quite slouched, then less than proudly. Unlike Dat Wah, who always seemed to stand at full attention, eyes scanning his surroundings, ready to take on the world, Ming appears tentative. He looks like he needs a strong partner next to him.

By this time Ming and the men surrounding him have also spotted her. Ming introduces Mai to his Uncle Ho Choi and to Guang, the real estate agent, translator, and all around go-to-person for transactions in English. After the initial pleasantries, the men start to speak about Ho Choi's restaurants. They talk simultaneously, interrupting each other, and Mai becomes aware that other airport patrons are taking notice of their group's presence. Perhaps it is because they speak in loud Cantonese tones—an angry-sounding village dialect that drowns out quiet conversations which sound like murmurs in comparison—that makes Mai feel conspicuous. She's relieved when the group starts to walk toward the cars.

She quickly takes the cue to compliment Ho Choi on the size of the car and the softness of the seats when she sees how proud he is as he opens the door for her to take the front passenger seat. Once on the road, Mai shares her honest belief that the car must be made of high-quality metal since she does not feel the movement at all when normally she experiences motion sickness on boats, planes, and even in taxis. She leaves out the fact that she rarely travelled by any of these modes of transportation.

Once they pass all the buildings and roads in the city it

seems like the highway never ends as they begin the four-hour trek to North Bay. Mai is perfectly happy to sit, looking out the window at the bright blue sky that resembles a painting because the colours are so clear and deep, and at the immense trees upon trees lining the highway. Ming, his uncle, and the agent trade gossip about the community she will soon call home. Occasionally, Ming tries to include her in the conversation, but she wishes he would stop.

"Lonely out here, isn't it? Mai says when everyone has quieted down.

"Yes, would hate to get lost in this area. No one to ask for directions except the moose and trees," answers Ho Choi with a grin.

"Like the country in China," Mai says.

"Except the moose don't speak Chinese," laughs Ho Choi at his own joke. Mai chuckles out of obligation.

"Thought it would be different," says Mai almost to herself.

"The people and how they live make it different. I'm Canadian now." Ho Choi straightens his shoulders and lifts his chin.

"What do you mean?" asks Mai.

"They respect their surroundings more here. There is not so much rushing about. It is calm, peaceful, almost like a village. Even the air is calm. Enjoy it."

Mai smiles politely but wonders if anyone notices her grimace at the thought of being anywhere that is like a village.

***

Another hour later on their road trip, they slow and pull off the highway at a large white sign. There are a few cars parked near a building with smoke gushing out the top.

"Are we here?" asks Mai concerned because there is nothing in sight except the smoking building.

"No, no. Stopping for a beef burger," says Ho Choi.

"Don't worry Mai, I made fried rice and *choi*, greens, for you. Didn't think you'd like the white ghost food yet," says Ming from the back.

"The cow's meat is very good and there are few places around here where you can stop next to the highway to get something to eat. Told Ming not to bother with making food. You have eaten Chinese food all your life. This you will want to try," says Ho Choi.

"You're right, I've never tried it," Mai responds.

"You will like Webers." His accent makes it sound like "Wabba." Line-up is short because it is a weekday," Ho Choi says, clearly pleased as if he was somehow responsible for the good fortune.

Mai gets out with the others and stretches. Ho Choi and Guang walk ahead telling Ming and her to get a table. Ming digs around in the trunk and comes up with a large paper bag with another plastic bag wrapped over it. He signals for her to follow him to one of the picnic tables, grouped beyond the parking area.

Lush green grass and huge trees like the ones they passed are all Mai can see. She never spent much time in the forest areas beyond the fields back home. She can't distinguish the different types of trees by name, but she notices the leaves have different shapes and patterns. Mai is concerned bugs might be near and the smell of the cars is so close she does not want to inhale the fumes. But she holds her tongue.

Ming starts to unpack the bag filled with a thermos of tea and several round foil and some sturdy cardboard takeout food containers. As he uncovers the tops of the containers, she tries to help organize the food. The scent of the fried rice, mixed greens, white and orange vegetables, and fried oil make Mai realize how hungry she is. Ming unpacks two small empty takeout cardboard containers to use as bowls. He fills one with food and hands it to Mai along with a pair of takeout chopsticks as she takes one of the paper cups and fills it with tea.

"Eat. Uncle will not mind if you start ahead of them. Still a little warm," says Ming.

"Thank you. Thoughtful of you," answers Mai. The familiar smells of the dishes make her feel at home.

As she expertly shovels food into her mouth, she notices a group of *gwai lo*, white ghosts, who sit close by with what look like round and long buns stuffed with meat.

"Mai, what are you staring at? Do you want one of those?" Ming asks.

"What are they? Chinese sausage? I'm just curious," she replies.

"Uncle's coming. You can see it up close," he says, chuckling. "It's pork."

"But I thought he was eating cow."

"There's both here," says Ming as Ho Choi and Guang bring over what Mai learns are called burgers and hot dogs.

"You'll go crazy eating cow and pig at the same time," Mai says with conviction.

They all laugh except Mai, who is completely serious.

"An old wife's tale. Try some," says Ho Choi.

"A lot of meat. Do we cut it up to go with rice?" asks Mai.

"No, you just take a bite. I used to not be able to eat all of it but now I can eat an entire burger by myself," says Ho Choi, patting his belly proudly like a little boy.

"Must be expensive," says Mai.

"Not too bad. More cows and pigs here than back home," says Ho Choi. "We got some for you and Ming. Try it."

"Oh, I'm getting full on the rice and vegetables. I really cannot eat more now. But thank you."

The portion per person, looked like enough to feed herself, Amah, and her siblings. What a luxury. Mai pushes the burger back toward the men, hoping one of them will take it. She is grateful when Ming says, "She's eaten a lot. Let's save this for later. You know Auntie loves them. I'm sure she'll eat it if we don't."

***

Back on the quiet highway, on the remaining half of the drive, Mai dozes off almost as soon as they start to move, waking to find herself alone in the car. She feels well rested and is at first happy to hear familiar loud, rough Cantonese tones through the open windows. There's a great deal of activity on the sidewalk up ahead, outside a large white brick building where a group consisting of Ming and two women stand. The short younger woman has Ming's eyes and sturdy build. She's carrying a little girl in her arms. A majestic looking older woman points in the car's direction.

Mai knows it must be Ming's aunt. She's very different but there's definitely a family resemblance to Ming's other aunt in Hong Kong. She tunes into what they are saying and realizes they are simply trying to decide whether they should wake her to come in.

Mai feels the weight of her body and her stiff neck as she stretches. Part of her wants to remain hidden in the car longer. It seems better than facing all these new people, these relatives-to-be. Mai might have fought with Amah about what to cook for dinner each night; she's still angry at Jung for not telling her earlier about Dat Wah's friends visiting, and they never had enough food in Hong Kong, or the village, but at least the problems and the people were familiar. All of that, all of them, are an ocean away now.

Mai refuses to cry again, as a wave of loneliness washes over her. She forces herself to sit up and get out of the car before she can think any more about them. The group moves toward her.

"Mai, you're awake. Feel better? Welcome," the short woman says, "I am Bao Jun, Ming's younger sister," she continues, barely taking a breath.

Mai finds Bao Jun is delightfully distracting, rattling on about whatever happens to catch her attention. Like Ming, there is no double meaning or hidden agenda in her words.

"Bit colder here than what you're used to, I bet. At least the snow has passed for this year. I remember feeling cold when I first arrived. You get used to it. Way more space. Lots to eat too."

"Welcome," says Aunt Fai Lok loudly enough to stop Jun's monologue. Mai cannot help but smile.

"And this is our Auntie. She is who we need to thank for being here today," Bao Jun finishes cheerily.

"Nice to meet you in person finally, Aunt Fai Lok. Thank you for your hospitality. My parents send their best wishes to you," Mai says.

At the same time, her attention is drawn to the large neon letters vertically lining the side of the restaurant closest to them as they suddenly light up, emitting a warm glow against the darkening sky.

***

If she can't busy herself helping with her wedding meal, Mai is happy to be away from everyone for a minute. Above the front door, the vertical neon letters, so lacking in elegance next to Chinese characters, are turned off. Mai has no idea how to read the letters yet, but she admires the simple, clean shapes. As she studies the lines, she is reminded of her arrival here, only seventeen days ago. She likes the plain white brick, and unconsciously nods her head in approval, as if she is an inspector assessing the sturdiness of the structure.

There are few people about, given it's the middle of the week and Uncle Ho Choi closed the restaurant to the public this evening for their reception. A few parked cars line the streets, and the store windows and signs look worn and tired. Mai finds herself enjoying the anonymity with the few passersby who do not know or care who she is.

The city reminds her of her nursing days in Jiangmen. And of Dat Wah. It's not empty but not bustling like Hong Kong either. Did she really gain anything leaving? At least there she had a potential career, an identity, and a clear path. Here, she's like a child unable to communicate with many of the *gwai lo*, without a job, and no idea if she can really help her family get here.

Aunt Fai Lok comes out the front doors looking like she needs a break from the commotion inside as well. When she sees Mai, she walks toward her.

"Mai, are you doing all right?"

"Yes, fine, Auntie. Getting some air."

She nods. "This must be a lot to take in, but Ming is a good man. This is a good place to start a life, a family. You'll get used to it. I did."

Mai says nothing, but nods. She is not sure if she meant in North Bay or in Canada. When the silence lasts a little too long, Fai Lok turns to head back in.

"Don't stay out too much longer. Guests will be here soon."

"Thank you again for everything, Auntie."

"No need for thanks, Mai."

Mai looks around and takes a deep breath thinking, *it has to be better here*, before re-entering the restaurant.

Mai smells fragrant sesame oil cooking with ginger and garlic as the sizzling sounds of meat in a wok greet her ears. She realizes she was outside longer than planned. The main dining room looks pretty and formal with all twelve round tables and chairs set with red and yellow napkins, lucky colours. Bao Jun is running around with her daughter, setting up Chinese fans as centre pieces, some gold and some red. There are red chopsticks next to the plates and small soup bowls lined up along the edge of the Lazy Susan.

The brightness of the main room stands in stark contrast to the dimness of the small bedrooms at the back of the restaurant. The first time she laid eyes on the apartment she and Ming were to share, Mai's heart sank. There was only one source of natural light, a west-facing window, and there was barely enough room for two people to fit never mind furniture. She didn't know what she expected but it wasn't this.

Mai pulls the garment bag with her pink *cheong sam* out of the small closet. Although traditional *cheong sams* are red, the dressmaker in Hong Kong told Mai—and more importantly Ming's eldest aunt who was paying—that while traditional red foreshadows a dynamic, blooming, and enthusiastic relationship, this dusty pink colour stands for love. Mai was hesitant to challenge tradition, but the substantial discount the dressmaker offered, because the wealthy bride who originally ordered it decided she wanted to go with red after all, was the deciding factor for all concerned.

She opens the dresser drawer containing all her worldly possessions, which hardly fill half the space. The larger of the two suitcases she brought contained the gifts of herbs, dried mushrooms, and teas Amah had packed for Ming's family.

Mai digs beneath her clothes and pulls out the velvet pouch holding the yellowed fortune paper, the gold chain, and the ring. She wants to see it. She wants to feel Dat Wah's presence for a moment. She pours them out of the pouch onto the dresser. She picks up the ring and stares at it. Even though it's been six years since he gave it to her, each time she sees the yellow of the gold and the deep green colour and shape of the jade, she is taken by its presence, his presence. She puts the ring on the fourth finger of her right hand but finds it is loose and the jade and gold centre so heavy it swivels to the side uncomfortably. It doesn't fit her any longer. After a moment she takes it off and puts it and the chain back in the pouch beneath her clothes and closes the drawer.

She turns back to the bed, unzips the garment bag, and looks at the hand-sewn sequinned dragon-and-phoenix dress. She quickly takes it out and slips it on. The dress wraps around Mai snugly as if it had been custom made for her. She looks in the mirror to ensure her face is clean and stands up straight.

"Look Mah Mah Ping! The soothsayer was right. Here I am."

She puts on her kitten-heeled shoes, holds her head high, and walks into the restaurant for the conclusion of her wedding celebration.

***

The menu consists of:

Roast Pork & Jelly Fish Combination Cold Platter
Deep Fried Crab Claws
Scallops & Vegetables
Shark Fin Soup with Crab Meat
Salted Ginger Chicken
Sliced Abalone with Chinese Mushrooms & Vegetables
Twin Lobsters with Ginger & Green Onions

Steamed Seasonal Fish
House Fried Rice
Braised E-Fu Noodles with Crab Meat Sauce

She and Ming glide between the tables to greet all the guests she does not know. Ming shakes hands with everyone and speaks the few words of English he has mastered. Mai smiles and nods. She carries herself in a sure, confident manner, over-compensating for her feelings of doubt. Some may even think she appears cold.

When dinner is served, Mai finds it uncomfortable and restrictive to sit in her skin-tight *cheong sam*. While Ming gobbles up the meat dishes barely chewing, Mai nibbles daintily. The deep-fried crab claws with the crispy bread texture, remind Mai of the meals she had in Jiangmen. She thoroughly enjoys the tasty whole chicken, freshly broiled in a bit of oil and a large vat of water. The head and feet are left intact for luck, before they are taken to the kitchen to be sliced and served. The meat is sweet and tender, more delicious once dipped in the diced ginger, green onions, salt, and hot oil sauce. It reminds Mai of the rare occasions they tasted meat back in the village, when they killed one of the chickens that no longer produced eggs.

By the time all the guests have left, Mai sneaks back into the kitchen to help. She finds only Bao Jun there.

"Mai, it's late. Go to sleep. We can finish in the morning."

"I don't want to leave it half done. You go ahead. I'll finish and sleep in."

"It's 2 A.M.! You must be tired."

"I'm fine. Too excited, I guess. You go ahead. I'll turn in soon."

"It's your wedding day. Let me finish with you at least."

"You have a little one who will wake again in a moment; you better rest," insists Mai.

Bao Jun leaves and Mai takes her time to finish. When she finally enters their room, she is relieved to hear Ming snoring. She walks to the dresser to take off the pearls borrowed from Aunt Fai Lok and finds a flower from one of the arrangements at the church. A note, a single Chinese character scrawled in large, childlike handwriting lies beside it. Double happiness. Mai inhales deeply as she studies the character, noting the lack of grace and flow of a sophisticated hand but recognizing the kind gesture from the man to whom she is now forever tied.

Mai goes to the bathroom to wash off what is left of the makeup she is unaccustomed to wearing. She studies her bare face in the mirror and recognizes herself again. She sighs as the longing in the pit of her stomach grows and a tear runs down her cheek falling on the counter.

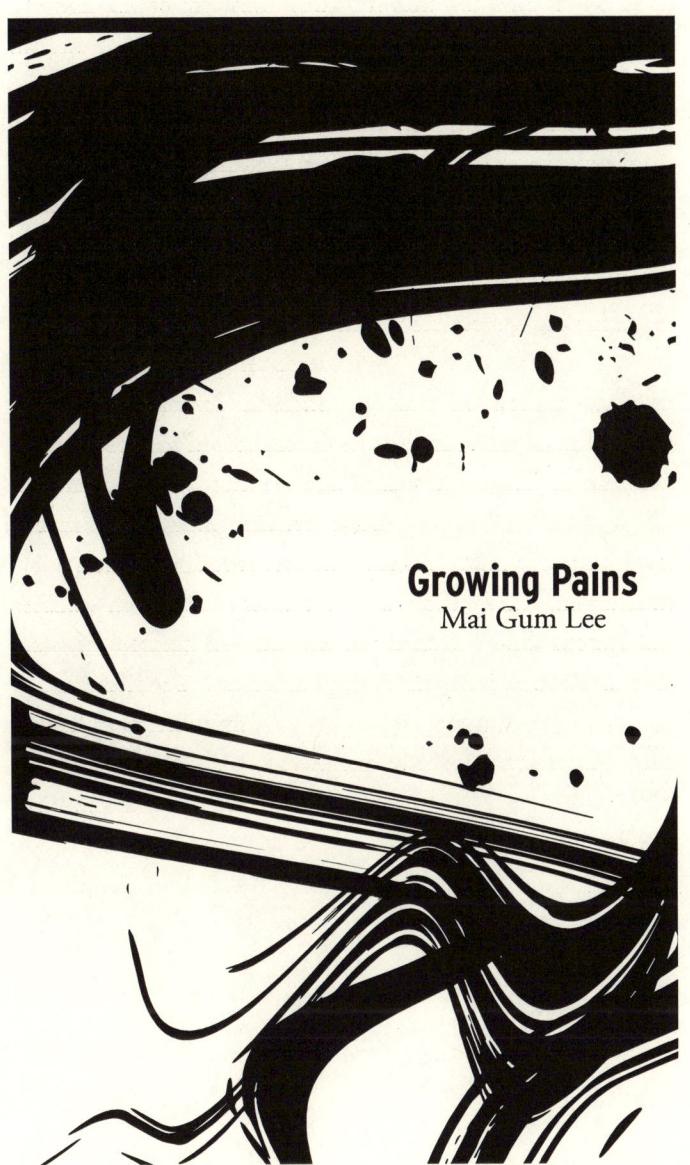

Growing Pains
Mai Gum Lee

9

"Did you eat your piece of candy and buy something with the money from your white envelope?" Before her husband can answer, Mai continues. "Did you walk around in a store or somewhere else before coming here? I don't want the death spirits following you in here. Did you rip up and throw the envelope away?" Mai fires questions at Ming as soon as he returns from Aunt Fai Lok's funeral.

Ming stands frozen with the door ajar unsure which question to address, but he eventually nods listlessly to all of it and gently shuts the door.

"We need to move." Mai states next. Seeing Ming's brow knit together in confusion irritates her. "We need more space," she adds, cooing at their two-month-old rustling in her arms as she jiggles from one leg to the other to keep her happy. "Even if we had a crib, there's no room for one. She'll be walking soon. There's no fresh air here. Sandwiched between everyone."

Ming's face remains blank. Then he nods again and closes his eyes before shuffling to his side of the bed where his worn work clothes hang on a hook.

"Hmmphh." Mai waits for Ming to give her and this issue the attention she knows it merits.

The room surprisingly fits the dresser, double bed, and side table they purchased after their wedding. When Ming brought in the small wooden desk Uncle Ho Choi no longer wanted, Mai complained it was too crowded, but they kept it because the thought of giving up something free and useful was worse than living in cramped quarters. It now sat between the dresser and the doorway of the closet, jutting out slightly past the frame of the door. And Mai discovered it was the perfect place for her to compose letters to Amah and Mah Mah Ping.

At first, a room behind Ming's aunt and uncle's restaurant seemed perfect. It was free, after all. They were close to people, family no less—at least Ming's family, who speak their distinct southern Cantonese dialect. But the downside of being so close to family and work was that the constant requests for help outside of his paid shifts soon overshadowed the benefits.

When pregnant, Ming was easily able to check on her during his breaks but that gave her little relief when she was holed up in their room during the freezing winter months trying to hide from the fried oil, fried fish and fried meat smells drifting in steadily from the kitchen, causing her to retch until only acidic bile came out. Combined with the general bodily discomfort she was never able to pinpoint, simply walking outside was more effort than she could muster. When she had enough energy to think that her day consisted only of naps and keeping a meal down, her lack of productivity and their accommodations repulsed her.

What had become of her? Less than two years ago, she had

a full-time job as a loom operator in bustling Hong Kong. And before that she was the most valuable student nurse at the Jiangmen hospital. Now look at her. She might be in Canada, the great Gold Mountain, but she's not earning a penny and barely accomplishing more than survival.

***

Watching Auntie get weaker, as her own stomach grew, seemed a cruel reminder of how things were never perfect. Between her morning sickness and Fai Lok's deteriorating health, the one thing which had helped Mai acclimatize to her new married life—the tea breaks with Fai Lok and Ming's sister—became a rarity.

Her feelings of inadequacy and fear of becoming insignificant increased as a first-time mother but Mai wasn't about to confess to Ming, or anyone, how ill-equipped she felt when alone with Baby Wei Qi or, as Uncle called her, Vikki. Nothing prepared her for the endless fits of crying and screaming, regardless of how much she fed, burped or bounced the baby about. Mai became a nervous wreck who, even if exhausted and sleep deprived, woke the moment the baby wriggled. Nothing she did seemed to please Baby Wei Qi for more than ten minutes at a time.

These frustrations made the only tangible problem Mai felt justified complaining about, their living conditions, that much more infuriating.

"Why now, Mai?"

"Because we can't afford you working all those extra hours without pay any longer. We can't afford all that money you send home to support your father and that stepfamily of yours who barely utter their thanks before demanding more money. For what? For them to live like kings while we slave to make ends meet here? Heh–Gold Mountain. If they only knew."

"I've told you Uncle Ho Choi can't calculate every minute I

work. I help him but he helps me too." Ming makes eye contact with her before adding, "And you."

"He's not the one who keeps asking you to start early or to do all the kitchen work those lazy, greedy waiters refuse to do. Half the time Uncle doesn't even know you're putting in all this time and that "family" in China you carry on your back certainly doesn't care about you. They're leeches. And you don't ever let him or them know what's truly happening here." Mai's voice grew louder.

"Uncle and Auntie have been good to me."

"I know they have been, but Fai Lok is gone now."

"I don't want to leave Uncle short-handed. He's family."

"Not telling you to leave but *we* have a family now." She holds the baby out toward him. "You need to look out for *us* first."

"Who says I don't?"

By Mai's calculations, the number of unpaid hours Ming worked made the room they lived in not just, not free, but ridiculously overpriced. She doesn't even want to think about the amounts he sent to China.

It is not a wonder Mai never made herself at home in the room. Nothing pierces the white walls except for the nail that holds up a wire-bound monthly Chinese calendar about the size of a school notebook. The top half features a gold *fuk*, the fortune or good luck character, against red backing. Mai agreed to hang it, in hopes it might really bring them fortune or at least good luck. Plus, it was practical. The calendar provides the Western dates, the lunar dates, and the full and half-moon dates. It also advises which days are fortuitous for purchases, sales, marriage, and just about anything important.

"We're stuck here between everyone. It's the smallest room

with only one window. And it faces west."

Ming pauses, confused. "It's the back. All the rooms face west."

"West is the direction the sun sets. It means endings. Aunt and Uncle's corner room has a second window facing south. South-facing windows offer more sunshine, for greater family harmony and an easier life. Besides, they own the place, so their west-facing window doesn't mean the same thing. Their luck is governed by the large east-facing windows in the front of the restaurant. East is the best direction. It's where the sun rises, it means new beginnings. Our luck is limited to the dumpster we face."

"How do you even know this?" Ming raises an eyebrow.

"Mah Mah Ping told me. And Fai Lok talked about it. Before—when we had tea together."

"Guess she wasn't so lucky. Just buried her." Ming resumes changing out of his suit.

Mai is silent for a moment, saddened by the truth of the statement as she pretends to fuss with the baby, until she comes up with a good response. "Her life was good before she got sick. Ho Choi brought her here to join him. Not all husbands could or did. Look at my Mah Mah's husband – he's been in San Francisco for decades. He couldn't or didn't help us at all." *Why won't Ming even look at me?* "Even a second window facing north like your little sister's room is better than just the single one we have."

"What's wrong with a north-facing window?"

"Facing north means you get less sunlight during the day. It's cold. Those who face it bear the brunt of the elements head on making life more challenging." Mai pauses and jiggles Wei Qi before adding, "But we're struggling as much, if not more than everyone else. We may as well have a little more space and fresh air to do it in." No response. *Is he even listening to me?* She gets louder. "So? Why does Bao Jun and her family have the other corner room with two windows?"

Ming turns to face her. "Mai, she married first, and they have their second child on the way. They need the space more than us."

"But you arrived first. You're older and you're a male. We too have a baby now. And if someone, anyone, had been more concerned about you getting married first, you might have had a child first. Who else do you know who waits until they're thirty-five to become a father? You're passing on your old brain cells to our children. Hopefully they won't be slow. The Chinese love their sons. With Fai Lok's son away at school, why weren't you the priority?" Mai holds her chin high.

"Just the way it worked out. No one planned it." Ming sighs heavily. "And you were the one who stopped writing to me for a year, remember?" He arranges his suit on a hanger.

Mai again fusses unnecessarily with the baby, stumped by the truth of the comment. "Anyway, ask the Jewish boy who comes in all the time. One of the waiters says his father has space above his shop."

"I will," Ming says loudly as he opens the closet door with such force that it slams into the desk. He jumps at the sound, exhales with his whole body, and returns to his regular volume. "Just let me get to work."

"Why are—" Mai stops herself when she looks up and sees his slumped shoulders and the tired expression on his face. *Why can't he just be angry?*

It takes energy to be angry but at least it has power and can yield results. It's much easier to deal with than this … this … despair that Ming wears. Despair is weak and futile. Something to be avoided. Mai despises how helpless it makes her feel.

***

She knows that Ming might think she doesn't care but she misses Fai Lok, too. It's one of the reasons Mai accepted the name Auntie suggested for the baby. The English "Vikki" sounds like Wei Qi, valuable energy. She is—was—the one person with whom Mai connected. It was probably because of those tea breaks together. Mai learned more about Ming and his family history during those breaks than he probably knows himself.

Their spot was the table in the back corner. One time the three of them, Fai Lok, Bao Jun, and Mai sat there watching Ming at the counter on his break, peeling an apple skin off in one long continuous strip. His sister commented on his creativity, lamenting how, despite Ming's patient and tireless efforts to teach her, she was unable to learn the art. Partly to bond, partly because she believed it, Mai laughed and dismissed Ming's activity as entertaining but useless.

When Bao Jun ran off to help her daughter use the washroom, Fai Lok started to talk, almost mumble, more to herself than Mai. She was staring not so much at, as through, Ming. Her quiet steady tone compelled Mai to listen harder, straining to hear over the clinking of glasses and dishes being set up for the dinner service.

"When their Amah and two youngest siblings died during the Japanese takeover, Ming and Bao Jun didn't even have each other. He was in Hong Kong. She was in their home, in our village, in China. Between the Japanese, and then the Communist takeover of Hong Kong, they may as well have been only children. Ming's father was in Hong Kong too, but he spent the days farming lands they rented. Their grandmother, my Amah, took care of Ming. Brought him everywhere, especially since there was no money to put him in school. When she too died, Fai

Nguk, my elder sister, helped. It was hard for everyone. Money was tight. Especially after Ming's father married again and had more children. Ming had no choice. Spent his days in the streets of Hong Kong selling and peeling apples in creative ways to earn a few dollars. He was just a child."

The memory makes Mai sad and then so angry she bounces and jiggles the baby more vigorously. It helps her understand why, when homeless men ask for change, he pulls everything out of his pocket, opens his palm, and lets them choose a coin or two before putting it all back. Mai scolded him the first time she saw him do that, fearful that the homeless man might take it all, or harm him. Considering their meagre savings and conditions, it was hardly a way to save for the life they, she, wanted. Why didn't everything that Ming had gone through, harden him? Make him smarter, more selfish? Why isn't he like his brother-in-law?

It's not personal. Mai quite likes Bao Jun. She's like Ming, trusting and honest. Too honest. Fai Lok did a good job arranging the marriage. Bao Jun's husband, protects and does what's best for her and their family. He certainly did not become head waiter because he's overly helpful and works without recognition. His parents pegged his future by naming him after the year in which he was born, the most powerful of the Chinese zodiac animals—*Lung*, dragon. Not only was he born in Canada, making Mai envious of his ability to communicate in English, but he was courageous enough to return here as a teenager, on his own, after his family moved back to Shanghai temporarily. With him, Bao Jun will be fine. But how can Ming—how can *they*—compete? It was up to Mai. Especially with Fai Lok gone.

She had helped Ming, protected him. Like a parent. If it wasn't for her, he'd be stuck in Hong Kong or China, where he'd surely perish. Or face a much more difficult life. He wouldn't have a family though. And like any parent, she did as much for Bao Jun. If Ming was more aggressive or shrewd, he'd have opened up a world of opportunity in the years before his sister arrived. After all, Uncle Ho Choi was easy enough to please. But as much as Mai wanted to blame someone, anyone, for Ming's (and her) current predicament, she knew it was no one's fault. Short of a parent to a child (and sometimes not even then) no one will hand anyone wealth or position; it has to be earned. Or taken. Unfortunately, Ming shows no such awareness or desire.

After everything she gave up to be here, she has no choice. She must make it worthwhile. Not like her grandfather who seems to have all but abandoned the family. She'll do what he couldn't or wouldn't do. Mai isn't sure how, but she knows it isn't going to happen stuck in this tiny room behind the restaurant.

Mai places Wei Qi on the bed and puts on Ming's parka.

"What are you doing?" Ming walks past her to the door.

"Going out to get some air. Stuffy in this tiny room." Mai hopes he feels her mood.

Ming continues to the door. "It's cold out."

"*Hmmmmmphhhhhh.*"

He leaves and shuts the door gently behind him, either not hearing or ignoring her reaction.

Mai fumbles to pick up the baby, unaccustomed to the parka's oversized sleeves. As she steps into the hallway, planning to head out the side door, voices from the kitchen make her pause. The deep baritone voice of one of the sneaky waiters is clear over the clatter of spatulas against woks and knives dicing on cutting boards at furious rates.

"Ming, Ho Choi says they need you to help in the kitchen tonight."

"Oh? He told me I was to wait tables." Mai sees Ming's back

at the entrance to the kitchen.

"He's pretty upset after just burying his wife. I wouldn't want to ask him now," says the sneaky waiter who Mai despises for his shameless sucking up to Ho Choi.

"Hmmm, whatever," Mai hears Ming respond as his back disappears and his voice fades.

"Told you it'd be easy to get you back in front for the extra tips," the sneaky waiter then says to whomever he is speaking.

Hearing this conversation, Mai feels the heat from her face warming her body, her jaw tightening, and a wave of tingling wash from her shoulders to her lower back. It was as if they heard her thoughts, illustrating her point with their actions. Too bad Ming doesn't notice or care. She resists the urge to march in and tell the sneaky waiter to go to hell. The baby, who stiffened momentarily when Mai's body tensed, now squirms and struggles, reminding Mai to move. Mai hugs the baby instinctively and tightens her grip before hurrying out the back door.

***

Sparse snowflakes flying wildly about at odds with the blindingly bright sun, force Mai to squint. She shivers as she feels the wind rush against her and the cold seep through the coat, cardigan, vest and shirt she has on. She is thankful the baby is wrapped in more layers than herself, wearing a little hat, and facing her. But when another gust of wind sweeps through, Mai wishes she dressed the baby in something warmer. Something like the warm, hand-knitted yellow sweater set Fai Lok had given Wei Qi.

It is the nicest of the few gifts they received. Like everything Mai deems valuable, she stores the sweater set in a drawer in the bag and gift box it came in, sometimes opening it to view and to unnecessarily add extra moth balls. It remains in its unused condition with the tags intact, safely tucked away, ready for the elusive special occasion Wei Qi may need to wear it.

How else is Mai to treat this gift? Despite her failing health, Fai Lok personally delivered it.

Mai stayed happily holed up in the hospital for several weeks, enjoying some privacy and the help of the attentive nurses. Like white noise, the muffled and hushed English conversations were easy to ignore because she understood no more than a few words. The baby was brought in for feedings before the nurses changed her and took her back to the baby room.

One day when Mai was in the hospital bed feeding Wei Qi, she heard Ming on the other side of the door. "Auntie, you didn't have to come all this way. They will be home soon."

"Nonsense, Ming. It's your baby." Despite Fai Lok's Toronto hospital treatments, her voice remained strong.

"I tried to tell her not to come," Ho Choi responded. "She should be home resting. This stale hospital air is filled with germs. It isn't good for you."

"You're like a superstitious old woman. It's been three weeks since she was born. These Canadian hospitals treat you like royalty. Let you stay as long as you please. Let me see the baby." Fai Lok pushed open the door at that moment.

Mai gasped and her mouth dropped open when she saw Fai Lok, and the bottle Mai was holding starts dripping milk on the baby's neck. At five feet, six inches, Fai Lok easily towered over Mai with her broad shoulders and perfect posture. But this was far from the woman Mai once mistook for one of the strapping white waitresses at the restaurant. Her head appeared to wobble on her thinned neck like the lollipops they handed to children. Her skin, once smooth, taut and tan was now wrinkly, shriveled, with a yellowish green tint. Her once full cheeks seemed to have caved in. Her clothes sagged off her arms and flowed loosely around her legs where they'd once wrapped snugly. The marks of death enveloped her.

Mai was surprised Fai Lok was able to move but resisted the urge to cry out seeing her so brittle. No wonder Ho Choi and Ming were nagging her about coming to the hospital. Coming to her senses, Mai busied herself wiping off Wei Qi's neck with a clean face cloth and repositioning the bottle tip in the baby's mouth.

Unexpectedly, Mai was overcome with the need to protect Wei Qi. She feared Fai Lok might suck out Wei Qi's delicate youth and impart her sickness.

Mah Mah had taken extreme steps to shield Mai from such events when she was young. Mai had tried to bring little sister Jie soup, when she was feverish and lying listless in bed after touching the sick pig, but Mah Mah shooed her away and held her back. And when Mai tried to follow Amah to comfort her during the burial, Mah Mah explained, unhappy spirits are most attracted to the innocence of the young, desperate to cling to the living, because they are not ready to voyage to the next life. For months after Mai heard this, she clung to Mah Mah and crept into her bed at night, seeking Mah Mah's protective arm for fear spirits might find her.

And so, at the hospital, Mai huddled closer to Wei Qi.

If Fai Lok sensed Mai's fears, she said nothing. She didn't even ask to hold the baby like the relatives of the white women did in the maternity ward. Fai Lok appeared content to proudly present the gift to Mai and the baby before sitting in the visitor chair Ming placed next to the bed. She smiled kindly, almost wistfully at Wei Qi, staring and occasionally patting her tiny arm as Mai finished feeding and burping her. Ming and Ho Choi provided background conversation, bouncing from fishing to restaurant gossip to the weather. Fai Lok added a comment occasionally but concentrated on Wei Qi. When the chatter lulled, Fai Lok appeared even more tired than when she entered.

For a moment, Mai wondered if Fai Lok sensed her concerns. Regardless, Mai thanked her again for the gift as Auntie squeezed her hand. Likely the only time she touched Mai. Mai hated being unable to do anything to help.

***

The blowing wind and Wei Qi's gurgling, pull Mai out of her memory, back to the restaurant they're standing behind. Mai takes in the picturesque view of the sun beating down and the intermittent clouds floating by in the crisp blue sky. Thoughts of Fai Lok whirl in her head as the wind whips the light layer of snow off the rooftops. The smell of accumulated rotten garbage from the large restaurant dumpsters reaches Mai. Fearing Wei Qi will catch cold, she turns around to grab the door to re-enter the restaurant. Before she touches the handle, something red flies right between the door and her face.

"Ohhhh. Baby, look! Birdie. Birdie. Look!"

Forgetting about the cold momentarily, Mai stares at the brilliant red against the snow dusting the building's surfaces. She is certain it is a sign of good luck. Birds have always meant happiness and freedom for her. And red has always meant life, warmth, and celebration for the Chinese. Mai watches the bird fly south, down the street, away from the restaurant, until it is out of sight. On today of all days, why would she see this bird? It must bring a message from Fai Lok or perhaps it is Fai Lok herself already living in her new form.

Mai's body suddenly feels heavy, overcome with helplessness. She wanted to attend the funeral to pay her respects, but the baby was just two months old. Even if Mai trusted someone to watch her, there was no one who dared not attend the funeral if only to suck up to Ho Choi.

Mai knew she herself was far from perfect, but she was genuinely fond of Fai Lok. She knew her, if only from their tea talks, which is why she was surprised when she overheard the obituary being translated to Ho Choi.

Mrs. Ho Choi Yee

Canon C. F. Large of the Church of St. John the Divine conducted the funeral service Monday at the McGuinty Funeral Home for Mrs. Ho Choi Yee, who died Friday in hospital at North Bay following a lengthy illness. Mrs. Yee came to North Bay 28 years ago.

Henry Fong offered prayers and paid tribute to Mrs. Yee in the Chinese language. The large number of people, who attended the funeral from Toronto, Sudbury, Montreal and North Bay, paid final respects to the very charming North Bay woman, whose husband has operated the Chicago Restaurant for many years and is also one of the owners of the Golden Dragon Restaurant.

Both restaurants were closed during the day out of respect for one of the leading Chinese families of this community. The exceptionally large number of floral tributes and the many who attended the service were indicative of the esteem in which the family is held in the community.

Anna Lee was born at Montreal Jan. 20, 1918. In 1948, she came to North Bay, where she married Ho Choi Yee and attended the Church of St. John the Divine.

Mrs. Yee is survived by her husband and son.

Mai knows the truth. Aunt Fai Lok was born in China in the late summer or early fall of 1918. Ho Choi and Fai Lok's original marriage ceremony occurred in China, years before Ho Choi and his brother made their way to Canada. Unfortunately, to gain entry, Ho Choi had to declare himself single. No way to change it after the fact, without creating unwanted problems or inquiries. After taking over the Chicago Restaurant, his second business venture, Ho Choi finally had enough money to buy the birth certificate of a Chinese woman, born close to the same year as Fai Lok, and bring her here.

Fai Lok assumed the identity of Anna Lee from the moment she stepped foot in Canada. Everyone called her Anna. At least the part about her and Ho Choi marrying (again) in the same church she and Ming married, is true.

It's one thing not to reference her real identity, but there was certainly no need to mention her false one. While the surname matched, nothing else did. She left another world, another life, to come here. But was her life before she arrived not worth even a footnote in her death?

Mai feels another door to her own past shut as she walks back into the restaurant.

10

A month later, Mai stands in front of the building where she lost sight of the red bird. Sol Waiser's Men's and Boy's Wear sits a few doors away from the Chicago Restaurant. Mai admires its solid brick exposure and the large second-floor window above the store front.

Wei Qi happily bounces about on Mai's back in the baby carrier Mai made, as she follows Ming, Guang, the real estate agent and translator Mai first met at the airport, and the landlord-owner, through the door, next to the department store's display window. The staircase is not terribly well lit but it's wide. There are four doors off the landing but only one is open, leading to the apartment closest to the top of the stairs. Everyone is standing inside. She joins them.

It turns out it is the largest apartment. Much to Mai's delight, the window in the living room is the one she admired from the street. It faces east with a view of Main Street. The kitchen is to the right of the entrance. Mai has no idea how she will fill all the cupboards. A counter separates the kitchen's grey linoleum from the hardwood floors of the living room.

The bedroom is smaller than their room behind the restaurant, but it has another window facing south. There is even a narrow door leading to a closet. Mai nods her approval before checking the bathroom, which sits between the bedroom and the kitchen. No window there but a noisy fan goes on when she turns on the light switch. Mai flushes the toilet and turns on the taps to ensure they work.

Mai feels the baby's hands pushing on her back and occasionally grabbing at her hair, gurgling happily. Another good sign.

When she was a child, Mah Mah Ping brought Mai with her to the home of a potential suitor for a distant relative. Mai wanted to stay by the pond and play but Mah Mah convinced Mai her presence was needed to perform a very important task meant only for her—to test the home for bad spirits. Since babies and children sense spirits stronger than adults, if they cry or feel upset in a home, it means the place is filled with unhappy spirits. Hearing this, Mai felt so important she ran ahead of Mah Mah. She wandered about the home as the adults drank tea and chatted. She waited and waited, at points willing herself to cry, but nothing came out. Three hours later, she left with a belly full of desserts, feeling no different. Mah Mah commended her on an excellent job as they strolled home at a leisurely pace.

"There's so much room here," Mai says. "The baby seems to like the place." Guang and the landlord have wandered into the hallway, leaving Mai and Ming alone.

"Kitchen's a bit small," says Ming walking into the kitchen area to examine the stove.

"We should've taken off our shoes," Mai says. "Don't want

to dirty our place."

"Ours already?" says Ming with a laugh.

"It has twice as much space as the room at the restaurant. And just a few doors down."

"We'll be paying rent though."

"Worth it for the extra space. Especially when Amah gets here."

"It's all you talk about. When your Amah gets here."

"What's wrong with me wanting her here? You see anyone else helping us? Any word on how the process is going?"

"Uncle just asked about it. Why the official gets whatever he wants from the menu, and I buy him a bottle of the best whisky when he comes in. He just hasn't been able to sort it out yet."

"Well, it's almost been a year and Amah is still not here. With all the free hours you work and all the money you spent on whisky, our entire village should be here by now, not just Amah and my two siblings."

"You don't understand how it works. We just asked about it recently."

"Well, ask again," Mai says.

"Forget it. You never listen," Ming waves her away and joins the other men in the hallway.

Oblivious to Ming's frustration, Mai walks over to the front window to admire the clear view of Main Street. This is better. East and south windows will surely bring better luck.

***

By the beginning of the next month, Mai is walking their clothes and few possessions down the street to their new apartment. Uncle offers to drive their bedroom furniture over and when he sees there is no kitchen table, he insists on bringing over an old, rarely used table from the restaurant basement along with a couple of chairs. After everything is set up, the apartment is still bare, with the small writing desk and a chair being the only furniture in the living room. To Mai, it's perfect.

She spends her days taking care of the baby and settling in. With Ming not constantly asked to "help" before and after his shifts, they are in each other's company constantly. So much so, that Ming eventually suggests he apply at the competing Chinese restaurant in the area, the Manshou Garden, for a part-time job bussing tables and helping in the kitchen. It suits them both when he is hired.

Ming had just walked in from his second shift of the day to find Mai at the kitchen table calculating their bills.

"Told you! You were losing money working all those extra shifts for free and sending all that money home. Even after rent each month, we still save more than before."

"Going to take a shower." Ming stumbles to the bathroom ignoring Mai's barrage of comments.

"Told you."

They save enough money that Mai eventually allows them to splurge, to purchase a deep freezer to store all the fish, meats, and other foods they buy in bulk, and an older model washing machine to help with all the laundry. Mai however refuses to pay extra for the latest styles, which are more than double the cost. Both purchases fit along the long wall in the kitchen, next to the appliances and help make their lives easier.

***

Mai quickly finds cleaning the apartment and caring for the baby does not keep her sufficiently busy. Only to Ming does she admit how mind numbing it is to care for an infant. Hungry for adult company she regularly wanders over to the restaurant when Ming's working, to chat with the wait staff.

She learns from them how official news reports advertise the end to discriminatory immigration policies. With no means to verify this information herself, Mai becomes obstinate about what she does not fully understand and pesters Ming to pester Uncle about her Amah's immigration application.

She forgets Ho Choi made no secret of her family plans. She also forgets some of the staff at the restaurant envy Ming because of his relationship to Ho Choi while others are jealous because they will never have the money to bring their own relatives to Canada.

"What do you mean they don't want to approve Amah's application because of my sister's leg?" Mai asks.

"The official told Ho Choi they think her leg is defective."

"She can't bend her leg at the knee but she's quicker than most. She just limps a bit. She will never be very tall, but she's healthy. It's not as if any Chinese are tall compared to the *gwai los* anyway."

"Stop yelling. Good thing our new neighbours don't speak Chinese."

"I'm not yelling. I don't understand this government though. She's not crippled."

"Well, the government thinks she might be. And it's why they are taking longer to review the application," Ming says, releasing a long breath of air.

"Tell Ho Choi to talk to that immigration official again. He's consumed close to a case of whisky by now."

"He did. Several times. On top of it all, family applications are just not getting approved quickly these days. Government policies change over time you know. There's a lot of racism against the Chinese still."

"I don't care. We need Amah here more than ever." Mai pats

her stomach. "Someone has to help me watch Wei Qi when this one is born."

At this point Mai is in such a tizzy she doesn't care whose information is accurate. When Wei Qi is napping and she has run out of household chores, Mai sits at the desk writing drafts upon drafts of letters to the government officials, engaging Guang to translate and mail them for her.

May 28, 1969

Dear Canadian High Official:

I am a permanent resident of Canada. I will be a citizen soon. My husband and our young daughter are both citizens.

I do not understand why it is taking so long to process my mother and siblings' application. I need them here. For the Chinese, it is traditional for grandmothers to help raise and teach their grandchildren so the parents can work. My husband's mother died when he was a child and sadly his aunt, a Canadian citizen, and the only mother figure in his life, recently died from liver cancer.

My husband works hard at two jobs. I also want to work but without my mother here to care for our baby, I cannot do this. Once she arrives, we will work shifts. One of us will always be here for the children.

My siblings are healthy even though my sister has a lame leg. She is young and already an amazing cook. My brother will go to university and give back.

Our family will be forever grateful if you permit their entrance to Canada, quickly. Please consider this in your assessment of their application. Thank you.

Yours truly,

Lee Mai Gum

All of Mai's frenetic activity and nagging comes to a standstill shortly before the leaves begin to change colours, when Mai experiences stomach cramps followed by heavy spotting.

"Good thing Dr. Ross is right across the street." Ming is holding Wei Qi but keeps an eye on Mai who hasn't said a thing since they left the doctor's office. Mai has no idea what the doctor said but she knows what's happened.

"We still have the cow bones from the restaurant in the freezer. I'll make soup when we get in." Mai doesn't caution him to watch how much salt he adds, and she doesn't review the ingredients to add to the broth like she normally does.

When they get into the apartment, she heads straight for the washroom and runs a bath.

She undresses quickly and slides in the scalding hot bath, but doesn't add any cold water. She forces herself to stay, wanting it to burn, to hurt, to sterilize her. She wants to punish her body, herself, for her failure. As the washroom steams up and her fair skin turns red, she sobs quietly.

When she finally drags herself out of the tub, the water is tepid. After wrapping a towel around her, she drops all the clothes she wore to the doctor into the bathtub of dirty water and starts to scrub them. She releases the water, adds soap, and repeats the scrubbing. She finally watches the soapy water drain and refills the tub to let the clothes sit and rinse. She had put on fresh clothes for the doctor's visit and would normally have saved them for a few more wears before washing, but she desperately wants to be rid of the invisible germs and negative energy.

"Mai, are you nearly done? The food is getting cold." Ming calls for the second time from outside the bathroom. She doesn't answer, but turns on the hair dryer.

The smell of the garlic and bones simmering, comforts her when she finally emerges from the bathroom. It's only 4:30 in the afternoon but the cloudy skies and the rain outside make it darker than usual in the apartment. By the time she gets out of the bedroom dressed in a warm pair of pyjamas, she sees Ming has prepared fresh rice, some boiled greens, and her favourite, a small plate of steamed salted fish with a few pieces of pork, drizzled with oil.

"Come eat something while the baby is still sleeping." Mai takes a seat at the table. "I think the soup will be done late tonight. It's simmering now. You can have it before we go to sleep." Mai nods. "I cancelled my shift tonight." Mai opens her mouth to protest but stops before anything comes out. "Dr. Ross said miscarriages are more common than people realize. No one's fault." Mai nods, but doesn't respond to any of Ming's comments. She picks at her food.

Ming starts to clean up the dishes without saying anything else. She's relieved. Talking does not help. All she wants to do is bury the day.

Mai wanders into the bedroom where the baby is sleeping in the bassinet, which looks tiny compared to Wei Qi now whose feet and head graze the ends. She walks over to her undergarment drawer and pulls out the velvet pouch hidden in the bottom. She pours out the gold chain and the jade ring leaving the fortune inside. She picks up the ring and strokes it. She even slips the ring onto her fourth finger. It fits again because her fingers are still a bit swollen from being pregnant. Tears fall as she recalls another time–waiting for the ferry to Macau–when she felt as lost and alone as she does now. The sound of the water draining from the kitchen sink draws her out of her grief. She swiftly removes the ring, dropping it and the chain back into the pouch and returning it to its hiding spot. Ming doesn't come in though. She slumps into bed exhausted but awake. Listening to the rain hitting the window, she eventually dozes off.

The next day is a haze for Mai. She barely manages to take care of Wei Qi when Ming's working. At some point the baby's crying awakens her and she automatically gets up to comfort her, eventually bringing her into bed and falling back to sleep.

Ming's snoring awakens her. For a split second she feels fine until she remembers what happened and a feeling of hopeless emptiness fills her. Then she remembers bringing the baby over. *Where's Baby Wei Qi?* She pats the bed around her. *Where's Baby Wei Qi?* She sits up, fully awake.

"Ming! Ming! Where's the baby?"

"What?"

She sees no bumps on the floor beside her and steps down. She rushes to the door to turn the light switch on. Ming shields his eyes from the bright light. She gasps as she spots the baby bundle at the foot of the bed. Mai rushes over and picks her up as tears stream down her face.

"She's fine, Mai. She's still asleep." Ming is standing beside her.

Mai feels the baby's head for bumps and starts to unwrap the blanket to check her body. All the activity wakens the baby whose cries match Mai's sniffles. Mai is relieved to hear her voice as she changes her diaper and instructs Ming to get a bottle.

What kind of awful Amah is she?

Mai stays awake the rest of the night watching Wei Qi and

Ming sleep. In the morning, she insists they take her to Dr. Ross to have her checked. Dr. Ross assures Mai the baby is fine and prescribes Mai some pills to help her rest.

"Is he stupid? It was because I was sleeping so deeply, I didn't know what happened to Wei Qi. I don't need help to sleep more deeply. Stupid *gwai lo*. We're not filling the prescription."

"Should I cancel my shifts today to help you and the baby?"

"Help? What help? You didn't even know the baby was on the floor until I woke you up. I need Amah. And we need the money. You go to work."

***

No one really knows whether the restaurant meals, whisky, letters or just the passing of time brings the result, and the explanation differs depending on who gives it, but the following year, Mai has one less thing to complain about.

11

"Amah!" Mai's voice pierces the noise of the crowds at the airport when she spots her mother and siblings.

"Big Sister, Big Sister," shout Jung and Yaing Gong as they run toward her, but they stop short of an embrace. Mai smiles and pats them on their arms as she walks past them to reach Amah. Mai takes the largest bag from her.

"Mai, you don't need to take it. You have the baby and so skinny now." Amah tsk tsks.

"I'm fine. Put away your passports and documents before you lose everything," Mai instructs Amah as she points to the document with a red date stamp of June 18, 1969. "You are well?" asks Mai as Amah struggles to shove everything into her purse.

"Good." Amah pauses as she blinks back tears. "We are good now," she adds quietly nodding continuously.

Mai rambles on about the drive, the weather, and the crowds, masterfully ignoring the emotion.

"Baby girl," Amah directs her attention to Mai's back as if she too is trying to shake off the sentiment she feels. Wei Qi reacts by fighting to get out of the carrier that she is quickly outgrowing.

By this time Ming and the others are beside them. Hoping no one sees her own eyes welling up, Mai makes introductions. Amah meets Ming, Ho Choi and Guang. The agent had insisted on driving an extra car to meet and pick up Mai's family when he heard their application had finally been approved.

Ho Choi plays with Mai's siblings, pretending to swipe Yaing Gong's nose and tap at Jung's shoulder from behind, but then pretending not to take notice of her, making her brother giggle with delight. Mai watches, not understanding why these silly adult pranks played with children are so popular. Ho Choi seems to be having as much fun as the kids.

Mai recognizes the outfit Amah wears. It's the nicest piece she owns, and rarely ever wore. It is a traditional two-piece Chinese collared-top with matching pants. It is formal, but dated. Nothing like the North American clothing Mai sees around her. Wei Qi squirms about on Mai's back trying again to get out of the carrier until Mai finally relents and has Ming lift her down to the floor. She topples about, part walking, part running and part stumbling around the adults, hanging on to pant legs as needed. Yaing Gong and Jung follow her around squealing with delight.

Eventually the group makes a noisy path to the two cars. After much discussion, Ming goes with Guang and the luggage, while the others pile into Uncle Ho Choi's car. Mai carries the baby on her lap in the front, while Amah and Mai's siblings sit in the roomy back. Mai's siblings look out the windows gawking at the tall buildings but once they leave the city's multi-lane highway, they take no interest in the adult discussions and pass time by needling each other. As they drive further north, the number of cars dwindle. Combined with the gentle movement of the car along the mostly deserted road, soon only the adults remain awake.

Ho Choi is in his element as tour guide and asks Amah questions in his usual animated manner, which partly impresses and partly frightens Mai as he occasionally takes his hands off the wheel to turn around and describe what he is saying. Mai finds herself enjoying the sound of Amah's voice. Only now she realizes how much she missed the familiarity of it over the last two years. As the drive continues, Mai feels a tightness leave her shoulders, eventually drifting off to sleep as the baby warms her lap.

Despite jolting awake each time the baby stirs, Mai feels more refreshed than she has in a long time when she sees the stone arches that mark the entry into North Bay come into view. Concentrating on the horizon, she enjoys the peace, and speaks quietly.

"Thank you, Uncle. Thank you for helping get them here."

"Mai. Of course. Our own people. Own family. No thanks needed." But Mai can't help but notice the look of pride on his face as he straightens his posture while he drives the remaining distance to their apartment.

***

"Wahhhh! All this space for the six of us?" Yaing Gong says when he walks into their apartment.

"Does anyone share our kitchen?" Jung asks.

"No, no. Just us. Our bathroom's there," Mai says.

"*Our* bathroom? For just the family?" Yaing Gong runs to where Mai pointed.

And from that day forward, the living room transforms into a bedroom at eight o'clock each night. Amah and Mai's siblings never complain about the old bed Ho Choi brought over before they arrived—even though a broken wire digs into the back of the unlucky person who lies in one particular spot.

***

The excitement surrounding her family's arrival quickly wanes for Mai once she finds herself pregnant again. Getting a job had already proven difficult because they were limited to working at the few Chinese-run establishments, a laundromat and the three restaurants because they didn't speak English. Now, it was out of the question because Mai wasn't going to risk anything happening to this baby. Amah takes the one dishwashing position opening at the Manshou Garden.

When Mai steps on a wet spot in front of the toilet after Yaing Gong pees, when she finds toothpaste smeared on the side of the sink, when she sees the hand towel blackening and smelling sour within two days with double the number of people using it, she shares her irritability with everyone.

"Ming, we need to call Guang again. It's boiling in here. Need the outlet fixed to plug in the fan in the kitchen." Mai sits by the window furiously waving a homemade paper fan for relief.

"He called the landlord. He will try to call again tomorrow." Ming hurries to gather his things for work.

"Why tomorrow? He's just downstairs. Tell him to talk to him. Your daughter's going to get sick," Mai continues as if he didn't answer.

"Guang has to work too. He called already."

"What are we paying all this rent for? Like an oven in the summer."

"Mai, we've done everything we can—"

"Until it's fixed, you have done nothing."

"Well, then you go speak to the landlord yourself," says Ming as he walks out the door for work.

"I will!" Mai says, whipping a spoon at the closing door. Her siblings and daughter scramble behind the bed in the living room. They hide there when Mai raises her voice, which seems to happen regularly these days.

Mai rushes off to the bedroom to hide her tears. Her armpits, the backs of her knees and her neck are slick with sweat. She wants to scream but she sits on the edge of her bed and rips squares of toilet paper off the roll in their bedroom which is there in lieu of tissues, to wipe her eyes and blow her nose. She squeezes the used paper into balls as her hands form fists. She hates relying on others, but the landlord barely acknowledges her when Mai complains in her broken English of the problems in the apartment.

Despite her efforts to follow the puppets mesmerizing her daughter and her siblings on the refurbished television they picked up for twenty dollars, trying to learn English has been hopeless. Dates are easier because there are numbers, and she knows the month. She's able to memorize most of the sounds each letter represents but once the letters combine to make words, it's impossible for her to follow. It's too fast and everything sounds garbled together. Besides, it's tiring enough running after her daughter and taking care of the apartment. She often ends up napping with Wei Qi instead of studying more. She can relate to why Jung is having so much trouble in school.

Her swelling stomach doesn't help either. The morning sickness isn't as bad it was with the first one but the very thought of another baby in a few months is tiring. And what if all her efforts to learn English make no difference? What if she ends up depending on others to translate, just as they have ended up struggling here instead of back home? Coming to Canada was supposed to make her life better, easier. Far from it. Wasn't she supposed to be happy by now? Where is the better life she imagined, the life the soothsayer predicted she was destined to have?

Mai wipes the last of her tears away with the back of her hand and exits the bedroom to help prepare dinner before Amah gets home from her lunch shift. Mai is a little envious of her mother's time away from the apartment and the kids. She wishes she hadn't told Amah about the miscarriage. Amah treats her gingerly now and always looks concerned. Seeing her that way only frustrates Mai more.

12

Mai is both offended and relieved that her daughter seems unaffected by her absence when she gives birth to a son and hides out in the warmth of the hospital for two and a half weeks.

Her shoulders slump from disappointment and guilt when she finally returns with the newborn to the chilling temperatures of the apartment even though Spring's supposed to arrive soon.

The landlord ignores their repeated requests in broken English to turn up the heat for the sake of the children. Driven partly by maternal protectiveness and partly by indignant outrage, she insists Guang contact the city officials to force the landlord to turn up the heat. At least this resolves the issue for the winter.

And as winter turns into spring, one of the patrons from Ho Choi's restaurant—who everyone fondly calls a *lo wah kiu*, an old Chinese bridge, because he was among the first to immigrate to Canada—learns of their addition to the family. He insists on meeting the baby after the first month passes. The old man abides by the Chinese tradition to leave new mothers and their babies in isolation for a month following birth, even though since her arrival in North Bay, Mai has not witnessed any other mothers host the red egg celebration that normally occurs after the month has passed. It is unclear whether this is due to cost, lack of time by new mothers, or simply a waning tradition in the face of a new country with so many other challenges.

"Waaaa! The place is so orderly, Mai. Baby is so clean. Nothing like your sister-in-law." The old man slowly makes his way around the kitchen and the living room, which takes only a few minutes even at his pace.

"She and Ming are not as uptight as I am."

"No one is as uptight as you, Mai," Ming says, laughing. "Come sit down," he adds, turning to the old man and gesturing to the kitchen table.

"This is your baby boy," says the old man making faces at the baby in Mai's arms. "He is very smart and handsome. What is his name?"

"Lee Wei Mak. Wei Qi, come say hello to our guest," Mai says. Her daughter obliges but runs back to draw at the desk right after the old man pats her head.

"A good name. Means powerful mark. What about his English name?"

"Uncle Ho Choi said Mak sounds like Mark," Ming for once jumps in before Mai can answer.

The old man nods. "Ho Choi is a smart man. Good heart. Helps everyone."

"Where is the rest of your family? I've seen them at the restaurant."

"Amah and my younger sister went to the grocery store. My little brother is outside. Playing or something." Mai walks around, jiggling the baby to keep him happy.

"So, how is the laundry store? Busy?" Mai asks the old man.

"Yes, busy most days. Keeps me out of trouble."

"You're lucky you own the business. All the work you put in translates directly to profit." Mai nods approvingly.

"Yes, but all the headaches are mine, too. Ho Choi will tell you. Deliveries are not always smooth and there are difficult customers. Sometimes I wonder if it's worth it. You know, there is one *gwai poh*, ghost woman, who does not like me. She does not think I work hard enough for her money. Instead of just giving me her laundry, she throws her dirty underwear behind the bed and makes me crawl under the bed to get it. Humiliating, but I do it. No choice. Need the money."

Mai shakes her head and purses her lips as a feeling of shame and anger rises in her chest; she fears tears might escape. She only realizes she has stopped jiggling when the baby starts to whimper, and she immediately starts again. The old man walks over to Mai to make faces at the baby to try and help, while Ming shares restaurant gossip.

"So, you are doing all right here?" The old man asks.

"Busy but we're all healthy." Mai is so grateful for the adult company she responds well before Ming has a chance. She greedily soaks up gossip the old man shares about others whose children have gone on to university or who have been struck by unfortunate illnesses. She is happily listening to the old man when Yaing Gong bursts through the door.

"Big Sister, three people stopped to have their shoes shined!" Her brother holds out the coins in his hand, grinning from ear to ear.

"Waaaa! Good boy!" says the old man ruffling his hair.

"Say hello to Abak." Mai leads her brother to use the polite title for addressing an older person, and he dutifully does as instructed.

"Why'd you come back so soon? Maybe more customers coming." The old man waits attentively for his answer.

"It's starting to rain. And the Chinese lady from the restaurant, who Big Sister doesn't like, says I'm like a beggar." Yaing Gong bows his head a bit, whispering the last few words. He was referring to one of the waitresses whose husband works as a cook at Ho Choi's. Mai openly cringes at how they always suck up to Uncle. To her, it's so inauthentic, it's laughable.

"Don't you listen to her! You keep working hard. The rich Jewish man who now owns a store three floors high and takes up an entire city block in Toronto started off just like you. Sold chestnuts on a street corner. Don't you listen to that ignorant woman." The old man angrily wags his finger in the air like he's scolding someone. He then mutters barely audibly, "Bad enough we have to deal with the bad white people but the Chinese who step on each other are even worse. One thing not to help, another for her to push down those making efforts. And a child too. Nasty woman."

As she continues to jiggle the baby, Mai is comforted by the old man who seems to voice her thoughts. Until she realizes what her brother said.

"Rain. Oh no. Rain! Yaing Gong get the bucket." Mai rushes to get rags from under the kitchen sink as she continues to bark out orders while carrying the baby. "Ming, we need to move the bed before it gets soaked."

Ming is already in the bedroom. Mai's daughter jumps out of her seat at the excitement and follows Yaing Gong.

The old man sits silently as he watches everyone running about. After a few minutes, the family files out of the bedroom but without the baby.

"Sorry, Abak, we need to keep the bed away from the window draft but the only other corner the bed fits, there is a hole in the roof," Ming explains as he sits down again. "When it rains, we have to put a bucket under the drip to catch the water."

"More tea until the rain stops?" asks Mai politely but looking at the clock. She is a bit embarrassed the old man witnesses what she now considers, the shoddy conditions of their living space.

"No. No. I only came by to meet your son and give him his red packet. It's getting late. I should get home before the rain starts coming down harder. Thank you for spending time with an old man whose own family only knows how to write when they need money." The old man pushes his chair back and starts to rise as he hands Mai a lucky red packet.

"No need for such formalities, Abak. We are not in China any longer." Mai makes an effort to refuse the gift.

"I insist. The new year just passed. We are celebrating a new decade. And the birth of a son. May the 1970s be fortuitous for you and your family." The old man bows so low, Mai automatically holds out her arms to catch him. When he rises again, Mai accepts the envelope.

"May it be fortuitous for all of us. Thank you." She grabs a plastic grocery bag from the drawer overflowing with them and tosses in two oranges from the bowl on the table before rushing into their bedroom for her old lucky red packets into which she stuffs a two-dollar bill from Ming's wallet before returning. "Take this. For good luck." Mai hadn't practised the Chinese customs for New Year since she arrived in Canada, but she thought it befitting to return the kind gesture from the old man, with the fruit, given its colour and shape, symbolic for wholeness and good luck and the token red packet amount.

"No, no. The kids need the food and money more than I do. They're little and growing," he says, refusing to take the bag Mai holds out as he struggles to put on his shoes and make his way out of the apartment. Mai follows him out and insists:

"You must take it. Good luck for everyone." They push the bag back and forth for a bit before the old man finally relents.

"All right. Thank you, Mai."

Ming walks in front of the old man down the stairs and opens the door for him while Mai stands at the top calling out her thanks as he leaves.

As Mai starts to prepare dinner, the old man's comment about his family floats through her mind and draws her to thoughts of her own grandfather in San Francisco. The only time he ever heard from the family, they were also asking for money. Just like with Ming's stepfamily. They seem to barely give a thought as to how much we're struggling and how crowded it's getting in our apartment. Maybe Grandfather feels abandoned like the old man, suffering to make ends meet and being called names behind his back by the *gwai* here and family at home, without anyone even inquiring as to his well-being. Maybe they shouldn't judge him so harshly.

13

By the fall of the next year, Ho Choi is driving Mai and Ming to the hospital for the birth of their second daughter. After a week and a half, her shortest recovery time, Mai returns to their apartment where fall rains have wreaked havoc because the landlord has yet to fix the hole in the roof. On top of the heating and cooling issues, the once roomy apartment is no more.

Only Ho Choi fusses about their new addition. There are no gifts or celebration. Mai however names her, Wei Ping, valuable peace. And Uncle Ho Choi suggests the English name, Amy because it sounds like Anna, Aunt Fai Lok's English name.

Mai busies herself in the upkeep of the home, mopping the floors–especially in front of the toilet where Ming and Yaing Gong seem to endlessly dribble–to washing and ironing diapers, scrubbing the bathtub and sinks, keeping the babies plump and clean, preparing family dinners, and balancing the family savings account and expenses. She views herself as busier than Ming who works two jobs.

One day after school, her brother bursts through the apartment door while Mai is preparing dinner and Amah is getting ready for her shift at the restaurant.

"Shhhhhh. Don't make so much noise. I just put down the baby."

He raises his eyebrows, and his eyes widen but he continues to grin.

"Go wash your hands," Amah says in a whisper, setting out food for him. "Where is your sister?

"Coming. She's just slow." He rushes into the washroom. By the time he returns, Jung is walking in.

"Here. Eat some yellow sponge cake for snack." Amah sets down a glass of milk and a piece of cake.

"He rushed off ahead of me. Again." Jung squints at her brother but no one pays any attention. "Why are you giving him more now? He doesn't even eat it at lunch." She finishes removing her shoes and puts on her slippers, all the while scowling at Yaing Gong.

"What? What do you mean he doesn't eat it?" asks Mai.

Delighted with the attention, Jung goes on as she walks to the washroom. "I see him squishing it under the lunch table ledges. He never eats it."

"What a waste!" Mai's outrage makes her forget to keep her voice down.

"It looks and tastes like a sponge. Dry and no flavour. Yuck! The other kids won't even trade with me anymore." Yaing Gong crosses his arms and scrunches his face at the cake.

"It doesn't mean you should—" Mai starts.

"It's all right." Amah sighs and raises a hand at Mai to stop. "I have to go but we'll try to buy something else for your lunches when we go shopping this week. You must eat. You're growing."

She pats Yaing Gong on the shoulder.

"Thanks, Amah. I have good news. I've been invited to a birthday party." Yaing Gong proudly holds up a card with a clown on it.

"You have? What does it mean?" Amah stops putting on her shoes to try to see the card he's waving in front of her.

"Means I get to go to my classmate's house, we eat cake, and he opens presents," Yaing Gong says, reading off the card.

"Presents?" Mai says alarmed. This time the baby starts to cry. Mai continues to talk as she walks into the bedroom. "Who has money to spare for children's toys?"

Amah tilts her head at Yaing Gong as Mai disappears into the bedroom and says in a quiet voice. "You're a good boy. We'll get something. Just don't say any more about it now. I have to go but both of you be good for your big sister tonight."

"We always are. Do you really have to go?" Yaing Gong bows his head and studies his feet as Mai comes out holding the baby.

"I have to make money to pay for food and to send some back to Abah and the others. I'll try to bring home some of that crispy beef tonight." Amah pats him on the arm again as she gathers her things. She waits for him to make eye contact to give him an encouraging nod.

***

That weekend, Amah and Yaing Gong repeatedly assure Mai she need not help with the grocery shopping, but Mai has been cooped up in the apartment all week, and insists on accompanying them.

"Stop putting the cookies back, Mai!" Amah frowns at her and for the second time, takes the cookies off the shelf Mai left them on, and returns them to the shopping cart.

"They're no good for you." She pauses before adding, "And

expensive. We're already buying a loaf of bread, and this sliced ham for their lunches." Mai points to the ham as she leaves the cookies on another shelf and walks on.

"I want a cookie now and then. Don't worry about what I buy for Yaing Gong and Jung Sum for lunch. I'm paying for it." Amah uncharacteristically speaks louder as she grabs the cookies and holds on to them this time.

Mai has stopped the cart to examine the pasta on the shelf, allowing Amah and Yaing Gong to catch up. "They're a waste of money. We don't have any to spare. Didn't you notice where we live?"

"I said, I'm paying for it with my money. It's not like this pack of cookies is going to make that much of a difference." Amah with the cookies in her hand and Yaing Gong at her heels, walk past Mai and continue down the aisle.

"We still need a present for the birthday party, Amah." Despite Yaing Gong trying to say it quietly Mai overhears.

"You see, more money wasted." Mai acts as if this somehow proves a point, eyeing the package of cookies in Amah's hands.

Before they round the corner of the next aisle, they hear Mai:

"Here. Here's a present."

Curious, Amah and Yaing Gong retrace their steps and peer around the corner to see what Mai's talking about. Her brother stops moving when he sees what's in Mai's hands.

"Chips?" He can't hide his confusion and disappointment.

"It's perfect. Kids love chips. You love chips. And it's not too expensive," Mai says proudly.

Amah shrugs, not sure what to think.

"Umm, I don't think that's a gift." Yaing Gong's eyebrows are pulled down, his nose is wrinkled, and his upper lip is pulled up.

"Sure it is. Do you not like chips?" Mai dismisses her brother's protests to Amah about being unable to wrap chips and how it's a treat, not a gift. "It takes an hour of work for Amah to afford a bag of chips. If you can find something else for the same price, buy it instead." Mai places the bag into the cart.

The colouring book and crayons at the front of the store are much more expensive and there is nothing else in the store resembling a present for the cost of the bag of chips.

Mai takes no notice of Amah and Yaing Gong's sullen mood as they walk home with the groceries. She also doesn't understand but is relieved and happy when her brother refuses to attend the next birthday party to which he is invited.

14

"We've been here almost four years and the roof still leaks." Mai complains as she gets into bed.

"Guang says we can fix it ourselves and deduct the cost of the tar from the rent," Ming replies as he turns away from her to lie on his side.

"We shouldn't have to do the work ourselves with all the rent we pay," Mai responds but the next day she urges Ming to go out to buy the tar right after he finishes his coffee.

On Ming's next day off, Mai and he climb out the bedroom window onto the fire escape, while Jung watches the kids.

"This is the problem with these flat roof tops." Mai stands beside Ming with her hands on her hips, staring out at the downtown landscape while he works at uncovering the lid on the tar.

"What is?"

"Holds water. Need a peaked roof so the water can slide off."

"Can't hang your clothes out to dry with a peaked roof," says

Ming, concentrating on painting over the hole.

"We'll have a backyard for the kids and clothes, once we buy our house." Mai says, as she happily basks in the sunshine, while Ming keeps painting. Soon a thick, ugly layer of tar is drying over the hole.

Truthfully, Mai is thankful the apartment's flat roof doubles as a bit of a playground for the kids in the summer, with Jung leading the way. In some ways her sister is quite maternal as she merrily herds the kids up the fire escape. This opinion changes quickly when she follows Jung one day and finds her on the roof teaching them how to catch pigeons. A delicacy they were never able to afford in Hong Kong.

"Turn the hamper upside down," Jung instructs, clearly putting on a bit of a show for Mai.

"Tie a string to the clothes pin and arrange it like this." She props up the hamper in one spot with the clothes pin. Now put the bread there." She points to a spot underneath the hamper as Mai's son, whom Jung favours because he's a boy, places a piece of bread underneath.

"Come on now. Everyone, hide." Like a school crossing guard, she directs the kids to scamper behind some containers. "I'll hold tight to the end of the string. It's tied to the clothes pin."

The trap works magnificently. Unsuspecting pigeons wander under the hamper trap to eat the bread as the kids hover eagerly behind boxes watching until just the right moment to pull the string. The clothes pin falls, trapping the birds in the overturned hamper.

As much as Mai enjoys the nutritious meal, she does not share her sister's ease with or stomach for the killing. The kids love the game until they realize they are not catching pets. And when her son learns the white pigeon he'd grown attached to has been killed, he cries non-stop for days. Exhausted from consoling him, Mai and Amah instruct Jung to stop the rooftop excursions.

***

As the wet weather turns stifling, Mai looks for relief from the sweltering apartment when Ming has a rare day off from both jobs. She suggests they venture to the beach to fish and cool down. She invites Amah and her siblings and is a little surprised that they decline, not understanding for a minute why they might want a break from her and the younger kids.

Mai works herself into a tizzy, directing her sister and Amah to help her bottle water, make sandwiches, find hats, and pack changes of clothes for the kids. Unlike Mai, Amah holds her tongue about the grandchildren also preferring sandwiches to the yellow sponge cake for snacks. Ming happily busies himself fixing the fishing line he borrowed from Uncle Ho Choi and ensuring the lid on the bait he and kids dug up at the park, is tightened for the twentieth time, if only to stay out of the line of Mai's commands.

Upon arrival at the beach, they find it quite empty. Mai and her son are equally excited when the fishing line tugs as they stand together on the shoreline struggling and squealing to pull up their bite. When the little fish pops out of the water, they laugh and giggle, watching it wriggle its body in S-waves mid-air.

Mai refuses to touch the squirmy bait or detach the fish from its hook. She calls Ming away from the girls who are happily taking turns with a toy bucket and a shovel, another child had left behind.

"How did you ever work in a hospital?" Ming teases, walking over.

"I just bandaged people up," says Mai shaking her head in disgust. "You prepare fish all the time."

"They're already dead; not trying to escape!"

To this, Ming laughs and drops the fish into the bucket of water.

Once the sandwiches are eaten and her son is tired of tossing the line into the water, Mai sits quietly on the beach blanket, under a tree, enjoying the gentle massage of the breeze coming off the lake. Her taut reddish-brown arms and legs glow with health. She watches the kids play in the sand and listens to the water roll up on the shore, enjoying a rare moment of peace.

It is late afternoon when they start walking back to the apartment. The kids are particularly cranky, with the two youngest fighting to ride in the single stroller.

"Look, look!" Mai suddenly yells out and points to the pair of cardinals flying near the big, rusted bridge.

"Wowww," says her son, jumping at the sight. "No eat Mammy," he says as he crosses his arms.

"No, no," she chuckles and hugs her son. "No, no. Too pretty. No eat."

The stark red feathers stand out so clearly against the cloudless blue sky, the group cannot help but stop and watch as the pair fly about in circles above their heads. Mai realizes she hasn't seen a cardinal since the day Aunt Fai Lok was buried. Wei Qi was only two months old. She's in school now and the youngest is walking.

How have so many years passed already?

The noise of her kids arguing disturbs her thoughts. The birds seem similarly disturbed and fly away.

"You frightened them away with your fighting," Mai says to the children looking stern but only hoping they will stop their bickering. The kids stare at her and don't say a word. Mai's mouth straightens into a line as Ming hoists their son onto his shoulders.

The group, now silent, retraces their steps to the apartment.

After dinner and baths, the kids fall asleep quickly, exhausted from the fresh air and activities. The youngest sleeps in the bassinet, their son in the stroller, and their eldest beside Mai in bed. Mai hates being stuck in the middle. There's no room to stretch out comfortably and she often awakes with neck cramps because of the awkward position of her head.

Not wanting to disturb the kids, Mai says in a low voice, "We need to move, Ming. All five of us are stuffed into this one room."

Ming grunts.

"Need a house. We have enough for a deposit now. We should've been searching already. Need to put Amah's name on it. To sponsor Abah and the others. It'll be easier for her once they're here. All this money going to rent. It's a waste," Mai continues more to herself than him.

"What about near the church? It's close to the library." Ming turns his head to Mai.

"No. Not here. In the big city. Toronto. Direction where the birds flew."

"What? Birds? What are you talking about?"

"There's nothing here. No factories, no businesses. Amah barely makes any money, and I couldn't find a job even if there was time to search. Only jobs for us here are at Chinese restaurants. Not like we own them or have a share in them." Mai's voice trails off.

"Who do we know in Toronto?" Ming asks.

"What does it matter? We know people here but except for Amah and my sister, we don't get help from anyone. Ho Choi tries but he is busy. Plus, he listens to all those scoundrels who surround him. You'll never be more than cheap labour there."

Ming turns away to face the wall.

"The kids need to be in a bigger city, too. Already so many years have passed. They'll be going to university soon. None here. May as well move closer to them now. Don't want them to be in another city alone," she says forgetting that she did exactly that at an even younger age. "Easier if we're nearby."

"Mammy too loud," says their eldest daughter turning onto her stomach and rubbing her eyes.

"Ohhhh. Go back to sleep." Mai pats her. By the time she turns back to Ming, he's snoring.

Mai quickly drifts off herself, but she dreams vividly throughout the night about flying with the cardinals to the airport in Toronto, somehow finding Ho Choi's restaurant there and seeing Mah Mah Ping waiting at a table for her. "How did you get out of China?" Mai asks to which there is no response. Suddenly a statuesque woman appears by the door of the restaurant and Mai realizes it's Aunt Fai Lok. She is alive and strong again. Mai hears her voice: *it's taken so long for you to get here. How much longer before you bring the family to join you?* Mai wonders, how am I to fly here with the family?

This is the thought in her mind when she wakes the next morning.

***

Before Ming knows it, he and Mai are scheduled to stay with his cousin in Toronto for a weekend so they can find a house. Much to the surprise of Ming and Amah, Mai insists they spend the extra money for a sleeping compartment on the train because of her motion sickness.

Mr. Li, the agent Ming's cousin introduces to them, warns them it won't be easy to find a place with all Mai's requirements and a bidding war going on in the city, but Mai thinks it's just a sales tactic. Her list includes:

- No homes facing north or west because the directions are not fortuitous.
- No dead-end streets because those living there will have dead-end lives.
- No houses with front doors lined up with back doors because all earnings will be lost as quickly as they are acquired.
- No schools, churches, or hospitals nearby because they suck away the wealth and fortune from the area.
- No cemetery nearby because the occupants of such homes soak up the sadness and misfortune associated with death even with a *bak gwa*, the eight-sided talisman hung facing outward in a window or to the side of the door to ward off misfortune.
- No homes too close to Chinatown because the area will be dirtier.
- No ghost (willow) trees which symbolize death.
- No flimsy stucco or wood homes; only brick or stone.
- No semi-detached homes because if the neighbour is noisy or dirty, it will leak into the other side.

After they submit offers on several houses Mai deems barely passable, only to be outbid each time, she realizes it might not be as easy as she hoped to find a home.

Disappointed at having lost Ming's weekend wages, plus the cost of the train tickets and the gifts they brought to Ming's cousin—with nothing to show for it—Mai and Ming return to their apartment.

Throughout the rest of the year Mr. Li keeps his promise to call with potential properties of interest, but before Mai and Ming have time to even consider plans to travel back to Toronto, they are sold.

15

In the new year, Mai's stomach and irritability swell simultaneously, for a fifth time. When Amah mentions they need another dishwasher at the restaurant, Mai insists on taking the job.

"*You* want to take it? Mai, you are only getting bigger. Don't want you to have any problems with this one," says Amah, flicking her chin at Mai's stomach.

"We can't stay here forever. This place eats all our money." Mai closes her eyes and stretches her neck as she rolls her shoulders back.

"Better than China," says Amah. "No one is going to take what's ours."

"What's ours? We have nothing still. This is the problem."

"You're so tired. You really want to work now?"

"A few hours a day. I'll be doing the same thing as here. Just washing dishes. Will bring home a few extra dollars. We need it. We need more than this," Mai says flinging her arm around the room.

"Will they be happy?" asks Amah, pointing at her son and youngest daughter.

"Jung can stay home and watch them."

"You want Jung to quit school?"

"She doesn't even like going. Can't blame her. Too hard to learn English at her age. She's in her twenties and in grade seven. Only because she's so small, they let her continue. Just the other day she complained again about the kids pulling her hair and kicking her when the teachers weren't paying attention. What's the point?"

"Let me talk to her when she gets home from school."

"What's to talk about? This will be better for everyone. We need the money."

"Mai! We still need to explain to your sister. Can't just tell her what to do. Don't be like that." Amah walks away from the table shaking her head and clearly annoyed.

It's true, even if Amah doesn't want to come to terms with it: No use wasting a good opportunity to earn money. Safer and more useful for her sister to stay at home. Yaing Gong has a chance, he's young, but Jung will never go to university.

***

Despite being tired from the pregnancy, Mai eagerly escapes runny noses, children's games, and unpaid household chores, to wash dishes and help in the kitchen at the Manshou Garden.

Amah's co-workers tease her about her pregnant state and how young she appears. She happily soaks in the adult conversation which has nothing to do with a toddler's eating habits or bowel movements.

During the first week, Mai makes an impression on her co-workers.

"Mai, you can just have the baby here. It's so clean after you finish with a pile of dishes," teases one of the waiters who helps her when business is slow.

"Sure. If Boss pays me, I'll just need a long lunch break," answers Mai grinning.

The kitchen staff, overhearing, chuckle as she wipes off the sink area with the damp cloth and checks for bits of food in the sink. She hates how messy it is when she comes in after the evening shift.

"Boss loves you. Says you're worth every penny," shouts one of the cooks from the stove.

"Means he needs to pay me more. You need more ginger and garlic?" asks Mai already moving over to the counter to pick up one of the cleavers. She always makes herself useful when there are no dishes to clean, more so because she hates idle time than to impress anyone.

"Thank you. Yes. Always. Just smaller pieces. You know the *gwai lo* don't like the pieces big enough to choke ducks."

"Silly *gwai lo*. I make it more worth their money." Mai quickly peels and dices as the cooks chuckle at her justification for her crude chopping.

Although her time at the restaurant is brief, and she is on her feet the whole shift, the $1.30 Mai earns each hour seems to renew her spirit before giving birth again.

***

"Mai, you back again?" chirps the nurse Mai recognizes from her previous stays at the hospital.

"Haaallow," Mai says in her faltering English.

"Here is your handsome baby boy." Mai takes him in her arms and accepts the warm bottle of milk the nurse gives her.

"You smart." Mai says pointing to her head while nodding vigorously but with her accent it comes out *see mart*. "Home …

no help. Me. All keeds." Mai points to the baby. "Eat … cry … pooh … me. Here," Mai points downwards and dramatically collapses her shoulders while exhaling loudly. "Here no work. Tank q you."

The nurse is nodding encouragingly as Mai struggles to enunciate her words. "That's right, you don't have to work here."

Though Mai doesn't know for sure, she feels understood. The nurses aren't perfect, but they're helpful and cheerful.

A few days later the nurse chirps, "You're going home already, Mai? Only a week this time?"

"Yessss. Keeds. Home."

"You take lots of formula and diapers with you for this little guy." The nurse touches the baby's face with her finger after setting down the case of formula and another package of diapers.

"Tank q you. Nice. Nice."

When Uncle Ho Choi drops Mai and Ming off at the apartment with their second son, her heart sinks a little as she takes in what she now sees as a grungy building. The dim light in the staircase barely allows her to see the rickety steps which creak in spots Mai has now memorized. A gum wrapper—there when she rushed out to the hospital—still sits on the third step from the top and her jaw tightens just a bit as she takes in the ripped wallpaper in the stairwell.

Mai sighs as her youngest daughter flings open their apartment door before her foot touches the landing and runs over excitedly to see the baby in her arms with Jung following closely behind. Mai softens as she watches her daughter's effort to imitate adult reactions.

"Hello baby! So cute," says her younger daughter as she tickles the baby underneath the chin.

"Are your hands clean?" asks Mai. "Don't touch the baby

unless you wash. Will make him sick."

The little girl examines her hands curiously and quickly runs to the washroom. Jung takes the baby from Mai and walks to the bed she shares with Amah and Yaing Gong where Mai's son and younger daughter meet them.

As Ming sets down all the supplies and Mai's hospital bag, Mai quickly trades her shoes for her slippers before going to the kitchen. She scrubs her hands at the sink before peeking into the steaming pot to find the afterschool snack for her eldest, and her brother—potatoes. She puts on the apron draped over the back of the chair, takes a bowl from the cupboard, and tongs from the drawer, to remove the potatoes from the water. Ming will have to leave soon to pick up Wei Qi and Yaing Gong from school.

She is comforted by the sight of Jung, her son and youngest daughter hovering over the gurgling baby, but the sight of the apartment depresses her.

When will they get out of here?

***

Mai stands at the living room window studying the snow coating the sidewalks, rooftops and cars parked overnight on the streets. The TV, tuned to one of the three channels they receive, keeps the children and Jung entertained as they sit in bed with mitts on to keep warm. The cup of tea she is sipping and the three layers she is wearing are not enough to keep out the chill. The turning of the door handle draws her attention away from the window.

"Good. For once you're not cleaning," Amah says, walking in as she brushes off the snow from her hat and shoulders.

"Snow already." Mai sighs and tries to sip her hot tea.

Amah removes her hat but keeps her coat on as she exchanges her outside shoes for slippers and walks into the kitchen to get herself some tea from the thermos on the counter.

"Just a bit today but winter always comes too soon here." Amah warms her hands on the steam rising from the cup she just poured.

"I'm going to get Ming," Mai says.

"Why are you waking him? He came in so late last night. Let him sleep."

"I know. But something we need to talk about, and you'll need to get ready for your shift soon," says Mai.

"Are you alright? Is there something wrong?" But Mai walks into the bedroom without answering.

Amah puts her tea on the table and returns to the cupboard for another cup for Ming.

"What's wrong?" Amah asks when she returns.

"Nothing's wrong," Mai says. "Just want to go back to work."

Amah's shoulders noticeably sink as she relaxes into a chair and takes her first sip of tea.

"Already? I don't think the restaurant needs anyone now. They replaced you when you had the baby."

"Need to save more for a house. We keep getting outbid. And we can't get an offer on a house quickly enough without being there to check it."

"You want to go to Toronto again?"

"Going for a weekend is costly and too rushed. Need to be there but Ming can't go, he has two jobs. And I can't because the baby and kids will want me here unless we bring them, and we can't bring them without a house. Since your name must be on the deed, to sponsor Abah and the others, I think you should move there ahead of us."

By this time, Jung has stopped pretending to watch TV and stands behind Amah as Ming comes in and sits down. Mai continues:

"You can stay at Ming's cousin's until you find a house. Pay a little rent. His cousin knows about a job opening. This way I can take over your job at the restaurant."

Amah says nothing for a long while.

"What about Yaing Gong and school?" Amah asks, finally.

"He's going to have to switch schools sooner or later anyway. He already communicates in English fluently. He'll be fine there. And Ming's cousin can help if needed."

"I guess it will work. You're okay with moving, right?" Amah asks Jung.

"Oh, no." Mai says. "We need Jung Sum to stay and help take care of the kids."

"But Yaing Gong will be alone if I'm working," Amah barely says before Jung starts whimpering.

"I want to stay with Amah," Jung manages to get out.

"Yaing Gong is mature enough to be on his own for a few hours. And Jung's not a child anymore. It's not forever. Just until we find a place and we all move out there." Mai directs her comments to Jung who promptly runs into the bathroom and slams the door. Mai turns to her mother. "You treat her like a baby. This is why at this age she still clings to you."

"Your bad temper and insulting comments have nothing to do with it, right?" Amah gets up and goes to the bathroom to speak with Jung. With all the commotion, the baby wakes.

Mai throws her arms into the air as she rises to tend to the baby. "What else are we to do?"

Ming sips his tea, but he doesn't know what to say.

***

Two weeks later, Mai listens to Jung sobbing the night before Amah and Yaing Gong are scheduled to leave. She feels bad, but she's also annoyed. When she was little, Amah was always pregnant or too busy taking care of one of her younger siblings to notice her. Mai was told she even called Mah Mah Ping "Amah" for a time. And she was at school on her own when she was just a few years older than Yaing Gong is now. Surely, Jung will survive this brief separation from Amah.

16

"Mai, I think I found a good house," Amah says. "It has three floors plus a basement. The main floor has two rooms, a huge kitchen with appliances and a cold room to store shelves of food and supplies. It's so much more space than we've ever had. The second floor has a kitchen with appliances, a full bathroom and two bedrooms. Both rooms are rented. The third floor has another kitchen and a bedroom. It's rented too. There's a school across the street but we're within walking distance to a grocery store and further down there are a few small Chinese stores just starting up."

Surprisingly, Mai doesn't interrupt Amah summarizing all the details, mostly because of the excitement in her voice. Apart from one other place Amah liked when she and Yaing Gong first arrived in Toronto, she hadn't found anything she thought worth an offer over the last month.

Between the kids, the trials of another cold winter, and her sister's disgruntled mood at being left behind in North Bay with them, Mai hardly had time to think about the task she had off loaded on Amah.

"A school faces the house?"

"Yes, but it's the only thing from your list. The house itself is solid. We've seen so many others. This is the best by far."

"What's the price?"

"Twenty-eight thousand, two hundred dollars."

With Ming and her working steadily, plus their savings—everything they ever earned apart from the necessities of rent and food—they had much more than the three thousand dollars needed for the deposit. Thanks to Mai's efficient, if at times inelegant, sewing skills, most of the children's clothes were mended and handed down; they never went out for dinner because she knew how dirty restaurant kitchens got and leaving a tip at the end of a meal was out of the question. They had a comfortable nest. Even if Mai didn't think it was enough.

"Do you think we should put in a bid, lower than ask?"

"No, no. Mr. Li told me the owners just turned down another offer for twenty-eight thousand. And have you forgotten how quickly the homes have sold over the year? If you and Ming want this one, I think you need to offer the full asking price."

Mai is unusually quiet before responding. "If you think it's worth it, then put in the offer for the ask price."

"Talk with Ming."

"No need. He just wants us to find something. Besides, we might not even get it. You know how many times we've been through this."

"Just tell him tonight. Nothing will happen now. I can call the agent in the morning."

"Fine, fine. I'll let him know and call you back first thing in the morning."

As Mai anticipated, Ming was agreeable to whatever made her happy, but they were both a little surprised when Mr. Li called a day later to tell them they now owned a house in Toronto.

That night alone in bed, Mai sighed. Seven years after arriving in Canada and four kids later, she finally feels she has something to show for all their work.

***

The noise of the TV and the kids building forts with kitchen chairs and blankets, filters into the bedroom Saturday morning. Ming returned from Toronto last night to sign the purchase papers with Amah.

"When are we moving?" asks Ming.

"The kids just started school a few months ago. Everything we know is here," says Mai.

"Your Amah wants us to join them. She seems a bit unhappy being there alone."

"I'm sure she's fine. Never said anything to me. And the restaurant called this week. Boss says the night shift dishwasher is not working out. Asked me to take over. Could use the money to pay off the house."

"But you can find a job in the big city. Like you said."

"Kids like their school too."

"They're kids. Will like any school."

They stop talking as Mark bounds through the door.

"Auntie Jung said we can't make French toast. Not enough eggs. And she won't cook. Said Daddy should because he doesn't have to work today."

Ming raises his eyebrows as he gets up. "And your sister sure wants to go."

Mai rolls her eyes as she puts on a sweater. "We better get out there before she sends all the kids in."

As the school year ends, Mai's sister excitedly takes the older kids to school to see the one teacher who was particularly kind to her and who had mentioned her husband's truck moving business. Mai had said once the school year finished, they'd be moving to Toronto to join Amah and Yaing Gong. The teacher provides a telephone number and Jung books him for the move to Toronto at the end of June.

"We need to move, Ming," Mai states one night.

"I know, Mai. I already told Uncle we'll be leaving at the end of the month. Your sister booked the truck."

"We need to find a house."

"What?" Ming does not hide his confusion.

"We need to find a house," Mai says again.

"Your Amah did, remember? You had a long shift today too, I guess." Ming chuckles at his own joke.

"No. We can't move there yet."

"But … what?"

"We need to find a house here. In North Bay."

"What? Why?"

"It's not the right time to move to Toronto now."

"Why is it not the right time?"

"Because we both have jobs here. What if we can't find jobs in the city right away? How will we pay for the mortgage?"

"You said there are more jobs in the big city. That's why your Amah and brother are out there. Why we bought a house there."

"But what if we don't find jobs right away?"

"I can ask my cousin or Mr. Li if he knows of any openings."

"It's just too risky. Too much work to move with all the kids and no job prospects.

Different if it was just us."

"Will have to do it sooner or later."

"Just need to save a bit more before we go. But we're wasting money paying all this rent."

"We have rent coming in from the upstairs tenants there. And your Amah is working."

"Rent is only enough for the expenses and part of the mortgage. And we can't take Amah's money. She needs to pay for her expenses, send money back home, and she just submitted the application for Abah. She needs to show she has funds."

"So, what do you want to do?"

"Stay here. In North Bay. For a little longer. But not right here. Don't want to waste more money on rent."

"So where then?"

"We can buy a house. Maybe near where your sister, Bao Jun and her family, just bought."

"You want to buy a second house? Here?" Ming is shaking his head as if to clear his ears.

"We have the money for a deposit. Your sister and her husband bought those two semi-detached homes. Renting one side out. I don't want a semi-detached, but we can rent a second floor and live on the main floor, like we're doing with the one in Toronto."

"But ... what about your Amah and brother?"

"They're fine."

"Your Amah wants you to move out there. And you know how your sister feels." He pauses and starts to get up. "This is crazy. Moving to Toronto was your idea!" Ming gets dressed and leaves without saying another word. His reaction is nothing compared to Jung's outrage and tears.

"The teacher is angry at me for cancelling on her husband.

You've ruined my relationship with her."

"It's not like you're in school any longer. I'm sure people have cancelled before. The teacher was probably only being nice to you to get business. Why else did she tell you about her husband's moving truck?"

"She told us in class, Mai. You don't know everything. I want to see Amah." She runs to the bathroom and slams the door.

With Jung so upset, Mai has no choice but to buy her a bus ticket to visit Amah and Yaing Gong in Toronto for the week. When she returns, she uses every opportunity to make her point.

***

"Auntie, make the yummy beef dish," says Mark to Jung as Mai prepares to leave for her dishwashing shift.

"I can't, we ran out of the oyster sauce and ginger. Only in Toronto. We'll have to wait until we get some," she says. The little boy runs immediately to Mai.

"Why can't we get oyster sauce, Amah?"

"Special Chinese products are only in the big city," Mai explains.

"Why?"

"Shipments from overseas go to the big cities where the airplanes and ships land. We have to wait for someone to go to Toronto and bring it back here."

"It's where Poh Poh lives now. She can send some."

"It's expensive to send things."

"So, we can't ever get it?"

"We can but we just have to wait for one of the delivery men who drives there to buy it for us."

"We can do it today then."

"No, we have to wait until next week."

"Why do we have to wait?"

"Because the delivery men don't go all the time." In fact, they just received an order from one of the two drivers who deliver Chinese products to the small cities. The salted fish, soya sauce, sesame oil, bean curd, cans of preserved shallots, black bean, preserved fish and dried packs of noodles were on the list. If she knew they were out of oyster sauce she would have ordered a bottle. It's something they use for cooking dishes regularly, but she'd been so busy, she'd no idea. Jung knew since she'd taken over most of the cooking. She purposely left things off the list. Anything to make life less convenient for Mai. Anything to try to get her to move to Toronto.

Amah, too, was unhappy when Mai first told her of the revised plan. No one seems to understand how this place is the only home Mai has known for the last seven years. It's the longest time she's ever lived anywhere. Leaving the comfort of all this familiarity is not something she is ready to do now. Or maybe ever.

17

Mai stands in front of the little garden, taking in the rose-like fragrance of the striking deep, dark red, peonies. From a distance, they appear black, almost lethal. This was what she thought the first time she stood across the busy street in Toronto, assessing the red brick house. It's hard to believe 1974 was five years ago.

The sound of a car horn makes Mai turn around and look down the street. The little yellow car Yaing Gong drives appears from around the corner, and he makes a U-turn to park in front of the house.

They're here. Finally. Yaing Gong and Abah climb out of the front seats. Abah promptly gets out and opens the back passenger door to help his mother climb out while Yaing Gong takes her single suitcase out of the trunk.

Grandmother is wearing a grey traditional Chinese two-piece outfit, a collared shirt, and a matching pair of loose-fitting pants that sway around her legs like waves when she moves. Mai holds back an unexpected urge to cry out as she sees her and freezes for a few seconds before rushing to her side.

"Mah Mah. You are well?"

"Mai. Mai. You're half the size you were when I last saw you." Yaing Gong and Mai laugh at Mah Mah Ping's observation as she reaches out and her fingers gently graze Mai's face. Grandmother is as thin as always, but wrinklier. This is understandable since she's in her late seventies and it's been close to twenty years since they were together.

"Are you cold? Do you want to go inside?" Mai gestures to their home.

"So nice out. How can I be cold? Crazy girl." Mah Mah looks at where Mai points.

"This is your house? Wahhhh. So big. And made of stone like ours back home. How many floors here?"

"Bricks. Very common in Canada. Three floors. Plus, there's a basement."

"Four floors! Much bigger than back home!" Grandmother walks to the steps of the house, flanked by Mai and Yaing Gong, studying her surroundings. She pauses to catch her breath before climbing the little staircase.

"Mai, I've never seen columns like these before. Very strong." Mah Mah pats the brick columns as she reaches the top of the stairs. Mai tries not to appear flattered.

"We just got them changed two years ago. The wooden ones were falling apart. I paid more for the brick to match the rest of the house. No one else on our street has anything like it." The columns support the sunroom attached to the master bedroom upstairs, creating a covered porch to sit in during the hot summer days. The columns remind Mai of those found at Buddhist temples and expensive grave sites. Mai loves how people can pick out their house from all the way up the street because of their eye-catching columns. She has no idea how peculiar it appears. Nor does she care.

"Oh, Mai this is good. The door ledge is not too high. The ledge at home was too high. Remember? Stopped the wealth from flowing in. After the *feng shui*, wind water, geomancer told us and we got it fixed, you were accepted into nursing school."

Abah, who is in the mud room already, turns around at this comment. "Crazy old woman. He was a con man. Just like the blind soothsayer you wasted our food on." Abah stomps off.

"What do you know?" Mah Mah waves her hand at him dismissively.

Yaing Gong chuckles quietly at the exchange and adds, "I remember the pig used to scrape his stomach getting over the ledge to get into the kitchen. One day, I used almost an entire bottle of Mah Mah's special oil to heal his cut and then bandaged him." He and Mai laugh.

"And when Abah smelled it and found out it was on the pig, he yelled so loud the neighbours thought someone was getting murdered," said Mai.

As they remove their shoes, Mai helps her grandmother while Yaing Gong hurries ahead and goes into his room. "Talk with you later, Mah Mah. I have to go back to school."

"Let's sit in the kitchen. Amah made a meal in case you're hungry." Mai says, walking slowly with her grandmother.

"Where is everyone?" Mah Mah Ping asks.

"At work, at school or sleeping. You'll see all of them later today or tomorrow."

"Last time I saw Yaing Gong, he was a little boy. Can't believe he's off to university next year. Can't believe you're a mother now. Four children."

They reach the kitchen where they find Amah busy at the stove. She calls out to Mah Mah warmly as if they were more than in-laws, and invites her to sit at the table, which is neatly tucked against the wall opposite the counter space and appliances.

"Oh, Mai! The kitchen is so big!" Mah Mah exclaims.

"I thought the same thing when I first saw it. Almost as big as a restaurant kitchen. Eight feet ceilings. I knew it was perfect for us."

"Ha! You knew it was perfect? I found it. Weren't sure if you were ever going to see it. And this was after you already bought the place." Amah points a finger at Mai accusingly as she deposits a steaming bowl of rice with meat and vegetables in front of Mah Mah. "I have to get ready for work, but I'll talk with you later." Amah pats Mah Mah on the shoulder before leaving.

Mai waves her off and says loudly after her, "Didn't say I found it. Just knew it was right when I first saw it."

"What is she talking about Mai?"

"Ancient news. You don't want to hear about it, Mah Mah."

"Yes, tell me. Everyone is running off and it's just you and me. Like when you were little. Get a bowl to join me. I can't eat all of this. You're so thin now."

"Eat it all, Grandmother. We have food now. Not like before."

"I will, but I don't want to dirty all of this if I can't finish it. Join me and tell me what your Amah is talking about." Mai brings another bowl to the table for Mah Mah to share her rice and toppings.

"Years ago, I convinced Ming to buy a house in North Bay after I sent Amah and Yaing Gong here and we had already bought this one."

"You had money for two houses?"

"We didn't pay them all off. Houses in the small city were

cheaper, too. But we had enough for deposits for two homes. Especially after Amah came to Toronto, and I took over her full-time job. Between Ming's two and my one job, we saved."

"Good. Your Amah couldn't have been upset about you making money."

"No, they were upset because she and Yaing Gong were here alone. No one to watch him when she was at work, but he was old enough. We needed Jung Sum to look after the kids when we worked. She hated it. Her whole life, she needs to be close to Amah. Even now. Grown woman and she sticks to Amah like a child."

"Don't be so hard on her. Jung has a bad leg. Your Amah had to look out for her. You're a mother now, too. You must understand." Mai sulks but says nothing. "But why didn't you buy a second house out here instead of in the small city? Then you'd be close to them."

"More expensive out here and the only reason we could afford any of it was because of our jobs. They were in North Bay. Not here. Was afraid we might lose everything if we didn't find work right away. Didn't want to move the kids until we had more money. More stable to stay there. Thought maybe we'd make enough to pay off the house, sell it and pay off this one. Safer. Less at stake."

"But if you had two houses, didn't you have double the expenses and costs?"

"Yes, but we had tenants here and in North Bay. The combined rental money took care of the expenses for one house. Our jobs took care of the other."

"Was the other house as big as this one?"

"No, no. This is much bigger. The kitchen was only half the size. Like the one upstairs or on the third floor. Will show you later."

"You have kitchens upstairs too? Waaaa! This is huge. You can do somersaults in this kitchen."

"The upstairs ones are smaller. But this place came with the refrigerator and stove."

"This table, too?"

Mai laughs. "No, no. Just the appliances. This table was the first piece of furniture we purchased in Toronto. Still in good condition, too." Mai pulls up the vinyl tablecloth which covers the surface, to show off the still-new condition of the laminate tabletop.

Many important conversations had already occurred around the table. It's where Mai and Ming argued about whether Ming had any duty to continue sending money to support his father and stepbrothers when, in Mai's eyes, Ming had been effectively abandoned; where Mai sat to compose letters to Mah Mah and to immigration government officials about Abah's application; where Ming recently agreed to quit working as a cook for a secure job with benefits at the large bread factory where Abah works; where Mai sits to hem pants or sew buttons; and where Mai calculates and assembles her time sheets from work or painstakingly writes cheques in English to pay the electricity and heating bills.

"Wobbly but modern looking," Mah Mah says as she examines the table. "What's on the feet of the table and chairs, Mai?"

Mai skips over the "wobbly" comment. "Oh. I didn't want the floor to get scratched so Ming wrapped the feet with old pieces of cloth. Tied on with string. Protects the feet and the floor."

"Good idea. Ming is creative. But what did you eat on, all those years before you purchased this table?"

"His uncle, Ho Choi, gave us an old unused table from the restaurant. Chairs too. They're in the upstairs kitchen now. That one is even more unstable because it has a pedestal leg. Had very little furniture before. The table there was one of the few pieces we brought." Mai points to the little wooden side table, which matched nothing, and currently stands beside the back door to the kitchen.

"So, you paid off this house after you sold the one in the small city? Or do you still own the other one too?"

"No. We sold the one in North Bay before we even owned it a year. No loss, no gain after all the expenses and taxes. Just a lot of work."

"Why? It was not a good house?"

"The house was fine, but managing tenants is very troublesome. Many headaches. And Amah was having a hard time here alone. Too much for her to do on her own. Plus, a Hakka woman at the laundromat was bullying her. Came home crying. Jung and Yaing Gong told me. Tried to get Amah to tell the woman to go die, tell the boss, or just slap her, but she wouldn't do any of it. Just suffered and cried."

Grandmother laughs. "She's not you or your Abah. Your Amah is gentle."

"Well, I couldn't leave her here alone, so upset. Everyone but Ming was happy when we finally left North Bay."

"Why didn't Ming want to come out here?"

"He wanted to come to Toronto, but he complained about me changing my mind so much. Said we should've gone right after we bought this house and never bought the small city house. Didn't talk to me for two days. But he knew I always wanted to come here. Just not when I originally thought. And no one told me about that bitch at Amah's work until after we bought in North Bay. If I'd known from the beginning, I would've come right away."

Grandmother pats Mai's arm. "You've always been such a loyal daughter, Mai. You can never bear your Amah struggling. Like in Hong Kong. You left but didn't even tell us you were sneaking over from Macau to join her. Ai yah! Scared your Abah and me to death when we heard you were with them."

Mai laughs at the memory. "Bet you Abah was angrier than he was scared."

"He's a man. Angry is all he knows. Not like he'll ever admit he's scared or worried." She pauses and thinks. "Your Amah's going to work now. She still works there?"

"No, no. Don't worry. She works at a garment factory now. Sews and helps with odds and ends. Made her quit that job at the laundromat when Ming and I found work here. But I went with her to that place on the last day. Yelled at the woman. Shamed her in front of her boss and co-workers. Hmm! Teach her."

"Oh, Mai. You and your father have such terrible tempers."

"The woman deserved it."

"Maybe so, but you get so excited. Is there any more rice, Mai?"

"Plenty, Mah Mah. Let me get it." Grandmother watches Mai take her bowl to the stove.

"Why are those cupboards a different colour than the others?" Mah Mah points above the stove top.

"Oh. We cook so much, the cupboards get greasy, so I wrap the closest with tin foil. This way I only need to change the foil every few months instead of scrubbing for hours. I wrap the drip bowl and rim of each burner with foil too." Mai points out her work to Mah Mah. "Saves so much time." Mai doesn't mention that repairmen advised her not to do it because bits of foil inevitably find their way to the inner workings causing the stove to short out.

"Makes sense." Mah Mah says, turning back around to eat

the new bowl of rice Mai sets in front of her. "Is there any soup, Mai?"

"Not yet but there will be *gua*, prickly bitter melon, soup tonight. Made with pig bones. It's been simmering for a couple of hours, but it's not ready yet. Did you want some more tea?"

Mah Mah nods and holds out her cup for a refill. "Good thing you remember how to make soups. I taught you and your youngest sister what I know. Your Amah never knew much. Her family had money and servants, so she never had to do anything for herself. Lucky I was there to help raise you and your siblings."

"The nurses at the hospital I worked at in Jiangmen talked a lot about what soups help if the body has too much heat or if we needed to bring back strength. Now, we can afford the ingredients, so I make soups at least once a week."

"What other ones do you know about?"

"Back in the small city, we used the fish heads and bones a lot, with black eyed peas, and garlic. Such a good use of the fish. Nothing wasted. The kids love steamed fish meat mixed with minced pork. Sometimes, the natives captured turtles for us. We made turtle soup to help Yaing Gong stop peeing in the middle of the night. Here, we get a lot of pig bones from the butcher for broth when we buy barbecued duck and pork. And everyone loves the black bean and oxtail soup. No one but me seems to like the liver and spinach. Last week I brewed carrots and greens with lentils."

"Where do you get the *gua*? Is it expensive here?"

"Ming and Jung grow it in the back."

"You have space for a garden?"

"Not a farm like back home but some space. You can see part of it from the window over there." Mai points beside the refrigerator. "Will show you after we finish eating."

Mah Mah concentrates on finishing her rice so she can explore some more. As Mai quickly cleans up, her grandmother wanders about the kitchen and peaks out the large window.

"You have a house out there too, Mai?

"Not a house. It's an old garage. Falling apart. Real estate agent warned us not to let the kids go inside because it's dangerous. Needs to be torn down."

"Why is it pink? It's ugly."

Mai laughs. "The neighbour complained about it. City sent us a notice to paint it because it was an eyesore. Didn't want to spend money on something we need to tear down and there wasn't enough leftover paint of one colour, so Ming mixed all the paint ends we have together. There was just enough to cover the garage."

"Good idea. So, you still have tenants upstairs?"

Mai laughs. "Mah Mah, if we had tenants upstairs, we'd be living in the rundown garage. Counting you there are twelve of us living here now. And only two washrooms in the house. Come on, I'm done. Let me get your shoes from the front and we can go outside."

***

Mai supports her grandmother's arm as they step outside onto the sturdy porch. Along with the columns in the front, years ago, Mai had both the front and back porches replaced with concrete, when the wooden ones started to deteriorate. They opted for metal railings, which she reasoned were sturdier than the wood ones they replaced. Besides, wood meant more maintenance, something Mai calculated would be more expensive over time.

"Do you want to go down the stairs or stand up here, Mah Mah?"

"Let's go down. I want to see the *gua*. Who made all these trellises?" Her grandmother points to the five-foot-tall wooden structures covering the yard.

"Ming did."

"He takes care of the *gua*?"

"He builds these crazy contraptions. But it's mostly Jung Sum who tends to the *gua*. She likes to use the kids' urine as fertilizer for the crops. Said it makes them grow bigger. Told her to stop."

"She's right. Nutrients in the urine. Surprised she remembered from when she was on the farm. Or maybe they learned about it in school. Why'd you make her stop?"

"Because the urine stinks and we didn't want the neighbours to complain to the city about something else."

"Too bad. It does make the crops bigger."

"Don't worry. She still does it. Can smell it sometimes. But now I just make her go out and water everything down if it smells bad."

"These are a good size though." Mah Mah points out the large *gua* hanging in the back.

"Yes. So big, the *kwai gwai jai*, naughty white boys, thought they were watermelons. Stole two of our biggest ones, last fall. Got pricked by the hairs on the skin when they bit into them. Threw them away in the alley. What a waste!"

"How do you know what happened if they stole them?"

"Ming found the *gua* with chunks bitten out, a few houses down."

"So how do you stop them now?"

"Think they learned their lesson. And we don't let them grow as big now. Cut them early."

"So much room to hang clothes out here." Mah Mah points to the three clotheslines, two strung between the house and hydro pole and the other strung between the house and the dilapidated garage. All are filled with hanging laundry.

"Yes. Perfect in the summer and spring. In the apartment in the small city, we used to hang clothes on the rooftop. In the winter, we sometimes go to the laundromat and pay to use the dryer because there isn't enough room to hang everything."

"Who washes all the clothes?"

"Jung handwashes some of it but Amah and I usually use the washing machine in the basement."

"You have a machine to do it? Show me the machine."

"Yes, bought it in North Bay. With the babies' diapers, it was much easier than handwashing. Now, with the whole family here, there's even more clothes. And I use the clean rinse water to wash the floors. It's perfect."

"I want to see the washing machine."

"Don't you want to rest a bit?"

"I'm fine. Let's go. Let's go."

***

"We need to wear slippers to the basement. Concrete floors. Cold. Just down the stairs here." Mai leads Mah Mah to the staircase at the side of the kitchen, flicks the light switch on the wall and takes the lead because only one person can fit at a time.

"What a large sewing machine!" Mah Mah points to the machine sitting at the bottom of the stairs.

"It's a Singer. Best brand. We bought it shortly after we moved here. I was working from home. Too bad the company didn't need us after a while. Now I just use it to make things we need, blanket covers, shortening pants, that sort of thing. I even sew my own underwear."

Mai doesn't mention how she often likes to disappear down here, partly to get away from the crowded house and partly because she loves bringing up a finished product after an hour or two of cutting and sewing.

"Do Amah or any of your sisters ever use it?"

"Ha! Amah knows how to use it but she's much slower than me. And the other two are hopeless."

"I remember you wrote me about your work in the fabric factory in Hong Kong. Where Amah said you lost all your weight. Is this what you do for work now?"

"I don't have to run around as much. I work in a knitting factory. Makes gloves, hats, scarves, and sweaters. A lot of military orders. You know French hats? I help make those. The tip on top. I'm the fastest one they have. My work always passes inspection."

"You were always a quick learner, Mai."

"Just not as slow as others. Still not smart enough, Mah Mah. If I were, we'd have a palace now instead of just this house."

"Oh, Mai. Will you ever think it's enough?"

Mai turns to point out the room with a bathtub and the separate room beside it that holds a toilet and sink before leading her grandmother to the laundry room, which is empty except for the washing machine and the deep laundry sink.

Mai shows Mah Mah where the clothes are put in the porcelain wringer washer tub, and how they crank all the clothes through the large rollers at the end. "This is considered old fashioned now. Newer styles don't need you to do anything except throw in the clothes and soap and press a few buttons. It's noisy and uses a lot of water but easier than washing bedsheets and blanket covers by hand."

"Don't need to tell me. Back home, the whole day can be spent washing and hanging clothes." Grandmother curiously pokes at the machine before saying, "You must have a lot of free time now."

Mai laughs even though her grandmother is serious. "Wish I did. Don't know what I do all day sometimes."

"What's over there?"

"Two more rooms. Just our deep freezer in there." Mai points to the room beside them. "And the last room has stairs leading outside. Not interesting. Come back this way, Mah Mah. Let's go upstairs."

As they walk to the stairs, her grandmother stops in front of the sewing machine to look around. "Where's that door lead? Is it a closet?" She points to the side of the basement Mai didn't show her.

"No. It's another room. Right under the front porch. Ming stores tools and his old reel-to-reel music player there. He has boxes full of reels of Chinese operas from when he worked in the theatre in Hong Kong."

"He was an actor?"

Mai laughs. "Only if you consider our lives a show. He did odd jobs. Building sets and things. Told me he eventually helped run a bed and breakfast for actors and crew with some friend. Cooked the meals, did repairs. He brought all this junk from Hong Kong to North Bay and now here. Still listens to those Chinese operas. I hate them. Loud and noisy. Don't know what else he keeps in there. I stay out. Just told him not to start a fire. Come on, let's go back up."

"Ming's hardworking. Good man despite growing up motherless."

"Yes. He is very honest and hardworking."

***

"Let's go sit in the living room for a bit before I show you your room, Mah Mah."

They walk through the kitchen and back along the hallway to the first room next to the front door.

"Sit, Mah Mah." Mai helps her to the three-person couch,

covered with an apple green, white dotted drop cloth. The couch's plaid fabric is concealed except near the wooden legs where the cloth won't reach. Mai sits beside her.

"Oh Mai, the Hundred Auspicious Birds!" Grandmother points to the painting hanging opposite the door through which they just entered. "Remember what I told you about the power of birds? Even pictures of them can carry earthly wishes to the heavens, to make them come true. The peacock in this one is beautiful. See how all the other birds are coming to see him. He attracts prosperity in abundance. Every bird in the picture brings something good—the doves for peace, the mandarin ducks attract mates for life and good relationships, the rooster signals morning and wards off dark spirits, the magpies bring children, joy, and new opportunities. No wonder you have had such positive luck here."

"Ming's father sent it with Abah when he came to Canada a few years ago. He works in the framing factory in Hong Kong, remember?"

"That's right. What a wonderful gift. Must have been difficult to transport and not break the glass all the way from back home."

"No, Mah Mah. He only sent the silk print, rolled up. We framed it here. I did it myself. Notice the matte is the same material as this cover." Mai points to the drop cloth over the couch they're sitting on. "The framer in the Chinese shops nearby wanted a hundred and fifty dollars to mount the painting. So, I bought the frame from him for forty-five dollars. Talked him down from fifty. Abah helped when he saw what I was doing. We spent every evening for a week, carefully pulling and pinning the silk print to the piece of cardboard in the frame. Then I used the scraps of fabric left over from the couch cover as matte. I sewed the four pieces on the sewing machine and lined each side of the frame."

"You did a very good job. If you hadn't told me, I wouldn't have known you'd done it yourself. Very professional."

It's a shame how it is hung after all the work Mai put into mounting the print. A coarse rope nailed to either end of the frame suspends the print from a screw in the wall but, because Mai does not trust it is secure, screws are also placed in the wall underneath the frame to add support. Ming then slipped small pieces of carpet between the frame and the screws to prevent scratching the frame.

"This room is so comfortable and bright Mai."

"Kids and everyone come in here to watch TV when they finish school. On Sunday nights though, they air the show with Wang Ming-Chuen, gamblers and kung fu masters. Everyone likes it. Whoever's not working comes in to watch. We even open up these doors to make more room." Mai motions behind her to the beautiful pocket doors that separate the living room from what should be the dining room.

"I don't know the show but of course I've heard of Wang Ming-Chuen. She's famous. Why don't you keep the doors open all the time? More room."

"Aiiii, Mah Mah. How can we? It's Yaing Gong's bedroom in there. This is the only communal room outside of the kitchen and basement. Told you, full house."

"Right. Right. You did tell me." She pats Mai's hand. "You're good, Mai. Can't wait until your grandfather sees what you've done. Your Abah told me they would not let him enter Canada right now, but I know you can make it happen. You can do anything."

Mah Mah Ping doesn't notice Mai stifle a gasp. What on earth had Abah told her?

18

Mai hurries to get Mah Mah settled in her room so she can nap, before rushing back to the kitchen where Abah and Amah prepare their bags to leave for work.

In a loud whisper she hisses, "Why does Grandmother think Grandfather is alive? Didn't she read the letter I wrote to both of you before you left China, Abah? She thinks we can bring him here from San Francisco for a visit."

Amah freezes in mid-scoop of her rice. Her eyes bulge but she says nothing.

"Why would I show her the letter? It would just upset her." Abah calmly continues preparing his bag, not even looking at Mai.

"He's been dead for over three years. He was her husband. She has a right to know. What am I supposed to tell her when she asks about him coming here?"

"Just tell her the government officials won't let him in. Like I did."

"He was her husband! Don't you think she has the right to know? It's *her* life. I'm not going to lie to her."

"Not about you. About keeping her happy. What does it matter if he's alive or dead? He hadn't seen her in over fifty years. You tell her he's dead and it will kill her. Not your decision. Tell Ming not to say anything either."

"Tell him yourself." Mai stomps out of the kitchen.

She wanted to say so much more but Abah was the one person with whom she normally held her tongue. With his bad temper, if she blew up at him anymore than she already had, he'd never speak with her again.

Mai slumps onto the living room couch with her arms and legs crossed, still fuming when Amah pokes her head in twenty minutes later with a concerned look on her face.

"Mai, we're leaving now."

She sighs when Mai doesn't respond but she lets out a long breath after the front door opens and shut, and she's certain they've left.

She recalls the summer of 1975 when Amah received the letter from the English-speaking relative in San Francisco who she learned managed her grandfather's money and affairs. Unfortunately, Mai suspected not everyone was as honest as Ming or his aunt and uncle.

Mrs. Chung,

Hope you and your family are well. I'm sorry to write with troubling news.

Your father-in-law has been hospitalized. The doctors are not sure how much longer he has to live. He has been asking to see his wife and son. I know they are in China still but is it possible for you and your children to come see him because you're closer being in Canada.

You are welcome to stay at my home. My phone number is below. Please call.

Chun Man Tat

Amah threw the letter on the kitchen table. "After all these years, this man wants to see his wife and son? He has no right. Why? Because he's dying? What does he think dying entitles him?"

Mai rarely saw Amah like that. She picked up the letter and read it herself.

"Amah. We don't know why Grandfather didn't send money all those years. Maybe this relative took it and said he sent it but didn't. Maybe he just doesn't have a lot. You know how hard it's been for us to save since we've been here. When I spoke with Grandfather on the phone after I married Ming, some money came." She leaves out the part about him calling collect. Good thing Uncle Ho Choi didn't mind. It's almost like he didn't know or didn't think of it.

Amah softened. "Maybe. But I don't have time to worry about him now. Just want to get Abah and the others here. What else do those officials want from us? Abah's application has been processing for almost two years now. Since the day we bought this house as collateral. I have a job, too. And you sent a letter, offering your and Ming's support. What is the holdup? Too bad Ming's uncle can't help."

"He tried but because we live here now, the officials are different than the ones in North Bay. Besides it's probably the Hong Kong officials who want black money." Mai studied the letter again.

"Well, I don't have money for that or any trip to San Francisco."

Mai said nothing for a long while, but she felt guilty she delayed moving to Toronto when Amah started tearing up. But why wasn't she stronger? Didn't she know Mai's juggled a lot, too? Between the mortgage and the kids and those troublesome tenants who kept clogging the toilet. Why wasn't Amah more like her? And what was wrong with those Canadian officials? They're supposed to be so humanitarian. It's all over the news. All those Vietnamese boat people they accepted under Trudeau. It was then, a thought crossed Mai's mind.

"You should go to San Francisco, Amah. Take Jung Sum. I can't leave the kids and Yaing Gong should concentrate on school. Cheaper for just the two of you."

"Are you crazy? Why would I waste money on flights and miss work? And Jung has school, too."

Mai tried to collect her thoughts, but she was annoyed with Amah's excuse. "Jung is only taking English courses for adults. She's been studying for years. It'll be a miracle if that government counsellor woman who visits finds her a job once she finishes. She can go with you."

"But why should we waste money on this now?"

"We need to send pictures and proof of Grandfather's condition to the immigration officials. Tell them this is the only chance left for Abah to ever meet his father. It's true. Think about it. Grandmother told me Grandfather had to get back to the U.S. right after Abah was born or he'd lose his status there. Not sure if it was true but he's never met Abah really. And Abah is a grandfather himself now. Not as sad as being a refugee, but it's similar. You know the Vietnamese refugees Canada's offering to help and is letting in? And it's partly because of the immigration restrictions Abah and his own father have never met. Need to show the Canadian officials why it's the right thing to do to let Abah in now. You have to go."

Amah's brow crinkled. "But it wasn't Canadian immigration laws that prevented them from being together. Your grandfather was never here. It was the U.S. laws if anything. And probably had more to do with your grandfather himself."

Mai rolled her eyes. "You don't know. None of us do. Laws here and in the U.S. restricted Chinese entry. The officials certainly don't know why exactly they have been separated for so long. Canadian and American laws are the same. Both are North America. Head taxes in both countries. We even call both Gold Mountain. Our letter to the officials won't say it was because of the laws. Just suggest it. And even if they don't agree with any of those arguments, it's still a sad situation. Tragic. Abah applied to come here instead of there because we're here. Just happens Grandfather is next door and dying. Not something we could have planned."

Amah nodded, finally understanding Mai's point. By the time Mai finished her speech, she believed her own arguments even more than she did when she first realized how grandfather's health challenges might actually help Abah.

The arrangements were quickly made for Amah and Jung to go meet Grandfather.

***

"How was the trip? Did he know who you and Jung Sum were? Did you take photos?" Mai was hungry for information and a part of her wished she could've gone.

"It was fine. Let me get settled and unpacked."

"I'll unpack for you. Just tell me what happened." Mai opened Amah's suitcase right on the kitchen floor revealing her used undergarments.

"Mai!" Amah pushed her aside as she retrieved her suitcase. "He's in the hospital. Gets tired easily. Called for Jung a few times. She clipped his nails for him."

"Did you ask him about why he didn't send money in the past?"

"No, he's in a hospital. I wasn't going to bring all that up. He's an old man. Sick. Dying."

"What was San Francisco like?"

"It's like being at home there. At least in Chinatown. Everyone speaks our dialect. The hospital was there. The relative showed us around a bit but he had to work. Jung and I walked over most days and picked up barbecued pork buns for meals. Didn't want to trouble his family any more than we already were."

"What was the relative like? Do you think he took Grandfather's money?"

"I don't know, Mai. He seemed nice enough. Let us stay with him and his family. Showed us where Bak Lai lives. Normally. A room on Jackson Street, near the hospital. Pretty run down. Like our place in North Bay."

When they picked up the developed photos, it was clear Amah's natural empathy in the presence of a man's suffering erased any bitterness about Grandfather that she first shared with Mai. The photos featured Grandfather in the hospital-issued blue gown lying in bed, flanked on either side by a sombre looking Amah and Jung. Mai selected the most pathetic of the photos, attached the letter she wrote, and delivered the package to the lawyer with clear instructions to translate her letter verbatim before sending it all to the immigration officials assessing Abah's application.

Two months later, Abah and one of Mai's siblings were approved to enter Canada. The other siblings still had to wait but, by the end of the fall, Abah and Dai Hong, Mai's second brother, arrived to join them in the red brick house.

Unfortunately, the American officials were less swayed by Abah and Grandfather's situation. They refused to let Abah enter their country because he was still a Chinese citizen and only a permanent resident of Canada. The reason for denial was that Abah was only a permanent resident of Canada, not a citizen. Mai knew that despite the U.S. leaders' attempts to normalize relations with China, many still did not trust the Chinese, and to some extent, she sympathized with that thinking. Five days after the Chinese New Year on February 6, 1976, Bak Lai died without any of his family around him. Abah never met his father.

Mai was thankful some U.S. official had the decency to finally permit Abah to accompany Amah and Yaing Gong to attend his father's funeral.

Back at their kitchen table, a day after the funeral Amah and Mai caught up.

"Your Abah, Yaing Gong, and I just followed the relative around after he picked us up from the hotel. Thank goodness your brother speaks English."

"Too bad you couldn't stay with the relative this time," Mai offered.

"No, it's bad luck. And too rushed. I don't blame him. No one wants the son and grandson of the deceased who are there only to attend the funeral to lure the dead spirits back to their house. Especially so close to the new year. Better we stayed in a hotel. Even if it was expensive."

"At least Abah got to see him before he was buried."

"And Bak Lai's at rest now." Amah sighed.

"Too bad Mah Mah won't see him again. It's been her dream

for as long as I can remember," Mai said so quietly Amah didn't hear.

***

Mai uncrosses her legs and arms as her hands hold her forehead.

The idea that Abah knows what's better for Mah Mah than she does herself! Even if he does, it's not up to him to withhold such important information. She has more right to the information than he does. He was her husband. Maybe if Mah Mah knew he was gone, she'd stop waiting and hoping for him to come back. Maybe she'd do something else. Maybe even meet someone else.

The idea of her grandmother finding a new love interest in her seventies makes Mai laugh out loud. But the arrogance of making such a decision for someone else and justifying it by saying it's for her own good, is so offensive to Mai, the urge to scream or hit something fills her and she clenches her fists so tightly her nails create deep imprints in her palms.

At first Mai doesn't understand why she is so upset. Then she realizes it's because Jung Sum had done this to her in Hong Kong. Sent those friends of Dat Wah's away without telling her. By the time Amah found out and told her, it was so late. Amah thought she could've chosen not to come to Canada. But it would've been a terrible mess; plus, how would she have found him? Technically, it was her decision in the end. Still, a part of her never forgave Jung for being so presumptuous, so high-handed.

Should she tell her grandmother the truth? What if she really does get sick from the news? Mai would have to live with it. Abah would never speak to her again even if she was fine. Or she can join the conspiracy Abah started. She'd want to know but maybe Mah Mah doesn't. Neither option appeals to Mai.

***

Mai realizes there's rumbling in the kitchen.

"Oh, Ming. You're up. Good."

"Hard to sleep when it's light out and everyone's moving about."

"I don't like you on the midnight shift. When the year's up, you should ask to switch right away. You never see the kids now."

"Your idea I take the job remember?"

"For stability. What were you going to do? Work in a restaurant all your life? Always told you this shift would be temporary."

Ming brings his cup of coffee to the table as Mai sits down.

"Mah Mah is napping upstairs."

"She got here all right then. Good. Does she like the place?"

"Of course. Bigger than any of us have ever lived in. Happy everyone is working and earning money. But you know how crazy Abah is?"

"Can't be any crazier than you." Ming chuckles at his own comment.

"He didn't show Mah Mah the letter I sent years ago. About her husband, Bak Lai. She thinks he's still alive. She thinks my great grandfather is still alive! Asked me today to help him come here from San Francisco."

Ming laughs. "Of course, your Abah did. He's the smartest. First day here at dinner, he sat at the head of the table like a king. Never helps to clear the dishes or clean up. Aunt Fai Nguk still complains about how he didn't even have the courtesy to put his paper down to greet her when she came to visit. As if she wasn't deserving of such respect. Does he even know it's our house, not his?"

"Don't talk about all this other stuff now." The irritation in Mai's voice tells Ming to back off. "Should I tell Mah Mah the truth?"

"Ha! You do and he'll never speak with you again. Besides you're afraid to challenge anything he says. You just ignore him if you disagree. Or talk about him behind his back. He usually doesn't interfere with our decisions. And you always do whatever you want."

"But this time it's different. Not something about me or our family. About his Amah. He's her son. But I know if it was my husband, I'd want to know. Something wrong with not telling her."

"It's been more than three years. Nothing she can do now except mourn. Maybe pray to him. What's your Amah say?"

"I could tell she had no idea Mah Mah didn't know. Said nothing when I was talking with Abah before they left for work. But she's only the daughter-in-law. She won't argue with Abah about this one. Maybe she even agrees with him."

"Think carefully before you do anything. Doesn't matter to me if your Abah doesn't speak to us again but it might to you. Not sure the kids like him so much."

***

The next day, when Mai is certain Mah Mah is napping, Mai approaches Abah and Amah in the kitchen again.

"You need to tell her the truth. I won't lie to her."

"What did you say to me?" Abah stops filling his metal food container and slams it down harshly on the counter.

"Mai, not now." Amah's eyes plead with Mai as she slowly shakes her head.

"If she asks again, I will tell her the truth."

Mai has always envied Abah's ability to yell and scold without raising his voice. Unlike her, who just gets louder as she gets angrier.

"What good is the truth if you kill her with it? It's selfish of you. I have a responsibility as her son to protect her. Don't you remember this from your schooling? You honour your elders by taking care of them because they've taken care of you. It's our way to pay her back for what she's done. We shoulder the news for her."

"It's *her* husband. How do you know she wouldn't want to know? Did you ever ask her? It's her choice. Not yours."

"I don't need to ask her. It will break her spirit if there's no hope she'll ever see him again. It's what she's lived for all her life. You speak of her choice and what she wants but it is clear with everything she's done the last fifty years. She's been waiting for him. Why do you want to destroy everything for her? You forget, we, as a family have a duty to her, to protect her for her own good. We undertake the burden, so she does not at this age need to do it any longer. You forget we are Chinese even if we live in Canada. All they do here is talk about individual rights and decisions, but this is a family decision. You have forgotten your roots. You are too Canadian now."

Mai is taken aback by his accusations. But he's wrong. Here, or in China, she's always believed individuals have the right to make their own decisions, for good or for bad. And no one, no government and no family member, has the right to take these choices away from a sane adult, even if it's for their own good. It's the very reason she escaped China after the Communists took over. Despite how tough the first few years were, the right to work as much or as little as she wanted, to save or spend, to move or not—these were her choices. She may bulldoze others to agree with her, but she didn't hide facts or change the truth to get agreement for her decisions. It's why she knows she belongs here, in Canada.

"What family decision? You didn't ask any of us or her. You made the decision and you just expect us to do as you say."

"I'm her son and your father. I get to make the decision for her and the family." Abah's voice is slightly louder.

"Not in my house," Mai blurts out.

Amah gasps and Mai is certain Abah is going to pick up the cleaver drying in the dish rack and whip it at her.

Instead, he says quietly, "Then we won't live in your house any longer."

By the next day, Amah has been instructed to contact Mr. Li, the real estate agent who helped them find Mai's house. Mai's siblings have been told of the plans to move out and they pool their savings with Abah and Amah to come up with a sizeable deposit. Abah and Amah spend every day off, viewing houses.

Despite Mai's attempt to engage Abah in conversation, at first telling him they need not move and later offering advice about searching for a home, he refuses to make eye contact with her, choosing instead to keep his newspaper in front of his face, and eventually leaving the room while she is mid-sentence.

Mai retreats to her room before her tears drop. She pulls open her undergarment drawer and takes out the velvet pouch. She dumps the contents into her hand and caresses the jade ring. Her body convulses as she sobs quietly, wondering why she gave up everything for her family, her ungrateful Abah.

Over the next while, Mai mops the floors, the stove, the bathrooms, anything to keep her busy when she's home. Anything to distract herself from being ignored and punished. She is hurt, but she refuses to show it.

Mai's siblings and even her kids know something happened, but Abah and Amah say nothing. Ming is sworn to secrecy. Friday evening family meals become unnaturally quiet when so many are huddled together at the kitchen table. Once the highlight of the week, the dinners are now a source of discomfort. Amah tries to help bridge the discord between them but there is no changing Abah's mind or position.

Despite her efforts to avoid it, Mai finds herself alone with Mah Mah at the breakfast table one morning.

"Good, Mai. We are alone at last. Everyone is so busy. What is happening with your Abah and you?"

"He's angry at me. Nothing new there."

"Whatever for? He should be thanking you. Everyone's working. Even Jung. Can't believe she has the best job out of all of you. Working in an office. Back home she would've been lucky not to be on the streets."

"It's only because she speaks enough English, and the government helps pay her wages because of her leg. But, yes, it's better than if she were in China or even Hong Kong."

"So, what is your Abah fussing about? He must know we could not stay with you forever. You're married. This is Ming's home, a Lee home. We are Chungs. It'd be nice if we could all live together like we did when you were growing up but it's not right."

Mai fiddles with her teacup. It's better than any excuse she could have come up with for why Abah wanted to move out. "Yes, you know Abah. He's very proud."

"Stubborn. He's been like that since he was a child. You can help him, but he will never ask. And he won't thank you either. Typical man. Everything always works out though. Look at you. He didn't believe it would happen, but it did. Your grandfather will be so proud when he sees all of this."

"He didn't help us achieve anything we have here, Mah Mah. Why does it matter what he thinks? Why do you care so much about him after all these years?"

"Mai. He is my husband."

"Even though you haven't seen him in over fifty years, and

I've never even met him?"

"Mai. We marry once in our lives. I bore him a son. We have an unbreakable bond. And I am lucky I was matched with the most handsome man I ever met. Fair skinned, large eyes and tall. I was born to be Chung Bak Lai's wife and your Abah's mother. No matter what they do or don't do, I am tied to them forever. It is my role in this life."

Mai gets up to start clearing the dishes. "Of course, Mah Mah."

With the commotion of Abah's house search and preparing for the move, her grandmother thankfully doesn't mention her grandfather again to Mai who wonders whether it was ever worth it to challenge Abah.

***

By the end of the summer, Abah, Amah, Mai's siblings and Mah Mah move into their new home. "I'll call when we're settled in, Mai. You'll all come over for Friday night dinner," Amah insists in front of Abah. Abah walks out without saying a word.

"We'll see, Amah."

Amah pats Mai on the arm and leaves.

Mai walks into the living room and sits down. Tears roll down her face. She quickly coils some of the toilet paper around her hand and rips it off to wipe her eyes and blow her nose when Ming and the kids come noisily down the stairs. The kids are excitedly telling Ming which rooms they want to take for their bedrooms now that it's just their family. She can't help but to smile as they argue and tease each other. Mai takes a deep breath and studies the birds in the painting. She lets out a deep breath.

A month before Christmas, likely at Amah and Mah Mah's behest, Abah calls and tells Mai and her family to come over for dinner on Friday night. Mai insists on contributing duck, barbecued pork, and a whole steamed white chicken. All Abah's favourites. No one apologizes or mentions what happened, it is simply considered over.

***

Two years later, Mai is sitting alone by Mah Mah Ping's bedside in the hospital. She jumps up from her chair when Mah Mah coughs.

"Have some *cha*, boiled, cooled down water. I also sneaked in some beef broth soup. To give you strength. Start with the cha." Mai supports Mah Mah's head and places the straw near her mouth who barely takes two sips.

"Mai. Such a good daughter." She struggles to get the words out. "Even as a baby, I knew…" Her grandmother coughs harshly.

"Mah Mah, save your energy."

"No, Mai. Listen to me. You're special. Stronger than your grandfather and your father. You made it possible for the family to come here. Few old women from China can brag about living in the great Gold Mountain, surrounded by their family before moving on to the next life. The soothsayer was right. It was you, all along. Tell your grandfather how proud I am of you when you see him." Mah Mah makes a choking sound and her eyes shut.

"Mah Mah! Mah Mah!"

Tears stream down Mai's cheek as she holds onto Mah Mah's warm hand.

"You let him know when you see him, Mah Mah. Please don't be angry at me for not telling you the truth," Mai whispers before she lets go of her hand.

Graduation
Amy Wei Ping Lee

19

"Would you like a coffee or tea?

"No. Thank you. I'm fine."

"May I at least take your coat?"

"No. Thank you. I'm a bit chilly still." Amy realizes this sort of contradicts her snubbing of a hot beverage, but she didn't want the quick exit she had in mind impeded with a search for her coat.

Amy takes a seat on the orange couch. The receptionist invites her to make herself comfortable, but Amy wonders if she should have cancelled. Instead of leaning against the back of the couch, she keeps her feet on the floor, resting her elbows on her knees, with her hands clasped together and her thumbs pressing against each other. She doesn't even take her purse off her shoulder. Her glasses have stopped fogging up after acclimatizing to the room temperature. She stares out the window to her right at the grey sky and leafless trees as her heel taps the carpeted floor.

A few minutes later, a woman in her late fifties enters. She wears a matching houndstooth skirt and jacket, white blouse, sheer black pantyhose and plain half-inch black heels. Her short, curly brown and white hair frames her face. The gold earrings, watch and necklace give away her vintage if the rest of her ensemble doesn't already.

Amy tenses a bit, but offers a smile, as is her natural reaction upon seeing a stranger, one of the habits lawyers and law students have said make her appear too friendly, weak, and not serious enough, unbefitting their profession.

"Hello. Amy Lee? I'm Dr. Noreen Walker, nice to meet you."

Amy notices she doesn't smile back but remains somehow welcoming as she makes eye contact, hands over her card, and starts flipping through her notepad in search of a fresh page. She takes a seat in the wooden, leather-covered chair situated directly across from Amy. A small round wooden coffee table divides them.

"Nice to meet you." Amy says as she accepts the card and nods curtly. She can't help but notice Dr. Walker's clean, trimmed, but unpainted nails. Glancing at the card Amy decides she likes the woman's style, simple, business-like.

"So, what brings you here today?" Dr. Walker asks.

Amy sits up straighter as if remembering to be on guard, "My family physician insisted."

"Why is that?"

"Something happened at work. It freaked me out a little." She then adds, "But I'm fine now."

There's an awkwardly long silence as Dr. Walker stares at Amy. "You probably noticed that no one else was in the waiting room with you. That was not an accident. All my clients enter through the front door and exit through the back, so one client doesn't see another. Appointments are timed to ensure it. The Royal College of Physicians and Surgeons also mandates a duty of confidentiality to all our clients. Our records are subject to physician-patient confidentiality. My card doesn't show my specialty as a psychotherapist. I only accept clients through referral. Your information is completely protected. Sometimes, it's useful to talk to a neutral party about things that are emotional. It gives you a chance to unload and perhaps reach a fresh perspective. We have an afternoon booked, so why don't you tell me about it?"

"I'm sure you have your obligations to your governing body regarding confidentiality but in the last year, I've been a student-at-law specializing in insurance defence. I know no confidentiality, except solicitor-client privilege, holds up in court. Your notes, letters, and even your recollection of this meeting can be scrutinized and reviewed under court order. So, unless you're a lawyer who I'm retaining, your privilege is not as secure as you might think."

Dr. Walker says nothing for a moment.

"Well, I don't have to take notes," she says as she drops the notebook on the coffee table. "And I don't have a great memory. Now. Can we talk?"

Amy can't stop herself from snorting, impressed with the woman's flexibility and in her head reviews the potential cons with speaking openly. "Ok. So ... just tell you what happened, right?"

"It's up to you. It's your appointment. Talk about whatever is on your mind. Whatever is bothering you. You're not restricted to just talking about why you were referred."

Amy takes a deep breath. "A couple of weeks ago, I went in to help organize a file I worked on that's going to court. This guy, this manager, used to be a friend, from the Claims Department, he … umm … he touched, grabbed me as we walked through a door. Touched me … here," Amy motions towards her chest, "And then pushed himself against me. I felt his … against my backside and … shit … sorry." Tears roll down Amy's face as Dr. Walker leans over to push a box of tissues closer. Amy takes a couple and wipes her tears away furiously.

Dr. Walker says nothing as Amy forces herself to get her breathing under control.

"Sorry."

"Please don't apologize."

"I'm not really sure why the whole stupid thing bugs me so much. It wasn't full on rape or anything but it just—" Amy sobs again and grabs more tissues. She concentrates on inhaling and then exhaling. Eventually the tears stop, she blows her nose, and her breathing becomes regular.

"Are you ready to go on?" Dr. Walker asks. Amy nods. "What did you do?"

"I went back to my office, grabbed my things and left."

"Did you tell anyone what happened?"

"Yeah. I called my fiancé. I mean—my ex-fiancé. When I got home. He didn't want to talk because I'd just broken off the engagement. He told me to tell my mentor. Everything's a bit of a mess." Amy's shoulders slump as she studies the floor and forgets to be on guard.

"Your mentor?"

"Sorry. A senior lawyer at work. He's been good to me. He taught me during my articling year. He's like a work dad, but younger. When I finally talked to him the next day, he said he'll make sure that the creep stays away from me."

"Is that what you asked him to do?"

"I was a bit of a zombie when I talked to him. I was crying

and I just kept saying I don't want to see him. All I know is I didn't want to deal with it—with him—anymore."

"But you're both still working there?"

"I think so. He's been there twenty-four years. I doubt he's going anywhere. He knows people. Our general counsel has been there the same length of time as him. They're old colleagues if not friends. My mentor's only second-in-command. I'm not sure what's going to happen. That is, I'm not sure my mentor can do what he said. I'm supposed to start after my Call. It's just a mess." A fresh wave of tears overtakes Amy.

When Amy's breathing returns to normal, Dr. Walker speaks. "What is it that upsets you most?"

"Everything. He's older. Supposed to be like a peer. A friend. It's just gross. I felt so dirty. Did I do something to make him think that would be okay? I thought I got a hire back because I'm good at what I do. Not because of—whatever the fuck he thought he was going to get."

Another wave of tears hits her.

"Let's go back a bit. By your Call, you mean your call to the bar?"

Amy sniffles and forces herself to breathe deeply. "Sorry. Yes. I articled last year, and I just finished writing the bar exams. I was flattered when they offered me the job because when I accepted the articling position, I was told that chances of a hire-back were nil. The fact that they want me back is unexpected, to say the least. Things worked out. Or at least I thought they did."

"And this is where you want to be? Where you're happy?"

"I don't know. I don't feel like anyone's on my side there anymore. We worked with the heads of all these departments on files. So did that creep. And him for a lot longer than me. Now they're talking about conducting an internal investigation about what happened. What does that mean? How can that *not* be biased. And the last thing I want to do is to have to keep repeating what happened. I didn't even want to tell my mentor about it. He wrote a summary of what happened, and even though I saw errors in it, I didn't point them out because it meant I had to again detail what happened. And relive it. Honestly, I'm not sure about anything right now."

"Have you talked to anyone else about what happened at work?"

"Well, kind of. I told my family what happened, but I didn't give them details."

"Who does that include?"

"My sister and older brother, they're both lawyers too."

"And what do they say?"

"My sister's torn. She's pushing me to go back because it's stable and she says not everyone gets a hire-back. My older brother's, a brother. He wants to kill the guy. He hasn't really said much about the job."

"Anyone else?"

"My dad and younger brother don't really get a chance to say much. Too hard to get a word in, I suppose." Amy gives a half-hearted laugh. "Mom. My mother. Mai Gum Lee. She's a force. She says if anyone ever comes near me, I should just claw their eyes out. I wish I had done something like that instead of being so … so … weak." Amy pauses and bows her head.

"Why does it matter how you reacted?"

"If I'd just punched him and walked away instead of falling to pieces—I don't know. Maybe I wouldn't feel so trapped now."

"How are you trapped?"

"I dread the thought of going in, but if I leave under these circumstances and apply for another job the next employer will ask for references. I've been looking. Someone will find out what happened. I'll be marked as trouble. No one wants to hire trouble. And if I stay—it'll be equally awkward. I'm not sure what will happen with their "investigation." I was just a student there. It's not like I've twenty plus years of history like that creep. Damn it! What a mess. I should've just shut up about it all."

Amy furiously wipes away her tears with the back of her hand before grabbing another tissue and blowing her nose.

"You know, unless you left something out, you didn't do anything wrong."

"I don't think I left anything out, but it sure seems like I did something wrong. It's like I'm under this spotlight and I'm being judged. About everything I did or will do. I'm not perfect and it won't matter that I didn't do anything. I'll be cast out. It's just a whole lot of attention and trouble I don't want." Through slow falling tears Amy adds, "To add to this chaos, a week before this thing happened, I broke it off with Joe."

20

"Joe's your ex-fiancé?" Dr. Walker asks.

"Yeah. And Mom thinks we'll get back together. In fact, she's pushing for it. That's her real concern." Amy rolls her eyes.

"Why do you think that is?"

Relieved to move on to another topic, Amy sits up. "My being settled is Mom's goal. My sister and brother graduated, got jobs where they articled, and got married to their partners. I was headed in the same direction before all this happened. Mom wants me to do as they did. I think in a way, it means her job as a parent for me is done then. To a certain extent anyway."

"You really think that's her worry?"

"Maybe not her only worry but it certainly takes priority over all else. She's a very practical person."

"In what way?"

"She likes to get things done. She likes order and accomplishment and finishing what she's started. My sister's married, working and has a kid. My brother's married, working, and his wife's pregnant. Check. Check. Check."

"Well, she must be proud of you and your siblings."

"Proud is a little strong." Amy laughs.

"Well, you're all finished school and you're lawyers."

Amy holds up three fingers, deepens her voice, and says, *"Three lawyers equal one doctor* is what Mom says about us being lawyers."

Dr. Walker laughs. "Your mother's demanding then?"

"I wouldn't say that. She just believes in humility, and she's Chinese. But nothing beats a doctor or someone who's good at math."

"She'll no doubt enjoy your call to the Bar."

"I doubt it; she won't be there. All we're doing is walking across a stage in our overpriced robes to pick up a piece of paper anyway. It's just a licence to work."

"I understand it's like a graduation though, isn't it?"

"Yes, but I haven't attended a single graduation since grade six. My parents have never attended. It's not like I won an armload of awards like my sister."

"So, no one's attending for you? Did she and your father go to your siblings' graduations or calls to the Bar?"

"Not their graduations but they attended their Calls. The difference is my sister was the first and my brother is the eldest male. I'm neither." Amy shrugs. "It's really not a big deal."

"What did they say when you asked them?"

"Well, I didn't. They work mid-afternoon to late-night shifts. Attending means taking a day off work and losing a day of pay. I can't ask them to do that."

"What kind of work do they do?"

"Crappy work." At this point Amy leans back against the

couch and stares out the window.

Images of her parents packing up their shoulder bags with their stainless-steel containers of overnight rice, meat, greens, and a thermos of tea or coffee fill Amy's mind. Whether it was so hot sweat dripped off just sitting still and the air felt so thick it was impossible to breathe, or it was so cold the snot in your nose froze when you inhaled, Mom and Dad trudged to the streetcar stop to weave through the city to their jobs. They were never late for their shifts and if offered, they always took extra shifts on their days off.

Amy unconsciously rubs her index finger and thumb together and starts biting the inside of her bottom lip. Her tone becomes robotic as she continues to stare out the window. "My parents are non-skilled menial labourers, according to government classifications. Dad was a cook at various dinky little Chinese restaurants for a while and now he works at a large commercial bakery, hauling carts of bread around. Mom works at a knitting mill. They are the definition of low-level factory workers."

"You don't like their jobs?"

Amy furrows her brow. "I don't like how much it takes out of them. And when you go to school with one of the grandsons of the family that owns the factory your dad toils at as a minion, it's awkward."

"Why does it matter?"

"Technically, it doesn't. Most of the time I don't care, but occasionally I'm reminded of who I am not. It's just that many of my classmates have parents who, at minimum, speak English fluently. Others have parents who run companies in their native countries or they're lawyers or in business. Our family is a bit different. A bit poor."

"Are you embarrassed by your background?"

Amy studies her shoes. The temperature of the room seems warm now. Buying time to think, she removes her coat, lays it beside her, and puts her purse back on her shoulder as if she's afraid to lose it. She readjusts herself on the couch. "No. I'm not embarrassed but I certainly don't talk about it. And sometimes I think I'm supposed to be."

"That's an odd way to put it. Why do you think you're supposed to be embarrassed? Are your parents?"

"Dad isn't. He doesn't say much. He's really laid back and just happy to get things done. To him, it's a bonus to get paid almost. Mom's not exactly embarrassed, either."

"What is she then?"

"Full of contradictions." Amy laughs at her own joke. "She's proud and self-deprecating."

"How so?"

"Well, for example, when I was about twelve or thirteen, I tried to sew this button back onto a blouse myself. Mom walked in and after a second said, you better study more because you're so clumsy threading the needle, you'll not make any money working with your hands. She then grabbed the blouse, her sewing materials, and reattached the button before I could think of a good response. When I eventually retorted that I could learn, she told me not to bother because I was hopeless. Adding, of course, the first time she picked up a needle and thread, she didn't fumble the way I had. I apparently have no natural skill. It's funny how some lines and thoughts stay with you, isn't it?"

"I see how that's proud but how is it self-deprecating?"

"Oh, at other times, she calls the work she and Dad do cow's work. Sounds better in Chinese. In other words, they use their brawn not their brains to earn a living. It's not high paying or professional work."

"She's a seamstress?"

"Something like that. She's been working in that industry since she was in Hong Kong."

"When was that?"

"The early sixties. You see, when she's bragging about her sewing abilities, she conveniently forgets how she's had decades to perfect her skills. She was studying to be a nurse but quit to go to Hong Kong. When she got there, she took a course and learned everything about operating wool looms in a couple of weeks, compared to others who took six months, and some who never got it. It meant she was able to find solid paying jobs to help pay the rent. They went from below the poverty line to just poor."

"They were tough times for her then." Dr. Walker follows Amy's stare out the window.

"Yes, but Mom always sounds so wistful when she talks about that time. It's like a mixture of pride and sadness. Sometimes I think she didn't want to leave nursing in China or the jobs she had in Hong Kong. I can't blame her, really. Who wants to leave a hub like Hong Kong for a freezing cold little city, in a country where you know no one and can't speak the language?"

"Toronto's pretty big."

"No. North Bay is where I was born and where we first lived. We moved here when I was a kid." Amy adjusts herself, finally taking her handbag off her shoulder and setting it beside her on the couch, on top of her coat.

"Your mom's been a seamstress since she arrived in Canada?"

"Well, not exactly. One of the reasons she was so anxious to get to Toronto was because of the promise of more jobs. She had a hard time finding work in North Bay. She washed dishes in one of the Chinese restaurants for a bit. That's when she was lucky enough to find work."

"They came to Toronto to find work?"

"In part. Mom also wanted to be close to universities. Even though we were only little kids, in her mind we were all going to university at some point."

"Then she became a seamstress again."

"Something like that. About a year after we got here, she got her sewing machine. Worked from home sewing stuff for the bag man."

"Did you say, 'bag man'?"

"Oh. Yes. She used to sew cloth bags, towels, and all sorts of small items from home. She was paid for every item she finished. This driver who was in his fifties and reminded me of Santa Claus, used to drop off the unfinished and pick up the finished items. We called him the bag man."

"I see."

"One time we helped her. What a disaster! You know those fuzzy dice that people hung up as car ornaments in the eighties? She made those."

"I've seen them."

"Well, the bag man was due to pick up the order of finished dice in a couple of days. She'd been too busy to finish for whatever reason, so she instructed us to glue on the pips. Those are the little circles on the faces of the dice while she finished sewing them together. She said it'd be easy, and we could do it while we watched TV." Amy closes her eyes and shakes her head.

"It was not so easy, I take it?"

"Exactly. The glue provided was terrible because it didn't stick. I don't know which of us came up with the bright idea that we use the white school glue with the elephant on the cover. On top of not sticking, the white glue dried and left ugly hard opaque stains while pips were falling off everywhere. It was a mess. Everything was stuffed into a bag and given to the bag man. I'm surprised she got paid for the job."

Amy sees Dr. Walker wincing. "Did the quality of the dice affect her payment?"

Amy studies the ceiling as she dissects the comment before continuing. "Mom got paid but I'll bet that's about the time she stopped getting work from the bag man."

Amy doesn't hear Dr. Walker's next question as she grapples with the realization that they lost that job for Mom. Why hadn't she put that together before? The job may not have been ideal because it was piecework, and there was no job security, but it meant Mom was home. Even if Mom always dismissed her work as menial labour, no one wants to be fired.

"I'm sorry, what did you say?"

"Does your mother work from home now?"

"No. After that job ended, she found jobs outside of the house, eventually landing where she is now. The knitting mill, which manufactures all sorts of wool and angora products like sweaters, leg warmers, hats, and scarves."

"What does your mother do there?"

"She's a tipper."

"What is that?"

"Have you ever seen a French beret? There's a little tip on the top; the decorative tail that creeps out the center. She makes those. It's called tipping."

"I didn't even think that was a job."

"I know. The first time Mom described what she did so I could write the word out for her to copy onto her time sheets, I thought she was misusing the word. It's not rocket science but it's harder than you might think. I certainly can't do it."

"Does she enjoy her work?"

"She's good at it. From what she tells me, anyway. Most of the factory's clients are military groups from all over the world. Each client sends their own inspectors to check the quality of the berets before they accept the whole shipment. Berets tipped by some of her co-workers have been rejected, which means the whole batch is wasted. Hers are always approved."

"Why are they rejected?"

"Because the holes for the tips are too big, too small or the tips are too short, too long or just inconsistent. It helps that she's been with the employer for about two decades now. They must like her enough to keep her around."

"She likes it there?"

"I think she likes the stability. And having work mates. A paycheque every two weeks as long as she shows up and does some work. She works hard. When there's no order for hats, she'll cut the ends off sewing strands for sweaters and other products. She doesn't take advantage of the stability. In fact, she hates sitting around. She recently mentioned something about learning a new machine, but I didn't pay attention to the details. Plus, there are benefits."

"It sounds like she enjoys her work and the environment."

"For the most part. She's cordial, but she stays away from the other Chinese workers. She prefers to stick to herself or the Italian ladies at the factory even though her English is broken and they can't really communicate. One year they took a company photo of all the employees. I couldn't find her at first because I was looking for her in the cluster of Chinese faces. She was in the front corner with a bunch of non-Asians." Amy laughs.

"Why do you think that is?"

"She doesn't like the gossip."

"That's healthy, if a bit lonely."

"She doesn't mind time to herself. She sometimes eats with the Italian ladies but she's perfectly happy on her own. She's just sure of herself."

"It certainly sounds like she's happy with her work."

"She has this habit of comparing herself to wildly successful businessmen like Li Ka-Shing who don't have to clock in or out. She marvels at how one day of work for a smart businessman is equal to six months of work for her. She laments not being as smart."

"Is that how you feel about her and her work?"

"I wish her work conditions were better. The building Mom works in, is in an industrial area, alongside other factories. It's poorly ventilated and with the machines running all day, it's hot. There are no windows except at the top of the wall, near the ceilings so you can't open them. She hates not having fresh air. Mom complains sometimes about inhaling the tiny fibres from the beautiful products they produce. She thinks it may lead to health issues, but she still goes every day. Mom heats her lunch or dinner on the radiators because she avoids the lunchroom if she can help it. It'd be nice if she didn't have to perform manual labour."

"What about the amount of money she earns? Does that bother you the way it does her?"

"Perhaps I misspoke. Mom both loves and hates piecework. On the one hand, she's fast so she earns a decent amount. It's just a shame she has to earn a living that way because it's not fun or mentally inspiring."

"Is piecework truly different from the work you do as a lawyer or me as a doctor? We only bill for what we do. Everyone has to account for their time."

"True, but our hourly rates are much higher and presumably our work conditions are more comfortable than hers. Don't get me wrong, Mom loves assembling her time sheets each Sunday night. She sits at the kitchen table calculating everything by hand for a good hour, without a calculator. She glues all her small slips of paper onto the large grid sheets. Each slip represents the number of pieces she finished, and each finished piece means a certain amount of money. It's like arts and crafts. She's pretty happy at the end." Amy laughs.

"What is funny?"

"I remember this one time when we were little, and she lost one of those slips. Absolute panic erupted. There was no TV that night. Everyone searched, under the couches, in her purse, the garbage, the kitchen cupboards, and even the bathroom. We couldn't find it. Mom went to bed grumpier than ever. It turns out, the slip wasn't lost. The manager forgot to hand them out for the last batch of hats they worked on. What a waste."

"Sounds like your mother has a right to be proud of her job."

"It's not as if she's living out a dream, tipping berets in a factory. She complains about sneaky workers who try to take her batch of work, supervisors who expect to be bribed with lunches and gifts, and bus drivers who don't wait for her. But she's proud she earns money, sometimes more than Dad makes."

"Many people don't enjoy their work. It's a means to an end. So, being proud of even a part of one's job is a positive."

"This is true. Mom loves sewing too. She made this." Amy points at the grey plaid miniskirt she's wearing. "And she mends or alters all our clothes when needed."

"That's a very nice skirt."

"Yeah, this is a good one. There's a pencil case I used all through school, and even now. It's made from a pair of old jeans. Can't find anything better. They're not always successes though. Some items are just ugly."

"It's a hobby for her then?"

"You're technically correct to call it a hobby, but she'd be reluctant to call it that. She likes taking a piece of fabric or material and turning it into something useful. It's sporadically fashionable but always useful. For her, it justifies the purchase of the sewing machine, especially after she stopped working from home. I can't think of much else she enjoys doing, except cleaning."

"Why does she have to justify buying something that makes her happy?"

"Well, I used to think it was a Chinese thing. Then I thought it was a poor thing. Now I think it's just our family thing. Whatever it is, spending on an item purely for enjoyment is almost sacrilegious. But if it helps you earn money or there's some practical use for it, then it's acceptable."

"Does something which makes you happy not matter?"

"Sure, if it's inexpensive."

"Is this how you feel?"

"It's hard not to believe in what you grew up being taught." Amy sighs and pauses before adding, "Damn. I guess it means I can't blame my aunt entirely for her behaviour."

"What did your aunt do?"

"When my mom started working outside of the house at night, my aunt, Mom's eldest little sister, babysat. She was the worst."

"Why?"

"She treated my brothers like kings, but I was Cinderella. Mom said her head was stuck in ancient times. She did what was done or expected of her."

"I still don't know what she did."

"If she had her way, I would have been cleaning the toilets and mopping the floors, but I was a bit young for those chores.

These days we'd call her a mean girl."

"Can you give me an example?"

"One thing I can't forget was when we were little and my brothers said they were thirsty after we'd all gone up to bed, she'd bring them downstairs and get them a cup of milk. When I said I was thirsty, admittedly because I wanted to see my parents, she told me to go drink tap water from the bathroom."

"I don't understand. Why's that so bad?"

"We never drink tap water. To this day, Mom boils water and lets it cool down. We keep containers or teapots of it readily available, *cha*. It's cleaner or something. Drinking tap water would give us wind or the runs, according to Mom. My aunt telling me to drink tap water from the washroom was equivalent to telling me to drink from the toilet bowl."

"You didn't like the different treatment?"

"I did not. She was just mean to me. Even when Mom was home, she'd make faces at me and tell me to wipe my little brother's butt after he pooed, or clean up if he made a mess even though she was asked to do it. But she only did these things if Mom was out of earshot or not looking."

"What did you do?"

"I ignored her when I could. When I worked up enough nerve to tell Mom and my grandmother, Aunt Jung denied it and convinced my grandmother I was making it up. Mom believed me but what choice did she have? She had to work. We needed the money. But for years, I hated Aunt Jung. She only started to treat me decently when I outgrew her and she had long since stopped living with us."

"Did your aunt recognize the fact that she, too, is a girl?"

"She had blinders on like Mom said. She just practised what she was taught. My grandfather, Lei On, who we lived with for a few years and who my aunt spends her life trying to please, is one of the most sexist people I know. This, even though Mom was the only reason he and any of the family ever escaped China and farm life."

"How is that?"

"After Mom married, she sponsored my grandmother, Aunt Jung, and her youngest brother Yaing Gong. If that hadn't happened, none of Mom's family would've been able to leave China."

"Your family must have appreciated her efforts."

"To her face, she receives a certain respect from her siblings, because she's the eldest but not with my grandfather. After Mom's family moved out and he came over, he'd walk in with his shoes on and stomp around. Mom was so angry she'd start mopping the floors where he walked even before he left and she'd complain about how if we did that at his house, he'd pop a vein."

"A double standard based on gender?"

"At least partly. But she'll never confront him about it. Especially not now since he's older. Fragile. Doesn't want to upset him."

21

"I take it your mother doesn't favour your brothers?" Dr. Walker asks.

"Like I said, she's full of conflicting views. She helps my brothers more. It might be because she feels they need it, or she has a duty as the mother of sons. At the same time, she's fiercely independent and hands down, runs our household even though she grew up in a family where daughters were not seen as important as the sons."

"Do you think your mother is unfair?"

"I'm not sure if I think about it much. I think Mom expects more from the girls. Maybe because we're more like her. But the bottom line is she does whatever she can to help all of us. I hate having to put more on her plate."

"How's your father feel about all of this?"

"Dad knows Mom protects him and all of us. She just does it in her own way. Dad rolls with it. Most of the time he ignores her tone if he can, even making a joke or teasing her. He only argues when absolutely necessary."

"What do you mean by her tone?"

Amy pauses, considering whether to answer because she doesn't want to make Mom sound as out of control as she sometimes seemed.

"Mom yells a lot."

"What does she yell about?"

"It depends. She hates wasting things. Money was and is always a concern. There was an egg tart incident."

"What was that about?"

"Chinese egg tarts. To this day, one of my favourite desserts. Served warm, the shell is flaky, and the custard filling has more egg than cream so it's sweet but not sickly sweet like the supermarket desserts my brothers preferred when we were kids. I didn't care for those Vachon Half Moons or Wagon Wheels." Amy's mouth salivates at the thought of egg tarts. She wished she'd eaten breakfast. "Dad said he was going to make egg tarts one night when he and Mom had a day off. I was overjoyed as I sat watching a rerun of *Charlie's Angels* on TV. The smell of sugar and flour in the oven eventually wafted into the living room and during the commercial break I ran to the kitchen to see how they were coming along. Before the second commercial ended though, it started."

"What started?"

"Mom was yelling full volume. Louder than the TV which was right in front of us. I ran out to the kitchen and saw it filled with smoke. Windows were open even though it was pitch dark out and the middle of winter. A distinct burnt odour had replaced the sugary, flour smell. I don't agree with it, but I get why Mom was freaking out. Something about an entire carton of eggs and what appeared to be a bag of flour were in the garbage bin.

Wasting anything, but especially food, has always been frowned upon. It was awful. All I wanted was quiet."

"Your mother has a temper?"

"Yeah. It's like she explodes but then she's fine. Sometimes, she's even laughing within minutes of yelling. That night, she went on for at least an hour until she tired herself out and it fizzled to muttering and complaining. It may have had something to do with her realizing her favourite show, *The Love Boat*, started. She finally stopped and joined us in the living room to watch."

"Is this her normal reaction to a problem?"

"It was pretty regular. It happens less now that everyone's older. She's just anxious and impatient."

"It must have been difficult living with such an explosive personality."

"We didn't know any different. And she didn't yell at us kids much. She got annoyed, but she treated us with, well, kid gloves. It's weird, I hated her upset and yelling, but she was justified most of the time."

"What do you mean by justified?"

"Well, wasted food was wasted money. And I knew we didn't have a lot of money."

"Do you think her reactions were disproportional to the problems?"

"Yes, exactly. Dad didn't mean to burn the tarts, use too much soy sauce to fry up the greens or leave a dish still dirty after washing. He just likes salt, and I haven't met any men who are particularly fastidious about cleaning dishes. Mom just hated when things didn't go right. And then there was Dad's smoking."

"Your mother didn't approve of him smoking?"

"Not one bit. She used to blast him for smoking because it's expensive and bad for him and everyone around him. We learned about the evils of smoking in school, so again it made sense that she was trying to get him to stop, but it sure made for noisy weekend mornings when she found a pack of cigarettes."

"She means well but she's excitable."

"That's a good way to put it."

"Why do you think she gets so angry?"

"I'm pretty sure she's frustrated. She's smart and capable but she's been limited in what she can do since she came here. She never had the time to learn English or to drive once we kids came along. She left a place where she knew the language and the community. Who knows what else she left behind?"

"You think she regrets coming here?"

Amy furrows her brow as she considers the question. "Not being a nurse? Maybe. It was a bit of a feat to get all that schooling from what she tells us and what I've read about the times she grew up in. But she arrived here decades ago, and she's never gone back, not even for a visit, like some of her relatives. I don't think she wants to go back. In fact, I think she's afraid she'll be trapped there. So, I don't think she regrets coming here. If anything, she regrets the loss of control she has over her life. I certainly can't imagine doing what she did. She's tough."

"You admire her?"

"Yes. I certainly do." Amy nods slowly. "She has said, and I don't doubt it, *If I spoke English, I'd be more than a lawyer in Canada. I'd be running the country.*" Amy sighs. "Unfortunately, I'm not like her."

"Why do you say that?"

"She left her family, crossed an ocean alone, and started a life here. Then she helped bring her entire family over, while raising all of us. Compared to that, I've done very little."

"What about calling off your engagement? That couldn't have been easy."

"That's hardly an accomplishment. In fact, Mom sees it clearly as a setback. She thinks I've made a mistake calling off the engagement."

"Everyone's challenges are different and what's easy for one is difficult for another. There really is no way to compare."

"I don't believe my mother would agree with you."

22

"Why do you think your mother disagrees with your decision to end your engagement?"

"I think she's afraid I'll be alone. I don't think she even likes Joe that much."

"What did she not like about him?"

"He's too bookish for her. There was an incident with a light bulb. I think she still holds it against him."

"What was that about?"

"Well, Joe's smart. Law schools rank the students. The top three get medals, gold, silver, bronze. Joe earned the silver although he claims he got marks equal to those of the gold medalist. Anyway, I think Mom was testing him. Our kitchen has one of those school lights. You know the fluorescent ones with two long tube-like bulbs. Mom and Dad were changing a bulb when Joe and I walked in one day. She asked if he could help. He said he'd not done it before and backed away. It was the wrong answer.

From then on, Mom basically dismissed him as book smart but not practically smart. In other words, a bit useless."

"Even though she thinks of him like this, she wants you to be with him?"

"Yup. I'm in my late twenties. She keeps reminding me how by my age, she was not only married but had a bunch of kids. As far as she's concerned, I'm past my best sell date. A couple nights ago we were watching TV when out of nowhere she says, *A rose only has so much time to bloom.*" Amy rolls her eyes. "Joe's dream job, teaching at a law school, is already a reality. At the rate he's going, he'll be done his Ph.D. within a year, and he'll likely be one of the youngest tenured legal professors in Canada. Despite what she considers are his flaws, he provides precisely the type of stability Mom wants for me."

"Why did you break off your engagement?"

Amy lets out a deep breath. "I'm not sure. Hard to put in words. I've been asked before and all I can come up with are unimportant issues. We didn't do anything fun, like going out dancing, making fancy dinners together or just going out for long walks. Joe was happy to stay in watching movies, playing video games, and making protein powder drinks for meals. Once, I made a nice dinner, thinking it might be like a date, but he accused me of trying to ruin his diet and he refused to help me with the dishes because, as he said, he never ate. Sometimes I felt more like his caretaker than his partner. I even had to find him an apartment at the last minute because he rented a cockroach infested place, sight unseen. And I didn't enjoy cleaning up the clogged toilet at his place because he said I was the last to go when it overflowed. As if that was all me. Nothing important, right?"

"Certainly, all the things you mentioned can be improved if everyone's willing to compromise. Relationships are hard work.

Do you want to get back together with him?"

"Is constantly feeling your partner might take what you say out of context to use it against you something that can be fixed with compromise, too?"

"What do you mean?"

"Joe's very logical. He used to take what I said or wanted and consciously or not it seemed he manipulated it to suit his position. For instance, I hate debt, given our lack of money growing up. Joe reasoned we shouldn't spend on nights or dinners out if I want to save money for a house and have less debt. But I know Joe didn't care about saving or buying a house. He just didn't want to go out. It was like he put it in such a way that I felt I was in the wrong to ask to do something I wanted. His solution, get the movie channels and more computer games to be entertained at home. Things *he* enjoyed."

"Did you ever talk to him about it? Explain how it made you feel?"

"I tried. He got defensive and he twisted things I said to make me look in the wrong. I probably should have tried harder, but I wasn't sure I wanted to anymore, after he talked with my brother."

"Why is that?"

"After talking with Joe, my brother said to me: you're not happy because you guys don't go dancing? I felt like such an idiot. I wanted to go dancing or something but it's not why I broke up with him. It's like Joe wanted to paint me as some unstable emotional woman who broke up with him for something trivial. Or maybe that's what he really thinks, which might be worse."

"Did you explain to your brother what you meant?"

"I said something like, I don't want to be divorced in a few years because I'm unhappy."

"What did your brother say to that?"

"He pooh-poohed the entire thing and said that's not going to happen. That was the end of it."

"Do you think you want to try and work things out with Joe still?"

"I'm not sure. There's something he's said to me which is unsettling even though it's nice."

"What did he say?"

Amy stares out the window for a while. "He says he doesn't want kids, but he'll have my kids because he loves me that much."

"I see. Why does this upset you?"

"Because I don't want kids with someone who's just doing it as a favour to me. I imagine him saying: *you're the one who wanted kids, you take care of them.* Just like with the dishes or the toilet. Maybe I'm making a big thing out of nothing."

"So, summarize it for me. Why did you break it off?"

Amy stares out the window for a long time before finally responding. "I'm not in love with him. And with all that's happened, I'm wondering if he ever loved me."

"Why do you question it?"

"I know Joe has every right not to want to be here for me with this work fiasco. But I just thought, after all the time we've been together and everything we've been through, he would be. I know if he needed me, if something happened at work or with his family, I'd be there for him just like I always have been. If he wanted me there. No matter what."

"It's probably hard for him to be a friend when he wants it to be more."

"This is what he says. Am I being selfish because I think he should be here for me?

"It sounds like you want different things. Don't worry about who's selfish or not. That's a blame game no one wins. Do what you need for you. Keep following your heart like you have been."

"Great. Mom will not understand then." Amy flicks her right hand before she starts rubbing the sides of her temple.

"Why not?

"Like I said, Mom's a practical person. She does what's needed or expected. Following one's heart is impractical and irrelevant."

"Is this why you won't really talk to her about everything you're going through now?"

"She knows what's going on. I'm not hiding anything from her." Amy's posture stiffens as she begins to regret what she's shared.

"I'm not judging, Amy. I'm just observing. I don't think you've told her how you feel about some of the things that have been happening."

Amy rubs her eyes with the heels of the palms of her hand.

"How I feel? Of course, I haven't told her how I feel. That's uncomfortable. For everyone. It's like talking about sex with your parents. And it's not what our family does. It doesn't help being uneducated in Chinese. All I know how to communicate are everyday things. Not feelings."

"Feelings matter and they impact everyone's interpretations and reactions to circumstances and events in their lives."

"Well, maybe I don't know how I feel!" Amy raises her arms and her voice in exasperation before letting her body deflate. Tears well up in her eyes again.

"Amy, it's perfectly reasonable for you to be confused with so many changes happening in your life right now. Do you remember the editing exercise from school where you read what you write out loud? Sometimes, just hearing yourself say how you feel or recount an event out loud gives you new insights."

Amy unclenches her fists as she stares at a spot on the floor considering this idea. They sit in silence for at least a full minute before Dr. Walker throws up her hands in surrender.

"And sometimes it does squat all. What do I know?"

Amy is grateful for the levity. She doesn't want to, but she likes this woman.

"I'm angry. At everyone. The creep from work who thinks he has some right to grab and touch me, my sister for being more concerned about a job than my welfare, my brother for actually thinking I broke up with Joe because he wouldn't go dancing, Joe for saying something so ridiculous to my brother and for not being here for me after everything I've done for him, my mother for wanting me to be with Joe even though he doesn't make me happy, and most of all me."

"Why are you angry with yourself?"

"Because I don't know why I didn't just hit the creep. Because if I was stronger, maybe Mom might get that Joe's not the one." The tears come streaming out and Dr. Walker waits for Amy to collect herself.

"Isn't it enough that you know he's not the one? And from what you've told me, your mother's too practical to believe in the one."

"She might be practical, but she strongly believes in fate."

"I find that contradictory."

"Welcome to my world. It's crazy superstitious but practical. Anything Mom can't explain, or she's stuck with, is fate. Even her arranged marriage is fate because it's where she ended up, so it was meant to be. Each year, after the new Chinese year begins, Mom makes a trip with my grandmother and the aunts to the big Buddhist temple on Bayview. They light incense sticks to pray to the ancestors, make offerings to the various gods, and most importantly get every person in the family a fortune stick to find out what kind of year they're going to have. Good, bad or average."

"Where does the practical come into play?"

"The type of work we're expected to undertake has to be stable, practical, nothing like acting or writing. The neighbourhood we live in should be near a bus or streetcar since Mom and Dad don't drive. It should also be near, but not too near, a Chinatown. Marriage is a union for procreation and, if possible, to advance your social status. Love is a type of fondness that develops after you're married but not the basis to find a mate. Mind you, finding the right job, house or mate has to do with your luck and your fortune."

"This is what your mother says?"

"Some of it's said. Some of it's implied. Mom vehemently opposed my desire to act."

"You were a thespian?"

"I don't know if I earned the title of thespian, but I did have fifteen minutes of fame. When I was a kid, our reading group was asked to try out for a role on a small TV show. I wore my favourite fancy clothes, a corduroy skirt Mom made from the material of a pair of Dad's pants where the hems had worn out beyond repair, and a pretty but itchy Chinese blouse some relative gave me. I remember being nervous and excited at the same time as our reading group walked together to the audition, each of us hoping we'd get the part."

"What was the show?"

"It was that Degrassi show on CBC but before it got popular. *The Kids of Degrassi Street*."

"I've heard of the show, but I never watched it."

"Mom didn't watch it either. Not even when I was in it."

"You got the role then?"

"Yes. Mom reluctantly signed the contract to let me participate. It was likely because I pestered her so much, but when I missed a week of school to shoot one of the episodes, she flipped out. School is more important. She warned me not to get lured away. She told me all actors end up starving and divorced. I made the mistake of arguing and telling her I was doing well in school. Her response was: *only compared to the students here you're doing well. Not compared to the kids in China and Russia.*"

"What does that mean?"

"That's what, regrettably, I asked her. Mom was only too happy to lecture me on why those from poor Communist countries are sharper and grittier because they need to survive and earn the chance to attend school, in other words, like her. Unlike us soft *jook sings*, who are required to go to school. Mom ranted about how Asian and Eastern European countries are smarter, as evidenced by their superior math and science skills. At the time, I wasn't sure how I'd ever be competing with students in China or Russia, but I wasn't about to ask her to explain further. Anyway, Mom made me tell the producer and director I wasn't allowed to miss school anymore."

"What's the phrase—*jook* …?"

"*Jook sing* literally translates to bamboo pole. The inside of the pole is hollow and compartmentalized between each node, so water poured in one end doesn't flow out the other end. There's no mixing. Similarly, we Chinese Canadians born here never fully mix or integrate with either the Chinese or the Canadian culture."

"Thank you for explaining. So, your mother wasn't supportive of your acting career?"

"She had my Uncle Yaing Gong take my siblings and me to

the premiere at Harbourfront and she didn't even watch it on TV when it aired. When the main episode my character starred in received an award and we were invited to attend the ceremony, I didn't even ask Mom to go."

"Did her lack of interest and support bother you?"

"It did a bit, but, again, I understood why she was against it. I knew it wasn't personal."

"What do you mean it wasn't personal?"

"It wasn't like she thought I was bad at acting, even though, in retrospect, I was. She just didn't want me to be an actor because it's a fickle business and lifestyle."

"But didn't you tell me she also didn't attend your school graduations either? So, was there a lack of involvement there, too?"

"You might see it that way, but I think it was just how parents did things back then. School was our domain."

"And you didn't mind her not taking an interest in any of these areas of your life?"

"Well, she took enough of an interest to share her opinions. She just didn't helicopter over us like parents these days. I can't blame her, really. She didn't speak English. And like I said, she and Dad had to work. Even if they were free some evenings, sitting through an entire concert or ceremony where you don't know what anyone is saying is boring and whatever the opposite of empowering is."

"Didn't you say she watched some English-speaking shows on TV though?"

"Sure, they watched comedies or a cooking show where the mannerisms or actions of the characters are funny or easily followed. But to watch a kid's show or sit in a stuffy school gym is an entirely different thing."

"How do they get by in the community if language is such a challenge?"

"Not sure who helped them before, but Uncle Yaing Gong used to be their main translator. Eventually my sister and I took over."

"Does this mean you're fluent in both languages?"

"Hardly. While my English improved with school, my Chinese sort of stalled at the grade school level. I understand enough to get points across so I can communicate with grocery store attendants, but Mom has to dumb her Chinese down, so I understand it. It's the reverse with English for them. I remember this one time—I must have been in grade six because I was home for lunch—the electricity bill had been delivered, and Mom was angrier than a hornet."

"Why?"

"Apparently, the bill was too high. Anyway, Mom's muttering and yelling about the bill. She insisted I call the company to complain. Until then, I didn't even know hydro dealt with electricity. The conversation went something like:

> Me: *We live at 244 Jones Avenue and my mother says our electricity bill is too high.*
>
> Attendant: *What do you mean it's too high?* The attendant is clearly an older woman who is not taking any nonsense from a child. I translate to Mom.
>
> Me: *We didn't use so much electricity. Why's it so high?* Mom is now angrily mopping the living room floor near me and feeding me responses in Chinese.
>
> Attendant: *You have a meter. We just read the meter. We can't control the price of the electricity.* To this day I can still remember hoping at this point Mom will be

satisfied with this logic and let me hang up because even though I know the attendant is being a bit difficult, I have zero desire to continue arguing with her.

Me: *My mother wants you to check the meter. She says it's broken.*

Attendant: *We can send someone, but I doubt it's the meter. Will someone be home between 9 and 1 P.M. on Thursday?*

"Of course, there was something wrong with the meter."

"Your mother must have been happy."

"Vindicated is the word I'd use. She insisted I call back to ensure we received a refund or credit. Remember, I'm twelve and not used to telling adults they're wrong, especially mean ones. But it was easier to argue with a woman I didn't know and couldn't see than to ignore Mom. Sort of like emails these days. Thankfully, it was a different attendant and the technician who came out noted the broken meter on our file, so we were assured a discount on the next bill."

"That's quite a bit of responsibility for a twelve-year-old."

"I suppose. Mom just needed help. By the time I got to grade seven, I was writing the cheques to pay for all the household bills because I could print faster than her and I wasn't as busy as my sister who was in high school. I was like a secretary. And after a while, I was much better at explaining problems to the utility companies, department stores, and doctors for Mom. I thought it was what everyone did."

"When did you learn it wasn't?"

"One day in high school, one of my friends came over to pick me up from lunch. We lived across the street from the school. She overheard me on the phone with the bank trying to figure out an error on a money order Mom noticed. She asked me what I was talking about. When I explained, she asked why I was the one who was doing it. When she pointed out her parents did things like that themselves, and she was Chinese too, I was a little embarrassed and I made a point to be more discrete about what I did for my parents."

"You were embarrassed for helping?"

"I was embarrassed my parents weren't seen as capable as others. I wanted to protect them. In retrospect, I know the girl was just being bitchy or trying to justify why she didn't do more, but I didn't see it like that at the time."

"It sounds like you and your parents have a co-dependent relationship."

"I never really thought about it much. It is what it is. I certainly don't want anyone to belittle Mom and Dad, especially not some stupid teenaged girl."

"You have no control over how others behave or view things, but you can control your reaction to others' behaviour."

Amy says nothing, but she considers the advice.

"You're right. That day, I resented it. Resented Mom, for a bit. I wished they spoke more English and knew how to drive like other parents. But even when I was upset, a part of me felt special because I was learning how to do things most teens don't."

"Is this how you feel now?"

"Definitely. I know I'm good at this lawyering business partly because of all the calls I made for them when I was young. After-all, getting what you need out of a growly telephone or hydro agent is arguably more difficult than convincing a judge a client isn't at fault for what he's done."

Dr. Walker chuckles. "It certainly sounds like a positive exercise. Were you at all kidding when you said your mother was not proud of you and your siblings for completing your schooling?"

"Well, she isn't overly impressed but I'm pretty sure she's happier than she would be if we failed school or worked grunt jobs like her and Dad."

"It sounds like she's hard to please but she's on your side. Again, just in her own way."

"Yes. It's just easier when she approves of a decision."

23

"It must have been difficult for you to end things with Joe."

Amy says nothing for another long while. "Yes. It would have been a lot easier just to marry him, I think. There would have been less backlash. I just knew I had to do something drastic when I had a horrid thought cross my mind." Amy stops, not sure if it's safe to say.

Dr. Walker says nothing.

"At one time, I thought the only way to get out of the relationship unscathed was for one of us to die. And, as imperfect as my life is, I certainly didn't want it to end, so it had to be him. Awful, right?" Amy holds her head in her hands.

"We're all human. Facing what I suspect you knew would come with your decision—resistance and disagreement from a lot of different people—you found different ways to end the relationship in your mind. It doesn't mean you actually wish him or anyone else harm. It probably would be helpful to have your mother's support on this one."

"Yes. I know it's more her disapproval of me being single than me being separated from Joe upsetting her, but yes, her support on this one would be nice."

"What if you're happy alone? Is this not enough for your mother?"

"If only if it was as simple. Practically speaking, if I'm with someone, it means I'm settled. There will be someone to take care of me in my old age or at least to keep me company even if all we do is argue all the time like her and Dad. And this bleeds into her religious beliefs or superstitions."

"What's your marital status have to do with religious beliefs?"

"She's old-fashioned. She knows more about Chinese traditions than her own mother. I'm pretty sure she learned it from my great-grandmother who basically raised her for a time. Anyway, the Chinese are patrilineal. We have a family shrine, but it strictly follows my dad's family line. What I understand is deceased, unmarried sons retain the protection of their birth family and name. But there's no place for deceased, unmarried daughters. So, if I die unmarried, not only am I alone and deemed a disappointment to my family during my present life but my soul is lost and unprotected for eternity and all my future lives."

"Wow. That's a heavy burden to carry."

"Yeah, tell me about it. It's probably why I waver so much when Mom pushes me to try and work things out with Joe. Maybe it is better than being alone."

"I think you know the answer, which is why you haven't caved yet. What's your mother's position regarding returning to this job in light of the incident?"

Amy scrunches up her face. "I'm pretty sure she wants me to go back."

"I see."

"Yes. I'd be disappointing her on all fronts if I don't go back."

"If this thing at work hadn't happened, would you want to go back?"

"I would for sure. There are parts I like and don't like but there'd be no question I would be going back if nothing had happened. I don't know many people who entirely love what they do. As you said earlier, many people do not enjoy their work. Do you?"

"I love a lot of parts of my job."

"That was not the answer I wanted." Amy laughs a little and then inhales deeply. "I like the court work and the thrill of a fight. I don't think I want to go back there, though. Not after everything that's happened." Amy finishes so quietly, Dr. Walker leans forward to hear her better. Amy is nodding. "I don't want to go back."

Dr. Walker remains quiet as she waits for Amy to make eye contact again. "How's it feel to say it aloud?"

"Satisfying. Scary. No partner and no job. Talk about failure." Amy groans.

"You have your call to the Bar. It *is* an achievement."

"It's hardly so, compared to the utter chaos that is my life right now."

"Have you read *The Art of War* by Sun Tzu? One of the more well-known lines is: *where there is chaos, there is opportunity*."

"Yes, I read it, but I didn't remember the quote. It's hard to see opportunities when I'm surrounded by wreckage. Like I said, I'm just not as tough as Mom."

"I think when upsetting events occur you need time to process and understand them. And what upsets one person might be nothing to another. You need not apologize to anyone or beat yourself up for your reaction to events. Nor should you compare yourself to how anyone else, not even your mother, might react differently to similar circumstances."

Amy sits perfectly still, and stares into space. "Even if she would handle it better?"

"It's easy to say in hindsight how one might react to a situation. And, in my opinion, it takes a braver person to walk away from a well laid out path both, professionally and personally, than continue simply because it's what people expect you to do."

"Ha! Well, I feel anything but brave right now."

"I think you need to give it time."

"Sure." Amy nods and noisily exhales. "I think I've talked enough."

"Good. My door is open to you."

"Thanks." Amy stands and starts to put on her coat. She feels better knowing what she wants to do but the thought of telling Mom her final decisions about Joe and work fills her with dread.

24

A few days later, Amy is driving with her mother in the passenger seat when her cell phone rings. Amy eyes her phone but keeps driving.

"Was it Joe calling?"

"What? Um … yeah." Amy wished more people had her cell phone number and Mom didn't know her habits so well.

"Why don't you call him back?"

"I'm driving."

"Pull over and call him back. Might be important."

Amy throws her a look of disapproval. "I'm on a highway. I'm not pulling over. I'll call him later."

"Maybe he wants to go out. You should call him."

"Stop it, Mom! We're not getting back together. We just hang out sometimes. Nothing more."

"Why are you shouting?"

"You think because we talk and hang out, we're back together or we're going to be, but we're not."

"But if you spend time together it's like going out."

"We're just friends."

"Men and women who talk and go out, are together. Like a couple."

"No, Mom. Men and women can be friends without being together like a couple."

"Doesn't last. You end up together eventually."

"Maybe in the past but not these days. Lots of girls are just friends with guys. It's different now."

"Give it time. You'll learn when you get older."

Amy grips the wheel until her knuckles turn white. Mom has this way of making her doubt herself even if she starts off a hundred per cent sure she's right. Her closest male friend from high school did end up wanting to date. And these days she hardly has any friends. When she and Joe started going out, she'd lost touch with everyone. Last year, most of her spare time was spent visiting Joe in Ottawa or talking to him on the phone. It's ironic how, according to Mom, on the one hand she's over the hill to start a new relationship but somehow, she's not old enough to understand how females and males interact.

"I just don't think we're getting back together. I think he's interested in one of his students."

As she exits the highway, Amy sneaks a peek at Mom to see how she's digesting this information. Mom has a poker face. Hopefully, when they reach Uncle Yaing Gong's house to visit with Amy's grandmother and grandfather, her mother will be distracted from talking about Joe.

Poh Poh Su Ling, Mom's own mother, is the only person who Mom ever listens to without yelling very much. Mom's father, Goung Goung Lei On, rarely sits with them when they visit. He was never very friendly even when they lived together. Amy was surprised her grandparents sold their own house and moved in with Yaing Gong a few years ago given how proud Goung Goung was of their house. Amy always thought they'd sell only when medically necessary.

"You've been together for years. If Joe's smart, he'll stick with you."

"Maybe I don't want him to stick with me. I don't want to marry him. If you like him so much, you marry him." Amy grips the wheel fiercely.

Mom laughs. "Why would I marry him?"

"Because you keep telling me to, even though he's not right for me."

"What happened? You were considering getting back together with him last week. What's changed? What is not right now? You know each other from law school; you're both Canadian born, and his parents find you acceptable like we find him. What more do you want?"

Amy was nervous that her increased obstinance about getting back together with Joe might lead to unwanted questions about her change of heart. The last thing she wanted to admit or explain was why she went to a psychotherapist. Having emotional breakdowns was bad enough but admitting to them and discussing them with an outsider was considered a show of weakness.

"Mom, he said he doesn't want kids, but he'd have them for me. As if he was going to do me a favour. I don't want to raise kids on my own. Besides, you know what he's done since we broke up? He's accumulated thirty thousand dollars in debt. He leased a car, bought expensive clothes and a new computer, all on credit. It's like saving the way we do went against his natural instincts."

"With the right person, he'll save. Like your father. If it

wasn't for me, he'd have no house or savings. He would've sent all his money home to that stepfamily, and smoked the rest. Your aunt and I changed more diapers than your father ever did. Men work. They don't care for the children."

"Things are different now, Mom. Both parents are supposed to help with caring for a baby."

"Not so different. Same problems and same goals."

"Maybe. I don't know." Amy contemplates telling Mom that Joe just doesn't make her happy.

"By the time I was your age, I had three of you already."

"Yeah, yeah, you've told me."

"What are you going to do, start over? You're going to be thirty soon."

Amy speeds up, hoping it'll scare Mom and make her stop talking. She and her relatives are so tactless. "Don't you think I know?" She pulls up to Yaing Gong's house, removes the key from the ignition, and slams the door. She grabs her purse and the bag of treats from the back seat, slamming that door too. Mom seems oblivious to her anger as she slowly gets out and walks to the entrance of the house. By the time Amy gets to the front door, Poh Poh Su Ling has already flung it open. A wave of heat greets them.

25

"So stuffy in here," Mom says as she walks in past Amy. "You should turn the heat down."

"It's not so high," Su Ling says. "Amy, come in quick. Cold out there."

"Poh Poh, how are you? Here are some oranges and dim sum." Amy hands her the bag as she steps inside. Mom's right. It's like a sauna inside. Amy removes her shoes and coat. "Where is everyone?"

"You didn't have to bring anything but thank you. Everyone is out shopping or working."

"Come pray to your great-grandparents," Mom says as she motions for Amy to pay her respects at the shrine in the dining room with photos of Mom's paternal grandparents, Ping Hao and Bak Lai. Amy obliges as her grandmother walks ahead of them into the kitchen where they always sit for visits.

When Amy joins them, Mom is already sitting with a cup of

tea and there is another cup on the table next to her.

"Drink your tea and have some cake." Her grandmother is busily cutting pieces of a bland yellow cake onto plates. Amy remembers the cakes from North Bay. Dry with just a hint of sweetness. She never liked them.

"No cake for me, Poh Poh, but I'll have the tea." Amy sits beside Mom at the kitchen table.

"You know, your grandfather doesn't think Joe's good enough for you."

Amy nearly spits out her tea at Mom's statement.

"Mai, don't tell her that," her grandmother says, furrowing her brow in Mom's direction.

"What do you mean? Goung Goung cares one way or another?"

"Your Amah told me you broke up with him and your grandfather overheard us talking," Grandmother says.

Amy is curious. "Why does Goung Goung care?"

Su Ling pauses but finally says, "He thinks Joe is too old for you. Doesn't like him being bald."

Amy laughs because she can't believe her grandfather commented. The last time Amy remembers him taking an interest in her life was one summer in high school when Mom told him she was working three jobs. It was the only time he asked to speak with Amy. She got on the phone, he asked if it was true she had three jobs, Amy confirmed she did, he asked if she was tired, she told him she was a bit. That was the extent of the conversation. It was really the only time Amy remembers him commenting on anything she ever did, until now.

"What do you think, Poh Poh?" Amy asks.

"I think it's great you get to choose your own partner. Get to figure out if you like them before you marry." She lowers her voice to a whisper. "If I'd had the choice, I would never have married your grandfather. And I bet his mother wouldn't have married that one in San Francisco who she barely knew or saw."

Both Amy and Mom laugh. Mom's parents bicker as much as Mom and Dad. Just more quietly. At least Mom and Dad had a choice to say yes or no to each other's photos before they married. From what Amy understood, Grandmother and previous generations didn't get that choice.

"I think Mah Mah Ping would still have married Yeh Yeh Bak Lai," Mom says.

Both Grandmother and I look at Mom.

"What? How do you know, Mom?"

"She told me. She thought he was handsome. Said he had excellent features. Looked like a mixed breed. Tall, big eyes, double lids, high cheekbones. Look at that photo of him in the shrine." Mom points in the direction of the dining room.

"I don't know if that makes up for never seeing him. Never met his own son, except for when he was a baby. Seven grandchildren and he only met one of them. You know," Su Ling points at Mom, "when your sister, Jung Sum, and I visited him on his deathbed, it was sad. Tragic, really." Grandmother looks away, and everyone is quiet for a long time.

"Too bad no one knows where he's buried. Should properly pay our respects to him at his gravesite," Mom says.

"Why don't we know where he's buried? Thought they went to the funeral," Amy says.

"Ai yah! Your grandmother and grandfather speak no English and your uncle was a child. They'd no idea where they were going in San Francisco. And then that relative wrote a few years after your great grandfather was buried, telling us they moved the grave. Probably got a chunk of money from the government.

Moved it without asking us. Just did it," Mom says, annoyed.

"It's true. He was buried near Chinatown. I remember. But your mother's right, we have no idea where they moved him. Would be nice to pay proper respect to him," Grandmother says nodding. "Whether he was good or not, he was family. But I still would never have married your grandfather had I been given a choice," Su Ling says to me. "He's bad-tempered and stubborn."

Amy can't help but to laugh at Poh Poh's definitive statement.

"But Joe's not bad tempered. They met in school. He's top of their class. Already teaching law before they're even lawyers. He'll have two jobs, one at the university and one at the law firm." Mom summarizes all of this proudly.

It was a bit infuriating that Mom, who was unimpressed by Joe before they broke up, is suddenly supporting him.

"None of it matters if Amy doesn't want to be with him," Grandmother says to Mom before turning to Amy, "What do you want?"

Amy almost wanted to cry. Poh Poh got it. "He is very smart. And he does have two jobs."

"You see Amy knows. She—"

Amy uses her court room voice to interrupt and be heard over Mom, "Mom! I'm sorry to disappoint you. I'm sorry *I'm* such a disappointment. But he doesn't make me happy." Amy's not sure if it's her volume or what she says which surprises Mom.

"This isn't about disappointing me. I'm your mother. This is for you. I want what's best for you. You don't argue with him. He doesn't make you angry all the time like your Abah makes me. You think I'm happy? I'd rather not be working all the time at a factory. I wish your father drove."

"Stop your mouth from running for a minute, Mai." Mom frowns at Poh Poh but obeys.

"Amy should be with someone who makes her happy. Don't want her to be like me and her grandfather or, worse, like you and Ming. Too noisy. Isn't this part of the reason you came to Canada? So your kids would have a better life? More choices? Not like China."

"She doesn't want to grow old without a partner either," Mom counters and then pouts.

"She's not old. I'm old. You had a choice, Mai. Let Amy have hers. You're not right about everything." Amy sometimes wonders how Poh Poh can be Mom's mother. She's so quiet and gentle even when she's adamant about what she's saying. Even her name means gentle compassion, Mom once told her.

Mom purses her lips and scrunches her eyes at Poh Poh to show her disapproval.

"I had to help you in Hong Kong. What was I going to do, keep going to school and living my own life when you were watching two little kids and trying to work and shuttle Jung back and forth to the hospital?"

Amy wonders if Mom regrets giving up her schooling more than she knew.

"Yes, you were a big help when you arrived in Hong Kong. But you didn't have to marry Ming. Or come to Canada. I told you."

"And what were we going to do? Stay in Hong Kong until the Communists took over? There was no choice."

"Well, it's 1998. More than thirty years since we left, China took back Hong Kong last year, and nothing has changed."

"The British are leaving," Mom replies. China will slither back in. They're strategic, sneakier than these western countries. Their true colours will show. Can't hide forever. Look at Tiananmen Square."

"Your brothers and their families visit regularly. Not only Hong Kong but our village is modern now. Houses are all stone. Bigger and nicer than this by a long shot." Poh Poh waves her hand around Yaing Gong's home, as she gets more excited and louder. "They have electricity. Fanciest appliances and furniture. Trains even go past there. Benefits for everyone. Not like when we lived there. Why would anyone want to come here and slave away like we did? Working all hours and hardly a weekend off. Yaing Gong is a pharmacist, and he still works six days a week. The only ones who haven't gone back to visit are us, Mai. You, Ming, me, Jung and Yaing Gong. The ones who arrived here first. The ones who have been away too long."

"This is why I told you to stop sending money back to relatives, for them to live like royalty." Mom sniffs and her face contorts like she smells garbage. "Weather's not always warm and maybe we're not living in the lap of luxury like they are back home but the chances of the government taking everything you work for overnight or getting thrown in jail because you say the wrong thing won't happen here."

Poh Poh nods. "Fine. This is why you chose Ming instead of the other one. Amy should be able to choose too." Amy feels her eyes widen and stares at her grandmother who is watching Mom. Mom looks lost in her thoughts. Who was Poh Poh referring to?

Until now, Amy never thought of Mom being with anyone other than Dad. Amy remembers Mom wondering a couple of times what happened to some military friend of hers. Friend or acquaintance. What did she say again? But Mom doesn't believe in men and women just being friends. She just argued with me about it. So, does that mean, this friend, was a … boyfriend? She opens her mouth and turns to Mom.

"Mom, did you date someone other than Dad?"

Mom narrows her eyes at Poh Poh, and her mouth sets in a straight line for a minute before focusing on her teacup with excessive interest, refusing to look at Amy.

"Not important what I did so many years ago. You just think carefully about what you're doing. I made a practical choice. I even turned your Abah down once. It just delayed our relationship an entire year, you know. Think carefully. You're not young long."

"Umm ... okay," is all Amy manages to get out while her mind reels from her sudden understanding that Mom may have had a life she never shared. And there was a change, a slight change, of attitude.

Now Amy isn't sure. It's true, Mom originally turned down Dad's photo. She'd heard the story countless times. Maybe she ought to see if she and Joe can work things out.

26

"When you start back at your job, if you want, you'll meet new people," Mom says.

"When do you start work, Amy?" Grandmother asks.

Amy's head swirls for a bit.

But just like the way she blurted out over the phone to Joe that she wanted to break up, she now unthinkingly says, "I don't want to go back. I don't want to take the job."

"What?" Mom screeches.

Amy closes her eyes. It may have been too soon to tell Mom.

"Because of that dead monkey? I told you, just turn around and claw his eyes out if he comes near you again." Mom starts ranting about how Amy can't be both unemployed and single.

"Calm down, Mai." Poh Poh says, tsk-tsking. "Why are you so anxious? It's just a job, not her soul."

Ignoring Poh Poh, Mom continues. "Your sister said there are lawyers who can't even get jobs. What are you going to do?

And where are you going to meet someone if you're not working?"

"Mom! Stop!" Amy is so exasperated she is louder than she intended. Amy takes a deep breath to regain some composure and then quietly explains. "I didn't say I wasn't going to work. I'm just not sure about going back there."

"You didn't tell them yet, did you?" Mom looks expectantly at Amy.

"No. No. I didn't say anything to anyone yet." Amy's face flushes red and she stares straight ahead, avoiding eye contact with her mother. "It's not just about that creep, Mom. Everyone there is miserable. Like bad karma or something. Divorces and accidents happening to everyone."

There's a long silence until Poh Poh comments. "Well, Amy must be a great lawyer if she has to argue with you all the time, Mai." It works. Both Mom and Amy laugh. "I'm not joking. Your mother is difficult to get along with. Always arguing and thinks she's right about everything. I know. I used to live with her. Never again."

"If I didn't argue with everyone, always following the rules, we wouldn't be here today. Have to be pushy to get what you need."

"Important to listen to others, too. You're just like your father. Think you know everything. Besides, you're always saying where there are people there will be money." Poh Poh speaks forcefully but at half Mom's volume.

Amy finds it odd, but she listens more carefully, afraid she might miss a word. She and Mom should learn from Poh Poh. And Amy couldn't agree more. Mom is like her father. Sharp and quick tongued, even when she means well. *Especially* when she means well. Amy thinks about all the times she yells at Dad.

"She has nothing to fear from that dead monkey. I don't

want her to give up a job because of him or anyone."

"Not everyone is like you. Sometimes people just want to move forward. Forget the negative. Why would you want her to work in a place where she is unhappy?" Poh Poh stops to drink her tea.

"I don't, but she shouldn't be the one to leave. She shouldn't be afraid of him. Or anyone."

"This isn't just about him, Mom. I see the lawyers there. They go from one case to another, fighting with everyone. Some of them are so tired of fighting, they just settle everything, right or wrong. It's like they have no purpose or will. It's depressing. One of the men working there committed suicide last year. Remember? I told you."

"There must have been more than work problems for him," Mom argues, never relenting.

"You're probably right, but the work conditions didn't help. Remember all the crazy things that happened last year? The entire floor we worked on flooded. Not the first or second floors, just ours on the third. And one of those metal filing cabinets, out of nowhere, fell on a secretary. You know how strong and stable those things are? Not good *feng shui*. Even Joe thinks I shouldn't go back."

Joe's angry words echo in Amy's head. *I can't believe you're even considering going back there to work. It broke us up and this creep touched you. What more needs to happen before you leave?* It was a surprising way for him to put it. He once described their Buddhist superstitions as similar to witchcraft unlike his superior Christian religion. But he was using her own beliefs to make her understand why she needed to leave. And he's right—something about that place is not right for her.

Remembering the conversation with Joe reminds Amy why

it's wrong to even try to get back together. She feels indifference towards him—at least romantically. When he talks about his interest in one of his students, she's jealous, not because she wants to be *with* him; she's jealous *of* him. She wants to find the real love of her life or at least have a date. She wants to have a job she loves like he does. The thought of being easily replaced, after all the years they were together, drives her bananas. Was it all a waste of time?

Amy sits back, knowing bad karma is one of the few things that trumps almost all of Mom's other concerns.

"What will you do then?" Mom demands rhetorically.

"I don't know. You're always saying you can't make real money working for someone else. Well maybe, I'll start off working for myself then."

"Working on your own is unstable."

Amy wonders if Mom says this to see if she is serious about practising on her own.

Grandmother gets up to refill everyone's tea. "Stability isn't everything," she says as she pours.

"And where will you meet people?"

"Lots of places to meet people. Amy's not ugly," Poh Poh says as she sips her tea.

Amy knows it's as much of a compliment as she'll ever get from any relative.

Mom mentions some cousin of hers she and Grandmother knew in Hong Kong who she thought was truly ugly and they're off gossiping about Mom's siblings and family. Amy tunes out thinking about what she will do if she doesn't go back. She's happy Poh Poh has distracted Mom a bit. She only gets drawn back to their conversation when Mom starts talking about Chinese newspapers.

"She must advertise if she's going out on her own. Probably better with *Sing Tao*. *Ming Pao* doesn't have as wide a circulation. She can get cards with Chinese characters, too." Mom continues, almost to herself, about finding office space downtown and how she can translate for the Chinese clients.

Poh Poh agrees *Sing Tao* is a better bet. She goes to a corner of the kitchen where a pile of newspapers sit stacked on a table and rummages about. She returns with a few sections she shares with Mom. "See, there are lawyer ads here." She points at a few pages. "Keep it simple. Don't need anything too complicated."

"So, you're okay with me not taking the job?" Amy stares at Mom suspiciously.

"If you end up working for yourself, you should advertise is all I'm saying. Just make sure it's what you want before you give up the job offer. Probably won't be there if you want it later." Mom says.

Amy's suspicious of Mom's words. Poh Poh reaches out and pats Amy on the arm as if to assure her, as Mom flips through the newspapers commenting on how one ad is too large, and another she thinks reads oddly. Amy still isn't sure she's making the right decision about Joe or work, but she knows she certainly won't be following her heart or instincts by staying with either.

Grandmother laughs a bit before saying, "Perhaps you can quit the factory and work for Amy soon."

"Can't put all your eggs in one basket. Maybe later." Mom completely misses or ignores the levity Poh Poh attempts to convey as she continues to study the newspaper ads.

"And I can't work with Mom. We'll be arguing with each other more than I would be arguing in court."

"Don't blame her too much. She was born like that. Must have the last word." Grandmother shakes her head disapprovingly.

A laugh escapes from Mom and she grins. "Lucky for you I'm

like this. Not for me, the lot of you would be stuck in that village in China."

"Yes, yes, you're the only one who did anything. No one else. All you." Turning to Amy: "All she does is brag." Poh Poh wags her forefinger at Mom in a scolding manner while turning to Amy, "When will you start searching for an office?"

"I don't know. Hadn't really thought about it, but I can call an agent to get some ideas about prices and available locations. Can't work until I get my licence next week anyway."

"I forgot you have to graduate." Poh Poh turns to Mom. "What are you wearing to it, Mai?"

"The ceremony is during the week. Mom and Dad would have to take a day off work to go," Amy offers, a bit surprised Poh Poh asked.

"Yes. Not like Ming or I understood what was going on for the other kids' ceremonies. Like *muk yun*, wooden people," Mom adds.

"You're not going?" Poh Poh frowns.

"Well, I didn't really give her the details." Amy doesn't want Poh Poh to blame Mom.

"Mai, it's one day of work. Not going to make that much of a difference to you or the family. How many times will she graduate?" Poh Poh gestures at Amy. "In one hour, she will earn what you make in a day once she has her licence."

"Well, I don't know about that," Amy says thinking about her paltry student income. "Not a big deal, Poh Poh."

"Your parents should attend. Even if they don't understand everything being said. Money's important but it doesn't make you happy. Need to celebrate occasionally."

Mom appears nonchalant about Poh Poh's rather passionate argument.

"Mom, do you want to go?" I ask.

She shrugs. "Either way. Up to you. If we go, you'll need to write notes for your father and me to get the day off."

"Hmm." It's ironic to Amy that her parents are like children in school.

"Make sure she wears something decent, Amy. Not one of those sweaters she made. Maybe buy something new for her. Your Amah is so cheap sometimes. Make sure she is presentable."

"What are you talking about? Those sweaters I sewed are nicer than anything you can buy in a store." Mom was in full defence mode now. "If you don't think they're good enough for going out, then I won't give you anymore."

Poh Poh winks and raises her eyebrows at Amy. Amy likes how she can poke fun at Mom, and is annoyed when her phone rings, interrupting the moment. It's Joe again.

"You need to take that? Go to the dining room to talk. Answer it." Poh Poh motions her to go to the dining room. Amazing how she and Mom are so different yet so similar.

Amy stares at Mom, who quickly looks down at the paper, pretending she doesn't care about the phone call.

"It's okay, Poh Poh. I'll talk later. Nothing important."

***

Three months later, Amy and her mother find an office right downtown on the edge of Yorkville, at the corner of Bloor and Queen's Park, across from the Royal Ontario Museum. The prestigious 206 Bloor Street West address is the fanciest part of the place. It sits on the second floor of a pre–Second World War building, above the chief tenant, a Pizza Hut. There is no elevator, and the rent agreement is month-to-month. Unlike Amy, who is uncertain if the rudimentary, dated space is appropriate because it doesn't resemble any of the offices she's worked in over the years, Mom believes it's perfect when she sees the south-facing front door and windows. Mom picks a fortuitous day on the Chinese calendar for Amy's grand opening.

At the same time, Amy's siblings convince her to lodge a complaint with the Ontario Human Rights Commission against her former employer and the creep, instead of just walking away. The process forces Amy to relive and record every detail of the incident, dragging her back to the past, leaving her at times so broken she can do little more than hide, and at other times leaving her so furious she lashes out at everyone near her. The end couldn't come soon enough for Amy.

After Amy's third and final meeting with Dr. Walker, Amy promises to do something purely enjoyable regardless of what anyone, including her mother, might think. This leads to the discovery of her favourite part of the office—its proximity to the University of Toronto where she attends karate classes every Monday, Wednesday, and Friday evening.

Closets
Zoe Lai Wah Nesbitt

27

"Why can't I use the money in my Spend account for a new dress for graduation?"

Mom—Amy Lee, and Dad—Andrew Nesbitt, give me allowance each month, and they make me divide it into four groups, Invest, Save, Spend and Give. I've been saving all my Spend, plus birthday and Christmas money, for months but now I want to spend it. Mom, of course, is telling me I can't.

I keep an eye on the houses as the car glides around the corner onto the street where Poh Poh Mai Gum and Goung Goung Hao Ming—Mom's parents—live. I consciously stop my face from scowling as the densely packed homes with cement and asphalt driveways appear. I like our neighbourhood better.

"Zoe, I didn't say you can't," Mom says. "I just don't understand why you need another dress when your closet is *full* of dresses. You've at least three in your closet that no one at school has ever even seen you in. They're hardly worn, and they're fashionable. Grandma Sophie says they're European. She got them at one of those sample sales."

It's not like Mom would know anything about fashion. All she wears are black, blue and grey suits she bought when she was still in university. "Everyone's getting a new one, and none of the ones I have are white or cream. Madison, Hailey and I wanted to do what the girls at St. Margaret's do for graduation. Everyone wears a white or cream coloured dress, so we sort of match, but all the styles are different so we're unique." I love the idea.

"Well, by all means, if Madison and Hailey are doing it, you certainly should." Mom rolls her eyes.

"Can you be any more sarcastic? I know you hate my friends."

"I don't hate them. I just don't think they're the best people to hang around with *all* the time. And don't you have the beige one Grandma Sophie bought just last spring? That's sort of cream coloured."

"Beige is not white or cream coloured. It's completely different. And I want the one I picked out at the store on Bayview. Besides, Dad said I can use the money from my Spend account on whatever I want. What's the point of having the Spend account if I never get to spend it? I know you were poor in the 1970s but we're not. It's 2011 and our family is different. Not the same as when you were growing up Mom."

"You talked to Dad about this already?"

Of course, that's the part she homes in on. I shouldn't have told her. Now Mom's eyes are bulging out. She hates it when Dad takes my side. "I talked to him generally about my Spend account. And why am I not allowed to talk to him about this?"

"The dress you want is expensive, and the material is cheap. The ones you have are perfectly fine, and they're already in your closet. This may seem like a big deal but it's grade six. I just don't want you to waste your money on this one night and have none for something you can really use later."

"Well, my friends and I agreed. Just because *you* never want to buy anything new, why do I have to suffer?"

"Suffer? Really? You have no idea what that even means."

"I live with you, don't I?"

"Really mature response. Can we just go visit with Poh Poh this morning? There are more important things to deal with than what you're going to wear to walk across a stage in your school gym. We can talk more with your father about this later, okay?"

"If that's how you feel, then you don't have to come. I know you think the tickets for the parents' dinner are too expensive. I heard you complaining to Dad. He can take me. At least I know he'll want to be there."

Mom doesn't answer for a moment. "I didn't say I don't want to be there, but I don't know of any other elementary graduations that are so over-the-top, with a privately hired school bus to transport kids to a membership racquet club where a professional photographer, party favours, grab bags, a DJ, a multi-course dinner, and bartender awaits them while the parents are served a formal sit-down meal in the adjacent patio. It's fancier than our wedding for crying out loud."

"Is this your way of telling me how you want to be there?"

"I just don't want you to get caught up in the hype. It's great you met the grade six requirements to move on to the next grade, especially since they're not allowed to fail anyone these days, and I know you're going to miss your friends who won't be going to the same school but just know—this is not going to define your life. There are more important things to worry about. Like Poh Poh." She takes a big breath after her rant. "Let's just talk about it later."

"What? Aren't we just cleaning up her closet today? Why are you worried about Poh Poh?"

Mom nods and appears to calm down. "You're right, we're just here to help her clean out her closet."

"Wait, you said she's fine. Isn't she?"

"Yes, yes, she is fine. She even mopped our kitchen floors the other day when she came to visit even though I told her to just sit. Remember?"

I knew it. Mom's just saying things to end the money discussion.

28

Poh Poh used to take care of me and come over all the time before she got sick. She makes the comfiest pyjama pants out of her good cloth scraps, but I only wear them at home. I wear the matching sets from Grandma Sophie and Grandpa Steve, Dad's parents, for school trips and sleepovers. I love Poh Poh Mai and Goung Goung Ming but if any of my friends ever saw their house, the way they dress or the way they do things, it'd be even more disastrous than the time I tried to share my lunch.

I never really thought of myself as different until grade four. Madison and I became best friends then. We ate lunch together every day. Well, I love Chinese dumplings, especially the ones Poh Poh makes. So, when Mom asked if I wanted to pack leftover dumplings for lunch instead of a plain old sandwich, of course I said yes. I even asked Mom to toss in a few extra to share.

What I didn't know, until after, is the combination of cooked pork and the thick steamed wrappers equals a serious case of bad breath. Mom knew. She should've told me. Not only did Madison not try the dumplings she told me to *stop breathing my smelly Chinese breath on her*. Hailey, who wasn't really hanging out with us much but wanted to, started to copy Madison, and the two of them teased me the rest of the day.

Despite all the water I drank and finger brushing my teeth, they kept up their eye rolls and jokes. They asked if I had *dumpster dumplings* for lunch the rest of the week. Stupid, but funny to them, I guess. I tried to laugh it off, but I felt my face turning red every time they said something.

By the end of the week, I broke down crying after school. Mom was great, at first. She hugged me and just listened. But then she got mad. Really mad. Mom wanted to speak to their mothers, my teacher, and the principal. I could tell by the way she said *speak*, she meant scream at them for *raising bitchy little vermin*. This is what I heard her calling them when she was talking to Dad. I had to look up what vermin meant later. It's one of the nicer things Mom still calls them occasionally, even though it's been two years.

This is the problem. Mom always tries to fix everything, which means she starts to verbally wipe out anyone she feels is wrong. She was screaming about bullying and racism. I didn't think it was either. I thought it was just my friends thinking they were funny and being a bit mean. It's like she forgot I had to see them every day and they're still my friends. At least I wanted them to be. What good is being right if everyone hates you?

Mom and I argued until Dad got home. Thankfully, he listened to me, which made Mom even angrier. Dad had her promise to not do anything and let me handle it my own way. I did what Dad suggested, I told them they were being mean and walked away until they stopped. It was hard because I didn't really have anyone else to hang out with, but after another week they seemed to forget about the whole thing, and everyone was fine. Except for Mom. Boy, can she hold a grudge. Anyway, the last thing I want is to emphasize my Chinese*ness* in case it leads to another scene.

I'm not stupid. I know no one's supposed to make fun of each other about being different. We learned all about Native rights, Black history month and kids with special needs, and the school makes announcements to recognize Hanukkah, Diwali and even Chinese New Year. But what the school does officially and what happens between kids on the playground isn't always the same. No one wants to be a tattletale, especially against your own friends, and, more importantly, it's hard to be different.

Most of the kids in our area are white. Pure white. I'm only part. Mom asked Poh Poh to give me a Chinese middle name, Lai Wah. It means something like future surplus. I wish she hadn't done that because my Chinese name shows up on my school records. Teachers who don't know me, like substitutes reading the class list, sometimes read out my full name. And I stand out.

I knew I was never going to have blonde hair like Madison or green eyes like Hailey, but I never really thought of myself as being different, until the whole dumpling thing. Dad says I remind him of those *anime* characters with black hair, oversized eyes, and pale skin. I just feel like I belong more with Dad and his family, than Mom and hers. Or maybe it's just what I want. I'm not sure but I worry about it sometimes.

It helps that Dad's family and I speak the same language. Mom says it's not fair to compare because I only see Grandma and Grandpa for holidays, vacations, and celebrations, but Poh Poh we used to see every day because she came over and helped us with basic chores like cooking and cleaning. Of course, it's not as fun. Then she got sick and now we don't see her much. Mom usually visits her parents alone, to drop off groceries or to take Poh Poh to some medical appointment.

29

I see Poh Poh peering out the large front window from behind Goung Goung's constantly growing colourful collection of house plants.

"Has he got more?" I ask.

"It keeps him busy. Makes him happy and keeps him out of Poh Poh's hair." Mom says while concentrating on parking.

"If he stopped transplanting them every few days, they might actually stay alive." Mom doesn't laugh at my joke.

"I shouldn't have given him the starter fertilizer. He just wants an excuse to use it." When Mom explained to her father why only new plants benefit from the starter fertilizer for the first month, he got around the rule by transplanting plants every few weeks. It's sort of funny. "Poh Poh must not know or else she'd kill him," Mom mutters more to herself than me before telling me, "Grab the bag of fruit and soup from the trunk, will you?"

"Yes, master," I salute her before undoing my seatbelt and jumping out of the car.

Poh Poh Mai opens the screen door wide as Mom and I climb the steep steps. The sharp smell of eucalyptus and lavender hits me. I see Mom wrinkling her nose and scrunching her face as she steps into the house.

"Goung Goung," Poh Poh says waving her hand in front of her nose and laughing a bit. He did seem to have a habit of applying Chinese herbal medicines heavily even though they're meant to be used sparingly for dire injuries, according to Mom. "Like baby." Poh Poh says, pointing to the kitchen.

I don't like the way Poh Poh's always slagging Goung Goung, saying he does things for attention. I don't think he is doing things for attention. He just takes ideas too far. Like with the starter fertilizer, he thinks if a little is good then a lot is better. Or he might just like the smell.

"Hi, Poh Poh."

"Someting jink? Eat?"

"No, it's okay, Poh Poh," I smile, answering in a voice I usually reserve for speaking to little kids. I figure if I speak slowly enough and keep my words simple, she'll understand me.

Mom and Poh Poh start talking quickly in Cantonese while I take off my shoes and put on a pair of the communal slippers from the closet. I know it's probably not fast, but it sounds fast to me since I don't understand them. It's like French class when Madame Gaultieri reads to us. She tells us she's reading at a normal pace, but I don't hear or understand more than a few words. It's not much, but it's still better than what I can pick up from Mom and Poh Poh when they speak.

Mom was disappointed because after three years of Saturday morning Chinese classes, which I happily exchanged for hockey practice, I still only know a few words. For once, though, Mom didn't accuse me of not trying hard enough in class, because even she found my homework hard to understand and it was kindergarten level. Mom speaks Cantonese but she never went to school for it, so she only understands simple everyday words and she doesn't read or write. Anything complicated, like the Chinese news reports on CFMT and OMNI, and she's as lost as I am.

Mom hurries over to the small family shrine sitting in the corner of the living room. She's always rushing around like we're late. She steps on the power bar making the warm red electric candle lights glow, lighting up the room. The red scrolls with Chinese characters painted in gold sit in the back of each of the three cabinet shelves. There's a picture of a beautiful fair-skinned goddess wearing a flowing white robe, on the top shelf.

I'm not sure if Mom really understands the shrine or if she just doesn't want to explain it to me, but all she says is that the shrine is supposed to protect the family. She never seems to have the patience to teach me, especially these days. She gets frustrated and yells, unlike Dad who's always trying to teach me something or other. I learned more from *Mulan* than her, and after the one trip to the big Buddhist temple on Bayview Avenue with Poh Poh and Mom, I searched for information on the internet.

I learned the beautiful fair-skinned woman on top is the Goddess of Mercy. The goddess governs fertility, helps to free souls from purgatory, and helps those who suffer. The stone statue of the goddess at the Bayview temple was enormous, at least two door lengths tall. We shook the can of a hundred fortunes in front of her to get our fortunes for the year. It was fun. At the temple, we also stopped to burn incense and pray before the statues of all sorts of gods. Originally, I thought we were randomly walking around the property, but Poh Poh was directing us to certain spots in the main and two smaller buildings. In one, we prayed before a wall of ancestral tablets sitting in a cabinet. It's like a cemetery plot but in the temple. There were hundreds of photos everywhere and it took a while for Poh Poh and Mom to find the relatives. Apparently, it's some great-aunt and uncle, from Goung Goung's side. I didn't understand any of it when we were there, but I did feel at peace while we wandered around.

Anyway, the bottom shelf of the shrine at my grandparents' is devoted to the Landlord God to bless all property belonging to the owners of the home. There's no picture because the god is formless and nameless.

The middle level is reserved to pay tribute to all deceased family ancestors starting with the most recent. So Poh Poh and Goung Goung's shrine honours all the Lee ancestors. Poh Poh said it's too crowded and they didn't have photos of Goung Goung's parents, so a red script with black writing has the family surname and some other words commemorating all the Lee ancestors. It's framed.

With everything we've learned about women's rights in school, I don't think it's fair only Goung Goung's and not Poh Poh's family line is honoured at the shrine. At the same time, I think if you had to honour both sides at every shrine, they'd need to be a lot bigger, and it'd be hard to keep track of all the family members. But I can't imagine not being considered part of Mom and Dad's family just because I might get married one day.

Mom is examining the hardened, dried-skinned oranges sitting on the plates in front of each shelf. She whips them into the waste basket and replaces them with the new ones we brought. She shouts something out loud to her parents who are in the kitchen. Whatever she says makes Poh Poh rush in. I can't help but laugh when Poh Poh tries to pick up the oranges Mom tossed out. Mom waves her away and fully opens the window beside the shrine.

Poh Poh brags about how the positioning of their shrine is much better than those sitting in darkened corners and hallways in other family homes. Here, the shrine receives natural sunlight ensuring a brighter and more fortuitous future for the ancestors and their descendants. On a practical note, it lets the strong scent of the incense flow out rather than hanging about in the house.

Mom strikes a match, lights three incense sticks, stands in front of the shrine, and bows three times while she murmurs in Cantonese before finally stabbing the incense into the sand filling an old tomato can. For Christmas one year, I wanted to buy Poh Poh one of the *expensive* plastic incense holders from Chinatown. They were only five dollars, and I had money in my Spend account but Mom told me not to waste my money because Poh Poh thinks they're overpriced, which doesn't make a whole lot of sense to me since she apparently spent hundreds of dollars for the shrine, electric candles, frames, photos, and Chinese scripts.

Poh Poh says something to Mom and then goes upstairs.

"Will you put down your phone and come pray? Why are you just standing there?" Mom waves her hand for me to come over.

"I'll do it before we leave." I only go through the motions to keep Mom and Poh Poh happy. I'm not sure what I believe yet and I really don't know what I'm supposed to be saying when I bow.

"Why do you always put things off?" Mom sighs. "Well, go with Poh Poh upstairs to see if you can use any of the clothes in their closet before we pack them up for charity. Your cousins already took what they wanted. Need to clear it out. Poh Poh wants us to bring whatever's left to the charity bin on the way home.

"Fine, but I seriously doubt the charity will take any of it."

"Funny. Just go."

I have no idea why Mom thinks I'm going to wear anything she or Poh Poh Mai owned from forever ago.

30

The main bedroom, Poh Poh's room, is cream coloured with a hint of pink. Bright and cheerful. There is a neatly made futon bed with clean but mismatched sheets and pillowcases, most of which Poh Poh made herself. The top of the old brown dresser from the seventies is full of framed photos of Mom, her parents and her siblings, which I've never seen before.

Weirdly for a bedroom, a small heavy diner-type table with a pedestal leg, a smooth burgundy-brown surface, and a metal trim sits in the centre of the three windows facing the front of the house, along with an S-shaped chair. The set apparently came from one of the restaurants Goung Goung cooked in over forty years ago. The table's covered with a clear plastic tarp, like the kind we get from Home Depot when we want to paint. Mom tells me the vinyl back and seat of the chair once matched the table, and it was in good condition even after years of use, but it didn't stop Goung Goung from re-covering the vinyl a few months ago with bright hot pink leather he scavenged during one of his neighbourhood walks on garbage day. It's tacky now.

I'm certain my friends' grandparents, the ones who come to our school events and hockey games dressed in modern clothing, have bedding and furniture that match. What a novel concept. Old furniture from a restaurant likely isn't used in bedrooms and nothing is covered with plastic protectors and homemade drop cloths, like everything in here.

Poh Poh notices me and points to the closet that takes up one whole wall of the room.

"Look, look."

"Okay, Poh Poh."

Unlike my closet, Poh Poh's is empty, in a way. There's room to hang more things but on the floor inside the closet is a filled garbage bag. I know what's inside before I even look—old clothes.

When things get worn down, lose their colour, or if I know I won't wear them anymore, I like to get rid of them to make space for new things. Not Mom. She still has clothes she wore in high school! Unless something is completely shredded, she likes to keep it. Mom will even wear clothes I want to give away. She doesn't care if the colour and the cut don't work at all on her if she can get more use out of it or if she thinks it's still stylish. It's no wonder she has garbage bags full of old clothes, some hers, some mine and some even Dad's, sitting at the bottom of her closet. She's just like Poh Poh.

The difference is Poh Poh has old clothes from Mom and her siblings as well because none of them took everything they owned when they moved out. Sometimes Poh Poh calls, threatening to throw it all out. She gets as far as putting everything into large industrial-strength garbage bags and tosses them all in the closet. Every six months or so Poh Poh gets frustrated with all the garbage bags of clothes, and she calls Mom or one of her siblings to take back what she's collected, or to drop it off at a charity bin—anywhere out of her house.

When Mom gets one of these calls, she complains to Dad or walks around muttering about how none of the clothes over at Poh Poh's can be hers because she *has* taken most of her belongings, but she ends up coming here anyway to make her mother happy.

I wonder how old and how long the clothes in this garbage bag have been sitting in Poh Poh's closet. I don't remember Poh Poh calling or Mom complaining about it recently. Either way, Mom seriously needs her head examined if she thinks I'm going through them to find things to wear. As if I'd ever find anything. No offence to them, but I've never seen anything Mom or Poh Poh has worn that I'd want to be seen in. Unlike some of the clothes Grandma Sophie has, like her black and white handkerchief top she wore for New Year's. It's silk. And you wear it crooked so it's like a poncho, but sexier. I think I saw something like it on a TV show! I'm hoping she'll give it to me one day.

I flip past Poh Poh's two pairs of Walmart jeans, one blue and one black. She always wears these, no matter the season. Mom has the same jeans. For more reason than one, I wouldn't dream of taking these from her.

In the winters, underneath her jeans, Poh Poh wears a pair of pyjama pants like the ones she makes for me to keep warm. I remember watching her arrive at our place to take care of me when I was little; it was like she performed a magic trick. She'd remove her pants, and she would still be wearing pants. I don't know why I found it so funny, but I remember laughing and laughing. One time she even got redressed to do it again because I was having so much fun.

Hanging beside her jeans are the golf shirts worn so often they're almost transparent. Her favourite home-sewn sweater and vest come next. A little bit further along the rod is the short puffy brown jacket she bought with Mom at Mark's Work Warehouse, which she considers fancy, so she doesn't always wear it. Next, come a few button-down blouses, the black blazer Mom gave her, and her grey and black trousers—her dressy clothes. Almost all of Poh Poh's dressy clothes are made of polyester. I hate the feel of polyester. It's scratchy. I'm sure Poh Poh doesn't want me to take any of these clothes either.

I dig further into the corner and find a few shirts with yellowed collars, an ugly worn-out leather jacket, and a sports jacket—all for men. I have no idea why these items are still hanging in here. Anyway, pass, pass, pass. Great, I'm finished one side.

I push the closet door closest to me. It glides about half a foot, stops, and bounces back slightly. I push it again, same thing. What's wrong with this thing? I spot the corner of another filled garbage bag on the floor, jutting out over the runner. I walk over to give it a quick shove, but it just bounces back at me. I push the top of the bag aside and see boxes sitting behind the garbage bag so there's no room to push it back in. It figures.

"Poh Poh, should I take this bag out?" She's next to me, standing on tiptoe trying to pull something off the top shelf. I step back to see what she's reaching for and see clothes haphazardly thrown up top.

"Want help, Poh Poh?" I walk over to where she is struggling.

"*Sam*" she says, meaning clothes I gather as she points to the top I'm wearing and then at the pile in the shelf.

"Clothes up here?" I ask her as I reach over her head to the shelf. I'm already slightly taller than Poh Poh but I still can't see up top clearly. I blindly start pulling pieces down and handing them to her. They turn out to be her homemade sweaters. She seems satisfied as she deposits them on the bed and starts to fold them into a pile.

31

I keep taking items from the shelf until a space is clear. At least I think it is until I catch a glimpse of something red. I haul out the large garbage bag to push aside the closet door a bit further before bringing over the hot pink restaurant chair to stand on.

On the shelf, I find two piles of what look like fancy school binders shoved against the wall. Each binder is about an inch thick. Two are orange-reddish and one is green. The other pile has two slightly thicker red binders sitting on top of a wide rectangular white cardboard box. The box is all yellowed.

I grab one of the red books assuming it's someone's old school notes to read the word on the cover. *Photos.*

"Zooeeee! Nooooo. Nooooo."

Poh Poh's shouting startles me, and I wobble on the chair.

"I'm okay, Poh Poh," I say reflexively, never wanting to excite her any more than she is naturally. But I quickly slap my hand down on the edge of the shelf to steady myself.

"What's going on up there?" Mom calls from downstairs.

"Come. Come." Grandmother is waving frantically at me to step off the chair. She's overly concerned with my safety. I'm only two feet off the ground. She holds out a hand to catch me if I fall. I quickly grab the closest pile of photo albums with both hands before I climb back to the floor.

"Ohhhh ... *Gao seng bou*," she says quickly taking the albums from me and putting them on the table before rushing back to my side. By this time Mom is at the entrance of the room. Poh Poh walks behind the door and picks up a rag.

"What's going on?" Mom demands. She appears angry it wasn't a real emergency that led her up here.

Poh Poh is busy wiping off the layer of dust on top of the albums and the yellowed box. With all this going on, I climb back onto the chair to grab the other pile of photo albums before either of them makes more of a fuss.

"Zoe, what are you doing? Those aren't clothes."

"Thanks, Captain Obvious." I set the other pile on the table in front of Poh Poh who automatically starts dusting them off with her rag. I clap my hands together over the little waste basket to get rid of the dust sticking to me.

"Why are you messing around with those? You're supposed to be going through the clothes." She goes on in the same tone, but in Cantonese, to Poh Poh.

"I wasn't *messing around*, and I already got through one side of the closet. Big surprise, there's nothing except Poh Poh's clothes and some dated men's clothes with permanent stains. And if you think I'm going through those garbage bags, you're crazy. I was just helping Poh Poh take down clothes from the shelf and found those. She got excited when she saw me standing on the chair."

"Fine," Mom says, but in a way that I know she's still mad

even when she has no reason to be.

I reach over to open the large box Poh Poh wiped down and pushed aside. It seems familiar, but I can't remember why until I remove the lid. A large white cover with the words *Wedding Album* written in gold script across the centre stares back at me. The album is covered with a heavy clear plastic.

"Hey! It's the same album as Grandma and Grandpa's. Grandma Sophie showed me it one Christmas after we opened all the presents."

Mom walks over to us. "They married around the same time. Your dad's parents were both from small northern Ontario cities too. Sudbury and Owen Sound, I think. Like us from North Bay. These types of albums must have been all that was available then."

"I didn't even know Poh Poh and Goung Goung had a wedding album. How come I've never seen it before?"

Mom shrugs. "Poh Poh used to always come to our place. We never stay very long here when we visit. I think the albums have been up there on that shelf since we moved to this house in 1990."

I open the album to the first photo. A young Poh Poh and Goung Goung stare back at me. Poh Poh sees it, laughs and says something to Mom who also laughs. "What's funny?" I wait for the translation from Mom.

"Poh Poh says it's when Goung Goung still had real teeth."

I grin at Poh Poh though I wish all her jokes weren't always making fun of Goung Goung, even if he seems to just ignore her.

"Why are some of the pages cut out and falling apart?"

"They had an argument."

"But. It was their *wedding* day."

Mom shrugs. "Poh Poh has a temper or at least she used to when she was younger. She's different now with you and your cousins. Besides, her and Goung Goung were an arranged marriage, so the wedding doesn't have the same sentimental baggage, like it does here, these days."

I know Poh Poh has a tough edge to her even though she's always smiling and gentle with me, but I never really thought about it, until now.

"Why didn't you wear her wedding dress instead of Grandma Sophie's?"

"The one Poh Poh wore was borrowed. From ..." Mom flips through a few photos and then taps at one, "this lady. I'm pretty sure Goung Goung's sister, my aunt, borrowed the same dress for her wedding a few years before this. His sister's marriage was arranged too."

"Sure makes the dress less special then."

Mom and Poh Poh lose interest in the album, leaving me to flip through it alone. All the photos are in black and white. It's almost like watching an old movie but in photos.

"Wow! Amazing dress. Poh Poh looks so chic." Mom takes her time coming back over.

"Oh. That's Poh Poh's real wedding dress. And it's a nice one."

"What do you mean, *real* wedding dress?"

"It's her wedding *cheong sam*. The traditional Chinese wedding dress. The white wedding dresses are a western tradition."

"Oh, like the second dress you wore when you and Dad got married."

"Yes, exactly."

"I always thought your red dress was more like a party dress. I didn't know it was a Chinese wedding dress. Was Poh Poh's *cheong sam* borrowed too?"

"No, that was hers." Poh Poh joins us.

"Why didn't you wear her *cheong sam* for your wedding

then?" I'd watched the video of Mom and Dad's wedding and went through their wedding photos all the time when I was little. All I remember is Grandma Sophie gave Mom her wedding dress to wear and at some point, she changed into this bright red dress.

"I wanted to wear Poh Poh's dress, but I never fit it. I'm built like Goung Goung's family except for the height." Mom laughs at her own joke, as my grandmother says something to Mom. "Poh Poh's getting it to show you."

"What? Her *cheong sam?* She still has it?"

Poh Poh leans awkwardly into the corner of the closet before triumphantly turning around with an old, dusty dry-cleaning bag in her hand.

"Ick!" I can't help but to say.

As she brings it over to the table, sunshine catches something inside the bag and I see a sparkle. She holds the bag above the little wastebasket and smacks it, sending dust flying everywhere except into the garbage. Poh Poh starts to pull the garment out and Mom grabs the bag as if holding a dead animal.

"I'm taking this outside to get rid of some of the dust." After Mom leaves, I see the beautiful muted pink dress.

"Soooo pretty, Poh Poh!" I lift the hem carefully because I'm afraid to ruin it somehow. "It's heavy," I say to Poh Poh and like when we play charades, I pretend I'm having trouble lifting the dress to show her. She nods and smiles at me.

"Try. Try." The smile Poh Poh has whenever she speaks to me is wider than usual. I can't believe she's the same person as the one in these glamourous wedding photos. I never thought of her as beautiful because she has slightly buck teeth and she wears funny clothes. But the skin on her face and hands is wrinkle free, not like some of the grandmothers I've met. And she might be older, but her hair is still mostly black.

"Oh, no, Poh Poh. Too small." It's an understatement. Poh Poh must have been tinier than she is now to fit into this. She hands me the dress and goes back to her folding. I carefully hold out the hanger in front of me. The dress is like a piece of artwork.

"The beads and sequins are hand sewn. Do you see the dragon and phoenix wrapped around the right side?" Mom is standing at the door staring at the dress.

"Yeah, I see."

"The phoenix represents the female, and the dragon represents the male. They're the two most powerful creatures and when they marry, they're invincible in all ways. At least that's the hope."

"It's so small. You told me Poh Poh was fat when she was younger." Mom speaks to Poh Poh and they both end up laughing.

"She *was* fat when she was young. She has no idea why because they were poor and had no food. When she quit school and went to Hong Kong, she eventually got a job that required she run back and forth the length of this room while holding her arms above her head. She was also too short to reach the machine, so she had to climb onto a chair at each end." Mom is laughing as she explains. "After three months, she was half the size she used to be."

I'm not sure if it's the image of a bigger Poh Poh doing what Mom described, or just Mom's laughing that makes me giggle.

"I thought red was the lucky Chinese colour. Why isn't Poh Poh's dress red? Like yours was."

"Most wedding *cheong sams* are." Mom shrugs and asks. "Poh Poh said they can be any shade of red, but hers was on sale because the bride who ordered it changed her mind and ordered another one."

"Figures. She got it because it was on sale?" I laugh.

"She didn't pay for it. Goung Goung's aunt bought it as one of her wedding gifts."

"Oh. It's a gorgeous dress and it fit her like a glove. The black and white photos made Goung Goung and Poh Poh look so classy, sophisticated. It's so different than what they are now."

"Real nice, Zoe."

"I'm not trying to be mean, but have you ever seen them like this other than in these photos?" I open the wedding album to the first page. Mom tilts her head and purses her lips as if considering it. I lay the dress down on the bed before returning to the album. Poh Poh slips the dress back into the bag and folds it over the pink chair.

As I return the album to the box, I notice a few loose passport-sized photos with serrated edges inside. I pick up the pile and look at the first one. A chunky girl with two pigtails stares back at me. She wears a Chinese top with a high neck.

"Who is this?" I hold it for Mom to see. She squints and walks over.

"That's Poh Poh! I told you she was fat." Mom laughs and then adds, "Your Goung Goung always says it looks like she was hiding a mattress on her back in this photo." I laugh.

"And you think I'm mean? She was so young."

"She was in her teens, I think." Mom shows Poh Poh the photo who laughs at the sight of it. "She was just starting nursing school then." Mom places the photo on the table.

She picks up the next one I set down. In it, a thin Poh Poh wears a dress or skirt that falls above the knee and a short matching jacket. It reminds me of a Coco Chanel outfit. I wrote a paper on Coco Chanel when we studied famous women from the twentieth century.

The outfit Poh Poh is wearing is a dusty blue. She's holding a small, matching rectangular clutch and she's casual, elegant, and professional all at once.

Mom studies it before speaking to Poh Poh non-stop for a bit. I wish I understood them. "This photo was taken in Hong Kong. It was one of the photos she sent to Goung Goung and his family before they got engaged."

"Where's the outfit? And why don't you ever wear colours like this, Mom?"

"No idea."

"She was so young and fashionable. Even her haircut was stylish." In the photo, Poh Poh's hair is cut just below the ears and pinned on one side. There's a slight wave too. "Why can't we go to a regular hairdresser to get fashionable haircuts like this?"

"Well, now she cuts her own hair and gets Goung Goung to help her trim the ends. Besides, your idea of a regular hairdresser would cost seven times what we pay in Chinatown for the same haircut."

"It's not the same haircut. They're better."

"How? They just charge you more because they're located in a pricey neighbourhood."

"Madison and Hailey's haircuts are always nice. They get their scalps massaged, hot chocolate, fancy coffee and if they want, those big cookies."

"Please. They barely trim their hair. I'll buy you a bag full of cookies and hot chocolate for half the cost of their haircuts. Consider yourself lucky. I was in grade eight before I got my first haircut outside the house. I stopped cutting your hair at home when you were two years old."

I know it's a hopeless argument. I go through the last of the small photos in my hand. "She's so young here, too. More casual but hip." In this one, grandmother has a bob cut with a hairband,

and she's wearing a white sleeveless blouse. Mom takes it from me and shows it to Poh Poh.

"She says it was taken just before she left Hong Kong. She needed it for immigration."

I pick up the last photo. It's in colour. "Is that your little aunt?"

"Yes, that's Aunt Jung Sum with my Poh Poh Su Ling, your great-grandmother. And in the bed is my paternal great-grandfather, Bak Lai, your great-great-grandfather."

"Why did they take a photo in the hospital? Were they in Hong Kong or China?"

"That was in San Francisco." Mom turns around and speaks with Poh Poh.

"San Francisco? What was he doing there?"

"He lived in San Francisco most of his life. Poh Poh says that was the first and last time anyone from their family met or saw him. My father, his only son," Mom is now pointing to the old man in the photo wearing the blue hospital gown, "never met him. Only went to his funeral."

"He never met his *own* son? Why didn't he just go with your mother and sister on *this* trip?" I wave the photo about with such force, it slips out of my fingers and falls to the floor.

Poh Poh is quick. She picks up the photo and studies it intently.

"Poh Poh says it was before my grandfather arrived in Canada. He was stuck in China still. The application to Canada was apparently stalled." Mom shrugs and goes silent as Poh Poh speaks, occasionally pointing at the photo.

"Oh no. What's wrong with Poh Poh?" I quickly wind some of the toilet paper sitting on the table onto my hand and give it to Poh Poh to wipe her tears. "It's okay, Poh Poh. Don't cry." I don't know what to do to make her stop. I've never seen her upset like this.

"Poh Poh is just saying maybe she should have invited her grandfather to her wedding or spent the money to visit him when he was alive. Goung Goung asked her to go a few times, but she always said it was too expensive. Told me not to wait to do things or to save my money all the time."

"See! Even Poh Poh thinks you're cheap and save too much. This is a woman who cuts her own hair and sews her own underwear."

Mom snorts and translates to Poh Poh whose tears turn into laughter as she pats me on the arm. "Seeemmart," she says as she taps my head before handing me the photo and returning to her folding. For once I was thankful for the way Mom and Poh Poh brush over their emotions. I didn't like seeing my grandmother upset.

I take one of the red-orange albums over to Poh Poh and sit beside her folded clothes. Mom follows me. I open the album and young versions of Poh Poh greet me again. She is surrounded by people I don't recognize and she has a bouffant hairdo and wears dresses in all the black and white photos on the first two pages. It's so weird, since I've never seen Poh Poh in a dress or skirt in person.

"So, where were these taken? Who is everybody?"

"She says some were from right before or right after she came to Canada. A lot of them were taken near the airports in Hong Kong and Toronto. She's not sure who was going or coming. Most of the people are distant relatives and you can probably recognize my Aunt Jung and Uncle Yaing Gong." Mom smiles as her eyes scan the photos.

"So, what happened to all these outfits in the photos?"

"She's no idea where they are now. Probably thrown out. I've not seen any of those except for the coat she has on in that one." Mom points.

"She has this coat?" Neither of them answers me, but Poh Poh looks over at the photo and stops her folding. She goes to the closet and starts digging. Eventually she brings out another dry-cleaning bag. I can't see inside it, but I know it's heavy from the way she carries it with two arms. She goes through the useless ritual of slapping the dust off over the little waste basket before laying it over the back of the chair, on top of her wedding *cheong sam*. She pulls it out.

I see the most beautiful vintage tan-coloured woman's coat. It has two large brown buttons. I can't help but to take it from her and put it on. The sleeves leave most of my forearms uncovered and the length falls just above my knees. It's heavy but there's a removable inner layer attached with buttons, not zippers. I adore it.

"Niceee. Niceee."

Poh Poh unpins the removable plush faux fur collar attached to the hanger. She motions for me to try it on and helps me do up the top button and clip on the collar. The soft fur brushes my chin. When Poh Poh's done she stands beside me, and we both stare at my image in the mirror.

"I remember your grandmother showing me the coat when I was little. I've never seen her in it except for the photo, though," Mom says from the bed, before diving into the garbage bag of clothes she's dragged over.

"Why don't you wear it?"

"Because. I have a work coat."

"I know you have one, but this one is more feminine. Try it on."

"It's too small," she says, waving me off, still not paying much attention.

"Try it without the liner."

Mom sighs, knowing I'm going to keep pestering her if she doesn't try it on. With Poh Poh's help, I unclip the collar and take the coat off. I start unbuttoning the inner liner. I hold the coat out to Mom when I'm finished.

"Fine," she says as she pushes the bag aside and gets up. She slips the coat on.

"It looks so much better on you than me. Why?"

"It's probably because you removed the liner for me," Mom says.

"You look younger in it."

"Very funny. Are you practising your Chinese compliments?" she says, shaking her head as if giving up on me, but I see her smile. I was being nice, but does she ever *not* know how to accept a compliment. "Really. It's a good colour on you and the shorter length doesn't drag you down like your black dress coat."

I avoid her eyes and stare at the coat.

"It's not very warm without the liner but," she says as she turns left and then right in front of the mirror, "it might be fine for the fall."

I nod, surprised at her agreement. It's so rare these days. It's like we're always bickering about something. Dad makes fun of us. He says it's time for the "Mom and Zoe Show."

"It's such a waste your grandmother never wore it," Mom says aloud. She rambles something off to Poh Poh and they chat as Mom slips her hands into the pockets and models the coat one last time before removing it, covering it with the dry-cleaning bag and laying it over the wedding *cheong sam*. Mom returns to digging in the garbage bag and I return to the photos.

32

There are coloured photos of Mom and her siblings, but I find myself drawn to Poh Poh's images. Logically, I know she was once young, but knowing it and seeing it are very different. I want to find the point when she went from someone who was hip and fashionable to this woman who wears homemade sweaters and cardigans. I study Poh Poh who is half standing, half crouching over the low futon bed, folding clothes at a furious rate. The doctors may say she's sick, but her frenetic energy suggests otherwise.

In one of the photos, she joyfully holds up a struggling naked baby, smiling broadly, the way she does when she speaks to me. Her arms are strong, and she's wearing a sleeveless white top with a sailor's collar that I saw her wearing in another photo.

"Is the baby you, Mom? And any chance Poh Poh has this top lying around?" I point at the photo.

"No. That's your Aunt Vikki. She's the only one who ever

had a formal baby photo taken. Your grandfather's cousin took it. And Poh Poh says the top turned into a rag at some point."

"Poh Poh was pretty."

Mom laughs and says something to Poh Poh, which makes them both laugh. I point out another photo to Mom. Poh Poh sits ramrod straight with a little boy on her lap and a little girl standing by her. She's wearing a top with a colourful print and an oversized collar. Apparently, Poh Poh always wore every colour in the rainbow, like her favourite homemade sweater vest she's wearing now. It's also one of the few photos of her with long straight hair, like Mom's. This time it's held back by a hair band.

"What about this one?" I ask.

"That's your Aunt Vikki and Uncle Mark," Mom says. "It was before I was born."

"Poh Poh was so young."

"She'd be in her late twenties there."

In another photo, my grandmother is sitting on the stoop of a building with short curly hair. A huge-eyed baby is on her lap and a little girl holding a ball is standing next to her. Despite the stories about Mom growing up poor, Poh Poh seems relaxed and happy in the photo.

"Is this Aunt Vikki and Uncle Mark again?"

"No, that's me standing, and your Uncle Billy in Poh Poh's lap. We're sitting outside the restaurant your grandfather worked at when he first came to Canada. In North Bay. It was Goung Goung's uncle and aunt's restaurant. You see this one?" She points to a photo on the next page with Goung Goung in a restaurant uniform, his work clothes, holding on to Mom.

"You sure like your ball."

"It's an orange!"

"Oh …" I laugh.

"We must have moved to Toronto shortly after." Grandmother places a finger on the photo, seemingly lost in thought as she and Mom talk. It lasts for only a few seconds before she goes back to her folding and Mom to digging in the garbage bag.

I flip through the two smaller albums and find a ton of photos of my grandparents, Mom and her siblings, in or around the red brick house Mom's mentioned. Mom and her siblings appear with matching bowl cuts in several of them.

"What are you laughing at?" Mom asks as she pauses over her garbage bag.

"You and Uncle Mark look like twins here. Shaped the same and same bad bowl haircuts."

Mom looks at the photo and laughs. "Told you, home haircuts. And I was in grade 4 or 5 there."

"Poh Poh's starting to look more like she does now in these photos. Where are these taken?" She has her signature pixie cut in almost all the photos in which they stand posing in someone's living room. Poh Poh and Goung Goung don't seem to age, and they wear similar outfits and hairstyles in all of them, but Mom and her siblings have acne in some, are fatter in others, and they wear some weird clothes I don't like in a few.

"We were at my grandparents' home, Poh Poh's parents, in all of those photos," Mom tells me as she points.

"Didn't you take photos after this?"

"Yes, but we stopped putting them in albums. There are tons of loose ones somewhere around here. I think those albums ended when I was only halfway through high school."

"You think we can find the loose ones?"

"You can try. They're probably around here somewhere."

I move on to the framed photos on the dresser. There's one of Mom in her court gown with Poh Poh and Goung Goung. It must have been when she became a lawyer. There's a good one of her and grandmother from Mom and Dad's wedding.

In all the photos, no matter the era or occasion, Poh Poh is almost always the only one staring straight at the camera, calm, as if she's challenging whoever is taking the photo. It's like she's in control.

"Nice dress, Poh Poh." I point at the photo of her and Mom from the wedding. It may not have been the latest style of the day, but it suited her. Poh Poh looks over my shoulder.

"Yesss. Me." Poh Poh is nodding repeatedly and points to herself, as she says something to Mom who stops her digging in one of the garbage bags of clothes to come over.

"So, did your sister not fit Poh Poh's *cheong sam* either? Or did she get her own, like you?"

"I don't know if she fit it. She's smaller than me but she didn't wear one for her wedding. She only had a white wedding dress made."

"Didn't Poh Poh mind?"

Mom is surprised. "No. Of course not. I don't think so anyway. No one had to wear one."

"Then why did you?"

"I wanted to. I may have been born in North Bay, but I *am* Chinese. Besides, your Grandma Sophie wanted to plan the reception and ceremony. It made sense because it was in Burlington where they live, but I wanted Poh Poh to have some part of the day. Before I met your dad, Poh Poh was scared I might never marry and she'd be stuck with me," Mom laughs. "So, when Dad and I decided to marry, it was as much Poh Poh's celebration as mine. Besides we had fun, finding *cheong sams*, wedding party favours, and material for the veil."

"Which dress did you like better, Grandma Sophie's or the

cheong sam?"

"I liked both. I think Poh Poh was happier than me when Grandma Sophie offered her dress. It was like she accepted me. And I loved the classic A line from the sixties. I felt a bit like a princess in it. But when we were out shopping, Poh Poh asked if I wanted to look at *cheong sams*. I got the feeling she wanted me to say yes. When I tried on the one I eventually bought, I felt sexy, even though I was completely covered. It was probably because of the neckline and the long slit along the side of the skirt. Poh Poh was the one who picked it out and told me to stop trying on others."

It was the first time I'd ever heard Mom describing how any clothes made her feel. I wish she'd do it more.

"Hey, the framed red silk cloth hanging in our dining room with all the signatures of the guests who attended your wedding, was that Poh Poh's idea too?"

"Yeah, I had no idea about that custom. It has a phoenix and dragon at the top of the cloth and the double happiness character sits between them for good luck."

"It's always about luck for the Chinese, isn't it?"

"A lot of the time, it is. Poh Poh even told me to perform the tea ceremony with Dad's parents for good luck."

"What is the tea ceremony?"

"Technically, it's the *real* marriage ceremony for the Chinese. On the day of the wedding, the bride is supposed to serve some type of red tea to the parents of the groom. When the parents drink the tea, it's symbolic of their acceptance of me into the family and my respect to their family."

"Really? What's the ceremony?"

"I knelt on one knee when I presented a cup of tea to Grandpa Steve and then to Grandma Sophie. Once they drank it, it was a done deal according to Chinese customs. We were married."

"You don't need rings or any paperwork?"

"Well, in modern times you need the paperwork but it's just a ceremony like the white dress and the ring is for western countries. I think they gave each other rings for dowry and stuff back in the olden days."

"Dad performed the ceremony for your parents too?"

"Some people have both sides do it, but Poh Poh said it's more important for the bride to be accepted by the groom's family. Like everything else with the Chinese, it's very paternalistic. They don't believe men join the women's family, so it doesn't matter as much."

"I don't think that's fair."

"Lucky for you we live in a modern world where I can't get rid of you even if I marry you off."

"Ha, ha. Did Poh Poh perform the tea ceremony, too?"

"She said Goung Goung's aunt and uncle, the ones who owned the restaurant he worked at, were stand-ins for his parents. His mother died when he was young, and his father never left China so they weren't around for their wedding."

Poh Poh is rummaging in the closet again. She comes back with another dry-cleaning bag that appears newer than the others and lays it over the back of the chair on top of the other items. She reaches in and pulls out a silver two-piece *cheong sam*. It's the one she wore to Mom and Dad's wedding.

When I get close to it, I see it is imprinted with what seems to be a circular Chinese symbol, bamboo leaves and branches of white flora. The decorative fabric buttons starting at the underarm to the front of the neckline are fake. A zipper runs two thirds of the way down the back with a small silver snap button at the top.

"Poh Poh got it at the same place I got my wedding *cheong sam*. Some no name store in the Dragon City Mall, downtown Chinatown."

I feel the dress. "I can't believe how much thinner the material is than Poh Poh's."

"They're mass-produced prints instead of hand stitched now. It's also not silk."

"Try, try." Poh Poh slips the top off the hanger and holds it out to me. I don't know where I'd wear it, but Poh Poh is excited, so I comply. I quickly pull off my T-shirt and slip on the top. I contort to try and zip up the back. When I finally manage to get the zipper up most of the way, Poh Poh finishes the job, buttoning the little snap at the top. The neckline is snug like a turtleneck, but it fits.

"Ohhhhhh ... nicey," Poh Poh nods her head in approval.

"She's right, it does fit you well." Mom doesn't hide her surprise. "Poh Poh says you look darker with it on though."

"Why does she always want me to be pale, like a ghost?"

"She wants you to be fair, not pale. It's got something to do with peasants having to toil in the fields under the hot sun but the wealthy getting to hide inside or being able to afford hats and shielding their skin from sun damage. So, if you're fair, it means you're wealthy."

"But everyone wants a tan these days."

Mom shrugs in response.

Poh Poh stands a slight distance from me, admiring the top. She studies me before stepping closer, lightly framing my chin and the side of my face with her index finger and thumb. Her thumb begins to rub my cheek. She speaks and Mom laughs.

"She says even with a *gwai lo* for a father, you're only slightly fairer than me."

I shake my head at them. "But she says you're sturdy, like the Samoans in Hawaii."

"Is that a compliment or an insult?"

"With Poh Poh, probably both."

"Do you think she'll let me borrow this sometime?"

"It's a little too Chinese for you, isn't it?"

I'm not sure if I'm more surprised or embarrassed to hear Mom knows how I feel about being Chinese. Felt. I'm not sure now. I'm not ashamed of being Chinese exactly, but I don't like standing out.

"I could wear it to a dance or maybe, maybe … even graduation."

"You want to? Really? What about your friends and wearing the same colour?"

"I didn't say for sure. I just want to see what it's like. Besides it's silvery white. Maybe I can find a pair of white or cream pants to match. I bet none of the girls will be wearing pants. Then I can wear my white sneakers and my feet will be comfortable for the dance afterwards."

It is really Chinese, but I like the way it shows off my shape instead of the baggy shirts I always wear. I'm completely covered but it's still sexy. Like Mom felt in her wedding *cheong sam*.

"Oh, I didn't know you were only planning to wear the top," Mom says, considering the idea. "It's up to you. I know you have your eye on that other dress." Mom promptly switches to Cantonese. "Your grandmother says to keep it. Not like she's going to wear it anywhere."

"Are you sure, Poh Poh?"

"Yesssss. Take. Take." Poh Poh laughs.

"Your grandmother says it will help clean out her closet, which is exactly why she wanted us to come over. And she says where would she wear it to, to mop the floors or go to Chinatown to pick up greens on sale?"

"Thank you, Poh Poh." Grandmother unzips it for me as I take off the top and start to assemble it back on the hanger with the skirt, and then she rushes off to her dresser.

I wander over to Poh Poh when I'm done and continue to look at the framed photos on top of the dresser as she rummages through her underwear drawer. Eventually she comes over and hands me a gold chain, motioning me to put it on.

"What is this Poh Poh? Mom?"

Mom looks up from her garbage bag and comes over. A flurry of Cantonese chatter erupts between them while I examine the gold chain. It's a thick dark yellow colour and much heavier than the silver chain I sometimes wear. It's not as chunky as the gold chains I've seen on rap videos but it's bulkier than anything I'd pick out.

"Mom, what is it?"

"Poh Poh says it's just one of the gold chains she brought with her to Canada. She wanted to give it to you, but I told her to keep it for now because it's not like you can wear it to school."

"Don't forget it's not exactly my style either," I say grimacing.

"Again, real nice, Zoe."

"Come on, I'm kidding. But why is Poh Poh trying to give away all her stuff? Is there something you're not telling me?"

Mom looks like she might cry but then quickly follows up with, "No. No. It's just Poh Poh trying to clean up." She shakes her head and returns to her garbage bag and ties it up before rushing downstairs with it.

"Thank you, Poh Poh. You keep it for now," I say returning the chain and watching her drop it into a velvet pouch and bury it in the corner of her drawer. Poh Poh pats me and looks teary eyed as she shuts her drawer and returns to her sweaters on the bed. I know Mom's not telling me everything but it's not like I can ask Poh Poh. I flip open one of the albums to check if I'm right about something I noticed. Mom returns. "Mom, why does Poh Poh never touch or hug you?"

Mom shrugs and hurries over to the remaining garbage bag of clothes, pushing it toward the door.

"Poh Poh never touches you or your siblings or Goung Goung. It's kinda weird."

"It's just not what Chinese people do," Mom says shrugging as if that's an answer.

"Come to think of it, I don't hug her. Like with Grandma and Grandpa. And she's not like you and Dad. It's like she doesn't care."

"It's just the way the Chinese are."

"Has she ever hugged you?"

Mom stops at the door and thinks about it for a while. "Can't remember the last time she did."

"Not even on your graduation or wedding day?" Mom and I argue a lot these days, but I can't imagine her not hugging me at night.

"Poh Poh didn't hug us, but she protected us. She cares in her own way."

"That's sort of sad."

"It works for her." After a pause. "One time I saw her holding Goung Goung's hand."

"When?" I ask, not sure if I believe her.

"We were in Hawaii for your Aunt Vikki's wedding. Everyone went sightseeing one day but Poh Poh didn't want to go so she and Goung Goung hung out at the hotel. At the end of the day, when we drove by the mall connected to the hotel, we saw them walking over the bridge. And there Poh Poh was holding Goung Goung's hand, chomping on gum, and strolling back to the hotel. It was surprising and funny. We should see if we can find photos from that trip."

"It was the only time you saw them holding hands? Like in your entire life?"

"Well, one of the few times."

"You and Dad are always embarrassing me, but it'd be weird if you never touched each other or me, I think." I'm not sure if Mom laughs at my squeamishness about her and Dad's affection or Poh Poh's lack of it.

"She cares about us in her own way. She protects Goung Goung."

"What does she have to protect him from?"

"Made him quit smoking. Makes him eat his vegetables. Plus, she plies him with restorative soups. She even "convinced" him to trade in his restaurant jobs for a stable factory job with benefits."

"Oh," I say, still not sure if it replaces a hug.

"When we were growing up, I heard them talking to each other early in the morning or late at night. Sometimes they ended up arguing but it's just how they communicate. It's been working for them for years."

"You and Dad talk in bed too. But shouldn't they have more together? They don't even share a bedroom now."

"They're older. They're from a different time. They married for different reasons. Poh Poh's parents used to bicker like the dickens, too, but those few years alone after he died, were lonely for my grandmother."

"It's like Poh Poh and her mom never got to fall in love or be happy."

"It's a different sort of love. Statistics show arranged marriages usually work out better than couples who pick out their own mates. And Poh Poh was happier than she would have been, had she been stuck in China."

"Well, I don't want you or Dad to ever pick out anyone for me, thanks."

Mom grins. "Remember, photos just capture a moment in time. They never show the whole story." She speaks to Poh Poh as I flip through another one of the albums.

"Poh Poh says photos are often misleading. Some people are nothing like their photos. Especially these days with filters and Photoshop. Check her sitting photos. Don't you expect her to be taller than she is?"

"Very funny, Mom." I roll my eyes at her.

"No, I'm not kidding. Look at one of her sitting photos." I open the wedding album at a photo of Poh Poh sitting in front of Goung Goung who is crouching over her with his arm around her shoulders. Both are smiling brightly at the camera.

"Hmmm, maybe." I hate to admit she's right but if I didn't know Poh Poh, and I only saw the photo, I'd think she was taller than she is.

"So, if you can't tell how big someone is by their photo, do you really think you can tell much by whether she's touching or not touching someone? Looks can be deceiving."

"Why does she put her arm around me sometimes?"

"You're younger." She pauses. "And she doesn't live with you like she did with us and Goung Goung."

"So, is she going to stop doing it when I hit a certain age?"

"I don't know. If we're lucky we'll find out. She's different with you and your cousins. You're her grandchildren."

Mom rushes over to the closet to carry the last garbage bag

full of clothes down.

"You know, I think I want to wear one when I get married."

"What? What are you talking about?"

"A red or pink *cheong sam*. I think I want to wear one when I get married."

Mom stops pushing the bag. "You do?" She nods and says something to Poh Poh that makes them laugh, before responding. "Well, it's a long time away. Why don't we figure that out when the time comes?"

I notice the shoe boxes behind the garbage bag Mom just moved. The lid is off and there are envelopes filled with photos inside. Poh Poh insists we take them home to sort. We add it to the growing pile of items we're taking home.

When we finish helping Poh Poh return all the piles of clothes she folded back onto the shelf in the closet, we load up the car with the garbage bags for the charity bin, the box of loose photos, and the clothes we're keeping.

As I return to the house to say goodbye to Goung Goung who's been happily hiding out in the kitchen the whole time, Poh Poh rushes upstairs. I remember to go pray in front of the shrine but before I finish, Poh Poh comes back down and hands me a dusty dry-cleaning bag.

"Mom, why is she giving us her wedding *cheong sam*?"

"She says you can get it altered or maybe your daughter or daughter-in-law will want it one day."

Poh Poh flashes her usual smile at me and pats me on the shoulder. Before I think too much about it, I hug her. She steps back, perhaps surprised or perhaps startled by the force of my hug as she laughs.

"Thank you, Poh Poh."

As Mom pulls out of the driveway, Poh Poh and Goung

Goung stand on their porch waving at us.

"Glad you found something you liked," Mom says. She's concentrating on the road or maybe she's avoiding eye contact when I respond, "Me, too."

Secrets
Amy Wei Ping Lee

33

"We need to resuscitate her. We have a protocol," says the fireman who seems to be in charge. He's the bully in the school yard toying with us. I hate him.

"The nurse made a mistake. She shouldn't have called 9-1-1. She's been gone for more than twenty minutes. We signed the Do Not Resuscitate form." This is the one time my sister Vikki's abrasive, military-like tone fits the situation and doesn't make me wince.

"The form isn't signed off by a doctor. It's invalid. Hook her up," instructs the asshole fireman. I imagine my heel stomping into his smug face.

"You can't. You can't use the defibrillator on her," Vikki shouts.

The heavy footsteps on the stairs draw everyone's attention to the room door. Two police officers have arrived. One speaks to the nurse in the hallway while the other joins us in Mom's room where the six of us, my two older siblings, me and the three firemen stand surrounding the rented hospital bed where Mom lies. The officer in the room speaks to the asshole fireman and then starts shepherding us out.

My brother Mark, inspired by my sister's vibe, addresses the officer, "What do you mean I can't stay in here? I'm a criminal lawyer. This isn't a crime scene. You can't stop us from remaining with our mother."

Mark's body and waving hands are within inches of the officer's face. His voice gets louder and his gestures more aggressive as he continues to argue. The officer may be trying to bring some calm to the scene but it's having the opposite effect.

We can't have them activate the defibrillator, a device that violently sends electric shocks to her heart. What if Mom's ribs break from the chest compressions? What if they scar her? The body is supposed to remain untouched; the energy of the person doesn't exit immediately after breathing stops. We need to ensure she gets to her next life, whole, unbroken. She'll never forgive us otherwise. Her voice in my head is saying, *Whole lot of good having three lawyers does me.*

Everyone is shouting. The asshole fireman appears bemused by the commotion he's causing. His two colleagues appear apologetic and embarrassed.

"Look, we're just putting the nodes on but we're not going to do anything else until we hear from the coroner or until EMS arrives, okay?" The non-asshole fireman holds up his hands to show us the nodes as he slowly starts placing the stickers on Mom's bare chest. He respectfully pulls the two sides of her shirt back into place to cover her up when he's done. The policeman turns his head slightly while keeping an eye on Mark and gives the non-asshole fireman a grateful look of thanks before facing us again.

"They won't do anything else yet. Please just step out of the room while we wait." He, too, holds the palms of his hands open to show they're empty but his eyes seem to be assessing whether Mark will resist. We may all be shorter than the men standing around us, but we're unstable—upset and angry.

Vikki suddenly tells us to leave as she stomps out and charges at the nurse, pointing her finger.

"I told you not to call 9-1-1. Fix this. Sign this form or get your supervisor to do it now."

The nurse pulls her phone out. The expression on her face clearly shows she's mortified for compounding an already desperately wretched scene and starts dialling a number on her cell phone.

Mark and I follow Vikki's cue and step out of the room. Standing on the outside of the bedroom entrance while the officer stands on the other side facing him, my brother continues to loudly explain why the officer has no right to do what he's doing. I stand behind him, peering in on Mom.

"She's our mother. We just need to be in the room with her." I hope by not quite shouting, I can reason with the officer, appeal to his sense of compassion, and get us back into the room. No luck. I back away from the bedroom door and stand at the top of the steps with Dad. He looks lost as the chaos swirls around him.

From downstairs come the sniffling sounds of the uncles, the uncontrollable sobbing of Aunt Jung, and the indignant loud Chinese translations about what's happening from my cousin, Mom's favourite niece.

What seems like hours, but is likely fifteen minutes, passes before the EMS team finally arrives. Their presence eases the shouting or perhaps everyone just tires out. Mom is officially declared gone, the unused nodes are removed, and the 9-1-1 entourage slowly leaves. Our relatives start to file out as well. Eventually it's just Dad, my siblings and me left. With the commotion gone, the reality of Mom's absence sinks in. She's gone.

I hate it. I prefer the bedlam to this chilling, odd silence covering us. I feel heavy. Something's stuck in my throat. The windows are open, the air is still humid and warm, but I shiver. I don't want to stare at a hospital bed and Mom not moving anymore. I just want this awful emptiness to leave me.

We pace and sit and wait for whoever picks up and stores bodies awaiting burial. Hours later, when the dark hearse-like car arrives, I almost cry out to stop Mark and the driver from loading her into the transport vehicle. My insides are hollowed out as I pass the now empty hospital bed. I instantly regret not sitting with her body longer.

I convince myself it'll be better once I get away from the house. I gather my bag to leave, certain I'm in no state to be driving. My body feels like it's floating, but on the outside I'm quiet.

"Keep the outside lights on until morning. We're all supposed to do it Mom said," I remind Dad and my younger brother in a loudish voice, so my older siblings hear. I know letting them know these were Mom's instructions from my grandparents' funerals, is the only way they might listen to what I say since I'm just a little sister. I want to make sure if Mom or her energy wants to visit any of us before she moves on to her next life, she can find her way.

It's after two-thirty in the morning when I get home. I take a hot shower and even wash my hair despite how late it is, hoping to scrub away the empty feeling clinging to my body. It doesn't work. I blow-dry my hair and it wakes me even though I want to collapse. I walk down the stairs in the dark to make sure the outside light is on for the third time since I got home. I set the alarm before returning to my office upstairs to send an email to my in-laws and a handful of close friends, as if writing the news will somehow make it better.

> From: Amy Lee amy@leelaw.info
> To: Amy Lee amy@leelaw.info
> Sent: July 31, 2012 4:28 AM
> Subject: Mom
>
> Just letting you know that Mom died a few hours ago. Will send details about the funeral soon. Thanks.
>
> Amy
>
> Amy Lee
> Barrister and Solicitor

It isn't better.

I finally get back to our bedroom where Andy is snoring, and I lift the bed sheet on my side of the bed to find Zoe lying next to him.

I stumble across the hall to Zoe's room and crawl into her bed. I'm unsure how long I lie there whimpering before falling into a restless sleep.

34

I realize that while I know some of the Buddhist funeral customs, I was never formally taught what the practices mean or why they're completed. I regret not asking Mom to explain more but it was taboo to speak of death. So, I search online and find a good article by the BBC.

> *Buddhists believe that human beings are born and reborn an infinite number of times, Samsara, until they achieve enlightenment, Nirvana. Through good actions, such as ethical conduct, and by developing concentration and wisdom, Buddhists hope to gain enlightenment or ensure a better future for themselves. These good actions are set out in the Eightfold Path, which includes right speech, right livelihood, and right concentration. Good actions will result in a better rebirth, while bad actions will have the opposite effect. Depending on the actions performed in previous lives,*

rebirth could be as a human, animal, ghosts, demi-gods, or gods. Being born as a human is seen by Buddhists as a rare opportunity to work toward escaping the cycle of Samsara and reaching Nirvana.

Knowing this is the goal, I gain a new perspective on the snippets of information I gathered from practices we took part in over the years. For the first time, I feel grateful for the time I found myself unexpectedly single in my late twenties, after the pressures of school were finished but before I met Andy, because Mom and I spent so much time together. Almost like friends.

Mom's been gone for twelve hours by the time my older siblings and I return to her house to start arrangements for the funeral service. Even though there are five of us, it's oddly quiet. We're relieved to learn from Uncle Yaing Gong that most of the funeral homes have employees who run the Buddhist services, and they will give us an official list of what we need to provide. Even though Yaing Gong arranged the funeral services for our great-grandmother and grandparents, Mom's sisters and sister-in-law seem to know way more about the Buddhist religious customs and ceremonies practised. Between the internet and the aunts, we gather items in preparation for the service before officially visiting the funeral home to get the checklist.

***

"We need to find something appropriate for her to be dressed in for the service. Let's find something now," my sister says as she walks upstairs to Mom's room. I follow as I recollect a conversation from years earlier.

I had just returned from some hearing, and I was changing out of my suit. Zoe was off at preschool. Mom wandered into my room because she had nothing to do, after prepping our dinner and cleaning whatever she deemed dirty.

"You shouldn't wear this anymore. It's all worn out." She was examining the frayed edges of the blazer I'd just taken off and thrown on the bed.

"Fits me better than any of the other black ones I have. I need a new one."

"What about this one?" She was in my closet, pulling at the sleeve of a hardly worn Calvin Klein blazer of a similar length.

"I don't like the way that one fits. Too boxy or something."

"I don't have even one decent blazer to wear to special occasions." Mom fussed with the blazer and pulled it out.

Feeling a pang of guilt for purchasing a jacket that I didn't even like, I urged her to try it on. She did that thing where she pretended to refuse as if she wasn't worthy. I took the blazer from her, removed the hanger, and held it out. Apparently, she'd made a sufficient show of refusal and finally slipped it on. I looked at her.

"Mom, take off your apron." She laughed, while she struggled out of the blazer, undid the apron and put the blazer back on. "It fits you well! Take it."

"How much was it?"

"Don't worry about it. Take it. I don't wear it. Do you need a pair of dress pants, too? I've too many dark ones."

"No, I won't fit your pants, but I need a good jacket to wear. You sure you don't want it? How much was it?" She was inspecting herself in front of the closet mirror, turning from one side to the other.

"Yes. Just take it."

"When the time comes, you can bury me in this and a pair of my dressy slacks."

"Mom!"

It was so unlike her to make a reference to death, especially her own, so casually, because she usually hushed any such talk.

I walk past my sister, reach into Mom's closet, and pull out the black blazer and her favourite pair of dress pants.

"Mom told me she wants to be buried in this."

"She did?" My sister's eyes open wide, unable to mask her surprise as I repeat the conversation with Mom.

***

"We need blankets for the casket. The aunts said we can get them from Chinatown," my sister says as we return to the dining table with Mom's outfit.

As my older siblings and Dad discuss when they can pick those up along with incense and paper money, I recall Poh Poh Su Ling's funeral preparations.

I had taken Mom to our Chinatown in the east end of the city. "Ours" because it was a short streetcar ride, or a twenty-minute walk if we were trying to save the transit fare, from the old red brick house we grew up in. Even though we now each lived in different homes and could drive to the larger and fancier Chinatowns in Markham or downtown, Mom always preferred the familiar stores and shopkeepers in the east end.

That day, Mom directed us to East Chinatown Gifts, one of the many cramped retail stores along that two-block strip. It seemed to sell everything from cold drinks and keychains to Buddhist shrines and funeral necessities. This store was conveniently located next to the one where Mom liked to pick up fresh vegetables, noodles, dried goods, and other Chinese specialties. As I parked in front of the stores, Mom relayed the plan to get the funeral goods first before we picked up the vegetables. She insisted I put no more than a dollar in the parking meter.

"We need to get some paper money to burn for the funeral," she said aloud without looking at me as we entered the first store.

I knew it wasn't for my benefit.

The woman manning the cash register heard and pointed to the nearest aisle. "Funeral money is down there." She spoke in an efficient, bordering on angry tone, which to anyone who is unfamiliar with the language, would have sounded rude.

"And blankets for the casket?" Mom asked as we walked by shelves of DVDS, two refrigerators with drinks for sale, and various glass charms.

The clerk pointed to the furthest aisle as she barked, "Over there. In the corner. Near the back. All sorts." There was no one else in the store but the clerk made no move to be any more helpful.

The first aisle held calendars, a host of ceramic and brass talismans of varying sizes, and red pieces of paper also of different sizes bearing fortuitous sayings. Mom reached the middle of the aisle and stopped in front of thick stacks of newsprint quality paper, bound together with elastics. The colourful bundles covered in Chinese characters reminded me of cheap board game money.

"Poh Poh will need lots of money, but your uncles and aunts will bring some too."

"What are these paper houses and clothes?" I assessed an elaborate cellophane-wrapped package.

"Some people burn those so the relative will have a place to live in the next life. There are paper clothes and jewels, too."

"Should we buy some?"

"Five dollars per home. Too expensive! If she has money, she can buy her own home and clothes. Leave it. Let's pick up the blanket." She gathered a few stacks of paper money of varying currencies and marched on.

I followed her to the far corner of the store passing small wooden shrines, large colourful porcelain, glass, and red wood

Buddhas, sitting on shelves gathering dust.

"These are just pieces of silk cloth. The edges aren't even well-hemmed. I can do much better." I looked over at Mom leafing through the death blankets. "Fifty dollars!"

"You want to make one? Now? Do you have material?" I asked.

"We have to get one for our family. If I had more time, I'd get the material and sew one myself. These are such a scam."

"The service is in a few days. We should just get it." I was thankful we didn't have to search for more.

We picked out Mom's favourite colour, a shimmering burgundy. The only reason she passed on the fancier one with a printed design of a hooked cross, like a backward swastika, is because it cost sixty dollars.

Months later, Mom and I found ourselves at Walmart.

"Twin sets for fifteen dollars. You get a fitted sheet, a flat sheet, and a pillowcase. What a good deal. Feel this one. Someone opened it up." Mom busily inspected the quality of the material between her fingers and opened the sheet.

"You know, instead of buying those expensive blankets for funerals from the stores in Chinatown, when I die buy a few sets of these."

I stopped my search for neutral colours and looked at her questioningly, certain I misheard or misunderstood.

"The material is thicker than the one we bought for my mother. A fraction of the cost and you get much more. More worth it than those silk sheets, plus you get to keep the fitted sheets and pillowcases. What a deal."

"What are you talking about that for?"

"Just telling you what to do when I die."

"But a bed is a lot wider than a casket. Do we fold it?"

"No, no. So stupid. Get it hemmed."

"Whatever you want, Mom. Did you find the colours you want for your beds yet?"

I never thought much of the whole thing until now.

"Mom didn't want those Chinatown blankets. She said they're overpriced. She told me to go to Walmart and get twin bed sets, one colour for each married child, cut the flat sheet in half, and have it hemmed. I'll deal with it."

They stop chattering because they know it's something Mom would say.

***

Choosing a suitable photo of Mom to sit by the casket is the only other item we can gather before visiting the funeral parlour. There are so many. A passport-sized photo my sister finds tucked in the box with Mom and Dad's wedding album is one option. An actual photo from Mom's wedding is another option but I quickly object to marrying such a happy occasion to this sad one. Intuitively, it seems wrong. As we search through albums and envelopes full of photos, we recall the holidays and events when they were taken, occasionally eliciting a chuckle or a story about Mom. After a bit, a photo falls out of the pile I'm searching. I scoop it up.

In it, Mom sits at her kitchen table, in her favourite home-made button-down multi-coloured sweater vest, and I know exactly what she was doing.

It was a Sunday evening. She was putting together the time sheets from the knitting factory, pasting on the little slips of paper to indicate how many pieces she'd finished that week to tally how much she earned on top of her base pay. Her cheeks are rosy, and her hair looks freshly washed. She's smiling, content, and her eyes pierce right through me. I know it's the photo.

My siblings aren't sure. They like the passport one as well. They decide to bring both in to enlarge, intending to make a final decision after it's done.

The next day Dad tells me, "The passport photo was too small to enlarge. We're using the photo you found. Your brother got copies framed for everyone to keep."

I look at Dad, clearly confused.

"There was a deal at Costco."

"Ohhhh," I nod, understanding.

35

I like to believe Mom and I were friends. She helped me decorate my first run-down little office above the pizza store and put the ad in the Chinese newspaper. She even sat in the car with me that whole year when I practised driving on my G1 licence.

One time, when I was trying to park, I was concentrating so hard on what was happening on my left side as I held out my right arm to the passenger seat, I didn't realize my hand was on her face. She was afraid to break my concentration, so she sat there quietly as I patted her face. When I finally realized what I was doing, we laughed so hard we teared, completely missing my sister who drove by in her car.

We complained to each other about the offensive behaviour of my sister who didn't ask, but demanded or expected assistance from either of us, the cheapness of Aunt Jung Sum and the haphazard overspending habits of my brothers and Dad.

We rarely argued so I assumed it meant we got along. At least it's what I believed until our first family dinner without her.

It was at Mark's home less than a week after the service. Family dinners were always at his or Vikki's place since neither of them thought mine or our parent's home were suitable. Now that they were highfalutin lawyers. As usual, the main conversation was between my older siblings and, occasionally, their spouses. What anyone else had to say was of little interest or importance and, as usual, I paid minimal attention until I heard Vikki issue an order.

"We need to combine their bank accounts and put our names on everything, including the house, in case anything happens to Dad. I've already called the bank to arrange it. They just need signatures. Each of you needs to go in to sign off."

For a few reasons, Dad, who was sitting at the table, was not part of this conversation. First, it was in English. Second, Mom was so dominant in their relationship, Dad became happily oblivious to many of their financial decisions. Despite their arrangement, I didn't believe any of us, as his children, had the same rights as Mom to assume decision-making powers without at least consulting with him.

"But Dad said there's already one of our names on each of the accounts. No need for anymore."

"Mom wanted it this way. Told me to take care of things." Vikki glowers at me clearly offended that I dared to challenge her.

"She told *all* of us to take care of things. She never said anything about accounts. And she also said Dad's still here. Why don't we just ask him? It's his decision."

She flushes, glares at me, livid, when I insist Dad needs to decide, not her. "Fine," she says.

I knew that "fine." She was not discussing anything with anyone. Especially not in front of our spouses, even though we'd all undoubtedly vent to our respective partners later. Fury oozed off her as she walked away from the dinner table. My older brother showed his allegiance immediately shooting me a look of disapproval as he advised aloud that what my sister said would be done—end of discussion. As if there had been one.

It was as if Mom's absence knocked down a dam holding back years of tension, competition, and resentment between my sister and me.

I had violated numerous unspoken household rules drilled into us as children. Revere the family above all else, don't share negative family incidents with outsiders, which includes spouses, and do not cause disorder or show disrespect to your elders, including older siblings—they're in charge.

I didn't know which was worse, the silent treatment that eventually followed which made me feel that I'd lost not only Mom but half my family, or the detailed emails listing everything they (and more importantly Mom) believed I'd done wrong.

Perhaps if emails didn't exist, fewer harsh words would have been exchanged because it takes a lot more courage and effort to confront someone in person or by phone, or to write a letter, than to send an email. Emails are instantaneous, leaving no time for reflection, and they cocoon the sender from seeing the impact of their actions.

***

At first, I tried to dismiss their emails and actions as their way of grieving. But what little empathy I managed to scrounge up dissipated as emails flew into my inbox dredging up every fault and insecurity I've had since childhood. When I gathered the nerve to read and, on the odd occasion, respond by explaining my side of things, the backlash was quick, harsh, and designed to shame me into agreement and compliance.

The exchanges eventually disintegrated into so much profanity they automatically hit my junk mail. These were easier to take than the emails embellishing and twisting facts until it was unclear where Mom's opinion ended, and their anger began. The underlying points driven home were: Mom thought I was an awful, disgraceful daughter and I had no right to oppose their decisions in any way. They were Mom's confidantes, not me.

The interactions hollowed me like when I was a teenager and got caught sneaking out to spend the night with a boyfriend. Mom lectured me but, of course, my sister chimed in. Each day I woke to the feeling of shame, wishing to somehow take it back, fix it, hoping the horrid feeling overtaking my body might go away.

Mom moved on within a day of such an incident, but my sister would ice me out. Communication was minimal until she decided enough time passed and I'd learned my lesson. Or until she got bored or needed something. Then we'd go on like nothing happened and it'd be done. I never saw it as bullying because I was in the wrong. This time, I wasn't sure.

***

After one of these colourful exchanges, I stand in my dining room staring at the framed photo of Mom, the same one we placed by her casket a few months earlier. I hold the plates I'm supposed to be setting on the table. I recall some of Mom's last words to me as she floated in and out of clarity:

Don't be upset with me for what I've said over the last few days. I've been delusional and feverish. I didn't mean any of it.

And in my mind, I respond:

What didn't you mean exactly, Mom? You didn't mean to complain about everyone behind their backs? You didn't mean to show us how to seize control without listening? Even if you were right, it was the wrong way to do it. You've let them do this to me and you left me alone to clean up your mess. I do hold it against you. It's your fault and you can't even fix it. You did this.

Andy and Zoe are buzzing around our dated eighties kitchen with the checkered tiles and chipped glass cupboard doors, preparing for dinner, but I feel very much alone. I am numb as my mind cycles through their accusations, self-doubt swirling.

Did Mom really think this of me? Was I a disloyal daughter? They're my siblings. My family. The people I grew up with. Why would they say these things if they weren't true? Are they right? But Mom criticized all of us behind our backs. It's how she vented, and in her mind, kept peace in the family. How could they not know her at all?

Tears flood out. My nose drips. Andy is beside me saying something, but I don't know what. I'm gasping for air. I see Zoe crying by the door leading into the dining room, watching me, afraid to come close. I can't help her. I can't stop. I feel myself fragmenting.

I stare at Mom's photo feeling completely lost until I have no idea how much time has passed. I hear Mom's voice in my head. Gradually, a strange calming sensation washes over me.

Don't cry. Everything will be fine. You know. You know.

Part of me wants to believe she's speaking to me from beyond. A part of me knows these words are lodged in my memory from when I was pregnant, and the second trimester ultrasound suggested a potential birth defect. Whether she believed it or not, her words and her support were unwavering.

You know. You know.

And then I realize, I do know. Of course, I'm thrifty. This isn't news to me. Mom said as much to my face. After all, I learned it from her. As did my sister, despite her attempts to hide or deny it.

I straighten my shoulders, close my eyes, and furiously wipe away the mess on my face with the back of my hands.

I know.

Despite how much I want the awful accusations and this fighting to stop, to say or do whatever they want to have them accept me again, I know I won't. I can't. For the first time, I see Mom's powerful, overbearing strength, as a weakness. She wasn't always right.

I'm finally aware Andy's arms are wrapped protectively around my shoulders. I push him toward Zoe, to help her, and force my breathing to return to normal as I walk to the kitchen to wash my face.

I am broken but I feel oddly empowered because I know the truth. The problem is I'm unsure what to do next and feel completely lost.

36

I arrive at Dad's the next morning to drop off groceries. It's been close to a year, but I can't get used to it not being Mom's place anymore. I haven't been able to take her name off my phone contact yet, so whenever Dad or my younger brother calls, her name pops up and for a split second, I think it's her.

Dad knows I'm still at odds with my siblings but he's unsure of the details. All our visits lead to some discussion of the situation.

"I just wanted them to do what you want. She's not Mom. They're not Mom. They should stop pretending they're following her wishes."

"Your brother and I are fine. It's okay. It would make me happy if you would just get along."

"Dad, we haven't gotten along for years. This was just the latest reason to argue." He sighs and sinks a bit in his chair. I wasn't going to tell him what he wanted to hear just to make him "pretend" happy like Mom did with all of us. But I don't want to upset him either, so I change the topic. "Let's go see what we can clean out from Mom's room."

We head upstairs. The morning sun streams in from the three large windows overlooking the front of the house. Dad has rearranged the furniture. I grab the garbage bag he has partially pulled out from the closet. I check inside and find it filled mostly with Mom's homemade sweaters and some very dated and yellowed collared dress shirts.

"Thought Zoe and I took all of these to the charity bin when Mom was around?

"You know your mom. She cleaned out more closets and threw in some of her crazy sweaters before she got the operation. Will you take this bag with you?"

"Sure. Are you going to clean out the rest of Mom's clothes?"

"Not yet." He opens the top drawer to peek inside and touch her clothes. "We don't need the space."

"You sure? Not like she'll need any of this now." I open the drawer closest to me. Underwear. Some of it is mended, some she's made herself. I pick them up and show Dad. He laughs.

I dig around and find a package of underwear I bought her a while back. It's unopened. As I start to dig further, I feel something odd. I pull out a velvet jewellery pouch I've never seen before. I pull open the draw strings and dump the contents into my hand.

"Hey, this was the gold chain Mom wanted to give Zoe a while ago. What's it doing here?"

Dad holds out his hand for the chain, curious at the find. "Chinese gold," he says as he examines it like a jeweller.

I return to the drawer and start to remove the underwear. I pull the drawer out further, and a chill travels along my spine at what I see. A small wooden box and a velvet pouch sit tucked in the corner on top of a regular business-sized envelope.

"What is this?"

I take it all out. The box fits on the palm of my hand. One, two three … eight. Octagon shaped. It's a reddish-brown colour. The smooth surface reveals the hours of sanding that led to its perfection.

The double happiness character is neatly carved on the top. It's one of the few Chinese characters I recognize because it's etched on the red wedding cloth hanging in our dining room.

I bring the box up close to my face and see detailed etchings cover the surface. "It's the dragon and phoenix," I whisper aloud but Dad doesn't seem to hear me. The dragon's body and tail swirl around the perimeter on one side while the phoenix does the same on the other side. The tails of each animal intertwine, and the heads meet. It's the most ornate jewellery box I've ever seen. And holding it, I feel an energy the way one senses the power of nature standing next to the ocean or the history one feels strolling along a cobblestone street in France.

"Have you seen this before Dad?" I suspect he hasn't because what little jewellery he and Mom owned used to be kept in a broken music box in an old suitcase. Even the colourful glass costume jewellery Mom once purchased from a street vendor almost every day for two weeks on the way home from work, was kept there.

"No. What is it? I need my glasses."

I lead him back to the hot pink chair in front of the restaurant pedestal table and hand him the box. Instinctively, I continue to support his hand as if it's heavy. As he examines it, I rush downstairs to fetch his glasses.

It's a shame no one has ever eaten a meal at the dining table. Mom's favourite crystal fruit bowl, a gift from one of her few close friends, has always sat in the center. It occasionally holds real fruit as well as message pads, paper clips, old batteries and other odds and ends. Today, it holds Dad's glasses. Unsure which pair he needs, I grab all three and run back upstairs.

I find Dad gently trying to twist the box like a jar to open it. It's always so odd to watch him handle delicate objects with his thick, factory worker hands. It's as if he's afraid the least amount of pressure might cause whatever he touches to disintegrate. I hand him all three pairs of glasses and take the box from him, eager to further inspect it myself.

If nothing else, the slightly uneven mitered corners give away the fact it is handmade. Dad has a pair of glasses on now and I hold the box by the bottom as he takes his time to scrutinize it.

"Double happiness." He points to the top. I fear he may be jealous. "Box is quite beautiful." He doesn't seem to care how it came to be hidden in Mom's underwear drawer.

I gently pull at the top, afraid to use too much pressure. After some jiggling the top comes off. I'm relieved to see no splintered wood or snapped hinges. Everything inside is lined in rich burgundy velvet. I gasp audibly at what sits nestled in the centre.

"Whose rings are these? Thought they took all the jewellery to one of their homes."

"Your siblings said it was safer because we had nurses coming to the house so often. Wasn't much anyway."

"I don't care about what they have, Dad. But what are these?"

"Didn't even know she had this box," he says.

I pluck out the more feminine of the two rings. A green jade stone, shaped like a leaf but with two pointed ends, is the centrepiece. When the ring is worn, the stone runs along the length of the finger. The gold holding the stone in place is shaped into tulip petals. Three on both ends. It exudes strength. Like Mom did.

Meanwhile, Dad tries unsuccessfully to wriggle the other ring out of the soft velvet nest. His thick fingers fumble with it. I put the ring I'm holding on the table so I can help him. I'm anxious to examine it as well, but I place it in Dad's palm.

I peer over Dad's arm. It is clearly a man's ring. The heavy, wide band is the same yellow gold as the other one. It holds a rectangle-shaped dark green jade stone. When worn, the stone is perpendicular to the finger. It too is held in place by eight prominent gold prongs shaped like claws.

"This a good quality jade. Yellow gold, too. Don't see much of it in Canada."

I reach out. Dad places the ring in my hand ever so gently and then picks up the other. I try on the man's ring. It rolls loosely around on my ring finger. I slip it on my thumb. Still too loose. As I remove it, the sunlight catches the ring and I notice markings on the inside of the band. I squint and make out two eternity signs.

I put it back into the box and check the other ring which Dad has returned. It's harder to see inside the much narrower band but sure enough, I find two eternity signs. The ring slips from my finger making a loud noise as it lands on the Formica table. Dad recovers it.

"Sorry." I'm not sure for what I'm apologizing. "Let me put it back in the box."

As I insert both rings into the velvet lining, I notice the liner has become a bit disheveled from our pawing at it. I start to tuck the corner back in but instead of unfinished wood, I see a hint of yellowish white in the back. I pull up the velvet.

"What is this?" I take out a very small black and white photo with serrated edges. An Asian man with large double lid eyes stares back at me. "Who is this?"

"Let me see," Dad says. I'm unsure how he'll react, but after hesitating a bit, I show him. "Maybe it's a relative?" I say hoping he buys it.

"None of your mother's relatives are this good looking." Dad is serious but I can't help but laugh. Partly because I'm relieved he's not upset, and partly because it's true—the man doesn't resemble Mom or any relative from her side.

I pick up the velvet pouch to slip in the gold chain when I feel something else inside. I reach in and find a yellowed piece of paper folded into a triangle. I gently unfold it.

"Can you read this, Dad?"

"The words are so faint, not really."

"What about this one?"

I hand him the envelope that sat under the box which is blank except for a few Chinese characters in the middle.

"This is your mother's name, Chung Mai Gum," Dad says pointing to the envelope.

The envelope has been opened but on the short instead of the long side. Dad blows it open and pulls out a piece of tracing-like paper with neat handwritten Chinese characters. He stares at the paper for a while.

"These glasses are not very good, and I can only make out a few of the characters. You know I didn't get much schooling. Just a few grades. Working since I was ten."

"That's okay, Dad." I don't want him to feel bad about his past so I place the letter and the triangle folded paper from the velvet pouch, into the envelope with Mom's name on it. "Where did all this come from?"

It was rhetorical but after a bit Dad responds. "I think a classmate brought it when she visited."

"You *met* him? When? Who is he?" I hold up the photo.

"No, no. I don't know who he is, Mom's classmate was a woman. Just arrived in Canada a few years ago. From Hong Kong. She stayed a long time when she visited. They talked for hours. Mom even invited her to stay for dinner. She must have known the man, the person in the photo."

I have no idea who he's talking about.

"Mom never invites, I mean invited, people for dinner. Unless they were relatives. And sometimes not even then." I hold up the box. "But why did she bring this to her?"

"I don't know."

I look at the photo and then Dad. "You're not upset?"

"Why?" He has a curious expression on his face until he realizes what I mean. "Oh, don't be crazy. Because your mom knew a man a long time ago? This guy doesn't know how lucky he is to have escaped your mother. He should be thanking me. I had other options too, you know. There was a woman I knew before I even came to Canada, but she didn't want to wait for me after I left Hong Kong. Another, I exchanged letters with when your mother stopped writing the first year. We swapped photos."

I can't help laughing as Dad goes on to tell me about the number of women with whom he exchanged photos and could've married instead of Mom.

"But your great-aunts liked your mother best. She was clever but no one else would have been able to stand her."

I laugh again. "So, you don't know who this is?"

"She mentioned some military man she once knew. He was stuck in China. Probably him."

"You know, now that you mention it, I remember her wondering what happened to someone she knew who was in the military. I always thought it was just an old classmate. She said something about him once when I was about ten and once again when I was a teenager. She wondered what he was doing and how life would have been if she never left China. And Poh Poh Su Ling said something when we visited her, but Mom didn't explain."

"No need to wonder. She would have been stuck in China and none of her family would be here today if she stayed with him."

"Probably," I say but all the unknowns send my brain reeling. I walk over to the framed photos on Mom's dresser. I pick up the one from my wedding. Mom stands there in her silver *cheong sam*. "Wish we could ask her." A thought crosses my mind. A sharp unpleasant sensation courses through my upper body.

Were they right? Maybe I didn't know Mom very well either. Maybe none of us did.

"Do you want to leave these here or give it to them to keep with the rest of the jewellery?"

"Why don't you take it? She was going to give Zoe the chain anyway."

"They were Mom's. Yours now, Dad."

"What am I ever going to do with them? Take them home." He holds the box out to me.

I inhale deeply. "Are you sure? What are you going to tell them if I do? I don't need another reason to argue with them." He sighs as another thought comes to me. "Who's this schoolmate of Mom's?"

"She attended the funeral. Really nice lady."

Again, I draw a blank. There weren't many people at the service outside of family, but I don't remember any woman who was a friend who arrived in Canada only a few years ago.

"Do you know how to reach her?"

"It's on the list of phone numbers on the wall downstairs.

Call and ask her."

"Sure. Maybe later." I feel my stomach flutter at the thought of speaking to Mom's friend. I didn't want to deal with whether Mom had bad-mouthed me to anyone else like my older siblings said.

"Wish Mom was here." I stare at her photo again. "Dad? Did Mom think I didn't treat her well? Like they keep saying to me?"

"Your mother criticized everyone. You and your sister are thrifty, your brother spends too much. Her one brother and sister are stingy, the nice sister is a busybody, another brother is too mouthy and all of them are cowardly. Unlike her. And it's not like you didn't hear her yelling at me all the time. Your mother complained about everyone. It's what she did."

"Why don't they know it then?" Still holding Mom's photo, I sink onto the bed. "They're so mean."

"Quick-tempered like your mother. When something goes wrong, your mother yelled but when she calmed down, we talked. Don't worry about them. I'll talk to them. Take care of yourself and Zoe. And take this stuff home. I'll tell them about it."

"But they only yell like Mom. They don't talk or listen to anyone. Ever. They just tell everyone what to do."

"I'll talk to your siblings."

I doubt anything he says will change things, but I don't want to discourage him. "I read the goal of Buddhists is to escape reincarnation and get to Nirvana. Think Mom's there?"

"Maybe. Your mother was loud and quick-tempered, but she had a good heart."

"You think she's with your family, Dad?"

"According to Buddhist beliefs she is. Why her photo is in the shrine downstairs now. Lets us pray to her and our ancestors."

"Zoe said it doesn't seem right that women lose their right to the family they're born into just because they marry."

"Just an old tradition. Just a name. Your mother will always be a Chung. Chung Mai Gum."

It's true.

"Funny, her given name is the slang for American money—American Gold. I never realized it until now."

"Not like you use her name. She was Amah to you."

"It's like she got lost and wound up here. In Canada."

"Your maternal great-grandmother, always thought they'd end up in San Francisco because of her husband."

"Mom never even met him, did she?"

"No. I told her to invite him to our wedding, but she said not to bother. Heard he couldn't cross the border. Rumours of a criminal record."

"Mom told you this?"

"Your mother never said anything bad about him. Probably because she bragged about him before we got married." Dad laughs. "Big talker your mother. Who knows what she really thought!"

"So, where'd you hear he had a criminal record?"

"Others from our home village who had relatives in the U.S. but who knows if any of it was true. Your mother's siblings talked about it a little. Said he and his brother were both scoundrels. One was a drinker and the other an opium addict and both were womanizers. Spent all their money on their habits, which is why they had no money to send home. Another rumour was he didn't read or write English, so he asked for help from a nephew or some relative. The relative was a liar and a thief, told your great-grandfather he sent the money, but never did. And still another story is that he married or lived with another woman. Possibly a white woman who took all his money."

"Really? Do you think any of those stories are true? Think Mom believed any of it?"

"Who knows? Not as easy here in the Gold Mountain as everyone thought it was. Tough to earn enough to send home all the time. You know how rumours get started."

I study Dad's face trying to figure out if he's saying this for my benefit or if he's really just talking about this great-grandfather of mine. He remains straight-faced. He's more observant and emotionally savvy than Mom.

"I suppose he could've been arrested for drinking or smoking opium. Or maybe just for being Chinese. A lot of racism back then. Right now, I'd rather know him than any other relative. At least I don't have to worry about Great-grandfather complaining or spreading rumours about me behind my back." I smile at my own joke as I return Mom's photo to her dresser.

Dad isn't sure what to say, so he goes quiet.

"You know, Andy and I are thinking of taking Zoe there on a trip. To California. Maybe we'll visit San Francisco. Pay our respects to him. Mom mentioned that she wished she had gone to see him. Almost like she regretted not doing it."

"You'll have a hard time. Doubt anyone knows where he's buried."

"Mom said that too. Something about the grave being moved. I'll see."

I wiggle the lid back onto the box and slip the photo of the stranger into the envelope before putting all of it including the velvet pouch into my handbag.

37

Over the next week, I frequently pull out and examine Mom's possessions. By the end of the week, all the items sit prominently on my desk, the box, the velvet pouch, and the contents in the envelope. All of it distracts me from work. What if she had stayed with this man? What did all of this mean? And I wonder about Great-grandfather and the rumours floating around about him. These alternate paths for Mom's life call to me.

My curiosity finally overtakes my desire to remain in hiding from family. I punch in the number of Mom's classmate that Dad had written down for me. I mentally prepare myself for more information I'm not sure I want to know. As the phone rings, I second guess whether I should pry, since Mom never told anyone about this part of her life. Before I can change my mind, a woman answers the phone.

"Hello. Is this Mrs. Mah?" I hope she understands me.

"Yes, it is. Who is this?"

"I'm Chung Mai Gum's daughter. I understand you were her classmate."

"Oh. Yes. So nice of you to call. I was very sad she passed away."

I'm relieved she understands me.

"Thank you. I was hoping to ask you a few things about my mother. Is that okay?"

"Yes, happy to tell you what I know."

"I heard she once had a boyfriend, but no one seems to know much about him. Do you know who he is or when he knew my mother?"

"Yes, she brought him to my family's home to visit a couple of times when they dated. Your mother was in nursing school then. And then years after she went to Hong Kong, he came looking for her."

"He went looking for her? Wow. Do you know what he did?"

"A pilot, I think."

"Do you know how they met?"

"No idea. Just know he wanted to find your mother. Came to my house shortly after she left for Canada. And showed me that ring."

"You mean the two rings?"

"Two? No. He had one ring. The one he was wearing. It was the largest piece of jade I'd ever seen. Rectangular shaped. Surrounded by gold. You have it right?

"Yes, but what about the woman's ring?"

"What woman's ring? I only brought her one ring. A man's ring." She pauses as we both realize what this means. "Your mother had a ring too? They must have been engagement rings."

"He left his ring with you when he found you in Hong

Kong after Mom came to Canada? Over forty years ago? You've had it all this time?"

"No. No. The beautiful box with the man's jade and gold ring was delivered to my home by courier with the letter from the lawyer asking me to ensure your mother received it. It arrived the year I was leaving for Canada, six years ago, in 2008. Only one week before I left. Inside the lawyer's letter was an envelope with your mother's name on it. It was sealed. I never read it. I brought it with me and delivered it to your mother still sealed. It was as if they waited until I was coming to Canada to bring it to her. Had it arrived any later than it did, I might never have received it. Odd how the timing worked out. Your family has it, right?"

I tell her I have the letter and the rings. I arrange to visit her the next day so she can read everything to me.

***

I pull out the box and show her both rings.

She gasps when she sees them. "They really are engagement rings. Your mother had hers all this time. She never showed me hers. Never said a word the day I brought his to her. She didn't even read the letter while I was there."

I hand her the envelope with Mom's name on it.

"This was the envelope I brought her from the lawyer." She confirms excitedly before pulling out the triangle piece of paper. I explain how Dad and I discovered the little slip of paper in the velvet pouch, separate from the letter.

"It's so faint, I can barely make out the characters," she says after adjusting her glasses. "It's dated July 12, 1950. It's simple. Like a prediction."

I shiver as she reads the words which describe what Mom had done.

"I can't believe someone knew that Mom was going to come

to Canada before she did it."

"Words have power. Perhaps it was because your mother heard those words so long ago, she set out to fulfill them."

I never considered it that way. It is at once a fresh and trite observation. Had it been destiny or sheer will that lead to Mom's life?

I take a sip of the tea before asking her to read the letter.

August 15, 2008

My dearest Mai,

If you're reading this letter, it means I am no longer a part of your world. I always hoped I'd see you again before I closed my eyes for good.

After receiving your note so many years ago, I eventually got over my anger and hurt and tried to track you down in Hong Kong. I was too late. When I learned you'd made it to Canada and married another man, I did not want to disrupt your life or your dream.

So, like you, I followed my dream. I climbed the ranks in the air force. I married a good woman introduced to me by a family member. This delighted my parents. I loved and was faithful to her and our three children. Ironically, my wife was anxious to send our children abroad to the great Gold Mountain for schooling. It was her talk of the United States and Canada which stirred in me the thoughts of you I tried to bury so long ago.

I realized a bit late how important your family was and is to you. I underestimated how loyal a daughter you are. I would have helped. I could have helped. All you had to do was ask. You're so stubborn and proud. It is partly why I admire you.

Your image and your touch never left me. I am grateful for the short time we had together. I hope you are happy and healthy, and it continues until I see you again in our next life.

Until then, this ring belongs with its mate. Keep it safe.

Forever yours,
Wong Dat Wah

Mrs. Mah and I are in tears as she finishes reading the letter that is shaking in her hands. I take a few tissues to wipe my face and sip the now tepid tea as we sit in silence. At one point Mrs. Mah leans over and holds onto my hand and tells me to take care of myself before I leave.

I become fixated with the need to show Mom that despite my many flaws I want her to know that I listened to her, that I understood her, that I miss her. And I set out to do one of the things she never got to do.

***

Pushing aside my own feelings about Aunt Jung, I call her.

"Do you know where Great-grandfather is buried?"

"No idea. All I know is a few years after the funeral, we got a letter from the relative who was taking care of his affairs. Told us the city was shutting down the cemetery and they were moving all the graves. The relative probably got money for agreeing to move it. Told us after he did it. Was your mother ever upset!"

"Can you give me Great-grandfather's full name and any other details you have? Date of birth? Date of death?"

"I'm the only one in the family who knows his date of birth, date of death and his two names."

I believe her because she knows everyone's birthdates—siblings, first cousins, second cousins, uncles, and aunts.

"What do you mean two names?"

"He changed his name when he married. It's a tradition in the part of China we came from. You can take different names in school and when you marry. Not the last name, just the given names."

I wonder whether this is accurate. She's known for insisting she's right even when what she claims is impossible. I make a note to check with Dad and the internet later as I take the dates down. I phonetically spell the names, which I need her to repeat several times before I'm sure I've got it. And she promises to have one of my other aunts write down the names in Chinese for me.

"Are the dates according to the lunar or modern calendar?"

"I don't know."

I realize it's going to be difficult.

***

From: Wong, Bonnie (ADM)
To: Amy Lee amy@leelaw.info
Sent: February 13, 2014 10:08 AM
Subject: 311 Request - Birth Cert Inquiry

Good afternoon, Amy,

There is no such thing as a public search for graves. An application must be submitted with the information of the person for whom you are searching. Since your great-grandfather was born in China, we will not have his birth information, but if he died in

San Francisco, we should have a death certificate on file.

The link to our application for death records is below. Please read through page one of the instructions before completing and mailing it to us. If our office cannot find it locally, we will be asking the Department of Public Health (who holds all death records in the state of California) for a more thorough search. It costs $21 for a search. Hopefully, they can find something close to the information provided.

http://sfgov.org/countyclerk/sites/default/files/Documents/ACCDC.pdf

Bonnie Wong
Deputy County Clerk
San Francisco County Clerk's Office

From: Amy Lee amy@leelaw.info
To: Wong, Bonnie (ADM)
Sent: February 17, 2014 9:08 AM
Subject: RE: 311 Request - Birth Cert Inquiry

Thanks for the response, Bonnie.

My challenge with sending in a "normal" request is I've no idea of the precise translation of my great-grandfather's name. It's a version of Chung but it could be Jung, Jang, Jun, Chong, Chang, Cheng, Chun ... I've no idea. The same problem goes for his first names, Bak Lai is how I've seen it, but it could be written Bak Li, Buk Li, Bok Lai, Buk Li. And to make it more complicated, according to some Chinese custom, he got a new first name after he married and returned to the U.S. The name is Su Fu, but it could be spelled Soo Foo, Siu Fiu, Sou Fooh or something similar.

I'm also not sure which birth and death dates were used. He was born October 13, 1903, by the Chinese lunar calendar. His death date was February 6, 1976, but my aunts and uncles are too young to know if the dates we have are in accordance with the lunar or the modern Gregorian calendar. This means his birth date might also be December 13, 1903, and his death dates could be January 5 or March 5, 1976.

Any options that won't bankrupt me? ☺

Amy Lee

From: Wong, Bonnie (ADM)
To: Amy Lee amy@leelaw.info
Sent: February 19, 2014 11:03 AM
Subject: RE: 311 Request - Birth Cert Inquiry

Hey Amy,

Since there are so many different possible name combinations and several different dates of passing, I don't know how accurately we can locate the record. We might be able to try a few versions of the names and dates of birth and death if you come in person.

Please keep in mind if we are not able to locate the certificate locally (within San Francisco) we push the search to the Department of Public Health where they can conduct a search throughout the state of California. But again, they might run into the same problem as us where they are not certain about the accuracy of the record.

If you want, you can write down two first names (eg: Antonio or Tony), two last names and both dates of death. That way we have a narrower search. However, we will not be able to work with more information than that. You may end up needing to send in more than one request form if you're unsatisfied with the results.

Bonnie

38

In the heart of the summer, we make a family trip to San Francisco. I am stupidly optimistic that fate will step in and help me find this needle in a haystack as I abandon sightseeing with Andy and Zoe, to visit City Hall.

As soon as I walk through the doors, I understand why famous couples like Marilyn Monroe and Joe DiMaggio married there; the domed foyer is breathtaking. I stumble across like a classic tourist gazing upwards instead of watching in front of me.

When I find the deaths, births and marriage licensing office, the clerk attempts a few of the name combinations and eventually gives up and charges me for one search even though she tried a number of names and dates of birth. Sensing my disappointment, she says,

"We'll send a written search request to the Department of Health. Their database is larger. You can provide up to two first and last names and two dates of death. Fill out this envelope with your address. The results of the search will be mailed to you."

My next stop is Chinatown. When I arrive on the bus, I feel at home. The smells of baked sweet bread, barbecued meat, and sour garbage remind me of the Toronto Chinatowns. Even the pushy shoppers are comforting in some bizarre way. I imagine seeing my great-grandfather walking down these very streets.

Different from Toronto though, are the many conversations in the southern peasant Cantonese dialect I always thought was our secret language. They surround me.

Mom used to complain about how our family never spoke the refined Hong Kong dialect. Before I was old enough to be embarrassed, I liked how others didn't understand us. Sometimes Mom laughed, sometimes she complained Dad, who was born and raised in Hong Kong, never used the formal dialect at home. She occasionally tried to speak to us using the upper-class dialect. The attempts only lasted as long as dinner.

The tidy window displays and decorative street lanterns end as I get closer to Jackson Street, to reach the Chinese Cemetery Association where I'm hoping to gain some clues to finding my great-grandfather's grave. Cars parked on both sides crowd the narrow street. I pass Gift Entertainment, Foot Reflexology, Wong Lee Bakery and Tung Shing Trading Co. before I reach an alleyway.

I check my map. Jason Court should be right here, next to this Tung Shing Trading Co. I must have missed it. I walk back the way I came. The shops are crammed next to each other. There's absolutely no space between them. I walk past the alleyway. More shops packed together like sardines. Weird.

I pick up my phone to call Andy but before I can dial, I see something between a store and street sign in the middle of the street, between the shops at the front of the alleyway I'd walked by several times already. *Jason.* But this can't possibly be a street. It's no more than five feet in width and there are no sidewalks. I wander along it. The two corner stores on Jackson have their side doors flung open, kept ajar by crates. Workers are running around in and out of the shops, moving boxes and speaking my dialect. I pass three or four buildings, which appear to have been abandoned, before reaching the end of the alleyway-street where the back of a building sits.

Sure enough, to the right is a short building with glass doors and floor-to-ceiling windows in dire need of cleaning. The yellow brick is filthy, the windows are so cloudy and marked I can't see inside, and there are paper notices taped everywhere. It seems deserted. But there is a small sign tucked beside a buzzer. CHINESE CEMETERY ASSOCIATION.

I feel unsafe and I hope someone has taken notice and will report seeing me if I go missing. I try the door. Locked. I can't decide if I'm relieved or disappointed. I'm about to push the buzzer when I notice a small handwritten sign, *Open at 1:00 P.M.* At the same time, a gruff voice speaks:

"Not open 'til one."

I look around. There is no one in sight. I look up to see if there's a window, even though the voice didn't sound like it came from above. The only people in sight are down near the entrance to the alleyway. Nowhere near me. I examine the buzzer thinking there might be a camera and microphone.

"Come back later. Open at one." The voice is behind me but all I see is a pile of garbage. I stare for a few more seconds at the pile and suddenly I see a pair of eyes staring out from inside what I now realize, is not a pile of garbage, but a handmade shack made of garbage. I gasp.

"Ahhh ... thank you." I walk quickly back the way I entered, a little freaked out about the homeless guy behind me.

There go my hopes of finding information on my great-grandfather with the Chinese Cemetery Association.

I pick up Chinese desserts from the bakery for Andy and Zoe and hop on the bus to get back to the hotel.

Maybe Mom didn't intend for me to find my great-grandfather after all.

***

"Why are we wasting our afternoon going to a cemetery in a suburb? You don't even know where the grave is Mom."

I hate that my thirteen-year-old daughter is aware of how futile my efforts may be.

"It's the most likely place for him to be buried. I Googled it. Maybe we'll get lucky."

"Did your aunts and uncles ask you to find him?"

"No, I only spoke with Aunt Jung to get information about Great-grandfather. I didn't tell anyone what I'm trying to do." I neglect to mention that Aunt Jung is the biggest gossip, so everyone probably knows I'm searching for him now.

"Do they even care to know where he is?"

"Well, I'm not sure. They're part of the reason some awful rumours about him exist but they also put his photo on the headstone beside my great-grandmother's and my grandparents, as if they were one big happy family. Doesn't matter. I'm not doing it for them."

"What rumours? Who are you doing it for?

"I'm doing it for Mom, your Poh Poh. Remember she said she wished she'd met him." I continue to share the stories Dad told me. She waits until I finish to respond. "So, why do you care about him if he was such a jerk?"

"They were just rumours. It's not like there's a damning

photo on Facebook." Zoe nods.

"You know Facebook is for old people. But I know what you mean."

I was such a mess after the funeral I hardly thought about the impact on Zoe. Most of the time she says nothing, but I've seen her take out and stare at Mom's cheong sam a few times since she died. She's also been wearing that gold chain since I brought it home to her despite how she once said it wasn't her style.

"Hey, this is all Poh Poh's family, right? Not Goung Goung's?"

"Yeah, why?"

"Didn't you tell me once Poh Poh married, she followed Goung Goung's family, the Lees? And she lost her right to be part of the family she was born into, the Chungs?"

Does she have to point out all the inconsistencies with this project? "It's true but it doesn't mean we can't pay respects to the relatives from her birth line. Besides, your grandmother's always been a bit different. You know her name is slang for American money? It translates to American Gold. I've known her name all my life but just made that connection recently."

"Really? Cool. Guess you're a bit slow." She grins. "So, what'd he look like?"

"Great-grandfather? You saw that photo of him from the hospital. The only other photo I've seen is the one on the grave in Toronto. The photo of him on the headstone and in Uncle Yaing Gong's shrine appears in Amy's head. "He looked sort of like, well, you—half Chinese and half white. Which is weird because he was full Chinese. He had almond-shaped eyes with double lids. His nose was slim with a short sharp tip. Full lips. And he had a genuine smile. You could tell because his eyes were squinting. Heart-shaped face and fair skinned. Tall too. The rumour is he was close to six feet."

"Did Poh Poh ever talk about him?"

"Not really. But it turns out she kept a lot to herself." My thoughts drift to the rings. Zoe thinks it was a great romantic story and she wants the ornate box but couldn't care less about the rings.

By this time, Andy is driving us through the arches of the Chinese Cemetery in Daly City, a city south of San Francisco. The place is vast, spotted with Monterey cypress trees and grassy patches surrounding the headstones. It's deserted except for construction workers near the entrance. We park near the only building in sight. It's like a traditional Chinese temple with a characteristic "resting hill" roof. Instead of finding an attendant in the temple, we find the building only houses public washrooms.

As we start examining the headstones, the impossibility of the task dawns on me. The newer and more expensive grave markers have photos with both English and Chinese writing, but the older ones have no photos, and everything is written in Chinese. Knowing only a few numbers and the odd character, like our surname, makes randomly searching the entire cemetery, which is the size of at least eight football fields pushed together, ridiculous.

"Look, it's the Chung character," I say finding a marker with English and Chinese writing. I quickly take a photo with my phone. "Now we can just search for this character on the grave markers if they don't have English on them."

"Clever," says Andy encouragingly. We go through the rest of the aisles with no luck. To me, the cemetery seems to be growing in size.

"Wait. This is Chung, too," I say finding another marker with English and Chinese writing.

"And the Chinese character is completely different than the

first one we found." I moan. Reluctantly, I take a photo of the new character.

"How many different ways are there to spell it?" Zoe asks.

"Who knows? I was always told there are only about five Chinese surnames. I assumed the spelling differed when the names were translated into English, but I had no idea there are different ways to write them in Chinese, too."

I stop and sit on the path, already tired of searching. I feel more apathetic than I did leaving City Hall. Andy comes over.

"Hey, we can't give up now."

"I didn't think this day was going to be such a total failure is all," I say as I stare over the hill at the number of graves we have yet to check.

"We're not done yet. Come on."

"Thanks, but if we had more to go on, or if I could at least read Chinese I might agree. It just feels so impossible right now. Let's just burn the incense in the middle of one of these rows and call it a day before Zoe gets too bored. It's gorgeous out. Let's go to a beach and stand by the ocean."

I lay out the oranges in the middle of the row of graves I happen to be standing in, strike a few matches to light the incense I bought in Chinatown and jam it into the ground. I put my hands together in prayer. I bow my head three times. I've no idea what words to speak. Mom never instructed me on the *proper* way to do this. I just remember her mumble something as she stood in front of my grandparents' graves or in front of the large Buddhist statues at the temple. It seemed an invasion of privacy and too personal to ask her what she said so I never intruded. I just watched.

When I was young and instructed to pray, I used to mumble what I wanted, sort of like to Santa Claus. When I was in school,

I asked for help to do well on tests and exams and after I finished school, I asked for help to land a job and to find the perfect mate. And at some point, I started having these one-sided conversations in my head or softly aloud if I was certain no one was around, with whatever ancestor or Buddhist statue I happened to be visiting. When Mom got sick, I asked for her to be healed; eventually I just asked for her to be free of pain. Right now, standing in the middle of this cemetery, frustrated, I wish I had asked Mom more as I spoke to him in my head:

Great-grandfather, I hope wherever you are, you have peace. Especially from the gossipy relatives. I know what it's like. You can always go and haunt them. I chuckle at my own joke. *Sorry I couldn't find your gravesite today, but I'll keep trying.*

It turns out, you and Mom had a few things in common. You both travelled to a Gold Mountain and you both have some secrets.

If you want to be found, send me a sign.

We all stand and watch as the incense burns. I hope for a sign. The smoke floats off in different directions and at one point it covers me. I read that when the smoke from incense does this, it means whatever you prayed about, reached the heavens.

"Look at the incense! The ashes are curling like candy cane tops. It's a good sign!" I really feel hopeful because of the hundreds of times I've burned incense I can count on my fingers the number of times it has burned this way.

"The strands in the incense must be stronger on the bottom to support the ashes above," says Andy.

"Aww, come on. Don't make it all engineering and logical. Can't we just say it's a good sign from beyond? Mom always said it was good luck."

"Er … umm … it's a neat balancing act. I'm sure it's a good sign."

I remember the last time it happened. It was at Mom's funeral. Getting Zoe to focus on it was the only thing that made her stop crying. I see her staring at the incense too. I wonder if she is remembering that day like I am.

39

Months later as I'm going through the mail, one envelope bearing my name and address is written in familiar penmanship. It takes seconds before I realize it's my own handwriting. I scan the upper left corner of the envelope. The stamp reads,

> San Francisco County Clerk
> City Hall, Room 168
> 1 Dr. Carlton B. Goodlett Place
> San Francisco, CA 94102-4678

I slide my thumb under the non-adhesive corner of the flap and tear it open. I take out a plain piece of folded white paper. It's a heavy weight. I assume my US $21 earns me a quality disappointment letter. I unfold it, revealing a blue sheet with a watermark printed diagonally across it, *INFORMATIONAL, NOT VALID.*

I let out a big sigh. Official failure. It appears they sent a copy of the search to show they did their job. As I stare, my eyes adjust, and I read the top lines: *State of California. County of San Francisco. Certificate of Death.*

"Wait. Oh my God! This is it. Holy crap. They found it," I whisper. And then loudly, "They found it!" I'm shaking.

"What?" Zoe comes running in from the kitchen, annoyed.

"It's the death certificate. It's Great-grandfather's death certificate. This is it. They found it!"

"What? No way! I thought you said there were like a trillion possible names to search and a bunch of birth and death dates."

"There were. But I got lucky, I guess," I say as tears start streaming. Zoe wraps her arms around my shoulders and squeezes.

The feeling of elation ends when I talk to Uncle Yaing Gong, days after I email a copy of the death certificate to him.

"My sisters don't think it's the right person. The name of his wife is not our grandmother's."

"Well, names are subject to whoever translated it for him when he entered the U.S. Those may not be a hundred percent accurate."

"They say they're not sure this is his, but I have heard he potentially had another wife."

"And it's unlikely another person had a similar name and the exact same birth and death dates as Great-grandfather," I say, refusing to let my aunts' doubts ruin my excitement, even though I fear they might be right.

"It's true. And this cousin listed, Richard Chu, sounds familiar to me," he says slowly.

As we talk further, Yaing Gong reminds me how Chinese organizations in large North American cities formed around common surnames to give members a sense of community and to offer help to its members. So, all the Jungs, Juns, Chuns, Chungs, et cetera, had one association and all the Lees, Lais, Leis, Lis, et cetera, formed another and so on.

I later learn such organizations continue to thrive in San Francisco, so I send an email to the Chung Association in San Francisco.

> From: Amy Lee amy@leelaw.info
> To: SF@Chungassociation.com
> Sent: September 9, 2014 12:31 PM
> Subject: Inquiry
>
> Dear Sir/Madam:
>
> I recently returned from a trip to San Francisco. My great-grandfather was CHUNG, Bak Lai. He, his brother, and his father migrated there in the early 1900s and they died there. Unfortunately, my family who spoke no English at the time, doesn't know where he is buried.
>
> I'm hoping to find his grave. Surprisingly, we found the San Francisco Death Certificate. Any idea how I might be able to track him down with this information? It's attached. Any help you can offer would be greatly appreciated. I'd really like to pay my respects to him.
>
> Amy

From: Arthur Chao [mailto:chaoart@hotmail.com]

To: Amy Lee amy@leelaw.info
Sent: September 11, 2014 7:14 PM
Subject: Re: Inquiry

Amy,

Looking at the death certificate, the cemetery name says Six Co. Colma. It looks like he was most likely buried in the Chinese Cemetery in Daly City because the Six Co. founded the cemetery. In Chinese it is called "six mountains cemetery" named after the six associations comprising the Six Companies Association.

It is very close to where I live. Since I have your information on his Death Certificate along with his Chinese name and village, I'll go there and see if I can find the gravesite and take a picture.

I'll have to find where they keep the records.

Arthur

From: Arthur Chao [mailto:chaoart@hotmail.com]
To: Amy Lee amy@leelaw.info
Sent: September 15, 2014 3:00 PM
Subject: Re: Inquiry

Amy,
No luck at the gravesite. Apparently, the records

are at the office for the Chinese Cemetery Daly City in Chinatown, SF. I'll go over there to see what I can find out. Did you go there when you were out here?

I am also told the Chinese cemeteries would not give out information on gravesite locations unless I can prove I am a relative.

So, I may have some problems. I'll let you know.

Arthur

From: Arthur Chao [mailto:chaoart@hotmail.com]
To: Amy Lee amy@leelaw.info
Sent: September 22, 2014 1:50 PM
Subject: Re: Inquiry

Amy,

Here's the latest.
I was able to contact a fellow Family Association member, Yuk Kwan, who knows someone on the board of the Chinese Cemetery. He has all the information on Chung Bak Lai. Just waiting now for a response.

Arthur

From: Arthur Chao [mailto:chaoart@hotmail.com]

To: Amy Lee amy@leelaw.info
Sent: October 3, 2014 8:23 PM
Subject: Re: Inquiry

Amy, just an update. All the records at the Chinese Cemetery Association were only ever recorded using the Chinese names. Someone must search the records by hand to find your great-grandfather's gravesite. Will let you know.

Arthur

From: Amy Lee amy@leelaw.info
To: chaoart@hotmail.com
Sent: October 4, 2014 9:08 AM
Subject: Re: Inquiry

What an administrative nightmare! No wonder they were so reluctant to help. Fingers crossed.

Thanks for the efforts, again. Let me know if you need anything from my end.

Amy

Amy Lee
Barrister and Solicitor

From: Arthur Chao [mailto:chaoart@hotmail.com]

To: Amy Lee amy@leelaw.info
Sent: October 17, 2014 8:23 PM
Subject: Fwd: Fwd: Attachments for the deceased

Amy,

Good news!!

We found your great-grandfather. See attached documents.
He is at Chinese Cemetery plot number indicated.
I live close by. I can see if I can locate the grave there.

Arthur

I did it. I can't stop myself from smiling as I email an enthusiastic thank-you back.

I quickly share the news with Yaing Gong, forwarding all the information and emails to him. He calls a few days later. I assume to thank me. I am wrong. He calls to cast doubt on my findings, again. And my sister, who by this time knows about my search, throws in her two cents suggesting I was likely scammed. I, too, start to wonder if perhaps this is the wrong gravesite.

To: chaoart@yahoo.com
Sent: October 21, 2014 9:08 AM
Subject: Fwd: Fwd: Fwd: Attachments for the deceased

Hi Arthur,

A few quick questions. I've had a few of my aunts and uncles look at the documents Mr. Kwan was kind enough to find.

1. What is a "pass"? Is this just the permit from the cemetery?

2. According to my relatives, the documents don't read CHUNG, Bak Lai but CHUNG, Mun Lai. I don't know if it means the paperwork is wrong or if the headstone may be wrong or something else.

Let me know what you think. Either way, I really do appreciate all the efforts.

Amy

Amy Lee
Barrister and Solicitor

From: Arthur Chao <chaoart@yahoo.com>
To: Amy Lee amy@leelaw.info
Sent: October 23, 2014 3:33 PM

Amy,

As you can see, I was able to find the gravestone and took a picture. See the attached. Yuk said the documents erroneously have the middle character incorrect, Mun instead of Bak, but the social security number matches, the dates of birth and death match, and the gravestone matches his alternate, married name you gave us. The "pass" is the gate pass for the internment.

When you come over, I can meet you to show you the gravestone location. It's very close to where I live.

Regards,

Arthur

I thank Arthur for his and his friends' efforts, a little embarrassed I let the family cynicism leak into my correspondence with him. I forward the information to Yaing Gong and Mom's other siblings via their children, my cousins. No one responds.

On the weekend, I take a red-eye flight to San Francisco and meet Arthur at the gravesite, my arms filled with bags of barbecue meat, all sorts of fruit, and Chinese desserts I picked up in Chinatown.

Arthur is an elderly but vibrant man who leads me to a plain concrete grave marker with the dimensions of a folding card table, half the size and much less elaborate than the one we bought for Mom. He eyes the packages I'm holding. He must know I'll have him take all of it home with him. It's the least I could do for all his help. He stands aside respectfully as I lay out the food.

I bring out a spade and dig a bit in front of the tombstone. I deposit the little velvet jewellery bag that held the gold chain Mom wanted Zoe to have and bury it.

I brush off my hands and wipe them down with wet wipes to

ensure they're clean before I light the incense, and bow. I speak to Great-grandfather in my head.

Thanks for helping me find you. It's been a long time since you left this world. I wish we could've met. I don't believe all the rumours. And if any of them were true, I'm sure you had your reasons. Hopefully you were happy, and you did what was right for you.

I'm going to do the same and not worry so much about what everyone else thinks or says, even if it's hard sometimes.

These are Mom's favourite foods. She wanted to meet you. She's the reason I came looking for you. I left you something that was important to her so she will have to find you for it.

She's still really important to us and making things happen here even though she's not with us any longer. I'm hoping you've met her by now. She's really something.

***

Shortly after I return to Toronto, Aunt Jung calls to remind me it's Mom's birthday.

I leave Andy and Zoe at home to visit Mom's gravesite. Luckily there's no snow and it's a sunny morning. She'll be happy I've come early, which was one of her many rules about how and when to visit gravesites. I park and walk over to Mom's grave marker, which I hate to admit is pretty, even if it's the colour my sister picked out. The burgundy is strong, her favourite colour, and different from the pinkish red colour most Chinese choose for grave markers. I pile the odd numbered oranges in a pyramid on the pie plate I brought.

They remind me of the morning Mom died. She hadn't really eaten since the operation over a month earlier taking only liquids in the final two weeks. So, I was surprised she was mumbling about wanting oranges. All they had in the house were those hybrid grapefruit ones. The peel was papery and thin, and stuck to the dry fruit. I ended up removing the membrane and putting the pulp into her mouth. She could barely chew. I ended up flossing most of the pulp out of her teeth.

The oranges I have today are juicy and sweet. The kind she liked.

I open the lid of the Tupperware container holding the extra T-bone steak I asked Andy to grill when we prepared dinner last night and I place it to the right of the oranges. Then I open the lid of the box of Chinese desserts I picked up, which contains Mom's and my favourites—egg tarts, coconut and pineapple buns, wife cake, and sweet red bean cake—and place the box on top of the bag it came in, to the left of the oranges.

I recall all the times Mom and I visited her parents' gravesite when there was hardly a breeze, yet we somehow would have to strike almost an entire book of matches before getting the incense lit. Today, I came prepared and easily light the incense with the barbecue lighter I packed. I bow three times and place the three sticks into the headstone's built-in holder. I stand there as the incense burns and stare at the photo of Mom in her twenties.

I originally resisted Vikki and Mark's insistence on burying Mom in Mount Pleasant Cemetery because Mom was so thrifty. I thought it sad one of Mom's most extravagant expenditures since arriving in Canada would not be a lavish home or an exotic vacation but her grave. What a waste. Mom was practical and the opposite of showy. I didn't think Mom needed or wanted to be buried among prominent members of Canadian society such as former prime minister William Lyon Mackenzie King, Canada's first female surgeon, Jennie Smillie-Robinson, renowned pianist Glenn Gould and now famous defence lawyer, Edward Greenspan.

But because there were no preparations, no words or conversations with Mom about a suitable resting place, because there were some things none of us knew about her, I had no energy to fight them. And now, I'm glad I didn't.

Here's your feast, Mom. I found Great-grandfather's grave. Too bad we couldn't visit together. He has something of yours now. To lead you to each other. I hope you meet soon if you haven't already. Thanks for letting me find your rings. I'm sorry you had to give up so much to get here but I'm grateful you did.

You belong here, Mom, among these famous Canadians. You're as important as any of them. And I'm proud to be your daughter.

AFTERWORD

You can't connect the dots looking forward; you can only connect them looking backward. So, you have to trust that the dots will somehow connect in your future. You have to trust in something—your gut, destiny, life, karma, whatever.

—Steve Jobs
2005 Stanford Commencement Speech

My mother is important to me. She died almost a decade ago and losing her sucked away a part of my soul. Writing and editing her story was my way of keeping her close and sorting through life with her absent. I originally just wanted to record Mom's stories for the next generation. But I never felt I had it right, so I kept rewriting and reworking it. It took many, many years of writing and editing before I felt what I wrote was worthy of being shared. Then many more rewrites before it became this book.

Mom's stories resonated with me, but I never really knew

why. From childhood, I delighted in listening to her talk about her life before I existed. She made me laugh and cry with her descriptions and recollections of China, Hong Kong and Canada. If only to me, it was interesting. While I loved to read, I couldn't wholly relate or connect to characters or people in the stories I read the same way I did to those in Mom's stories.

In university, history—in particular, Canadian history—was my chosen major. (Much to Mom's chagrin since she believed history was pure memory work.) I revelled in analysing events and decisions made by notable figures who had an impact on our country's development. Surprisingly, one tutorial assistant dissuaded me from writing about the Chinese presence in North America because of my personal ties to the topic—great-grandfathers from Mom and Dad's families migrated to San Francisco and Vancouver in the late 1800s and early 1900s. While I knew the concern, a caution that my analysis might be tainted by personal feelings, was sincere, the comment unsettled me. I never wrote about the topic.

I've been an immigration lawyer now for more than twenty years. My job is to capture the essence of a client's life—either on the page or in a hearing—and marry it to Canada's immigration goals. I enjoy the work. To me, it's an art form. Canada offers freedom and opportunity but receives economic and cultural benefits from immigrants in return. The relationship is symbiotic and that is why the stories of immigrants are relevant to our shared national history.

Being the voice for so many Canadian immigrants over the years, I found my mother's story prodding me. The desire to write it down, to preserve her memories, began well before she died. After, the need was overwhelming. While Mom was not a renowned politician, famous actor, athlete or economic guru, her decision, and that of my Dad's, to leave their families and come to a country where they didn't speak, read, or write the language had a ripple effect that shaped my life and contributed to changing the face of our country. For me, writing this book meant connecting the dots, connecting the things that matter to me—family, history, and country.

This book is a fictionalized memoir, not a traditional biography. I've taken a poetic licence with some facts and created some episodes, in part because I've always been fascinated with stories featuring female characters—good and bad—and what makes them tick. And because, in part, all you have when you write about family members who lived before you were born, is a reasoned guess. Nevertheless, I believe these stories reflect the true spirit of events that occurred.

NOTES

1. Unlike North American family titles such as grandmother, grandfather, aunt and uncle, the Chinese have different family titles for paternal and maternal relations. For example, a maternal grandmother is called "Poh Poh" and a paternal grandmother is called "Mah Mah." There are also different family titles for maternal versus paternal aunts, uncles, cousins etc.

Reference: https://littlechinesethings.wordpress.com/2019/01/26/relatives-in-cantonese/

2. There are different ways to refer to people of European descent. There is the more polite term, *lo fan*, which means "white people". However, a common and technically derogatory term is *gwai*, which means ghost. A white man is a *gwai lo*; a white woman is a *gwai poh*.

3. Red packets of money are given for many occasions—births, New Year, marriage and even at funerals for pall bearers—all meant to bring good luck or protection to the receiver.

Reference: https://artsandculture.google.com/story/8-things-you-should-know-about-the-lucky-red-envelope/PwKiICEFJXMOJg

4. The Chinese culture favours boys because boys carry on the family name.

Reference: https://www.theguardian.com/world/2011/nov/02/chinas-great-gender-crisis

5. Some Chinese believe it is better to spare their parents or family from knowing the truth of important aspects of their own or family member's health, including death.

Reference: https://www.nytimes.com/2019/07/24/movies/the-farewell-family-lies.html
https://www.ncbi.nlm.nih.gov/pmc/articles/PMC6294856/#:~:text=This%20study%20shows%20majority%20(98,traditional%20Chinese%20culture%20%2D%2D%20Confucianism

6. During the Second World War, the Japanese invaded and held Hong Kong between December 18, 1941 and August 30, 1945—three years and eight months.

Reference: https://military-history.fandom.com/wiki/Japanese_occupation_of_Hong_Kong

7. On October 1, 1949, the People's Republic of China was founded, making the country Communist. During the Second World War (1939–1945) there was popular support for the Communists but there were also many who disagreed with the Communist agenda.

Reference: https://history.state.gov/milestones/1945-1952/chinese-rev#:~:text=On%20October%201%2C%201949%2C%20Chinese,Republic%20of%20China%20(PRC).

8. There are several drawbacks to being an unmarried Chinese woman. One is that women are only able to acquire membership in a descent line through marriage. A woman who was unmarried in life cannot be worshipped at the altar of her birth family after death. Hence the importance for parents to marry off their daughters. Ghost marriages were a viable solution to give a deceased unmarried daughter affiliation to a male descent line, so someone would worship her soul.

Reference: https://en.wikipedia.org/wiki/Chinese_ghost_marriage#Providing_a_deceased_daughter_with_a_patrilineage

9. Webers is a famous fast-food restaurant north of Orillia, Ontario, that many pass, travelling on Highway 11 to cottage country. It was established in 1963 and has grown in popularity and size in recent decades, with its hamburgers now available for sale in supermarkets.

Reference: http://webers.com/#home

10. The Chicago Restaurant at 167 Main Street West in North Bay, Ontario, came into the ownership of Young Sing Eng, my great-uncle, in the 1930s. It was eventually taken over by his son, Ed Eng, and closed in 2017.

Reference: https://www.baytoday.ca/local-news/the-chicago-cafes-owners-thank-you-for-80-years-worth-of-memories-gallery-618359

11. There is a document from the Department of the Interior, Chinese Immigration Branch, listing the details of Anna Lee's departure from Canada as a child at two-and-a-half years old. This document coincides with the birth information listed in my great-aunt's obituary on page 96.

12. Many graves located in downtown San Francisco, California, were moved from the main parts of the city to nearby smaller communities, including Daly City and Colma. I was able to locate my maternal great-grandfather's grave and paid my respects to him.

Reference: https://www.kqed.org/news/10779164/why-are-so-many-dead-people-in-colma-and-so-few-in-san-francisco

ACKNOWLEDGMENTS

Thank you to the writers who share their work and inspire me to do the same. Thank you to Robert Rotenberg, Lara Hinchberger, Douglas Whiteway, Matt Joudrey, and At Bay Press. Thank you to my family and friends who supported me—you know who you are.

Nancy Lam is a Toronto author. As a child and teenager, she lost herself in stories by Canadian writers, in university she majored in Canadian History to earn a Bachelor of Arts before acquiring her law degree. As an immigration lawyer she now helps prospective Canadians write and present their life stories to government officials. *The Loyal Daughter* is her debut novel.

Thanks for purchasing this book and for supporting authors and artists. As a token of gratitude, please scan the QR code for exclusive content from this title.